All the Things
I Should Have
Known

All the Things I Should Have Known

TIFFANY L. WARREN

Dafina Books

KENSINGTON BOOKS
www.kensingtonbooks.com

DAFINA BOOKS are published by

Kensington Publishing Corp.
119 West 40th Street
New York, NY 10018

Copyright © 2020 by Tiffany L. Warren

All Kensington titles, imprints, and distributed lines are available at special quantity discounts for bulk purchases for sales promotion, premiums, fund-raising, and educational or institutional use.

Special book excerpts or customized printings can also be created to fit specific needs. For details, write or phone the office of the Kensington Sales Manager: Kensington Publishing Corp., 119 West 40th Street, New York, NY 10018. Attn. Sales Department. Phone: 1-800-221-2647.

Dafina and the Dafina logo Reg. U.S. Pat. & TM Off.

ISBN-13: 978-1-4967-2369-7
ISBN-10: 1-4967-2369-4
First Kensington Trade Paperback Printing: February 2020

ISBN-13: 978-1-4967-2370-3 (ebook)
ISBN-10: 1-4967-2370-8 (ebook)
First Kensington Electronic Edition: February 2020

10 9 8 7 6 5 4 3 2 1

Printed in the United States of America

Acknowledgments

I've gotten to another "the end" and I couldn't be more thankful for this journey. This book reflects on relationships with the men in our lives and the sister friends that hold us together in between the love affairs. Hahna, Kimberly, and Twila are fictional representations of all the sister friends I've known over my forty-plus years. Their bond is incredible, and I would be proud to call any one of them my bestie.

First, as always, I must thank my husband, Brent, and my children. I always thank them because they help write these stories. Their patience and support while I opt out of housework and movie night is impressive. My youngest child only knows me as a writer. I published my first book shortly after she was born. My writing career is part of their journey too.

To my team at Dafina—you are amazing! Tara, thank you for your patience and encouragement. Thank you for sticking with me as I write the stories that are in my heart. Samantha, thank you for helping me get the word out about my books and coming up with the coolest giveaways. Sara, I live for our talks which run the gamut from the state of politics in our nation, to racism, to raising children—and oh . . . sometimes we get around to talking about books.

Next, I'd like to thank Kandi and Todd Tucker from the *Real Housewives of Atlanta.* No, I don't know them at all (cause I know some of y'all gonna ask me). Their love story played out on national television and gave me hope for the characters in this novel. Many blessings on your continued success and happiness.

I couldn't have crafted this story without all the sister friends in my life. I think of our conversations—how we call each other out, how we pray for one another, how we have one another's backs. These relationships are fundamental to my views of sisterhood and how the stories unfold. So, a toast to the lovely ladies who hold me down at all times—Shawana, Afrika, Leah, Brandi, Cybil, Staci, Victoria, ReShonda, Renee, Helen, and Robin. Love y'all to the entire moon and back. Thank you to my work sister friends (Lorraine, Ronnie, Heather, Lauren, and Annie) who read my books and share them with everyone (even when I don't talk about them in the office, LOL).

Thanks goes out to the wonderful women of Alpha Kappa Alpha, Delta Sigma Theta, Sigma Gamma Rho, and Zeta Phi Beta. Although I am not in a sorority, I love the support and ride-or-die fierceness of these organizations. I hope my fictional sorority, Gamma Phi Gamma, exemplifies all of the best characteristics of these ladies I admire.

There are a couple scenes in my book where I blow kisses to all my book club readers, friends, and supporters. Your support by purchasing books, showing up for signings, writing reviews, and sharing what I write with your avid reader friends is appreciated so much. It humbles me when I get your kind words, and even when you get mad and throw the book. Ha. Your passion for the written word ignites my passion for creating stories. I would name some of you, and then I would inevitably leave someone out, so I won't do it—but you know who you are, you fierce sharers of Facebook posts! I love you all!

And finally, I give all thanks and honor and praise to God who is the source of all good things—including my vivid imagination.

Hope you all enjoy this book, and maybe even see yourself in there. Happy reading!

Chapter 1

A year ago today, Torian was a ghost.

Hahna's Facebook page reminded her of this fact. Was there a filter on Facebook to delete the bad memories and only remind you of the good ones? She slowly scrolled the page and remembered. That fateful morning, she'd woken up to a note. Five words had changed her life.

Baby, I can't do this.

Hahna had no idea what this one thing was that Torian couldn't do, because his note wasn't specific. She had a few ideas, though. He couldn't be faithful. He couldn't commit. And he damn sure couldn't tell the truth.

Or maybe it wasn't just one thing. Maybe Torian couldn't do any of the things she wanted him to do—or be any of the things she wanted him to be. Just because he was a chocolate-covered demigod who made her quiver with a glance; and just because he'd showered her with expensive shoes and jewelry and vacations; and just because they'd probably make cute kids—it didn't mean that Torian Jackson truly wanted to have a life with her.

So, he'd disappeared, and he'd left a note as a good-bye.

Hahna placed her phone facedown on her huge cherry-wood desk. The desk she'd splurged on when her consulting firm, the Data Whisperers, exceeded twenty-seven million dollars in annual revenue. The desk that made her office smell like old money, even though the money that bought it was brand-new.

Hahna walked over to the large bay window that she'd had custom-installed to give her a panoramic view of the lake and magnolia trees behind the old-style Buckhead mansion that she'd renovated and turned into her company's main office. She met with clients there and gave them gracious Southern hospitality. Sweet tea, biscuits and honey, and proposals that opened their eyes to all the ways their small companies could use the data they hoarded on laptops and tablets.

Hahna gazed out the window, twirled her right index finger through her honey-colored curls, breathed, and found her peace. Those small actions had become muscle memory for her. She'd made it a habit to calm herself when anxiety threatened to consume her spirit.

Sylvia, Hahna's assistant, stepped into her office. "Hahna, I ordered the car service to take you to the airport. Is there anything else you need me to do before I get out of here for the weekend?"

Hahna looked over at Sylvia and smiled. It was only Thursday, but Hahna was giving Sylvia a long weekend because she was taking one. Her annual spa retreat with her best friends, Twila and Kimberly. They would make her forget Torian, the ghost, and make new memories for her Facebook timeline.

"You're free to go, Sylvia. What do you have planned for the weekend?"

"My grandbaby is coming over, and we're making jewelry and having a fashion show."

Hearing Sylvia talk about her granddaughter made Hahna feel warm inside. The idea of doing fun activities with a little person was a dream that Hahna used to have—before she hit forty and her ovaries decided that they wanted to turn their full-time job into a part-time I-show-up-when-I-feel-like-it gig. And before she had a ghost boyfriend.

But this weekend was not about the ghost, or her sometime-y

ovaries. Spending time with her girls was about rejuvenation, restoration, and relaxation. Some of her favorite *r* words.

"You have a good time with your beautiful granddaughter. I'll see you on Tuesday morning."

"Tuesday? You're being generous."

"I decided that I won't be back until Tuesday, so you get the benefit of my wanderlust."

Sylvia laughed. "Wander on, baby, but be careful about that lust. Don't come back here from that island with one of those green-card seekers."

"I can't import a man? You don't care about me importing furniture, but you won't let me bring back some hot chocolate."

They shared a long laugh that felt good. Laughing, along with breathing, twirling her hair, and gazing out of her bay window, held Hahna together when her cracks started to show. That's why the spa retreats were so important. She was going to laugh, probably at Twila's antics, breathe in the ocean air, and twirl her hair while gazing upon every fine piece of sculpted chocolate that passed her on the beach.

"You don't need to import a man, sweetie. God is going to send you one."

Hahna accepted this as fact because Sylvia believed it, not because she had any evidence of God being concerned with her singlehood. This blessed man who might fall from the heavens was clearly on God's time.

"I know. If I put out positivity, I will attract positive energy."

"Unh-uh. Don't start talking to me about the universe and attracting. You know good and damn well, I'm talking about Jesus. 'Bye, chil'."

Hahna chuckled some more as Sylvia muttered, *My sweet Jesus* and *Oh, the blood of the Savior,* all the way down the stairs. Sylvia loved the Lord but would also cuss you out about Jesus.

Hahna walked back over to her desk and shut down her laptop. For a half second, she was tempted to bring it with her, but then she quickly changed her mind. There wouldn't be any relaxing, rejuvenating, or restoration if she was checking emails all weekend. Plus, if any emergencies popped up while she was out of the country, her staff was more than capable.

Corden, Hahna's senior data analyst, peeked his head into the office.

"Oh, good," he said, "you're still here. I thought you were gone already."

"Almost. The car service will be here in a bit. What's up?"

"Just a teeny-tiny client issue."

Hahna read Corden's body language. His usually tucked-in button-down was half out of his skinny jeans. He shifted his weight from one foot to the other, and his nostrils were flared. This was not teeny-tiny. He wouldn't be standing in her office, fifteen minutes before her car whisked her away to vacation, if it was.

"Do I need to sit down?"

"No . . . well, maybe . . ."

"Shit."

Hahna sat down, placed her hands on the desk, and waited. She hoped it would be quick. She didn't want to miss her flight.

"Aliyah mistakenly sent table data from Shale Accounting to We Work Employment Agency. It was an honest mistake, but the data had sensitive personally identifiable information of Shale's customers. Should we disclose the data breach?"

"Shit, shit, shit."

"I know."

Hahna never strategized on this type of thing without sleeping on it first, but there was no time to sleep on it this time.

"We have to disclose it. To both parties. We Work and Shale. The issue is how we do it. We don't want them to lose confidence in our processes."

"Right. So, Aliyah was sending a dashboard with sample table data over to Shale's database analyst for review. She started typing the name Regina, but Renaldo popped up. She was going so quickly that she didn't realize the email address was wrong."

"Have we already asked We Work to delete the data?"

"Yes, we sent a communication that said the information was

sent in error, and we requested that they delete it as soon as possible."

"So, here's how we will handle Shale. First, create a new secure process for sharing data with their staff. I suggest we use our secure upload site. Then, explain what happened, and assure them that their customers' data is secure."

"Are they going to believe it?"

"I've got a good relationship with Julian Cortez, one of the partners at Shale. I think that I will be able to smooth over any rough edges when I get back."

"Thanks, boss, I hate to bring this up right before you leave for the beach."

Hahna relaxed in her chair, although she was anything but calm about this situation. If Julian and the other partners at Shale felt strongly about this data breach, then they could end up losing one of their biggest clients.

"Also, finish their damn dashboard this weekend. I don't care how many hours y'all have to work. Take some days off next week when I get back. We can't deliver bad news without that dashboard being completed. And I mean ready to go, not in pilot mode. How close is Aliyah to finishing?"

"She's close. I think if I work with her, we can deliver the dashboard and the email on Monday."

"You're not just blowing smoke up my ass, are you?"

"No. She has been testing every page on the dashboard and is only working out a few quirks. We'll get it done. Go enjoy the beach."

"I'll try."

"No, you will. Did you get that bathing suit you showed me?"

"The low-cut white one?"

"Yes, *that* one. The husband maker."

Hahna cracked up. The swimsuit was sexy, and she'd asked Corden what he thought. The man had impeccable taste, and although he had a longtime fiancée and a daughter, he felt more like a girlfriend than a male subordinate.

"It's in my bag, Corden, I don't know if I'll be bold enough to put it on."

"If Twila sees it, you will. You have fun, honey. I'm gonna go catch Aliyah before she leaves and let her know it's gonna be a long weekend."

"Thanks for holding this together."

"This is what finances my comfortable lifestyle. We're not losing this client."

Hahna jumped up from her desk and hugged Corden. He had been with her from the start and was as invested in the Data Whisperers as she was.

"Have fun, boss lady."

Corden left Hahna's office to round up Aliyah, and Hahna exhaled. That could've been a vacation-cancelling emergency. If it had happened a couple of years ago, no one could've convinced her to get on a plane. But she had developed her staff, and she trusted them.

Hahna gathered her luggage from the closet when she heard the SUV pull up in the drive downstairs. As soon as she got to the airport, the shenanigans would commence.

Relax. Rejuvenate. Restore. Her mantra for the weekend, even if/when Twila pulled up with drama.

Chapter 2

Twila had stopped at the adult store on a whim, on her way to the airport. Now she wished that she'd done this the day before. She had no idea what to select in this toy emporium, not to mention their flight to Saint Lucia left in three hours.

"Can I help you find something?"

The deep voice that asked the question came from a sinfully fine man. Golden bronzed skin with hazel eyes that were probably contacts, but she didn't care. Locs down to the center of his back, probably faux, but whatever. He should've been *her* man. Then she wouldn't be in the store looking for a penile replacement.

"I don't know where to start," Twila said. "I've never been inside a store like this."

Twila lied. She didn't want him to think she was desperate or that no one wanted her, because she had options. Plenty of options. The options were unemployed, not-all-the-way divorced, old and boring, but still, when it came to scratching an itch . . . they were options.

But she'd been inside several stores like this shopping for bachelorette party gag gifts and whatnot. Just not for something to please herself. Mostly 'cause the singles ministry at her church said masturbation was fornicating with yourself and that those orgasms were from the devil.

So, Twila was no longer in the singles' ministry.

"Well," Golden Bronze said, "it depends on what you like. Do you want clitoral stimulation or penetration?"

Twila swallowed hard and looked around to see who'd heard Golden Bronze. He was talking too loud about what her vagina wanted. Right now, what she wanted was to turn on one heel and run. She should've brought Kimberly with her, because she'd know how to answer these questions without falling apart.

"I . . . um . . . guess I don't have a preference."

Twila wasn't a virgin, but for as many options as she had, her body count was pretty low. She could count the men she'd been with on one hand, and the ones who were decent lovers on two fingers. She had no idea what women meant when they said the words *mind-blowing sex.* But she wanted to know.

"Let me show you some that can give you both sensations."

"Okay . . ."

Golden Bronze led Twila to a wall of fake penises, some in pastel colors, some in flesh tones. Some had beads, some had little appendages with butterflies on the ends. Twila blinked, and then blinked some more. The flight part of her fight-or-flight reflex was about to kick in. Didn't they have any female workers at this store? Would Golden Bronze think she wanted him if she picked the jelly penis that was the same color as his skin?

Golden Bronze took one of the penises from the wall. She wondered if this challenged his masculinity at all—handling fake penises. Maybe he was gay and was used to handling them. *Oh, my goodness, I'm lusting after a gay man.*

"This one," Golden Bronze explained, "is self-thrusting and has a clitoral stimulator as well. It has eight thrusting speeds and ten vibrating settings. It will give you a mind-blowing orgasm."

"It will?"

"I've used one on my girlfriend. She loved it."

Twila relaxed. Thank God her gaydar wasn't broken. She needed that in Atlanta.

"Well, okay. I'll take that one, in umm . . . dark brown. How much is it?"

"This one is on sale today. It's one hundred twenty-nine dollars."

"What? Over a hundred dollars for a fake jelly penis?"

Golden Bronze doubled over from laughing, but Twila was serious.

"I mean, I'm going to Saint Lucia. That's probably someone's income for the month. Shoot, I could probably buy some real penis for the whole weekend."

"You probably could. But Mr. Fake Jelly won't get you pregnant or give you a disease you can't give back."

Twila snatched the package from Golden Bronze. "Just gimme this. Thank you."

Still laughing, Golden Bronze led Twila to the register, where they also talked her into buying lubricant (did she look like she had sandpaper vag?) and toy cleaner. The employees acted like there was nothing to be embarrassed about, but then they sold jelly penises all day long.

"We put two packs of batteries in there for you," Golden Bronze said. "I don't want you to run out while you're on vacation."

"Thanks," Twila said as she grabbed the bag off the counter.

She couldn't get out of that store fast enough, but since this weekend was all about getting her relax on, she'd trust Golden Bronze that this little (kinda large) battery-operated boyfriend was going to blow her mind.

She wondered if it was waterproof. 'Cause Mr. Fake Jelly was about to get all this ocean action.

Chapter 3

Kimberly glanced at the clock in her bedroom and felt a tiny bit anxious. Three hours until her flight to Saint Lucia with Twila and Hahna, but she wasn't done packing. They'd picked a late afternoon flight, so traffic wouldn't be an issue, but she still only had about twenty minutes left to decide.

To swimsuit or not to swimsuit.

She liked the idea of walking out onto the beach and straight into the crystal-blue waters of the Caribbean Sea, with her ample cleavage and juicy buttocks getting all the sunshine they could stand. But she also felt a little self-conscious when she pranced on the beach beside her tiny friends. No. They pranced. She jiggled.

Kimberly sighed and took her Torrid swimsuits from her dresser drawer and stuffed them in her luggage along with her cover-ups. If she didn't bring swim attire, Twila and Hahna, with their body-positive selves, would just force her to find one on the island that inevitably wouldn't fit properly. Because for some reason island gift stores thought one-size-fits-all included two hundred fifty pounds of black girl magic.

Every year for the past five years, Kimberly had promised herself that she'd lose weight for their girls' trip. Every year they chose some beachfront location. *What about Paris? London? Ain't no beach in London.* And it never failed, that she hated the pictures that Twila and Hahna posted on social media. The comments were always sweet.

You go, girl!

You *wearing* that swimsuit!

But Kimberly just wanted, for once, to have small arms, a flat stomach, and thighs that didn't rub together until her skin chafed. Was that too much to ask?

And she hated to share anything about her weight-loss journey with anyone. Even the other big girls were split. Some said she should love her body. Others were where she was—on the diet roller coaster and having either a win or a loss. And the ones who'd actually done the work and had the after picture where they looked oh-mazing, she hated them the most. They made her feel guilty about her laziness and lack of discipline.

The thin girls, like Twila and Hahna, were even worse than the pre- and post-big girls. They mostly didn't know what to say about weight loss, and they didn't understand the struggle. And when they started to apologize for the insane amount of food they consumed while she ate chicken Caesar salad at every meal—Kimberly didn't feel body positive at all. It reminded her that she was almost allergic to all of the foods that she loved. She couldn't eat a plate of lasagna and not gain seventy-eight pounds. She couldn't have a glass of wine without throwing herself out of ketosis. Because, yeah, ketosis was where you had to be to lose weight on a no-carb diet, else you were depriving yourself of food for no reason.

Kimberly hated that she was an expert on weight loss, but still fat.

The f-word. She *was* fat, although nobody wanted to say that either. Now she was plus-sized, fluffy, big and beautiful, and one of the ladies at the office had called her robust. Ro-freaking-bust. Kimberly hadn't even known how to take that. If the woman wasn't one of the partners at her law firm, she probably would've cussed her out for that. Robust.

Outside of the stresses of beach attire, Kimberly was looking forward to this trip. She needed this trip. Her work crush, Jason, had flirted with her incessantly for two years, but never once asked her out on a date. At least she *thought* he was flirting. But maybe he wasn't, because a week ago, he'd announced his engagement—to the office intern. They were having a Memorial Day wedding, and everyone was invited. The intern was twenty-three years old, and he was forty-seven. He was taking a child bride. Probably wanted to have a bunch of kids with his exposed-to-the-elements, probably radioactive sperm.

To make matters worse, Jason had whispered to Kimberly on his way out of the office. *There's still enough of me to go around. She's a pony. I might need a thoroughbred.*

Thoroughbred. As in a big, grown-ass horse? That was worse than robust.

Then, on top of everything else, Kimberly was working the hell out of her side hustle. Her natural hair care products had gone viral after she'd got all her naturalista sorority sisters to model their hair regimens on social media. But the side hustle, along with her ridiculous main hustle workload, was too much some days—most days.

Anyway, Kimberly needed some peace. She wanted a full body scrub with something that smelled like coconut, sunshine, and better days ahead. She wanted cocktails that made her forget caloric content, ketosis, and grown-ass horse references. She needed to hear Twila and Hahna's struggles, so that she knew she wasn't alone.

That's what their spa weekends were for—pure, gently intoxicated bliss. And Kimberly was here for it. She just hoped that next year, they would find a good spa location in Denver, Colorado.

No beaches in Denver.

Chapter 4

Hahna inhaled the island air, a mix of ocean and lush green vegetation, as the bellhop drove her, Twila, and Kimberly to their over-the-water bungalows in an oversized golf cart. The check-in process had been easy, just like their flights. Easy, breezy was going to be the theme for this trip. Because that's what she needed. Drama need not knock on her bungalow door.

"You ladies are here alone?" the bellhop asked.

"We're here with each other," Kimberly said.

"Ohhhhhhhh. . . ." the bellhop said. "Well, my name is Peter. Anything you need, and I do mean *anything*, please make sure that you ask for me."

The way Peter wiggled his eyebrows and his pelvis let Hahna know that his "anything" included sexual favors. She rolled her eyes and continued to gaze out at the landscape. Why were men always offering unrequested sex?

"You think we're down here to get our groove back?" Twila asked.

"Aren't you?"

"My groove is just fine and in one piece," Kimberly said.

"Well, speak for yourself," Twila said. "I might just call you, Peter. Depends on what you're working with."

"I am working with a lot. You've never seen this much work."

"I'm sure I have, Peter. All you men think your junk is the greatest, and there's always better."

"One man's junk is a bad girl's pleasure," Peter replied, except he said *girl* like *gyal* with an island twang.

"Boy, you talk a good game, you better be ready."

"You talk big, big too, and you're such a little one. I may want to try your friend. The quiet one in the back. She's got more for me to hold on to."

Peter winked at Kimberly in the rearview mirror, and she promptly blushed and looked away. Hahna giggled, and felt a fun mood settle right in her spirit.

"I'm not here for your *junk*," Kimberly said. "I'm here to relax."

Peter was right about Twila, though. She was a little one. She was barely over five feet tall and needed a fine tailor to fill out a size zero waistline. But then she always needed that tailor to let out the hip area, because her waist-to-booty ratio was unreal. Size below zero waist and size eight hips and booty. Most men looked at her like an amusement park ride they had to try out.

"How you just gone be offering it to everybody in this little golf cart?" Twila asked. "You just messed up your chances with me, big fella."

"Oh, no," Peter said with fake sorrow that made Hahna burst into laughter. "There's plenty of Peter to go around."

"Boy, if you don't get us to our finely appointed lodgings, there will be hell to pay," Twila said. "I need a cocktail."

Up over the next hill, the path finally opened to a road that went down the center of the beach. The over-the-water bungalows were Twila's idea. She wanted to see fish swimming under her feet. Hahna kept thinking about the open ocean floor beneath her and got a little nervous about sleeping on top of it.

The bungalows were beautiful, though, and not very far from the shore. The narrow road was built right over the water, with the bungalows connected like little branches from a tree trunk. The drive in the golf cart was a bit unnerving since it was dark outside.

"Which one is ours?" Twila asked.

"The big one on the left," Peter said. "Two bedrooms, one master and one single king size."

"I call dibs on the single," Twila said.

Hahna glanced at Kimberly and smiled. Twila never had to call dibs on the single room. No one wanted to share with her. She liked to walk around in her naked glory, randomly clapping her behind, and she snored. Plus, she took all day in the bathroom. Anytime there was a room-sharing situation, Hahna and Kimberly were always together, ever since the three of them had met in college.

Peter pulled the golf cart right onto the little narrow piece of road that led to the cottage. He jumped out and opened the golf cart doors and then went to remove their luggage from the back. Hahna and Kimberly had both packed sensibly—one bag apiece. Twila was extra, and extra came with more baggage.

Inside the cottage, Hahna and Kimberly walked straight into the huge master bedroom while they waited for Peter to bring in the luggage. One of the walls was a giant sliding glass patio door with a view of the water. The floor wasn't entirely glass, but there were lights built into the window frame, showing Kimberly the fish swimming below.

The large king-sized bed, with what seemed like a dozen or more pillows, was a bed for lovers. For a brief second Hahna wished that she was here with the love of her life instead of her girlfriends. Not that she'd ever had the love of her life. She was waiting to feel that swept-away feeling that women gushed about, where they couldn't eat, sleep, or breathe without thinking about their man. She'd had relationships and situations that were almost relationships—situationships—but she'd never been swept away.

Hahna had pretty much convinced herself that these women were faking that nonsense. They were ignoring some tragic flaw that their man had. He might be chocolate with abs like a god and a six-figure income, but something was broken. They just weren't sharing it with everyone else. Perpetuating a fraud all over their social media pages. And then they were quieter than a toddler in a jar of Vaseline when their fraudulent loves went awry.

Hahna had never met a man who didn't know how to take the wind out of her sails instead of blowing her away.

"This room is incredible, right?" Kimberly asked, snatching Hahna out of her negative spiral of thoughts. She was glad to be interrupted too, because the fun spirit that had settled earlier scurried right away when she thought about relationships.

"It is. I can't wait until the morning so we can go to the beach. You brought swimsuits, right?"

Kimberly rolled her eyes. "Yes, I brought swimsuits. We're on an island. Duh."

"Okay. You can say 'duh' all you want, but I know you."

"You think you do, but you don't. I even packed a two-piece."

"Shut your mouth, you body-positive heffa! That's what I'm talking about."

Kimberly gave Hahna a blank facial expression. Hahna bit her bottom lip. Maybe she was being too over-the-top with her excitement, because Kimberly was never excited about a swimsuit. The fact that she'd brought one without weeks of cajoling was epic.

"Yes. I'd like to go snorkeling out on the coral reef. We'll have to take a boat out there and jump off."

Hahna nodded her approval. "Look at you, being a daredevil."

"I thought it would be fun."

That's different for you, but I'm down. I don't know if Ms. Thousand Dollar Sew In is going to . . ."

"You hoes in here talking about me?" Twila asked as she burst into their room, her sundress billowing behind her like she had a wind machine prepped for her entrance.

"No, we were just saying your weave probably wasn't going to be submerged in the ocean."

"First of all, I got this weave for the ocean. It can get wet. And second, I tried to give Peter a tip . . ."

"Peter tried to give you the tip," Hahna said through a muffled giggle.

"You nasty. Anyway, I tried to tip him, and he wouldn't take it. He said, no tips allowed here. I did good when I picked this resort. The bar is stocked, the damn ocean is under my feet, and there are on-site spa services. I'm 'bout to get my life."

"I wanna see your room," Hahna said.

Hahna, Twila, and Kimberly all left the master bedroom for Twila's private accommodations. Her room was equally stunning, with the same sliding door and glass floor.

"This is incredible," Kimberly said.

Hahna narrowed her eyes and looked around the room. "Do y'all hear that humming sound?"

"Is it wildlife?" Twila asked. "I don't do wildlife. Not crickets, not lizards . . ."

"Not snakes," Kimberly added.

Twila jumped on the bed. "Definitely not snakes. Where have I brought us? I thought it was safe here. Did one of the sea creatures get inside? I don't want to be shark food."

"Be quiet, so I can hear where it's coming from," Hahna said.

She concentrated for a moment, and then walked in the direction of Twila's bags.

"I think it's coming from your big suitcase. Some bug or lizard probably got on it when we were outside."

Twila shrieked. "Get it! Whatever it is, kill it!"

"I'm not gonna kill it," Hahna said. "I'm going to take it outside. It didn't get on your stuff on purpose. It was probably an accident."

"Yo' old *Bug's Life* ass better get it out of here," Twila said. The words were loud, but there was a quiver in her tone.

As Hahna got closer to the bags, the humming noise seemed to be coming from inside the bag and not outside. It was muffled a bit.

"I think it got in your bag somehow."

"Oh, my God, there's a lizard in my Chanel? Please don't let it lay eggs."

Kimberly was done. Fell out laughing right on the floor next to the bed. Hahna hollered, too, because Twila was dead serious.

Hahna figured out which bag it was coming from and slowly

lowered the zipper. She didn't want anything jumping out at her out of surprise.

"Oh, my goodness," Hahna said as she grabbed the *lizard*. It was more like a snake, though. "What the hell is this?"

Before Kimberly could scramble to her feet, Twila lunged from the bed over to Hahna. Hahna, however, waved her findings in the air.

"Give me that!" Twila yelled.

Kimberly's jaw dropped when she saw the buzzing creature. It was Twila's gigantic vibrating thingamajig.

"I knew I should've left it in the damn package," Twila said as she hastily pressed the OFF button.

"Ewww . . ." Kimberly said.

"That's why she wanted the single room," Hahna said. "She got a rendezvous with her little friend over there."

"Look, y'all can clown if you want, but I ain't had none in a long time, okay?"

"Me either," Kimberly said.

"Well, I haven't either, but I'm not gonna stick inanimate objects up my coochie."

"It looked animated to me," Kimberly said. "All that whirling and twirling."

"And thrusting," Twila said. "It thrusts on its own."

"It what?" Kimberly asked. "Let me see that thing. I need one of those."

Still laughing as Kimberly and Twila made the toy light up and gyrate, Hahna sat down on the edge of the bed.

"Is this what we've come to?" Hahna asked. "Are we that desperate?"

Twila shut the toy off, rammed it into her suitcase, and then joined Hahna on the bed. Kimberly plopped down in a white wicker chair near the patio door.

"I'm not desperate," Twila said. "I just don't want to go through it right now."

"Through what?" Kimberly asked.

"Meeting someone, really digging them, feeling hopeful, and then getting it on."

Hahna nodded. "It's the feeling hopeful part that gets me. I'm tired of thinking he's the one, and then he's not."

"I think it's the kind of men y'all date," Kimberly said.

"This coming from Ms. I'm-Saving-Myself-for-Jesus," Twila said. "The kind of men I date are fine. It's just that I keep picking the rotten ones out of the bunch."

"Me too," Hahna said. "Rotten to the core."

"Let's try not to think too hard about being single while we're here," Kimberly said. "We've got great careers and our bank accounts are fat."

"That's enough for now. Y'all wanna drip some melanin at the restaurant we passed on the way back here?" Twila asked.

Hahna nodded, and followed Kimberly back to their bedroom, so that they could freshen up and change into sundresses, but Twila's words lingered. *That's enough for now.*

But it wasn't enough.

Success, finances, and sister-friend vacations were only some of what Hahna needed. She wanted love. That '90s rhythm-and-blues love. That if-lovin'-you-is-all-that-I-have-to-do kinda love.

Why did Hahna have everything except *that*? She'd probably trade some of what she had for a twin flame love. Not her sister friends, or her success, but shit, not her finances either.

"Why do we have to trade?" Hahna asked Kimberly.

"Trade what?"

"Why can't we have everything we have, *and* have a man? Why do we have to give anything up?"

Kimberly looked up from the two sundresses she had spread out on the bed.

"Who said that? I'm not giving anything up."

"You're not?"

"No. But stop stressing yourself about not having a man right now. That's not why we're here."

"You're right. It was Twila's rubber thingy that got me feeling all destitute. I'm fine now."

"Good. 'Cause I need you to help me get into this girdle. It's a two-person job."

They laughed again, because it was needed. The air had become thick with grief and despondence, and that had nothing to do with relaxation, rejuvenation, or restoration.

Kimberly's superpower was replacing dark clouds with laughter, and Hahna loved her for that. Plus, Kimberly didn't have to know that some of the tears that came out with her belly laughs were leftover tears from Torian's betrayal.

Chapter 5

Hahna walked over to the edge of the pool and stuck one big toe into the chilly water. She quickly pulled it back and marched over to the pool chairs where Kimberly and Twila lounged while waiting for drinks.

"That water is frigid," Hahna said. "They need to heat it or something."

"It'll be hot by noon. It rained last night, did y'all hear it? It was so peaceful," Kimberly said.

"I just wanted to finish flushing the toxins from the massage out of my body with a nice swim," Hahna said. "Those spa treatments were heavenly."

"Ain't nothing like an oiled-up ebony man, using his God-given muscles and talents to massage joy back into your joints," Twila said with her eyes closed as if she was reliving the experience.

"You need a cigarette?" Kimberly asked.

"No. I need some sex, because that toy isn't a man. But since neither one of you heffas is my type, I'll settle for a toxin-filled cocktail."

Twila flagged down the pool server, and Hahna stretched out on the pool chair between Kimberly and Twila. The pool was cool, but the morning sun was warm and renewing. Hahna could feel herself getting energized.

"When did you get so horny?" Hahna asked. "I remember when you used to say you could do without sex."

"I don't know what is wrong with me," Twila said. "It's like I hit forty and my body decided it was going to make up for all of the sex I didn't get in my twenties and thirties."

"Your coochie decided to be a ho, girl?" Kimberly asked.

"Yes. And it didn't give me the damn memo."

"Do you ever let your lady parts get sunlight?" Kimberly asked. "Maybe your yoni isn't a ho. Maybe she just needs a little sun."

"Who does that on purpose?" Hahna asked.

"I do it every morning. I go out on my deck, sit on my deck chair and spread my glory out toward the heavens. I swear it feels like battery power."

Twila burst out laughing. "She sitting over there with a photosynthesized coochie."

"Except I'm not a plant, and photosynthesis is how plants process sunlight."

"Well, what do people do with it then?" Twila asked.

"We turn sunlight into vitamin D. There are nutrients in the sunlight. Sunlight is food to me."

Hahna stared at Kimberly and shook her head. There was always a metaphysical explanation for all the weird stuff Kimberly did.

"Don't say I didn't tell y'all. When you're all dried and shriveled up, you're gonna wish you were sunbathing your lady parts all along."

"What difference does it make whether I'm dried and shriveled up?" Hahna asked. "I haven't been with anyone since Torian ghosted me. What if that last time with him was my *last* time?"

Twila gave a laugh that sounded like a snort and a hoot put together. A snoot.

"Girl, you can get some anytime you want," Twila said. "Shit, we all can."

"Since we're determined to talk about the male species, let's be real, ain't nobody trying to just get some," Kimberly said. "I need it to be meaningful."

"I want meaningful," Hahna said. "I want it to be earth-shattering. I want to feel loved."

"Right?" Kimberly said. "Can I just mean something to some-body? Can he look into my eyes instead of focusing on what this stomach roll might or might not be doing?"

"Who in the hell is looking at a stomach roll when they have a naked woman in their bed? Anyway, you betta find somebody to grab that stomach roll," Twila said. "Lots of brothas like that."

"What else they like, huh?" Kimberly asked. "Cause both of y'all look like you go to the gym every day and all y'all eat is spinach and quinoa lettuce wraps on beds of lettuce. Like for real. If y'all can't find someone, my chances are slim to none."

"Maybe we're all just too picky," Twila said.

Hahna shook her head. "That's what we're not about to do. We get to have standards. Just because I'm not interested in an unemployed felon doesn't mean I'm too picky."

Twila held up one finger while she ordered her cocktail. A rum runner with a rum floater on top.

"You getting it in early," Kimberly said.

"Don't judge me. It has orange juice in it."

"Well, then that's breakfast," Kimberly said. "Bring me one too."

The pool waiter winked at Kimberly right before he walked away. He was as delicious going as he was coming. Hahna won-dered if he knew his white shorts were just a tiny bit too small. They gripped his glutes and made all his manual labor worth-while.

"Now, back to your standards. I'm not talking about unem-ployed felons. I'm talking about Todd Tucker."

Hahna scrunched her eyebrows together trying to remem-ber if she knew Todd. Was this a man from Twila's past who had resurfaced? And if he had, then why was she in need of her whirling, twirling, and thrusting apparatus?

"I keep forgetting your bougie self doesn't watch *Real House-wives of Atlanta*."

"Todd is a character on that show?" Hahna asked.

"Well, it's a reality show, so he's not a character. He's just himself."

"You're trying to hook up with him?" Kimberly asked. "I'm confused."

"No. Todd is Kandi's husband. I know y'all know Kandi from Xscape. The singing group?"

"Oh, yes, of course," Hahna said. She was a Georgia peach, and that R&B group was homegrown.

"Anyway, Kandi married Todd. They have a little boy and everything."

"What do two people getting married on TV have to do with us?" Kimberly asked.

"Because Kandi is rich. A boss chick. She's got millions. And Todd was just a regular guy with a good income. He was on the camera crew of the show."

"She met him while filming?" Hahna asked.

"One of the other cast members, I think Phaedra, introduced them. And they hit it off. He's fine, and Kandi didn't care if her money was longer than his. She is one happy sugar mama."

"She was cool that he didn't make as much money as she did?" Kimberly asked.

"I mean, I'm sure she thought about it. How could she not? But in the end she just wanted love, and a baby," Twila said.

"I *need* a man to have money, though," Hahna said. "I've been poor before. I don't want that ever again."

Kimberly and Twila had no clue what it was like to be as poor as Hahna had been growing up. She'd never had enough underwear and socks. Barely had enough to eat every night. She was the kid who ate the entire school lunch, no matter how terrible, because it was free, and it would fill her up. Food at home for dinner was never guaranteed, just like her college tuition hadn't been. Hahna remembered her grandmother telling her to go into the military if she didn't land a full tuition scholarship. Luckily, Spelman had come through, and it had changed her life.

Hahna was never going back to being poor.

"We need to find a Todd," Twila said.

"Where am I gonna find a Todd?" Hahna asked. "Looks like Kandi already got him."

"A guy like Todd, of course."

"A cameraman?" Kimberly asked.

"No. The kind of guy you crossed off your list for having potential, but not reaching it yet. The guy that's got two baby mamas. Or three."

"Three?" Hahna asked. "Three might be too many."

"It's not the number that's important. It's the fact that we cross dudes off our list so quickly. One strike and they're not a contender."

"Oh, I got you," Kimberly said. "Like no college degree is a no for me."

"Turn that no into a yes," Twila said.

"But if a man doesn't have a degree . . ."

"Listen, Kim. You can't do this if you're going to justify your strikes."

"Okay. A man has no degree, and I just say, no problem?" Kimberly said.

"Yes. You don't worry about that."

"What about a felony?" Hahna asked. "We forgetting about those too?"

Twila shrugged. "Depends. When did it happen? Is he dangerous? Is he a sex offender?"

"I'm not dating a sex offender," Hahna said. "Game over. It's a wrap."

"I'm not telling you to date a criminal. I'm saying some of the things on your list shouldn't be there. Erase all the stuff from your list that doesn't make the man a bad person. If you do that, I bet you'll have a lot more men to choose from."

"Are you gonna do the same thing?" Hahna asked. "Or are you experimenting on me and Kim? Because you have been known to do such a thing."

"Yeah," Kimberly said, "like that whole let's-date-a-white-guy thing. You didn't even try it. You just used us as a social experiment."

"I'm doing it too. I think standing in that store buying that contraption and drooling over the guy who sold it to me, convinced me."

"Was he single?" Hahna asked.

"He said he had a girlfriend."

"Wouldn't that be awkward anyway?" Kimberly asked. "Since he hooked you up with your current flame?"

"You're such a miserable heffa," Twila said.

"Time-out." Hahna said. "I'm trying to wrap my brain around this. Okay, so when I get home, I'm going to break all the dating rules. I have no idea what that looks like."

"I don't even know all my rules," Twila said. "But when one pops into my head, I'm gonna dismiss it."

"Why the hell not?" Kimberly said. "If Kandi can be a sugar mama, so can I."

"I'ma need you to know who Kandi is, though," Twila said. "You can't use the reference if you don't know."

"I know 'cause you told me."

"The next guy that asks me out on a date," Twila said, "I'm going."

"Why does he even have to ask you?" Hahna said. "Isn't that a rule too?"

"It is. How about, the next man I want, I'm having him?" Twila said.

Hahna had to hold her side to keep from cackling. She knew her friend, and she meant that. She was going to *have* the next man she desired, in all the ways a man could be had.

"So, we're all-in," Hahna said. "It's the first weekend of April now. When do we report progress?"

"Memorial Day," Kimberly said. "Mostly because Jason is getting married that weekend, and I need a date."

"Wait, work Jason?" Hahna asked. "The guy you've been digging for the past five years?"

"Yep. He's marrying the intern."

Twila shook her head. "Damn."

"I know. How the hell can I compete with a twenty-three-year-old?" Kimberly asked.

"We don't have to," Twila said. "They might have rock-hard abdominals . . ."

"I used to have rock-hard abdominals," Hahna said.

"They might have tight little bodies," Twila continued, "but we have things they don't have. We don't need anyone to buy our weave bundles or pay our tuition."

"There's men out there paying tuition?" Kimberly asked. "Where were they when I was in college? I needed a tuition bill or two paid."

"Girls are out there scamming left and right, but we don't have to do that," Twila explained. "We have everything we need. We just have wants and desires that need attention, and if we put it that way, I don't think we'll get turned down."

"That doesn't make us sound too nasty?" Hahna asked.

"No. It makes us sound grown. Are y'all in?"

Kimberly nodded. "Yes, girl. I'm ready to try anything at this point."

"Me too," Hahna said. "I mean, not anything . . . but something. Shit, anything. I'm ready to try anything too."

"Since Kimberly needs her date by Memorial Day weekend, I think we should check in the first weekend of May. That gives us three weeks after we get home," Twila said.

Three weeks to find a man in Atlanta. Twila should've started this challenge off with, *Your mission, Kimberly and Hahna . . . should you choose to accept it . . .*

"That's a tall order," Hahna said.

"Only if you keep all your rules intact. Only if you meet men where you've always met them. I don't know about y'all, but I'm pretty excited about this. I have a feeling we've been missing out on some great opportunities."

"You just want to get rid of that jelly dingaling," Kimberly said.

"Yes. There's that too."

Hahna wasn't as excited as Twila, but she was ready to replace the memory of Torian with someone new. If she could do that in three days, three weeks, or three months, it would be welcome. And if it took erasing a few rules, then, she welcomed that too.

Then, maybe next time she visited an oversea bungalow, she could go to the spa with her girls during the day and curl her toes at night.

Chapter 6

The long weekend had gone by too quickly, and none of Hahna's clients had taken the days off with her. Her email in box was overflowing with messages from the last five days, and she was only halfway through them at three o'clock.

Aliyah's one-on-one meeting with Hahna couldn't have come at a worse time, but Hahna didn't want to reschedule. She needed to have this conversation.

Aliyah walked into Hahna's office without knocking and sat at Hahna's conference table. Everyone else always plopped down right in front of her desk, but Aliyah preferred the table.

Today, Aliyah had waist-length braids with blue tips. Her royal blue dress matched the braids. The blue hair gave Aliyah a hood edge, but her schoolteacher glasses and full, glossy lips softened it. The girl had body for days too. If she wasn't a data scientist, she could just as easily slide down the pole for a living or be some celebrity's trophy wife.

"Hahna, can you tell Corden to lay off?"

Aliyah had gotten right to business. Hahna appreciated her candor, because she didn't have time for a long, drawn-out meeting on this topic.

"What is he doing other than holding you accountable?" Hahna asked as she joined Aliyah at the table.

"It's not the accountability that bothers me. It's the lack of trust."

"You have to earn his trust, Aliyah, and accidentally sharing our customers' data isn't quite the way to do that."

Aliyah rolled her eyes. "I owned up to that mistake, but he made it bigger than it was. The customer didn't even know what they were looking at. No one was hurt during that situation."

"No one was hurt that time. Give me my speech about data."

"Your speech?" Aliyah asked.

"Yeah. My talking points. You ought to know them by now."

Aliyah rolled her eyes again. If she could only get past her attitude, she might be a senior executive somewhere someday. She had the chops for it. This was why Hahna was patient with Aliyah. She saw past the girl's exterior and found brilliance.

"Data is an asset, and data has value."

"What else?"

"With data analysis, our customers can make information-based decisions."

"Correct. These are not just random incidents that don't have impacts, Aliyah. This time we were able to fix it. Too many more of these, and we lose credibility with our customer base. No customer base means . . ."

"No company, no job. I get it, Hahna."

"Okay, good. I'm glad we had this talk."

"But that still doesn't deal with Corden. I think he doesn't like me because he's gay."

Hahna scrunched her nose. "Corden's not gay, though."

"He's not out. I'll say that. The streets of Atlanta have lots to say about his proclivities."

Corden wasn't just an employee—he was a friend—so, Hahna wasn't going to allow Aliyah to sit in her office telling lies on his character.

"Corden has a lovely fiancée, and you would do well to cast rumors aside. The only issue Corden has with you is your lack of attention to detail. Plus, you report to me, and you work with Corden on projects. He's not your supervisor."

"So, he can't fire me?"

"No. Has he ever threatened to?"

"He just sucks his teeth like a little punk and says stuff under his breath like, 'She gotta go,' or 'I ain't gonna be able to do this.'"

Like a little punk. This girl hadn't heard anything she just said.

"Corden isn't gay, but if he was I wouldn't care," Hahna said. "I need you to be clear about that, because you're slipping into some intolerant behavior."

"Well, if I have to tolerate him, he needs to tolerate me."

"I'll talk to him."

"Thank you."

"Aliyah, I called you in here to tell you that you did a good job cleaning up that data breach and finishing the dashboard. I appreciate it. Corden told me that you did most of the heavy lifting."

"I did. Corden didn't even know where to start on that dashboard."

Hahna ignored the dig at Corden. "Thank you. Why don't you take the rest of the day off? Get some rest, and then come back tomorrow feeling inspired to be a part of this team."

"What if I can't find that particular inspiration?"

"Then you should be inspired just to have a job."

Aliyah smiled as she stood, but it wasn't a warm and cheerful smile. It was the perfunctory smile a subordinate gives her manager when the meeting has been adjourned. There was going to be more conflict with those two in the future. Hahna knew it was inevitable, but she had no idea how to prevent it.

Aliyah passed by Sylvia on her way out. Sylvia put the mail on the corner of Hahna's desk.

"Have you caught up yet?" Sylvia asked.

"Almost. I put out the most important fires, anyway. Corden and Aliyah did the dang thing on that data breach situation."

"They were here all weekend."

"I know. And it looks like Shale has decided not to inform their customers of the data breach. Not what I would've done, but they have a lot to lose when customers walk away."

Sylvia shook her head. "As long as we were ethical in *our* dealings. We can't control what they do or don't tell their customers."

"Exactly. I'm reading emails from Brexton Inc., the pharmaceutical company in Miami. I may have to fly out to Miami for a face-to-face meeting. Hale Brexton is old-school. He's not used to making deals with a company over the phone or video-conferencing."

"Is Brexton worth the cost of the trip?"

"Absolutely. This one client will bring in another two million dollars in revenue. We need bigger clients, anyway, because I would rather deal with a few large clients than hundreds of little ones."

"When are you available to travel?"

Hahna sucked her teeth slowly. "We can travel on Saturday and meet with Brexton on Monday. I need Corden to get our presentation ready. He'll travel with me too. See if he wants to bring his fiancée and get airfare for the three of us and two rooms."

"His fiancée? Okay, big spender."

Hahna shook her head. "No, this is a bonus for him handling the Shale situation while I was on the beach. I take care of my people, you know that."

"What about Ms. Aliyah then?"

"She caused the breach. She should be happy I didn't fire her."

Sylvia nodded. "You're right. I'm glad you didn't."

"I didn't *this* time. She really needs to tighten her game up."

"And her attitude," Sylvia answered.

"See, I didn't even say all that. I'm going to put her on a mentoring plan when all the dust settles. But first, we're going to land Brexton. What else do I have for today? Do I have time to put together some talking points for Corden?"

"Well, your calendar says you're supposed to leave today at three thirty p.m. for a book signing."

"That's right. The Eric Jerome Dickey signing in Buckhead."

"Are you going to cancel?"

"Ugh. No, I can't. My sorority sister just opened a bookstore and needs numbers at her events to attract bigger authors so that people will come out to her store and spend money."

"You can't do everything, Hahna. You're going to wear yourself out."

"I know. And you're right. But I am going to do this. I'll shoot Corden some talking points later this evening. Plus, Eric Dickey is my favorite author."

"Is he single?" Sylvia asked.

"Girl, I don't know."

"I'm just saying, you might want to put on a little makeup and take your hair out of that severe-looking bun."

"Really? I'm not a groupie. I'm not going to holla at the author."

"You need to holla at somebody."

"Sylvia."

"I'm just saying."

Hahna wanted to laugh at the pose Sylvia had struck: hands on hips, lips poked out, and neck ready to roll. Then she remembered the challenge, and she snatched the ponytail holder out of her curls.

"That's what I'm talking about. Now, get on out of here if you're going to beat the traffic."

Hahna typed furiously, and then hit SEND on one more email.

"Corden will handle the rest," Sylvia said. "Just go ahead and go."

Hahna was glad that she got to the book signing early. The small event space was elegant, but packed, with close to standing room only. Hahna's feet were not made for standing room only, though, so securing a seat was a necessity.

As soon as she sat, she texted Corden. *Make sure you include our customer service and innovation. No one is speaking to data the way we are.*

Hahna was seated at a table with strangers. Some appeared to be members of a book club, since they were all wearing matching t-shirts, and there was a man with a stack of Eric Jerome

Dickey books on the table in front of him. He nursed his drink, something brown, and didn't engage with anyone.

Typically, Hahna wouldn't speak to a guy like this. He could be mean, or her awkward jokes could fall flat. These kinds of guys had the potential to make her feel stupid, and feeling stupid would drain the peace right out of her body.

But she was supposed to be atypical Hahna. No rules. Just fun. That's what they'd decided in Saint Lucia. This was the first practical application of their plan. Plus, he was fine.

Hahna cleared her throat and the man looked up at her, eyebrows raised like asking, *What is it?* In that moment, she almost chickened out.

"You might even be a bigger fan than I am," Hahna said as she motioned at his stack of books.

"I am a pretty big fan," he said. "I usually don't make it out to the signings, though. Something always seems to come up."

"I know, right. Like life? But we've got to support our artists, you know?"

"That's one hundred percent right. He's one of our generation's finest griots. I'm Sam Valcourt."

"Hahna Osborne."

"Pleased to meet you, fellow book lover."

"Pleased to meet you as well."

Hahna exhaled. Sam was friendlier than she'd thought he'd be. Not so friendly that she'd find him creepy, but cordial enough that conversing with him was an option.

But now what? She had no idea what to ask him next. Couldn't ask her normal top three, because she was supposed to not be caring about where a man worked, where he went to school, or if he had children. She hadn't planned this well.

"This little space is so nice. The bookstore is new, but I didn't even know the building was tucked away back here. All this time I've lived in Buckhead, I've never been to anything here."

Sam nodded his agreement. "It took me a while to find it. A bit of traffic getting here from Lithonia, but not too much."

Was Sam purposely not giving Hahna anything to go on? His answer had nothing she could springboard to, but his smile was inviting. More noteworthy was his beard, salt and pepper with more salt. The hair on his head matched. It was a sexy contrast to his dark chocolate skin and wide, expressive eyes. At least he was in the right age range.

"Do they have a full bar?" Hahna asked. "What are you drinking?"

"They have a full bar. I just have bourbon. Would you like me to get you something?"

Now Hahna returned Sam's smile. "I'd like that. If the bourbon's good, an old-fashioned. If you didn't like it, a vodka cranberry."

"The bourbon is good, but it needs a cigar to go along with it."

"I like cigars and bourbon."

Now Sam seemed to be assessing *her*, which was good. He could help her do some of the work.

"It's a unique pairing, like wine and Brie."

"I am a fan of unique pairings."

Sam gave her a quick nod and then headed to the bar. She watched him walk away. Yes, wide shoulders, strong-looking back, nice behind—he must work out. He was slim, but grown-man slim.

"He's fine," one of the book club ladies said. "I shoulda hollered at him first."

Hahna laughed. *Too late, thirsty.*

"Oh, you don't have to worry about me, I'm just playing," the book club lady said. "I'm here for Eric Jerome Dickey, honey. At his last book signing, he wrote, 'Hey, Boo' in my book. I should've given him my number then, but I was slipping."

"You were slipping," Hahna said. "But this time you're gonna secure the bag."

"Yes, I am. He ain't ready."

The other book club ladies giggled and snickered. The Eric Jerome Dickey fangirl must be the fun character of their group.

"Well, good luck, girl."

"I don't need it, but thank you anyway."

"Um . . . okay."

Sam reappeared with liquor in his hand, and Hahna was happy to see him again. Or maybe she was just happy to be rescued from the book club conversation.

"Your old-fashioned, and there were no cigars, but I did grab some snacks from the table. Didn't know if you'd had anything to eat already, but they looked good."

"They put out snacks?" the book club lady said to one of her friends. "Girl, watch my stuff."

"Thank you, Sam," Hahna said as she stifled a giggle. "Looks like those snacks will be gone in no time."

Sam sat back down at the table, ever so slightly moving his chair closer to Hahna. She noticed and liked that. That meant he wanted to converse further.

"What's your favorite EJD novel?" Sam asked as Hahna took a sip of her old-fashioned. It was delicious. And strong.

"I think *Dying for Revenge* is my favorite. I really liked the villainous assassin with the penchant for shoes."

Sam nodded. "One of my favorites too. But if I had to choose one, it'd be *Genvieve.* That was before he started writing the darker titles, but I really enjoyed that one."

"Me too. There's not a book of his I haven't enjoyed, and he reduced me to tears with *The Blackbirds.*"

"Yep, that one was a culmination of so many of his other stories, but it was good. I love his constant evolution."

"So do I. When I read his reviews, I don't think all his readers get it . . ."

"They don't, but as a writer, I totally get it. An artist can't stay stagnant. As soon as we have to color in the lines, it's no longer art. I refuse to do what everyone else does."

"You're an aspiring writer?" Hahna asked.

"Not aspiring. I am a writer."

Hahna noted his clipped and defiant tone and wondered if she'd ruined their good start.

"Oh, I'm sorry. Did I offend you? I didn't mean to."

"You didn't. I've only published two books, and I haven't had as much exposure as I'd like. You probably haven't heard of me yet."

"I'm sure it's only a matter of time."

"That is correct."

Hahna liked his confidence. "Tell me about your books."

"I write quirky romances, about lovers who meet under impossible circumstances."

"Now I have to hear more."

"Like, for example, what's happening right now, this dialogue between us, could be the start of one of my books."

Hahna's eyebrows rose. "Is this an impossible circumstance?"

"Sure. An unknown author attempts to impress the finest woman in the room when she only has eyes for Eric Jerome Dickey."

Hahna's laughter rang out, maybe a little too loudly, because the book club ladies dropped their conversation and stared. She didn't care, though. The laughter felt incredible and freeing.

"See?" Sam said. "Impossible."

"You had me at 'finest woman in the room,' " Hahna said.

The applause for Eric Jerome Dickey drowned out Sam's response, and any hopes of pulling that conversation thread. Hahna's insides felt like warm, mushy goo, and not because she was seeing her favorite author live and in the flesh. This was what a confident, sexy man did to her. Reduced her to gelatin.

Hahna barely heard anything the man of the hour had to say about his new book, or the questions from the audience. She spent the entire time stealing glances at Sam and memorizing his profile. His strong jawline and prominent and masculine nose was sexy scenery, and she enjoyed the view.

As they stood in line to get their books signed, Hahna tried to talk herself out of asking Sam out on a date. He was right here, and he was clearly feeling her. Why didn't he just man up and do the asking? If she had to take the lead in asking for a date, would she have to lead everything in their potential relationship?

Then she listened to herself.

How many opportunities had she missed out on because she was too old-school to make the first move? Wasn't she supposed to be doing something different? Just because Sam wasn't in her face with toxic masculinity, that didn't mean he wasn't a man.

She waited, though. Couldn't stop herself from thinking that a rapid date request was a desperate one.

Hahna's stomach grumbled loudly from the stress of it all. It didn't help that the room was quiet, because everyone was trying to listen in on the little conversations Mr. Dickey had with each reader. Hahna squeezed her eyes shut, hoping that Sam hadn't heard. Her back was to him in line, so maybe . . .

"Snacks weren't enough for you, huh?" Sam asked.

Embarrassed, Hahna shook her head. "Maybe it was the old-fashioned."

"Would you like to score a few more snacks when this is over? The Fish Spot is across the street."

Wait! A date! Well, maybe not quite a date, but an ask. Her first instinct was to turn it down. Because that's what a smart woman did when a man asked her on a spur-of-the-moment date. To go on the date would make her seem too available. But she was available. And she was supposed to be breaking her rules.

"I've been meaning to try their catfish nuggets," Hahna said. "I've heard great things."

"The catfish nuggets are everything."

"You've convinced me."

"Good. I'm not quite ready to end our conversation. We were just getting started."

"I agree."

Finally, it was Hahna's turn to get her book signed. She smiled at her favorite author and mumbled something complimentary. He made a joke about her name that went over her head, but she laughed anyway. But her attention was elsewhere. She'd left the room. In her mind, she was already on her date with Sam.

She took her signed book and stood to the side while Sam had his moment. He gave Eric Jerome Dickey a copy of one of his own books.

"Hahna, do you mind taking a picture of us?" Sam asked.

"Might be too much fine for one photo, but I'll try," Hahna replied.

She was rewarded for her flirtatiousness with a beautiful smile from both men, although she paid more attention to Sam's.

She whipped out her phone and took several photos.

"You'll text them to me?" Sam asked.

"Sounds like he's just trying to get your phone number," Eric Jerome Dickey said.

"Oh, I was already getting that," Sam said with a laugh. "Thanks, my brotha, for leading the way and for opening doors."

They shared a warm bro-hug that Hahna also captured with her phone.

"You ready for those catfish nuggets?" Sam asked.

Hahna nodded. She was ready for a lot more than that, though. She wanted a taste of him as well.

Chapter 7

Sam held the door as Hahna walked into the Fish Spot restaurant. She noticed his manicured nails as he did so and silently approved. Nice nails meant that he, at least, had enough money for some extras. She sure couldn't tell by his shoes—Nike sneakers.

Dammit. Hahna stopped herself from assessing Sam. This was what she always did. She assessed a man, made marks, took score. Then, if they'd made it to the end of the test without being in the negative numbers, they got a second date. She wasn't going to do that tonight. She could assess Sam later; this night was for enjoyment.

The restaurant was busy but not packed, which meant they didn't have to wait for a table. The waitress showed them to a small table. One side was a booth on the wall, but the other side had a regular chair.

"We can both sit on the booth side if you want," Sam said. "It'll be a little cozy, though. Is that cool?"

Sam smelled incredible, like spices and earth and male pheromones. He smelled like lust, and she indeed wanted to be cozy with that aroma.

"I'd like that."

There was just enough room in the booth that their thighs

didn't touch, but Hahna would've welcomed it. She refused to lie to herself about the things she wanted, and after one conversation she wanted this man.

There was a DJ set up in the middle of the dining area, giving the restaurant a club feel. Hahna liked this too. If she didn't want to talk, she could snap her fingers and sway along with the music.

"It's half-price wine night," Sam said. "Would you like to split a bottle?"

"You like whites or reds?" Hahna asked.

"Both, but I prefer a cool, refreshing white."

"That works for me. I'll have whatever you order."

"It works, but do you like white?"

Hahna smiled. "Not really. Not unless there's nothing else available."

"We're having red, then. I'll defer to you. How's a nice Malbec sound?"

"It sounds divine."

As Sam signaled the waitress to place the wine order, Hahna wondered why she always did that—always deferred to whatever the man wanted on a date. It would've been just as easy to say that she didn't care for white wine, especially after Sam said he liked both.

"I gave Eric Jerome Dickey one of my books," Sam said. "I hope he reads it."

Happy to escape the judgmental voice in her head, Hahna perked up. "I saw that. Do you think he'll give it to his agent or publisher?"

"I wasn't thinking about that. I just wanted him to read my book, and maybe feel how he's influenced me. His books have taught me everything I know about writing. Not just his, but all of the great writers I've consumed."

"You didn't go to school for writing? What did you think you were going to do with your life before you started writing? I love to hear stories about reinvention."

"I've always known that I would write. I just didn't have any male mentors to show me that was an option for my life."

"Mentors are a blessing, I wouldn't trade mine."

The waitress brought the bottle of wine and attempted to pour the glasses. Sam stopped her and poured each glass himself.

"Would you all like to place an order for dinner or appetizers?"

"I know we'd both like an order of catfish nuggets," Sam said. "Hahna, was there anything else you wanted to try?"

"For now, the catfish nuggets are fine."

The waitress nodded and walked away. Her body was unreal—almost certainly surgically enhanced—but Sam hadn't seemed to notice at all. *If* she had been taking score, that would've been a plus mark.

"Tell me about your work," Sam said.

Hahna pressed her lips together and tried to think of a way to describe her business to Sam in a way that he would understand, but also not insult his intelligence (which she almost did when she'd asked about him going to school for writing).

"I take data and transform it into information. Like, say, for instance you have a stack of shopping lists that you've made for the past five years. For the average person, it just looks like scraps of paper with random food items. To me, that looks like how to market to you, how to forecast your health over the next ten years, and if I have one other type of data from you—like, perhaps, your receipts from the grocery store, because, of course, you always buy more than is on your list—if I have *that*, I can analyze your personality. I can tell if you're impetuous or strategic. This information is gold to a company like Starbucks or Amazon. And they treat it like gold, or shit, platinum."

Sam stared at Hahna. He sipped his wine, and he stared. His silence unnerved her, because she knew she had just blurted a river of information. She couldn't help it. And usually she refrained from the blurting, because she'd found that men didn't want to hear it, and they ran away when she did. She was ready for Sam to say, *check please.*

He didn't.

"That was amazing," Sam said.

"Data transformation *is* amazing. It's why I've spent so much time and money building a business around it."

"No, not data transformation. Hahna transformation. We were sitting here having a decent date—had me thinking maybe it would be the last one, 'cause maybe you weren't feeling me. Because your mask was on real tight."

Hahna sighed. She thought she'd left her mask in Saint Lucia. That was the promise she'd made to herself. But Sam had felt the internal wall that she always threw up. It was the wall she used to assess a man. The wall she used to figure him out before he figured her out. But Sam had done the figuring.

"Then you started talking about your passion, and your mask melted away."

"I've never called it my passion before. It sounds so Iyanla-esque."

"She sure didn't invent passion; Oprah, either."

They both laughed at this. They laughed again and sipped more wine. The bottle was nearly gone from their sipping.

"I think we need another bottle," Hahna said.

"I have some at my apartment."

There. He'd put it out there. Hahna wondered if he was going to ruin their evening somehow. Because it was going too well. She was feeling him too much, and she wanted him, but she didn't know if she could handle the *question* on a first date. A half date at that, because this wasn't planned.

"I understand if you don't want to go to my apartment," Sam said when she didn't respond.

"Okay."

The hope that'd crept into the recesses of Hahna's heart quickly fizzled. The questions that she'd been holding at bay pushed their way to the surface. Is he a scam artist? How many women has he slept with on the first date? Is he a rapist? Would he take it if she didn't say yes?

The silence felt awkward, but she was stuck in the moment of him inviting her to his apartment.

"Why would you ask me that?" Hahna asked. "Do I seem like

the kind of woman who would go back to your apartment with you on a first date?"

"You look like a woman who likes wine. I have an extensive collection. It wasn't a request for sex, although I can see how you thought it was."

Was he trying to make her feel stupid now? Of course, it wasn't a direct request for sex. It never was.

"The sex is never an outright ask."

"Unless you say yes?"

"Correct."

"You're right. It usually is, and I understand your reaction. I just know I didn't mean it that way."

"You don't want to have sex with me?"

"Not tonight. No."

"Wow. I don't know how to take that. I thought men only approached women they wanted to have sex with."

Hahna couldn't believe the words coming from her own mouth. Maybe it was the wine, or maybe Sam had irritated her by asking her back to his apartment. Either way she was giving responses like she gave zero cares about making a good impression.

"Men approach women who attract them. Sex isn't the only attraction."

"I see. What attracted you to me?"

"I liked that you started the conversation with me. I've been told I don't look very friendly."

"You don't. I thought you'd be mean."

"But you spoke anyway. You're brave. Unkind men are dangerous to women."

"Brave or really, really stupid. Not sure which one I've been tonight."

Sam grinned. "I *do* have a confession to make, though. The reason I invited you back to my place."

"I thought it was just for more wine."

"It was. It's also because I've exhausted my entertainment budget. The hardcover book, bottle of wine, catfish nuggets, and a tip have me tapped out. My wine at my apartment is free."

Hahna did a quick calculation in her head. Thirty bucks for the book, twenty for the half-price bottle of wine, catfish nuggets at twelve dollars each. Even with the tip, that was less than a hundred dollars.

"What if I had wanted an entire meal?" Hahna asked. "Would you have been able to afford it?"

"I would've been able to pay, but something would've suffered next week. I typically plan ahead for dates. This was unscheduled. If I had the money, I'd order five more bottles of wine to extend our evening."

Hahna got the waitress's attention. Sam's honesty had changed her vibe again. Something about it felt pure and unguarded. He'd just opened himself up to judgment from her, because most women would think him crazy for admitting that he couldn't afford a hundred-dollar date without planning ahead for it. But Hahna wouldn't judge him harshly. She'd been lied to by so many men. Torian had been the king of lies. Sam had told a simple yet embarrassing truth when he could've lied.

"Can you bring us another bottle of Malbec?" she asked the waitress, then turned to Sam. "Or do you want to go with a white this time?" Hahna asked.

Sam's smile was so warm that Hahna felt a surge of heat. She was feeling him regardless of what he could afford. She wasn't ready to go back to his apartment, but if the cost of a bottle of wine was the only thing keeping them from extending this date, she wouldn't let that be the reason.

"Malbec is fine," Sam said.

The catfish nuggets arrived at the table with the second bottle of wine. Both were devoured with equal fervor.

The DJ switched up the music and slowed it down with ballads. When Mary J. Blige played over the speakers, Hahna danced in her chair and bobbed her head.

"You want to dance?" Sam asked.

Hahna looked around the restaurant. "There's no dance floor."

"So?"

Hahna giggled as Sam got up from his seat and pulled her from hers.

"We can dance right here," Sam said.

Hahna didn't know if it was the wine or his woodsy, earthy scent that had her feeling high. Sam was tall enough that even in her heels, she could rest her cheek on his chest. Even though they barely rocked to the music, his heart raced. He was feeling this just like she was.

Hahna tilted her head until her lips brushed the base of Sam's throat. She placed a small kiss there and felt him shudder. She waited to see if he would escalate and make the next move, but he just pulled her in a little tighter and rocked to the music.

So, Hahna rested in Sam's arms and rocked with him. Danced to Mary J. Blige in a restaurant in the middle of the week, with a man who couldn't afford two bottles of wine. And it might've been her best first date ever.

Rules definitely broken.

Chapter 8

Kimberly looked at the time on her phone and sized it up against the line at Starbucks. Did she have enough time to wait for the coffee she so desperately needed? It was eight fifteen, her meeting was at nine, and she still had to drive another ten minutes (although in an Atlanta rush hour ten minutes could be thirty) and set up for the meeting.

If this meeting hadn't been game changing, she'd have foregone the coffee. But she had to be coherent for it. A major distributor wanted to put her Curlpop line of natural hair products in Walmart, CVS, Walgreens, and every other grocery store in the United States. This was about to take her mid-six-figure income to millions.

Kimberly looked at the time again and pressed her lips together. The line would be moving if not for the woman at the front of the line ordering a half-caf, three-shot, no-whip, foam-whip whatchamacallit.

Kimberly texted her assistant, LaShea, *Hey gurl. Can you put water, mints, and a box of tissues in the conference room?*

LaShea texted back, *Is this an Usher board convention?*

This made Kimberly smile, and her nerves calmed a little. She'd thought about telling Hahna and Twila about this opportunity while they were in Saint Lucia, but she didn't want to have to tell them if it didn't work out. All three of them were successful, but Twila and her cosmetic dentistry to the Atlanta stars and Hahna's data consulting had made them both millionaires. Kimberly's career as a lawyer put them on the same level intellectually, but she was not ready to stomp with the big dogs when it came to cash flow. She still had student loans from her time at Harvard Law.

Kimberly felt a tap on her shoulder and she turned around. It was one of the Starbucks baristas, and he had a look of concern on his face.

"What's wrong?" Kimberly asked, immediately thinking the worst.

"I need to show you something over there by the cream and sugar table."

When the young man winked, Kimberly almost didn't catch it. He wasn't very good at winking, but his dimples and his caramel complexion were easy to look at, so Kimberly didn't hold it against him. She followed him to the table.

"Now what?" Kimberly asked.

"Wait here two seconds."

Well, shoot, this had better be good, because now she'd lost her place in line and about five people had walked in since she'd followed this barista boy on good faith.

Kimberly couldn't and didn't contain her smile when the barista reappeared holding a cup of coffee in his hand. He grinned and the dimples in his cheeks deepened. She always did have a thing for dimples and big eyes, and he had both.

"You looked like you were in a hurry today, Ms. Kimberly," he explained. "And you always order the same thing, venti blonde roast."

This was one of the benefits of customer loyalty. He remembered her name and her order. Nice.

"Thank you, young man. I am in a hurry. How should I pay?"

"'Young man?' You say that like I'm a teenager."

Kimberly took the coffee from him. "I didn't mean that. I mean, clearly you're . . ."

"Grown. I'm Shawn."

"Okay, Mr. Shawn. My bad."

He smiled, and Kimberly wanted to add "sexy" to that "grown." Grown and sexy. And young.

"Don't worry about the coffee, Queen. You can buy me an after-dinner cup if you want."

"After dinner?"

"Yes. This is me wondering if you'd like to have dinner. I see you every day, and I'd like to get to know you better."

Kimberly needed an extra pause before responding to this. It was a test, of course. Her first break-all-the-dating-rules test. Here, this fine, chocolate, and sexy *adult* was asking her on a dinner date—not out for coffee or lunch—but dinner. She knew nothing about him except that he worked here, and she saw him every day.

"You caught me off-guard this morning, Shawn."

"Well, you're the one in a hurry. I typically like to take my time with these things."

Kimberly swallowed hard. Okay, the young man was dripping innuendo and sexiness, and she needed all of it. For a split second, she imagined her naked body being ravished by his full lips and big, *big* hands.

"Um, okay then. Dinner. When? Where?"

Shawn took Kimberly's phone from her hand and dialed a number—she assumed his.

"I will reach out this afternoon. I've got to see where I can make a reservation."

Somebody raised him right. He was making reservations? On a barista's pay? Maybe he had another job, and this was just what he did for extra funds.

"All right then."

"You have a fantastic day, Kimberly. You've already made mine."

She noticed that he'd removed the "Ms." from in front of her name. Done away with the formalities. Gotten personal.

Kimberly left Starbucks with a smile on her face and peace in her spirit. She'd almost forgotten about her important meeting. Was that what a little bit of attention from a fine man would do? She wondered what she'd forget after their first date.

Chapter 9

Twila sat at her kitchen table and stared at the screen on her tablet, as a beautiful man the color of butterscotch made a frittata. And he stared right back at her—well, into the camera, but it felt like he was looking at her. His muscles seemed to ripple for her. He wore a tiny apron pulled taut across his midsection, but because there was no shirt, and lots and *lots* of oil, his muscles glistened and shone as they rippled.

Drool collected in the corner of Twila's mouth. She swallowed. This man was delicious.

The frittata looked good too, though not as yummy as its maker.

Then he smiled into his webcam with his dreamy gray eyes and invited all of the women (because there had to be men watching this, too) who wanted the recipe to his eggplant frittata to send a message to his in box. A direct message about the eggplant. No. The eggplant frittata.

But Twila wasn't interested in the frittata.

She knew that this man was probably the equivalent of a video vixen. He was a thirst trap. A honeypot set to capture and destroy.

But he looked so delicious. She wanted a taste. He wasn't a snack or a meal. He was a butterscotch buffet.

She didn't send the direct message. She clicked the little heart underneath the video expressing appreciation at him being eye candy. Then she closed the application, turned the tablet off, and slid it across the table.

But even with the tablet turned off, his image still burned in her mind.

After a deep, deep inhale and a long sigh, Twila stood from the table. She had to get dressed. She had her first patient in an hour. Ungodly eight o'-damn-clock in the morning. Too early to be awake and ready to install veneers on her pickiest patient. But the money was beyond good, so it was a shower first, then out the door.

The vixen would have to wait until later.

The vixen sat in the waiting room of Twila's office. She wanted to pinch herself, because this was clearly a dream. She had just been watching him make eggs, and now he was sitting in her office. He was with her patient, Joseph, a male model with the ego of an A-list actor, except he hadn't done any acting work outside of Atlanta.

Joseph looked at his watch when Twila walked in.

"You just now getting here, huh?" Joseph asked.

Twila laughed. "When you're the owner, you get to make your own hours. You should be glad Mai was here to let you in."

Mai was Twila's receptionist. She worked for very low wages and dental work. She was, like the majority of Twila's patients, on the come up in Atlanta's entertainment scene. Mai stripped at night and tried out for reality shows when she wasn't booking appointments for Twila.

"Come on back, Joseph," Twila said.

"Can my friend watch? He's interested in getting veneers too, and I told him you were the best in town. He wants to see how it works."

"I don't usually like to have observers, but I'll make an exception this time."

Joseph and the Instagram friend followed Twila back to her examination room.

"Did I just see you on my Instagram feed this morning?" Twila asked, knowing good and damn well that God wasn't answering her lust prayers, but that somehow this morning's object of desire was sitting in her office.

"See, I told you tagging me would get you more views and followers," Joseph said. "If Dr. Twila saw you, then you've got a wide reach."

So that's how he'd appeared. God hadn't sent the butterscotch buffet. It was simple marketing.

"Yes, you saw me. I'm Marcus in real life. Marc_able on the Gram. Did you follow me?"

Twila laughed. "No, although I do want to try that eggplant . . . frittata."

"You can have the recipe. DM me, and I'll share."

"You should put it in the caption of the video," Twila said. "You seem like a thirst trap if a person has to direct message you for the recipe."

Joseph cracked up as he slid into the dentist's chair. "Bruh. Dr. Twila isn't your market."

"She should be. She's the one with discretionary income to purchase tickets to shows."

"Are you a singer?" Twila asked.

Marcus nodded. "Yes, and my agent keeps telling me that I need to become a viral sensation."

"But you're not singing in the video."

"Exactly. Which is why I don't see the point of it."

"The point," Joseph said as Twila draped a paper bib around his neck, "is to gain fans. You're trying to soak Atlanta to become a local sensation. Don't neglect home. Plus, the Instagram videos get you modeling gigs."

"Yeah, I'm on the cover of about fifty street lit novels."

"That last one is the best so far."

"Joseph is being funny. The last one was called *This Ho Has Roaches: An Urban Love Story.*"

Twila chuckled. "That doesn't sound like something I'd read."

"It doesn't sound like something anyone would read," Marcus said. "But the photo shoot paid seven hundred fifty dollars."

"Gotta get your coins," Twila said.

"All money isn't good money. I'd give that back if I could."

"I'm about to do the final install of Joseph's veneers," Twila said as she pressed lightly on Joseph's shoulder to get him to lie back in his chair.

"Yep, I'm about to get all the print advertising jobs with these pearly whites," Joseph said. He wouldn't be able to keep talking, though, if he wanted the veneers on his teeth.

Twila looked up from her work, because she could feel Marcus's gaze. He wasn't looking at Joseph's veneers. He was staring at her booty. She couldn't blame him, it was glorious.

"How did you get into cosmetic dentistry?" Marcus asked, shifting his gaze to Twila's face.

"Both of my parents are dentists. There's a lot of money in cosmetic dentistry here in Atlanta, where everyone's trying to be pretty."

"I like the imperfections in my teeth," Marcus said. "But Joseph thinks that I need to make an appointment to see you."

"Let me see your teeth. Smile for me."

Damn. His smile was sexy without even trying. He had a small gap between his two front teeth that could indeed be fixed with a retainer, but it didn't need to be fixed.

"I can fix them, but they don't need it."

"I'm good then."

Joseph tried to mumble something, but his mouth was full of tubes, and his jaw was propped open.

Twila turned back to Joseph to finish her work. She added an extra arch to her back as she bent over her patient, knowing that she might as well be a twerk girl on social media the way she was displaying her ass. It worked its wonders, though, because when she glanced back at Marcus, not only was he leaned back against the wall, openly gawking, but he was biting his bottom lip as if imagining all the angles from which he could take her.

She was open to all the angles.

Twila took her time installing the veneers, giving Marcus plenty of time to get his nerve up. He was not her typical selection—starving artists had never been sexy to Twila—but she'd decided to be open to new things since Saint Lucia.

She grabbed a mirror and handed it to Joseph as she adjusted his chair into the upright position. He smiled at himself in the mirror, then held the mirror at arm's length and smiled again.

"What are you doing?" Marcus asked.

"This is my selfie pose, had to see what my teeth would look like in a selfie."

Twila laughed. "You'll look great in selfies and close-ups. You're ready for that film gig."

"Look out, Idris. I'm coming for your spot."

"Idris's teeth seem kinda jumbled on the bottom," Marcus said. "And the women still love him."

"I can fix his teeth," Twila said. "When y'all meet him, give him my card."

"You didn't even give me your card, and I'm a potential client, standing right here," Marcus said in a low tone. The way he licked his bottom lip and grinned let her know that he wasn't trying to get dental work. He was trying to get that *work* work.

"How old are you?" Twila asked.

"Old enough to have a dental plan."

Joseph laughed. "Shoot your shot then, bro!"

Twila whipped out one of her cards and slid it into Marcus's shirt pocket. And dammit if he didn't flex his muscles a little as her hand traced the front of his shirt.

"Call me when you're ready to make an appointment," Twila said.

"I will."

Twila thought of so many freaky little jokes that would continue their banter, but she didn't want to seem too thirsty, though she was parched.

"Joseph, make sure you handle that copay on the way out."

"I got you, Dr. Twila."

Marcus stayed behind when Joseph left the room. He touched his shirt pocket where her card was stored.

"I'm twenty-nine. Is that too young?" Marcus asked.

"Too young for what?" Twila countered, because everything she could think of doing with him was perfectly legal with a twenty-nine-year-old.

"To be your man."

"I think a man's experiences expand his worldview and add richness to his years."

He chuckled. "So, I'm not too young then?"

"Haven't determined that part yet."

"I'll call you."

"Good. 'Cause I won't be sliding in your DMs. That's for little girls."

Marcus chuckled again as he walked out the door. He tried to exude confidence with his shoulders back and a wide-legged stance, but Twila knew he wasn't ready for her.

But that didn't matter, because she was more than ready for him.

Chapter 10

Hahna opened her eyes to glaring sunlight, through window blinds she didn't recognize. She closed her eyes and shook her head in the unfamiliar bed and remembered the previous night's events.

She and Sam had started dancing at the restaurant, then they'd wanted to dance some more, so they'd left and gone to a real dance club. And there was more wine. Way more than she would typically consume on a night when she had to go to work the next morning.

Work. She groaned and fumbled for her phone. She needed to see the time and let Sylvia know she'd be late.

There'd been no sex, no making out. That part she did recall vividly. Not because she didn't want it, but because Sam refused to pursue all of her obvious signals. But he'd felt bad for taking her to a dance club far from her house, and he offered her his bed. He'd slept on the couch.

Hahna threw back the comforter and smiled at her sleeping attire. His sweatpants and a t-shirt. The smell of coffee and breakfast lured her out of the bedroom.

"Good morning," Sam said with an already-plenty-awake smile. "Are you a coffee or tea drinker? Or neither?"

"I'm a both person, but after last night, I'd love some coffee.

With cream and sugar, please. But first, do you have an extra toothbrush?"

"What? You don't want to use mine?"

"Ewwww. No."

Sam laughed. "Yes, I do. Look in the top drawer in the bathroom. You'll see a package."

When she looked around for where the bathroom might be, he pointed to metal barn doors, right off the apartment's main room. Two steps and she was across the room and into the tiny bathroom.

The entire place was small and snug. Enough for one person, but it would be problematic for two. But even though it was small, it wasn't cramped, and each corner and crevice was decorated meticulously, maximizing the space. The bathroom had a narrow shower space that was tiled with bricks all the way to the ceiling. The same brick lined the rest of the walls. A towel rack over the toilet was decorative enough to be considered art.

Hahna opened the small drawer beneath the sink and found a package of four toothbrushes. She didn't know if she should read something into that or not. Did Sam have many overnight guests, or was he just careful about his own dental care? If it was the former, should she even care? She hadn't yet decided if this would be anything past their first date, so maybe not.

While she brushed, she wondered where he kept the extensive wine collection that he'd bragged about. There certainly didn't seem to be room for one here. There was barely room for the sofa, table, and chairs.

Hahna finally emerged from the bathroom with a washed face and brushed teeth. Her curly hair was fine to do whatever the hell it wanted. She didn't have the tools with her to tame her mane.

"Ready for breakfast? I didn't know what you liked, so I kept it continental. I've got fruit, cheese, bagels, English muffins, and coffee."

Hahna smiled and sat down at the table in front of the expertly presented tray of food. She was more of a bacon, scrambled eggs with cheese, and grits kind of breakfast person, but she'd take this.

"Welcome to my home," Sam said. "I can give you the tour from your seat."

Hahna laughed. "Well, I've already seen the bedroom and the bathroom."

"You're halfway done, then," Sam said while still standing in the kitchenette.

"This is the living space. I cook, eat, write, and entertain here," Sam said. "Oh, and speaking of entertaining . . ."

He reached down and turned to what looked like a piece of the floor, but was clearly the top to something. When he pulled, out of the floor came a small wine rack with six rows and three bottles stacked neatly on each one.

"My wine collection."

Hahna chuckled but felt relieved that there was wine at his home, and that he hadn't made that part up. She found small lies to be the worst kind. If a person lied when there were no consequences for telling the truth, he could never be trusted. Torian had done that—lied about small things that hadn't mattered. What *had* mattered was his dishonesty, but now he was a quickly fading memory.

Sam screwed the little wine cellar back into the floor and joined her at the table. "I'm enjoying our date. I'm looking forward to the next one."

"I guess we are still on the first date. I'm still here. Haven't done the walk of shame yet."

"No walk of shame here. Even if I'd twisted you into a pretzel to taste every orifice, there'd be no shame in that."

Hahna's eyebrows shot up. "Every orifice? Oh my."

"I'm sorry. Did I offend you?"

"No. I was just imagining what that would be like."

He smiled. "I'm sure your imagination didn't do it justice."

Hahna wanted to steer the conversation away from sex, because she was the one who'd started it, talking about doing a walk of shame. Why had she said that? They hadn't been intimate, plus she didn't even believe in the shame part. A woman's body was her own, so there was no shame in finding pleasure. But *still* she had said that. Why?

And why was she being so introspective on a Wednesday morning? These were Sunday morning thoughts.

"I think I'm not going to go to work today. I should call my assistant."

"You aren't going to miss anything important, are you?"

She shook her head. "There's always something going on in my office, but I don't have any meetings on my calendar today. I will have to get on a conference call with my senior data analyst sometime this afternoon. We have a meeting with a potential client in Miami on Monday. If I was in the office, I'd be drinking lots of tea with sugar and honey."

"Sugar and honey? Not one or the other?"

"Both. Does that tell you something about me?"

"Nothing new. I'd already gathered that you're sweet. I looked in the mirror this morning and saw the start of a cavity. I think you gave it to me when we were dancing."

This tickled Hahna. "I gave you a cavity? Well, one of my best friends is a dentist, so she'll hook you right up."

"I like the sound of your circle already."

"My other best friend is a lawyer, so don't try to sue me for the cost of your dental work."

"Sheesh. Y'all roll deep, huh?"

"Shole do. We're deep, and thick. Been best friends since freshman year of college."

"Where'd y'all go? Let me guess. Spelman?"

Hahna nodded. "Yes, Spelman."

"You exemplify the image of the Spelman woman. I'm surprised that you'd be interested in me."

"Who says I was interested?"

Sam spread cream cheese and jam on a half of a bagel. "You were, weren't you? You started the conversation. You made the first move."

"I did not."

"You did. A conversation started by a beautiful woman is a first move."

Hahna couldn't wipe the grin off her face if she tried. "Okay, now it's your move, then."

"I'm going to take you on a proper date. What are you doing this weekend?"

"Nothing . . . oh wait. Shoot. I have to go to Miami for work. I have a meeting on Monday."

"It can wait until you get back then."

"Or you could just fly to Miami with me."

The shocked expression on Sam's face made Hahna want to gobble her words back and rescind the invitation.

"Wow," Sam said when he finally responded after a few long, awkward moments.

"I mean, I just . . . you know what? No. I meant that. I'd like you to join me in Miami if you're available."

Hahna doubled down even though she wasn't sure if Sam was feeling her or judging her. She didn't know him well enough to read him.

"I would like to join you, but . . ."

"Don't worry about your entertainment budget. This one is on me. The whole weekend. You can plan the next trip."

"You just made two moves in a row."

"I guess I did."

Hahna chomped into her bagel, feeling the need for sustenance from all her boss moves. She didn't think she'd be a good sugar mama, but so far, this felt good, and it was going to feel even better having a date of her own in Miami.

Chapter 11

When Shawn asked Kimberly to wear comfortable shoes on their first date, she wasn't sure what to think. Especially with it being on a Saturday morning. Who needed reservations anywhere on a Saturday morning at nine o'clock?

Shawn hadn't given her any additional clues about where they might be going, so she wasn't sure what to wear besides comfortable shoes. It was an unseasonably warm weekend in Atlanta, so if it was outside she didn't want to be uncomfortable. But she also wanted to be cute, and cute required her hold-in-all-the-rolls girdle.

Kimberly decided on a maxi-dress with a blue jean vest. This was dressy enough for a nice brunch, a museum, or a tour of some sort. Plus, with her girdle she looked like a thick video vixen.

Her two-stranded twist-out had come out perfect with her Curlpop styling cream. She picked up the small jar of lavender-and bergamot-scented cream and smiled. The styling cream was the staple of her product line and was what all the retailers wanted. That and the finishing gel that gave all of her hair models their perfect look. When the distributor had given her the check for 1.2 million dollars, she'd almost cried. When he'd said they'd need the first order ready in three weeks to ship to one hundred test stores, she'd almost fainted.

But as soon as the meeting was over, she got to work. She called suppliers and secured a warehouse facility where she would manufacture the first order. She wouldn't be accused of changing or watering down her formula like some of the other natural hair companies that went from garages to the store shelves. She wouldn't be accused, because she would personally oversee the production. Even if that meant taking time off from her law firm. The partners had understood and had even given her a vote of confidence.

Kimberly gave her reflection a final once-over and sighed. She didn't have time for a date today, but she figured that since they were going in the morning, maybe she'd be able to finalize the production plans later. But always putting work before play was a rule she needed to break.

Her doorbell rang at eight fifty-seven. Young and punctual? She hadn't expected him to be on time, so this was a plus.

Kimberly pushed her feet into her comfortable flip-flops and rushed to the door. She opened the door to Shawn dressed in athletic shorts, a t-shirt, and sneakers. Where could they possibly be going with him dressed like he was going to play ball? Were they going to the gym? Kimberly had never cussed a man out on a date, but she would today, if she had to.

"Hey, Ms. Kim. You're looking really nice this morning."

Kim found herself melting at the sound of his voice. There was a familiarity to it that she hadn't noticed before. Maybe it was because she heard him speak every day at Starbucks, although it seemed like something different that she couldn't pinpoint.

"Hey, Mr. Shawn. I thought we'd gotten to a first-name basis."

He smiled, and his dimples came out to greet Kimberly as well. He was so handsome. Too handsome, in fact. He could have any young woman his age. What did he want with her?

"Am I overdressed?" Kimberly asked.

"No. As long as you have on comfortable shoes, you're perfect."

"Well, where are we going?"

"First, breakfast. The rest is a surprise."

"Okay, I'm going to grab my purse and then I'll follow you in my car."

Shawn gave her a confused look.

"You're not riding with me?" he asked.

Kimberly smiled as she shook her head. "Not on a first date. Have to get to know you first."

"Oh. I see. Well, I'll be in the car."

Kimberly closed the door and locked it while she got her purse. She wouldn't have had to explain to an older man why she wasn't getting in his car. He'd know immediately. He'd either respect her decision or be annoyed with it, but he wouldn't be confused by it.

Was this what it would be like dating someone younger? Would she be educating him on grown people shit all the time? That must be the "mama" part of "sugar mama."

Kimberly pulled her car out of the driveway and followed behind Shawn. Since Hahna was in Miami for a work trip, she called Twila.

"Hey, girl," Twila said.

"Hey, girl, hey."

Kimberly's response was how they always greeted one another on the phone. If the "hey, girl, hey" didn't happen, the sistafriend on the other end was on high alert that something was wrong.

"You on your date with that lil' baby?" Twila asked.

Kimberly hollered, "You can't talk with your Instathot."

"Sure can't. He's coming over tomorrow."

"For real? He's coming to your place?" Kimberly shook her head in disbelief. Twila was fearless.

"You don't think he should?"

"Girl, no. You don't know him."

"We have a friend in common," Twila explained. "Plus, you know I have plenty of weaponry in my house."

"I forgot Ms. NRA."

"This is America, girlfriend."

"Well, I called to tell you that I'm following Shawn, and that I texted you his license plate."

"Where y'all going this early?"

"He says breakfast, and the rest is a surprise."

"We're too grown for surprises. Tell me where the hell I'm going, so I can know if it's worth my time."

"Okay! All he told me was to wear comfortable shoes. He's dressed like he's going to play ball with his homies."

"He got on gray sweats?"

"No, why?"

"'Cause I was gonna tell you to peep out the eggplant print."

"Eggplant? Oh . . . eggplant."

"Yep!"

"You're nasty. Looks like we're exiting. Must be going to Cinnamon's for brunch."

Twila sighed. "Really? A chain restaurant on a first date?"

"This guy isn't even thirty yet, girl. He doesn't know any better. He probably thinks this is fancy."

"It probably *is* fancy for him. You'll have to elevate his life experiences."

Kimberly sighed. "I don't know if I want to do that. And I'm supposed to be finding a date to the wedding. I can't take his ass."

"Why not?"

"My coworkers will be there."

"You have to stop caring about what other people think. This sugar mama thing isn't gonna work if you don't."

"You're right, girl. I'll call you back, we're at the restaurant."

Kimberly pulled into the parking spot next to Shawn. It pleased her when he rushed over to her car to open her door. At least she wouldn't have to teach him chivalry.

"You ready to get your grub on?" Shawn asked as she stepped out of the car. "I love this place."

She would rather have gone to someplace where the menu wasn't plastic, and they served mimosas instead of all-you-can-eat pancakes, but she nodded happily anyway. No need to ruin the date because of it, plus she still had the surprise.

Oh, the surprise . . . it was going to be a long day.

Chapter 12

It had cost her an unmentionable amount of money, but Hahna was able to get Sam a plane ticket for the same flight that she, Corden, and his fiancée, Symone, were taking to Miami. Hahna held her breath as she and Sam walked up to the gate where Corden and Symone waited. She should've warned Corden, because the look on his face was already doing too much. His eyebrows nearly touched his hairline, and his mouth hung slightly ajar.

"Corden. Symone," Hahna said as she hugged Symone. "Long time, no see, girl."

"I know. Thank you for inviting me," Symone said.

"Thank you for letting me steal Corden last weekend while I was on vacation. He saved my life, like he's always saving my life."

"Enough of this," Corden said. "Introduce us to your travel companion."

Hahna narrowed her eyes at Corden. She had already decided that she wasn't going to tell him anything about the fact that she'd only met Sam a few days ago, and that this was their second date. That was unnecessary information for him.

"Oh, this is my friend Sam Valcourt," Hahna said. "Sam, this is my right hand at work, my senior data analyst, Corden John-son, and his beautiful fiancée, Symone."

Sam extended his hand and gave Corden a firm handshake, and then Symone.

"Pleased to meet you both," Sam said.

"Same," Corden said. Symone smiled and nodded.

"So, you decided to make this work *and* play, huh, boss?" Corden said. "I'm not mad at you."

"This is the conversation I'm not having with my subordinate," Hahna said.

Corden bit down on his bottom lip and gave a slow nod. Hahna hated having to go there, but he was not going to act right. They were boss and subordinate, but Corden was also a good friend. She'd have to make up for this later.

"Um . . . I'm gonna go grab a coffee," Sam said. "Do you want one?"

"Yes, thank you."

"Cream and sugar, right?"

Hahna nodded and she watched him as he walked away. When she turned around, Corden was staring at her.

"I'm gonna let that subordinate thing slide, boss, because I know you don't want to tell me about your new man yet," Corden said. "It's cool. Your business."

Corden and Symone sat back down in their seats, and Hahna sat down next to Corden.

"You *are* my subordinate," Hahna said.

"I know."

"It wasn't an insult."

"I didn't say it was. You were shutting me down, though."

Hahna scoffed. "Yeah. I didn't want you scaring him off."

"Yeah, you were coming on kinda strong, babe," Symone said.

Corden looked at her and scrunched his nose. "I was not. I simply wanted to be introduced to this new dude who rolled up with my boss friend. I'm part bodyguard too."

Hahna laid her head on Corden's shoulder. "You are. Thank you."

"Mmm-hmm. How does he know how you like your coffee? Y'all had breakfast together? You only drink coffee in the morning."

"Dammit. You get on my nerves."

"I should've been a private detective," Corden said.

"We have had breakfast together, but it's not what you think. It's a long story."

Symone leaned forward to talk over Corden. "Did you meet him in Saint Lucia?"

"No, I didn't."

"Well, then, he's not trying to use her for citizenship," Symone said.

Corden nodded. "Good question, baby."

"Stop it, you two. He's coming back."

Hahna, Corden, and Symone couldn't help but giggle as Sam handed Hahna her coffee and took an empty seat across from her.

"What's so funny?"

"Oh, we were talking about the sights on South Beach in Miami. Have you ever been?"

Sam nodded. "I have. I used to go with my friends for spring break."

"Me too," Corden said. "We look close in age. Where'd you go to undergrad?"

"North Carolina A&T. You?"

"Morehouse. That's where I met Hahna. She's a few years older than me, but she's one of those Spelman alumnae who give back. She goes to the job fairs every year."

Sam grinned. "I'm not surprised about that. I'm still getting to know Hahna, but that aligns with what I've already learned about her."

"How long you been getting to know her?" Corden asked.

Hahna elbowed Corden in the ribs. "Enough."

"It's cool, Hahna. It's good to have people looking out for you. But Corden, I think you're wrong about the age. I think I have a few years on you. I'm forty-three."

This was information that Hahna hadn't even discovered.

Maybe she ought to let Corden go on with his diarrhea of the mouth so she could get all the details. Just that quick he'd gotten Sam's alma mater and age. Corden needed to teach a class on first date interrogation, because he sure had it down.

"Well, it's cool to have you on this work trip, where we hopefully have a little time to play."

"Why do you think we're going so early?" Hahna said. "You and I will have some work to do on our presentation tomorrow afternoon, but we're going to get some downtime in."

"I have to work on my novel. My readers are waiting for the next installment in my Georgia Peaches series."

Symone's eyes lit up.

"I knew your name sounded familiar," she said. "I love those books."

Sam grinned. "It's rare that I get to meet a reader. Thank you for your support."

"Did you know how much Hahna loves to read too?" Corden asked. "When she's not whispering to data, she's reading. She's got a full library in her office."

"That part I did know," Sam said. "We met at a—"

"Let's keep our story to ourselves for now," Hahna said, not wanting Corden and Symone to know that she'd just met this man a few days ago and was already traveling with him.

Sam gave her a look she couldn't decipher. If he stopped talking, she didn't mind what he thought about her ending the conversation. She'd explain it to him later when they were alone.

And they *would* be alone in Miami. The only question Hahna was asking herself was, when she was alone with Sam, would her clothes be on or off?

Chapter 13

Kimberly stared in disbelief at the SIX FLAGS OVER GEORGIA sign as she followed Shawn's car into the parking lot. Was *this* the surprise? An amusement park? It couldn't be. Maybe they were lost, and Shawn had just turned into the parking lot to turn on his GPS and get his bearings, because she knew damn sure he hadn't just brought her to an amusement park.

No, they weren't lost, because Shawn had turned off his car ignition and was getting out. Kimberly's car was still running. She didn't know if she could stay. Amusement parks were not her thing. Too much walking and too much sweating, and she had on her good girdle too. The one that would roll right on down and underneath her stomach if sweat got between her skin and the fabric.

Shawn walked up to her window and tapped. She pressed the button and it slowly opened.

"Surprise! I hope you like roller coasters."

She didn't.

Well, she'd liked them when she was a teenager. She hadn't ridden one after her twenty-first birthday. She hadn't been to this Six Flags since college. Kimberly raised the window back up again.

Shawn tried to open the door for her, but it was locked. He

gave her a confused look through the window, and she gave him a half-smile, half-grimace.

Finally, she unlocked the door and he opened it. She stepped out and tried to muster a smile. She mustered something, but she couldn't be sure it looked thrilled to be at Six Flags.

"You don't like the surprise," Shawn said.

"It's not that I don't like the surprise. It's that I wasn't expecting this. For one, I would've dressed differently."

"You look fine to me. I see lots of girls in the park in sundresses."

Operative word—girls. Not a grown-ass forty-year-old woman whose inner thighs had such an intimate relationship that they kissed one another all day.

"Come on. It'll be fun. We'll eat caramel apples, ice cream, and burgers, and ride the rides like when we were teenagers."

"It wasn't that long ago for you."

"I'm twenty-six. It's been a while for me too."

In the end, it was Shawn's dimples that did the trick and made her decide to go along. That warm and friendly smile made her think she just might enjoy getting more steps on her step counter than she had in months.

"Question," Kimberly said. "Why did you need reservations for this?"

"Oh, well, I was going to take you to Ray's on the River for brunch, but I thought this would be a lot more fun and adventurous."

Ray's on the River would've been perfect.

The sun beamed hot, making Kimberly swoon for a moment as they walked up to the entrance gate. She needed ice water and quick, before she started to overheat.

Kimberly tried not to notice that Shawn paid for them with a buy-one get-one-free park admission. Not only was this a surprise, it was a cheap surprise. He might as well have taken her to an Applebee's two-for-twenty special. To bright-side it, though, at least she hadn't had to pull out her wallet.

"We're here early, so we can get in a few rides before the park gets crowded."

Kimberly struggled to walk next to Shawn, as his strides were long and hers were short. She was trying to conserve energy, and he had it to spare. She felt sweat collecting in the small of her back. This overheating situation was not going to be a good one.

"Let's get on The Monster," Shawn said. "The line for that one is usually bonkers by lunchtime."

"Does that one have a lot of twists and turns? Like, does it go upside down?" Kimberly asked, trying to hide the anxiety in her voice.

"I mean, what's a lot? It's a roller coaster, so yeah it has some twists and turns."

Kimberly took a deep breath and tried to relax. It was just a roller coaster. It would only last for two or three minutes. She could do this. She didn't want Shawn to start thinking of her as his mama; she was older but not *that* much older. He'd found her attractive, and maybe even sexy. It'd been so long since that had happened that Kimberly wasn't ready to let it go so quickly, and not over an amusement park ride.

"All right. I'm down. Let's do it!"

The line was long—two-hours-or-more-wait-time long. Kimberly was glad. It gave her enough time to get her nerves up.

"Kimberly, do you like to go by Kim?" Shawn asked.

Shawn was such a handsome man, almost pretty, and the way he held eye contact was very sexy. It made her feel at home.

"It doesn't matter. People call me both. My girlfriends switch up depending on the day."

"What do your boyfriends call you?"

Kimberly chuckled. She could count on one hand all the relationships she'd had in her forty years. And every single last one of those boyfriends had called her Kimberly. She wondered if she hadn't made any of them feel comfortable enough to give her a nickname.

"You can call me whatever you'd like."

"Then I'm gonna go with Kimberly. It sounds important, and I think you are. You look like a boss."

She laughed. "I am a boss, baby. You got that part right."

"What do you do? You always look so serious when you come to get coffee in the mornings."

"I'm a lawyer, but I also have my own natural hair company called Curlpop."

"Wow."

"Wow? What are you thinking right now?"

Shawn chuckled. "I knew you had a career, but not like that. Shit. I'm still in grad school."

"I knew you were young when I accepted the date, Shawn. I'm not surprised you're in grad school."

"And you're okay with that?"

"I said yes to the date, didn't I?"

He took her hand and squeezed. "Yep, and I'm glad you did."

Kimberly swallowed hard. She felt nothing when this fine young man squeezed her hand, except the urge to shake his hand off her as he pulled her through the line. Kimberly dodged eye contact with the younger girls who stared at her and Shawn. They were probably wondering the same thing Kimberly was wondering.

What in the hell was she doing with him?

It felt wrong, and not only the age difference. He was just a baby in his thoughts and in his actions too. She couldn't see herself kissing him, and she damn sure couldn't see herself sleeping with him. This date was a mistake.

"You want to sit in the front of the car or the back?" Shawn asked as they approached the front of the line.

"It doesn't make a difference to me."

"The front then."

Shawn pulled Kimberly to the front of the line, and she felt her nerves start up again. She reminded herself that it would be over in a couple of minutes, and then she could get through the rest of the day and never call this boy again.

Kimberly cocked her head to one side as she looked at the roller coaster track. It was above them instead of on the ground.

"Why is the track up there?" she asked Shawn.

"Oh, because this is one of those coasters where our feet dangle."

"Dangle? What do you mean dangle?"

Shawn pointed to the coaster car as it rounded a corner. She'd been so preoccupied with how they looked as a couple that she hadn't noticed what the ride was actually doing.

"Oh, my goodness," Kimberly said.

"You okay?"

"Yes. I'm okay."

She was *not* okay. Her knees felt like jelly, and her stomach flipped. Two minutes, though. She could make it for two minutes.

Finally, it was their turn, and she slid into the seat next to Shawn. She'd been so worried about her dangling feet to notice the other potential problem: the overhead restraint that was unfriendly to big girls. She eyed the metal contraption and tried to quickly estimate if it would even close over her triple-D breasts.

Before she could decide, the Six Flags employee walked by and slammed the bar down until it locked. And it did lock, but she could barely breathe. Her boobs were crushed and in pain, and nearly choking her. It felt like a mammogram.

Kimberly closed her eyes tightly, just wishing she could fast-forward through the next two minutes. She didn't complain, though, because she didn't want to bring attention to her fat, which was smooshed between the bars.

Shawn grabbed her hand again, and she cringed by accident. She was stressed, and his hand-holding creeped her out.

"Woo-hoo!" Shawn yelled, seeming not to notice Kimberly's cringing.

The roller coaster took off from the platform, and Kimberly swooned when there was nothing but sky beneath her feet. The scariest part of a coaster was always climbing the first hill, and Kimberly was indeed terrified, but it was worse because she couldn't tell how close they were to the top. Beads of sweat popped out on her forehead, tears streamed out of her eyes, and she tried not to hyperventilate as she snatched bits of oxygen into her compressed lungs.

After the first drop, the rest of the ride was a blur, but it wasn't fun. It was torture, the longest two minutes Kimberly had ever lived.

They pulled back into the platform, and Shawn hollered.

"That was great! Want to go again?"

Kimberly didn't respond verbally. She couldn't. She just shook her head.

The restraints unlocked, and Kimberly threw the metal bar off her boobs and took in a huge gulp of air. She shook as she crossed out of the car and onto the platform.

"Kimberly, are you okay? I'm sorry. I shouldn't have convinced you to ride," Shawn said.

He looked truly concerned, which made Kimberly wonder how she looked. There was no mirror nearby, but she could imagine. Her stomach turned as wave after wave of nausea struck her. She swallowed back the salty taste in her mouth that signaled vomit was on the way. She refused to throw up.

"Kimberly, are you going to be sick?" Shawn asked.

She shook her head. "Just give me a second."

Kimberly stumbled over to a wooden post and held on tight while taking long, deep breaths. After a few moments, the nausea passed, and she stood up straight.

"Sorry," Shawn said.

"Not your fault. I haven't ridden a roller coaster in twenty years. Didn't know it would hit me like that."

She listened to herself. Twenty years ago, they hadn't had roller coasters like The Monster. Twenty years ago, this boy had been six years old.

"You probably just need some more food in your stomach," Shawn said. "You didn't eat much at breakfast."

"You're probably right."

"If we go over to the picnic pavilions, I'm sure my family has already started to barbecue."

"Wait. What?"

"That was the surprise. I brought you to my family barbecue."

"You brought me to your family gathering on our first date?"

Kimberly felt herself go into panic mode. She'd just met this boy. She didn't want to meet his family. What would his family think of her? They'd think she was some thirsty cradle-robbing cougar. And she'd thought this date couldn't get worse.

"It'll be fine. My family is cool. I had forgotten about the barbecue, and I didn't want to cancel our date. Plus, they're used to me dating older women. I haven't ever dated a woman my age."

"Shawn . . . I don't think we're *dating*. I appreciate you asking me out and trying to show me a good time, but—"

"But what? I'm too young?"

"All of this is too young, baby. This isn't me."

Shawn bit his lip and nodded. "I understand. You thought you were ready for this, but you weren't."

Kimberly was almost tickled that he tried to flip it, so she decided to let him save face.

"You're right. I'm not ready—at all. I'm probably missing out."

"I promise you are."

He was almost sexy when he said that, but Kimberly had, in her mind, reduced him to a Similac-behind-the-ears baby.

"Well, let me at least grab you something to eat from the picnic. You don't have to go in. I'll walk you over to the tables and get you a burger."

"That sounds amazing. You're such a gentleman. I appreciate you for that."

Shawn helped Kimberly down the stairs from the roller coaster platform. He steadied her with a hand on her back as they crossed the park to the picnic area. She started to feel better as the nausea passed.

"Sit here in the shade," Shawn said. "I'll be right back."

"Okay. Thanks again, Shawn."

Kimberly took out her phone and texted Twila. *Girl. I'm over this. I'm not cut out to be a cougar.*

The first reply Twila sent was a string of laughing emojis. Then she sent another text.

You can't give up before you get some of that good loving.

Kimberly held her head back and hollered. Leave it to Twila to put things in perspective. She wasn't going to get any loving from Shawn, though.

"Kimmy Kim!"

Kimberly looked up from her phone and narrowed her eyes. There was only one person who called her Kimmy Kim.

"Big Ron!"

Kimberly jumped up from the table and smiled hard as Ron closed the space between them. He was holding a plate of food, but that didn't stop him from scooping her up with his free arm and kissing her on the forehead.

"It's been too long, Kimmy Kim. You look good!"

"You do too, Big Ron!"

They sat down at the table, and Kimberly couldn't stop grinning. Ron wasn't big at all, he was tall, thin, and chocolate. They'd called him Big Ron as a joke, because he was so slim. He was the Morehouse brother who'd tutored her in calculus her freshman year at Spelman. He was a sophomore at the time, and a math genius.

"What happened to you after graduation?" Ron asked. "I know you went to Harvard Law, but I didn't know you were back in Atlanta."

"You would if you came to homecoming."

Ron chuckled. "I know. I know. Life just got busy. Family and all."

"Oh. You're married?"

"No. Not anymore."

Kimberly wondered why the marriage failed but didn't ask. Ron was twenty years older, but he was still fine. That chocolate skin was still smooth, those dimples were still deep, and his eyes still twinkled when he smiled. His beard had a little more salt than pepper, but that was all good too.

"So, what have you been up to, Kimmy Kim?"

Kimberly remembered when he'd started calling her Kimmy Kim. The only boy who'd ever given her a nickname. They'd been sitting in the Atlanta University Center library, and he'd been grilling her about a calculus review.

He'd said, "Kim, did you do the reviews I gave you for homework?"

"Kimberly."

"That's what I said."

"No. You said Kim. My name is Kimberly. Three syllables. Real easy."

Big Ron had cracked up. "Okay, okay. Not Kim. How 'bout Kimmy Kim? That's three syllables too."

He'd won her over with that smile, and those dimples. And Kimmy Kim it was, for the rest of their time in college.

"You practicing in some fancy law firm?" Ron asked.

"Not fancy, but we do a lot of business law. It's boring, to be honest. But I have a line of hair products too."

"You always were doing someone's hair on campus. You kept all your girls looking good."

"What are you doing these days?"

"I rehab houses. Rip out floors, install floors, tear down walls, all of that."

"You went to Morehouse and got a mathematics degree to rehab houses?"

He laughed. "Yeah. I worked in corporate America for a while doing statistics, but this is what I love, and the money is good."

"Okay, then. I'm proud of us. We got all those student loans only to make money doing what we've always loved."

"Kimberly?"

She'd forgotten all about Shawn getting her a burger from his family picnic.

Ron raised his eyebrows. "You know my son?"

Kimberly put one hand over her mouth. Shawn was Big Ron's son? No wonder his eyes and dimples had seemed so familiar. He looked like his daddy! This was the most embarrassing thing that could happen. No. It would've been worse if she'd slept with him. Ewww . . . she'd almost slept with her college crush's son.

"Dad, you know my date?"

"Your date?"

Shit. This was getting worse.

"I met Shawn at Starbucks. He invited me out, and he was so respectful and mature that I accepted."

Big Ron burst into laughter. "Son, if you're gonna be going after grown women, we need to talk about where you take them on a first date."

"Well, Kimberly told me that we weren't dating, so I don't think it matters anymore. I was just bringing her something to eat."

"Kimmy Kim, you broke up with my son?"

Kimberly laughed. "This is insane. We weren't dating."

"Well, son, you have good taste," Big Ron said. "I always wanted to ask Kimmy Kim out on a date when we were in college."

"Man, whatever!" Kimberly said. "Your daddy wasn't thinking 'bout me."

"Son, Kimmy Kim and her sorority sisters would be strolling on the yard. They'd be like this."

Ron got up from the table and performed a pretty accurate replication of Kimberly, Twila, Hahna, and the rest of their sorority sisters' stroll. He even made the appropriate calls.

When he was done, Ron plopped back down at the table and took a bite out of his hot dog.

"All that strolling took your energy, huh?" Kimberly asked.

"It sure did."

Shawn looked from Kimberly to his father and back to Kimberly. She tried to think of something to say that would make this situation less awkward, but nothing came to mind.

"I hope you like the hamburger," Shawn said. "I'm gonna let you two catch up."

"Kimmy, why don't you come on back to the picnic?" Ron asked. "The kids are riding rides, but we're back there playing spades."

"Some of the adults are riding rides too," Shawn said.

"Oh, you're right, son. My bad," Ron said.

"Do you mind if I stay?" Kimberly asked Shawn. "Your dad and I were really good friends in college."

Shawn shrugged. "I think our date was over when we got off that roller coaster, so you're good."

Shawn took his own plate of food and jogged over to a group of young people eating hot dogs and burgers.

"Is he angry?" Kimberly asked.

"I don't think so," Ron replied.

"Okay, 'cause he really tried to show me a good time today. I just . . ."

"What made you say yes to him?"

Kimberly looked away, then decided to tell Big Ron the truth. He could always see through her anyway.

"Twila, Hahna, and I have this challenge going to throw away our dating rules. After we left Saint Lucia on vacation, we agreed to say yes to the next guy who asked us out. For me, it was Shawn."

"Well, he does have my swag," Ron said.

"Your looks too."

"You think? I see his mama there too."

Kimberly shook her head. "Those dimples and those eyes. I kept thinking he looked familiar, and that was because he looked like you."

"Well, come on back to our pavilion. I hate to swipe my son's date . . . wait, no, I don't. I saw you first, Kimmy Kim."

He had seen her first, and Kimberly was happy to see him again. She was looking forward to picking up where they'd left off. She just hoped that Shawn would be okay with losing his cougar date to his daddy.

Chapter 14

Hahna checked into the hotel with her company card and gave hotel room keys to Corden and Sam. She couldn't read Sam's expression—he had perfected the blank stare—but she wondered if he'd thought they would be sharing a hotel room.

She had considered them sharing a nice suite but had changed her mind. What if things went south and she wanted her own space? That was a possibility since she'd only known him a few days.

"Let's get together tomorrow afternoon after you've had time to finalize the presentation," Hahna said to Corden.

Hahna wanted to set the understanding that this trip was not a double date. And although Corden had gotten her some very critical intel, she didn't want him interrogating Sam all weekend. Nor did she want Corden to know that she was paying for everything for both herself and Sam.

"You don't want to have dinner together?" Corden asked. "I know some great Cuban spots."

"I think Sam and I are going to venture out on our own."

Corden opened his mouth to say something else, but Hahna lifted her eyebrow and tried to give him "the look," like a black mama communicating to her child to stop cutting up. Corden seemed to understand this, because his mouth snapped closed.

"I'll meet you at your hotel room at noon tomorrow, then," Corden said.

"Sounds good. Have fun, Symone. I know you like to dance, and there are lots of great clubs on the strip," Hahna said.

"I can't believe you put us in the middle of South Beach, boss lady," Symone said. "I'm here for all of this."

Not just the middle of South Beach, but at a five-star hotel. This was how Hahna liked to travel, and she wouldn't put her staff in lesser accommodations.

The foursome crossed the opulent lobby that smelled of lavender, eucalyptus, and rosemary and entered the glass and marble elevator. Every step they took screamed wealth and status. Hahna had seen how Sam lived, and now she wanted to show him how she lived. She'd earned her millionaire status and was damn sure going to enjoy it.

In the elevator, they pressed three separate buttons for three separate floors. This was done purposely too. Hahna didn't want to run into Corden in the hallway as she was doing a mad dash to or from Sam's room. Not that hot, steamy sex was a given on the trip, but it would be welcome.

Corden and Symone's floor was first. As they exited the elevator, Corden gave Hahna a look. She laughed.

"Y'all be good now," Corden said as the doors closed.

Sam exhaled. "Finally, I can relax. I felt like I was being assessed. Does he have some scorecard he's using?"

"I have no idea. We're very close. He's just trying to look out for me."

"Corden doesn't need to worry about me. I'm really feeling you, Hahna. I realize it's only been a few days, but I just want you to know that."

"I'm feeling you too."

"I want to take you somewhere special to me," Sam said. "Do you want to change clothes?"

"I would like to freshen up some. I'll meet you in the lobby in thirty minutes."

The elevator stopped on Sam's floor. Before he exited, he took a moment to brush Hahna's curls out of her face.

"Damn, you're fine," he said as the doors closed.

Hahna bit her bottom lip and squealed. She wondered if Sam had heard her, then realized that she didn't care. She wanted this man, no matter how Corden assessed him.

When Hahna got to her suite, she quickly pulled out a sundress and sandals to wear outside to Sam's special place. She started the shower but also took out her cell phone. She had to tell Twila and Kimberly about this.

She called Twila first.

"Hey, girl," Twila said.

"Hey, girl, hey! Let me get Kimberly in on this call too, so I only have to tell the story one time."

"Well, damn. How about, hey, are you that busy? Do you have a man over who's about to make your toes curl?"

"Do you, heffa?"

"Naw."

Hahna cracked up. "Okay, well, I'm about to call Kim."

"She's on a date with that young boy she met at the Starbucks."

"Really? I wonder how that's going."

"Chil', he took her ass to Six Flags."

"Oh, shit. Well, I'm gonna call her anyway. She might need rescuing."

"Okay."

Hahna dialed Kim's number, and she picked up on the second ring.

"Hey, girl," Kimberly said.

"Hey, girl, hey! I'm about to bring Twila on the line."

Hahna connected the calls.

"Y'all," Hahna said.

"What, girl? Make it quick," Kimberly said.

Twila laughed. "Oh, your date going better now?"

"Yes, actually, but it's because I found someone else. Y'all remember Big Ron from Morehouse?" Kimberly asked.

"How could we not remember him, Kimmy Kim?" Hahna asked. "You were in love with him."

"I was *not*."

"You were," Twila chimed in. "But how you gonna ditch your date for your old crush?"

"Chil', Big Ron is Shawn's daddy."

Twila and Hahna hooted and hollered so loud that if someone had walked by Hahna's hotel room they might've called security.

"This heffa pulling fathers *and* sons! You done surpassed sugar mama!" Twila said.

Hahna could barely pull herself together from laughing so hard.

"W-wait, y'all. I called to tell y'all about *my* boo," Hahna said. "I flew him out to Miami with me for a work and play trip."

"You flew him out? Damn, y'all taking this sugar mama shit seriously," Twila said. "I gotta step my game up."

"What's he like?" Kimberly asked. "Where'd you meet him? Is he fine?"

Hahna gave Kimberly and Twila the lowdown on how they met and the ridiculous fineness of Sam. She even told them about her spending the night at his place on the first night, although she was worried about their judgment on that part of it. When she finished, they were silent.

"What y'all think?" Hahna asked when neither Kimberly nor Twila said anything.

"Be careful," Twila said.

"Yeah," Kimberly said.

"So, y'all think this is crazy? Stupid? What? Am I not doing what we said we'd do?" Hahna asked.

"You are," Twila said, "but I didn't say don't be safe. That man could've raped and killed you at his house. We're not college freshmen anymore. We don't do dumb shit."

"Don't go out with him alone. Isn't Corden there?" Kimberly asked.

"He and his fiancée."

"Perfect," Kimberly said. "Take them with you. It's probably fine, but I don't feel good about you wandering around Miami with a stranger."

"I don't get a bad vibe about him, though, y'all."

"Then he's probably one of the good guys," Twila said. "Just take Corden with you. At least on this trip. Until we've seen how he moves."

"Let me get back to this card game," Kimberly said. "Be safe, Hahna. Love you, girl!"

"Love you too," Hahna said back.

Kimberly disconnected, but Twila remained on the call. Hahna could hear her tapping keys on her computer.

"What's his last name?"

"Who? Sam? Valcourt."

More clicking of keys.

"Are you doing a background check on him?" Hahna asked.

"I am. You done got on an airplane with a stranger."

"You said I should break my rules."

"I didn't tell you to get yourself robbed or killed."

Hahna closed her eyes and tried not to feel annoyed. She trusted her instincts about Sam. He didn't feel like a stranger. She'd stayed at his home and hadn't been harmed or molested. Nothing had been stolen from her.

"I don't think this is necessary," Hahna said.

"Hmmmm . . ."

"What?"

"You sound pretty anxious for someone who doesn't think this is necessary."

Hahna sucked her teeth. "Just tell me."

"Preliminary search didn't turn up anything. Not even a traffic ticket."

Hahna let out a relieved sigh. She hadn't realized that she was even holding her breath.

"I still wouldn't go out with him alone," Twila said. "If you do, please turn on your GPS, so I can find your ass if you turn up missing."

"Twila, I wish you could meet him. Then you'd see why I'm not worried. I've never met anyone like him."

"Well, don't hesitate to reach out if something doesn't feel right."

"I will."

"Love you, girl."

"Love you too."

Hahna disconnected the call and felt a bit of her excitement dissipate. She wished she hadn't told them about Sam yet. Now her friends were going to be worried for no reason.

That call had taken much longer than she'd thought it would, so she had to hurry and change her clothes to meet him in time. She took a five-minute shower, pulled her damp hair into a bun, and refreshed her makeup.

When she exited the elevator and crossed the hotel lobby, she saw that Sam was waiting and that he'd also changed clothes. He wore a fitted and colorful soccer jersey and khaki pants. The look was casual and stylish at the same time.

"Sorry I'm late," Hahna said as she approached.

He smiled. "I had no expectation of you changing and being ready in thirty minutes."

"What? I'm usually very punctual. I just called my friends and Kimberly ran into her college crush. We had to talk about that."

"Lots to unpack there, sounds like."

"Yes, there was. Are you making fun of me?"

Sam gave her a warm hug. "I wouldn't do that. I'd love to be a fly on the wall when you and your girlfriends talk about me."

"What makes you think we're talking about you?"

"You're not?"

"Maybe . . ."

Sam took her by the hand and spun her in a circle. "You look beautiful. I appreciate the few extra minutes."

Sam didn't let go of Hahna's hand as they walked to the taxi stand outside the hotel. He laced his fingers through hers and stroked her palm with his thumb. It was a sensual touch that made Hahna's insides feel warm. She closed her eyes and inhaled his cologne. It was an earthy scent that reminded Hahna of jasmine and cedarwood. She changed her mind and didn't want to go out anymore. She wanted to snuggle up against him and lay her head on his bare chest.

She wondered what his bare chest looked like. Her imagination told her that there were rippled muscles and smooth ebony skin. She imagined it glistening as her fingers glided over its beauty.

Hahna shivered, though she was anything but cold.

"Do you like the hotel?" Hahna asked.

"It's great. Typically I would never go for a hotel like this, but I am loving it so far."

"Really? This is the only kind of hotel I want. Nothing less than four stars, and that's only if there are no five-star hotels."

Sam nodded, but didn't add anything else, making Hahna think she'd said something wrong. She didn't get to ask a follow-up, though, because the taxi pulled in front of the hotel.

Sam gave the taxi driver an address. The driver smiled and said, "*Byenveni lakay frè.*"

"*Mesi. Li bon pou lakay,*" Sam replied.

"Are you French?" Hahna asked.

"Haitian," Sam said. "Haitian Creole sounds similar to French in many ways, but we've made it our own."

"Ah, I see. What did you say to the driver?"

Sam chuckled. "He welcomed me home and I said I'm glad to be home."

"I didn't know you were from Miami."

"I grew up in Atlanta, but my mother grew up here, and I spent summers here. I'm taking you to a place that reminds me of her and home."

Hahna relaxed and allowed herself to take in the beautiful and art-filled Miami landscape while Sam chatted with the taxi driver. And even though she didn't have his full attention, Sam's hands never left Hahna untouched for the entire drive. He stroked her hands, face, hair, and neck, keeping her nerve endings pleased, and making her want to fast-forward to whatever came next.

The taxi driver stopped them in front of a small building that was painted with bright colors like the Haitian flag. On stepping out of the taxi, Hahna's stomach growled at the scent of garlic and some kind of meat. She was hungry, but she also wanted to dance to the Caribbean music that was playing loud enough to be heard in the streets.

"Come on, beautiful," Sam said.

Everything this man said made Hahna melt. How could a man like this be unattached? Hahna's mental question sobered her a bit. There was probably a trail of heartbroken women to be found if she only looked for them.

Hahna was surprised that the building was a bookstore. Each wall had a bookcase that went to the ceiling, filled with new and used books. The music had come from the band that was entertaining a small group of people at the front of the store, and the food scents came from the restaurant in the back.

"This is where I spent my summers."

A short and muscular man came from the back of the bookstore. A huge smile lit up his face when he saw Sam.

"*Pi popilè Sam Valcourt la!*" the man said.

"Papa Michel."

Sam embraced Michel in a warm hug. Hahna could see the resemblance in the two men. Sam had gotten his height from somewhere else, but his face and Michel's shared many similarities. Mostly, their kind eyes and prominent noses.

"Hahna, this is my uncle Michel, but I call him my papa, because he has been a father to me. Papa Michel, this is my very special friend, Hahna," Sam said.

Papa Michel looked Hahna up and down and gave his nephew a congratulatory clap on the back.

"Are you hungry?" Papa Michel asked. His English dripped with his Haitian accent, making his words sounds musical to Hahna.

She nodded. "I am starving."

"Well, you are in for a treat. I just finished a pot of stewed chicken. Come sit down and let me feed you."

Michel led Sam and Hahna to a small private dining room at

the rear of the restaurant. It was separated from the other seating, and had a family feel to it. Hahna wondered if it was where Sam ate meals as a child.

Hahna promised herself she wouldn't be a glutton in front of Sam, but as soon as the food came to the table, she felt all her resolve disintegrate. There was stewed chicken, rice and peas, and buttery bread.

"Oh my God," Hahna said. "I'd be three hundred pounds if your uncle was my man."

Papa Michel laughed. "Has Sam not cooked for you?"

"Only a little," Sam said. "I haven't had the chance to yet."

"He is outstanding," Michel said. "I wish he would come back here and work with me, but he loves Atlanta and books more than the kitchen."

"I hear he's a phenomenal writer," Hahna said between bites.

"Oh, you haven't read his books yet?" Michel asked.

Hahna swallowed her food slowly. This was a question where she needed to score points with her response. Of course, she was going to read Sam's books; she had already purchased them.

"We just met on Wednesday, Papa," Sam said.

Michel's eyes widened, but then he settled on a smile. "Well, you have time then. After you two get done being swept away."

Michel excused himself and left Sam and Hahna alone in the dining room.

"Did you eat here as a little boy? In this room?" Hahna asked.

Sam nodded. "Yes. My cousins and I spent the summers eating here and working in the restaurant. Except I always helped my aunt and mother in the bookstore."

"Where is your aunt?"

"Matante Celestine died two years ago. She had an aneurysm."

"Oh, I'm so sorry."

"Thank you. She was wonderful. She and my mother were best friends. My mother introduced her to Papa Michel."

Hahna didn't know what to think about being invited to

Sam's family's restaurant. It felt very intimate for their new relationship.

"I feel honored that you brought me here," Hahna said.

"You're the first one I've ever introduced to my papa. He must think we're going to get married."

He was in his forties and had *never* brought a woman home? Hahna felt alarmed and flattered at the same time.

"What are you thinking?" Sam asked.

Her first instinct was to withhold her feelings and say something innocuous about the food or surroundings. It wouldn't technically be a lie, because she was thinking about all those things too.

"A lot of things. Like how intimate this feels when we just met this week, and how you've never brought anyone here."

"I know. I feel the same way. It was crazy to me how you brought me to Miami on a date. Your move brought us to somewhere special to me. Felt like kismet."

"It does. I thought that too, but I've never trusted fate with anything in my life. I do things. I don't just let life happen to me."

"Thank you for just letting *this* happen," Sam said. "These few days feel like weeks or even months."

Hahna felt it too but had been afraid to vocalize it. Sam was braver. Or maybe he had less to lose. She had everything to lose.

"It doesn't seem like three days at all. It feels like you've always been here."

Sam scooted his chair closer to Hahna's. He took her hand and kissed it again. It was still warm from his touch in the taxi. He enflamed every part of her body with his small yet intimate touches.

This time, he took his touches further, and he leaned in to kiss her waiting mouth. She could taste the spices from the stewed chicken, the garlic, onion, and tomato. It was okay, though, because those same flavors swirled inside her mouth as well.

His lips had become the second course of her meal.

He softly sucked her bottom lip, pulling it into his mouth and savoring the soft skin. His hands traveled wherever they pleased, and she encouraged him by twisting in her seat to give him access. It had gotten warm in the dining room, and it wasn't due to the humid Miami spring. It was the forest fire that Sam had started with his kisses.

But Hahna didn't want the flames doused. She wanted to be engulfed.

Chapter 15

Twila turned Marcus's card over and over in her hand. She'd been talking herself out of calling him all day, but after the phone call with Kimberly and Hahna, she wondered what the hell she was waiting for. She'd told Kimberly he was coming over because that was the plan, but she hadn't executed it yet. She was the one who'd started this challenge, but she was the one hesitating.

Kimberly had gone on a date with a youngster, then swapped him out for his daddy, and Hahna had flown a brand-new man out to Miami. She was probably getting that good new sex in the Atlantic Ocean, while Twila sat on her living room sofa with the key to her own good time in her hand.

There was nothing alarming about Marcus, outside of the fact that he was probably a starving artist, so it wasn't that she was worried about her safety.

Has it really come to this?

The thought blared in her mind like a six-in-the-morning alarm after a night of drinking. It woke her when she didn't feel like awakening. Because, yes, it had come to this. It had come to worse than this. She'd fallen to her lowest rung. And on that rung was a silicone, shivering, quivering, and thrusting fake penis.

Instead of dialing Marcus's number, she went to his Instagram page.

There was that oiled-up chest again, but this time without the apron. The complete washboard abdominals were on display, and his gray sweatpants rested low on his hips, showing off all the excessive time he had to be spending in the gym. The gray sweats also highlighted something else. Unless Marcus had stuffed a pair of socks down the front, the outline on the front of his gray sweats was enough to retire Twila's battery-operated substitute.

Twila double-tapped the picture. He deserved that little heart next to the photo that said Twila loved it. He deserved the 2,300 other women who'd placed that little heart there too.

Maybe that's what it was. The 2,300 women. Twila had never seriously dated anyone who had groupies or Instagram stalkers, and she was sure that Marcus did. So, was this a waste of time, since she could never be serious with someone like that . . .

That outline in the front of his sweatpants convinced her to at least ride the ride, before she swore off amusement parks.

Finally, she dialed.

"Hello," Marcus said.

Twila panicked. Wanted to disconnect the call. She hadn't thought of what to say, or what to converse about.

"Hey there, Marcus. This is Twila. The cosmetic dentist."

"Did you think I forgot you?" Twila could almost hear his smile through the phone.

"I hope not."

"I didn't think you'd really call. I hoped, but I didn't think you'd want to talk to me."

Twila wrinkled her nose. She hated self-deprecating men. Even the ones who were using it as a game, like Marcus was clearly doing.

"I don't necessarily want to talk to you," Twila said. "I want to see you again, though."

Marcus let out a loud hoot. "I'm just eye candy to you?"

"Not if you have something interesting to talk about. Then

you'll be eye candy and a great conversationalist. But if talking isn't your thing, eye candy is certainly enough."

"Only if you plan on tasting the candy, though. That's the only reason I'll accept it."

"You'll accept what I offer you," Twila said, feeling powerful with her role-play. "I might offer you wine. I might offer you a good meal. But I might not be talking."

"Do you want to go out on a date, Dr. Twila?" Marcus asked. "Maybe that'll make it easier."

"No. I don't want to go on a date with you."

Twila was one of Atlanta's best cosmetic dentists—no, she *was* the best. Her clients were singers, actors, athletes, and the other Atlanta elite. She wasn't going to be seen out in the streets with an Instagram video vixen, no matter how fine he was.

"Ummm, wow. I don't know what to say to that. Why'd you call me if you didn't want to see me?"

"I didn't say I didn't want to see you. I said I don't want to *go out* with you. You can come over to my crib, though. We can spend some time together here."

"Like Netflix and chill?"

"A definite yes on the chill part, but I think we can find more creative things to do besides watch Netflix."

"Hmmmm. . . ."

Twila felt herself becoming impatient. She had invited this underserving man into her space, and he was acting as if there was room to negotiate. There wasn't.

"Aren't you concerned with inviting me to your home?" Marcus asked.

"You really don't think I invited you over without doing a background check, do you?"

Twila had, of course, done a background check, and he was cleaner than Big Mama's kitchen. Besides, she had weapons stashed all over her home. If he was feeling froggy, he'd leave without a frog leg or two.

"Well, what if I *want* to go out?" Marcus asked. "Maybe I don't feel comfortable coming to your house."

Twila sucked her teeth. "I'm sorry. I thought I had called a grown-ass man on the phone."

"I'm grown. But maybe I want something more than sex."

"Very presumptuous of you to think I'm offering sex at all. Are you interested in coming over or not?"

"Of course, I'm coming over."

"I'll text you the address. Bring your ass."

Twila disconnected the call without waiting for his response. He would show up with his tongue wagging and his hopefully long tail between his legs. And she would decide what transpired from there.

Twila felt powerful. *Is this what it is like being a man?*

Chapter 16

Hahna stumbled to her hotel room door, pulling on clothing as she went. Someone was knocking on the door like a police officer on a trap house raid.

"Hold on."

The sound of her own voice made Hahna's head pound. She hadn't been hungover in years, and she wasn't now, unless it was from the multiple orgasms that Sam had given her. And the lack of sleep. They'd made love until dawn, and she'd only just fallen asleep when the knocking started.

She looked out the peep hole and it was Corden. What the hell was he doing at her door first thing in the morning?

Hahna opened the door, but not wide enough for Corden to see any evidence of Sam sleeping in the bedroom.

"This better be good," she hissed.

"Somebody woke up mean and nasty," Corden said.

Hahna narrowed her eyes and snarled, "What is it?"

"I have been trying to tell you since last night, but your ass wasn't answering your phone."

"Watch it . . ."

"Oh, are we on the clock now, boss? Because if we are, I have something very important to tell you. Dr. Brexton and his wife have invited us for Sunday brunch."

"Oh, my goodness." Hahna's head throbbed.

"Yes. So, go take some Tylenol for that hangover . . ."

"I am not hungover."

"Well, get some coffee or something, because you look like hell."

"I was sleeping until you woke me up."

Sam cleared his throat from the bed; he was still asleep, but could be heard. Corden grinned. Hahna twisted her lips to one side, not willing to confirm or deny anything.

"My bad boss lady," Corden said through irritating giggles. "I didn't know you had a guest."

"When is brunch?"

"Three hours from now. It's at their Fisher Island estate, so I'm expecting it to be extravagant."

"Shit. I don't have anything to wear, and I'm sure Sam doesn't either."

"So, we are taking the boy toy."

"Dammit, Corden. I don't have time for your jokes. Who do you know that can get us outfitted in three hours?"

Corden closed his eyes and opened them again. "I know a girl, but it's gonna be a little tense. She's my ex."

"Tell her to bring something nice for Symone too, then."

Corden rubbed his hand across his forehead. "You're trying to get me stabbed in Miami."

"With this big old ocean to dispose the body in."

"I really need to send my résumé to a headhunter."

"Love you too, Corden," Hahna said. "Get your friend here in an hour."

"Yeah, I will. You and Sam make sure you're decent when she gets here."

Hahna nodded and closed the door slowly. Then she tiptoed back to the bed. The soft pillows called her. If only she could have fifteen more minutes. But she knew that if she crawled back between those soft sheets, she would sleep through the afternoon.

She tickled the bottom of Sam's foot and he stirred.

"Wake up, lover," Hahna said in a husky whisper.

Sam smiled and stretched, but barely opened his eyes. "What time is it? It feels like we just went to sleep."

"We did, but my client, the one we're trying to land, has invited us to Sunday brunch on Fisher Island. He will probably be offended if we don't go."

"And that'll cost you this account?"

"Maybe not, but it sure wouldn't put him in a good mood when we sit down at the negotiating table. This will be Brexton trying to feel us out and make sure that we're a good fit for his organization."

"Are you sure you want to bring me?" Sam asked. "I wouldn't be offended if you didn't."

"I wouldn't have brought you to my bed if I wouldn't take you to brunch."

For the first time since she met him, Sam didn't seem to exude confidence. "I might not know what to say to some of these people. You said it's a pharmaceutical company, right?"

"About pharmaceuticals, I'm as clueless as you are. I'm a data geek. We'll figure it out together. Corden is sending over a stylist in an hour."

"A stylist?"

Hahna shrugged. "It's not as fancy as it sounds. We need something to wear, and this girl has clothes."

"If the stylist is coming in an hour, I suppose I should shower," Sam said with a gleam in his eye that Hahna read as an invitation.

Hahna started to disrobe in front of the bed. "You know, I think you're right. I *am* feeling kind of dirty."

Hahna dashed into the bathroom with Sam at her heels. She wished she didn't have to put on her work face and woo her client. She'd rather stay holed up in the hotel suite to woo this man. Or was he *her* man? Hahna pushed the thought away before it had time to marinate or fester. Even if she was breaking the rules, it was too soon for that kind of thinking.

Still, the words lingered at the edges of her thoughts, nearly willing themselves to solidify into truth. Her. Man.

The warmth of the water cascading down her back, and the strength of Sam's arms as he encircled her, made Hahna feel more refreshed than anxious. More at ease than at risk. In fact, she couldn't ever remember feeling more at home in anyone else's arms.

Hahna just hoped that Sam felt at home in her world too.

Chapter 17

Twila opened her door before Marcus got the chance to knock. She'd seen him walk up the path to her brownstone in the security cameras.

"It smells good in here," Marcus said.

It did. Twila had lit a dozen candles, so the scents of frankincense, cedarwood, sandalwood, bergamot, and lavender filled every corner of her home. It was a smoldering scent. It was boudoir-esque.

"Glad you like it," Twila said. "I felt like some aromatherapy during my massage."

"Oh, you got us a couples' massage?"

Twila laughed. "I got myself a diva massage. Unless you're not up for it."

"Wait."

Twila's laugh got louder, but she knew Marcus was up for whatever task she set before him. The way he took in her thick thighs and round behind, made him look like a starving man gazing at his next meal. Her tiny fleece shorts that allowed the bottom of each cheek to play peekaboo didn't help, and neither did the tiny tank top that barely contained her breasts. Or they *did* help—because Twila's goal was to set Marcus on fire.

"Yes, you're the masseuse. I saw your hands, and all I could think about was you working all the stress from between my shoulders and my lower back."

Marcus chuckled. "Is that all? I mean, I can think of a few more things my hands can do."

"Don't know," Twila said. "Right now, my shoulders are feeling kind of tight."

Twila led Marcus to her favorite room in the house—her glam room—where Twila usually got her thousand-dollar weaves installed and her eyelashes done. There was even a pedicure chair, where Twila got serviced like a queen.

Today, Twila was going to be serviced like a goddess. Or maybe served was a better word.

She climbed atop the leather massage table that she'd unfolded and placed in the middle of the room.

"You can wash your hands in the bathroom right there."

"You're serious about this," Marcus said.

"I am. You don't want to run your hands all over my body?"

He didn't reply. He just turned and walked into her glam bathroom.

Twila removed her tank top, stretched out on her stomach and waited impatiently for Marcus's hands to work their magic. She hoped he wasn't clumsy.

"You look so sexy on that table," Marcus said, "that I just want to mount you."

The Taser Twila had affixed under the table would be a severe impediment to Marcus sticking that mount.

"I really wish you wouldn't," Twila said. "That would ruin things. The lotion is warming right over there."

"I don't want to ruin things."

And Twila knew he wouldn't. He was too turned on. The bulge in the front of his pants almost made Twila change her mind about the mounting, but she knew she had to make him wait.

Marcus started with the center of her back and radiated out to her shoulders. He first made wide circles, but then started to purposefully knead the tense space between her shoulders.

"You are so tight. Lots of stress, huh?" Marcus asked.

Twila's response was a moan.

Marcus rubbed the warm lotion into the small of her back. This was one of her erogenous zones. Marcus's fingers rubbed all of the tension out of her body and caused a waterfall of moisture between her legs.

But Marcus wasn't going to have any idea that she was turned on. This was about teasing him to the point of insanity, and then sending him away. That way, when she finally did let him in, *if* she let him in, it was going to be explosive.

Twila tried not to moan again when he used his elbows to penetrate her muscle groups deeper. He leaned forward until she felt his breath on the back of her neck. He was closer than close. If she didn't stop him soon, Twila was going to lose her resolve.

"That was nice," Twila said as she held up one hand to stop Marcus from continuing.

"We're barely getting started here. I can do this all day."

Twila laughed. "I just bet you could, but my back was truly bothering me. I have some work to do."

"What kind of work? Are you seeing patients in your house?"

Anger flickered in his eyes, but Twila didn't feel nervous. She'd probably be angry too if she was a man. He thought he was going to get some, and it wasn't going down.

"The kind of work that's none of your business."

Marcus looked at the floor and back up again. There was no longer anything on his face or in his smoldering gray eyes that signaled anger. She was glad about that part. She didn't want to hurt him; she just wasn't ready to have sex with him yet. They barely knew each other.

"You know what?" Twila asked. "It is somewhat rude of me to ask you to come here, just to give me a massage."

"You're damn straight it is."

Twila smiled. "Brunch will be here soon. You hungry?"

"Do I have to cook it?"

"No, you don't have to cook it," Twila said with a little giggle. "Although I wouldn't mind tasting that eggplant frittata."

"You can have that the morning after."

"Okay. That's something to look forward to."

"That's all you're looking forward to?"

The doorbell rang, saving Twila from having to answer that question. She pulled her robe tightly around her body and went to let her caterer in with brunch. Marcus's eyes were glued to her body as she walked out of the room. One of the good things about being a woman was that a man could only guess that she was turned on. A man couldn't hide his excitement.

Marcus was very excited.

Katie worked quickly to set up three different kinds of quiche, a sandwich platter, a tray of fruit, a small pan of macaroni and cheese, an assortment of muffins and biscuits, a carafe of mimosas, and a fresh brewed jug of coffee. It smelled amazing, as it always did. Katie made everything from scratch down to the crusts on the quiche. There was enough food for ten people.

"Thank you, Katie," Twila said as she paid her bill with an app on her phone. "You did your thing on this one."

"You're welcome. I'll get out of here so you can finish getting dressed for your company."

Twila looked confused for a moment and then laughed as she looked down at her robe. "My company is already here, girl."

Katie shrieked in a high pitch that only white girls could manage. "Get it, then! I am not mad at you."

"Good, 'cause I'm grown."

"Grown-ass woman all day." Katie did a little dance that let on that she liked Cardi B and sometimes went to the club with her black girlfriends.

Katie danced right on over to the door singing and laughing the whole way. Twila gave Katie a little extra push out the door. She wanted to get back to her company.

As if he'd been listening from the glam room, Marcus emerged and walked into the kitchen. He'd unbuttoned a few of his shirt buttons during the massage, and she could see the top of his strong pectoral muscles as he approached.

"You hungry?" Twila asked.

"Ravenous."

"You should be. You put in some work. My muscles are gonna be loose for a week. Come get a plate of food."

Marcus piled his plate high with everything and then filled another. He sat down at the kitchen table and started to dig in. He shoveled food into his mouth so quickly she wondered if he even tasted it.

"You're not gonna wait for me?" Twila said.

"I'm sorry. I was just so hungry. I haven't eaten since last night around dinnertime."

She lifted an eyebrow at him as she hastily made her own plate. The way he was eating, it didn't seem like he'd had a meal in days. Maybe she hadn't ordered too much food.

Twila sat down at the table and tasted her own food. It was delicious. She was tempted to shovel food in too, but her manners kept her acting like a lady.

"This is good," Marcus said. "You said a caterer made this? They need a restaurant."

"She will have one soon. She's just trying to get the money together."

"And you're supporting her with your purchases. That's what's up."

"I support small businesses. Shit, I'm a small business that needs supporting."

Marcus twisted his face. "You're not really a small business, though. Everybody in Atlanta is trying to book an appointment with you for something."

"I do get a lot of business, but we're still small. I'm the only dentist in my establishment."

"You didn't get all this," Marcus said as he waved his arms around her home, "by being small. That's a technicality."

"I do well, I'm not gonna lie, but I could always be doing better. I'd like to expand and add a dentist."

"I wish I knew how to do that work. I'd take the job in a heartbeat."

"I'm sure you would. Let me hear you sing."

He looked up from his plate, with a mouth full of food, chewing slowly. Then slower and slower until he actually stopped.

"You want to hear me right now?"

"Yes, right now. Have you eaten too much? Are you one of those singers who can't sing on a full stomach?"

"No. I just . . . this is weird, Twila."

"What's weird?"

"I've never had anything like this happen before, like I'm legit nervous."

Twila laughed. "You never had a woman invite you to her home?"

"Not a woman like you. No. This is some next-level shit."

"I am a next-level kind of woman. You aren't wrong about that. But there's nothing weird about this. I find you attractive, and I wanted to see if there was any potential."

Marcus swallowed another bite of food. "So, you invite me over to rub all over your naked body."

"I had on panties."

"Seriously, this is weird."

Twila felt like Marcus was calling her bluff. She didn't know what she was doing with this sugar mama stuff. Twila was new to this game. She wished she knew Kandi, so she could call and ask how she'd snagged Todd.

"These aren't boss moves?" she asked.

Marcus set his fork down on the table and cracked up. "Is that what's happening here?"

"Yes. I'm bossing up on you."

"Well, I don't have a problem with that at all. I wish you had told me up front. I thought some reality show cameras were about to pop out the corner or something."

"Really?"

Marcus nodded. "This is Atlanta. Everybody is producing a reality show."

"You're right. But I still haven't forgotten."

"What?"

"That I asked you to sing. I really want to hear you."

Marcus took a sip of water and cleared his throat. Then he belted out the hook to "One Last Cry" by Brian McKnight. His voice was so smooth and expressive that she felt the melancholy that was written into those lyrics and melody.

"Wow, Marcus. You can really sing."

"Thank you. It's just tough here. Everybody can sing. Everybody can act. Shit, everybody gets plastic surgery so my face ain't even all that marketable."

"You just need the right connections to get you on."

He nodded. "I've got a single done. Once I get my money together, I'm gonna shoot a video. Then maybe I'll have enough to do an independent project."

"Don't you want a record deal?"

"These days, record companies are looking for prepackaged artists, with an album done, and a built-in fan base. Unknowns aren't getting deals anymore."

Twila still felt chills from Marcus's singing. This kind of voice needed to be on the radio. He could blow up, for real.

Marcus was just the kind of guy who needed a sugar mama.

"I think I want to help you," Twila said. "Maybe I could be your manager."

"Can I hug you? Would that be a problem?"

Twila shook her head. "No, it's all right."

She'd almost added, *come to mama*, but didn't. That might've made Marcus feel weird again, and this was just starting to feel right. Besides, when she was standing next to him on the Grammys red carpet, no one would care a bit about her giving him a little push in the right direction.

"I feel like I was supposed to meet you, Twila. Do you feel like that too? Like this was supposed to happen?"

Twila thought about how she'd seen his face on Instagram and then how he'd turned up in her dental office. One could make a case for destiny, or a very convenient coincidence. Either way, she was feeling his vibe, so she'd go with it.

"I think it was," Twila said. "Do you feel like going to the movies or something? I am not ready for our day to end."

"I graduated to going out in public. That must've been a great massage."

Twila grinned. It was a great massage, but the not going out in public had been a last-minute rule she'd thrown in the mix. It was up to her if she wanted to break that rule. She was taking her Instagram boo out among the people and wouldn't care what anyone had to say about it.

Chapter 18

Hahna's nerves had never been this bad at a client meeting, but then she'd never taken a man with her to meet one of her clients before. This was new. Another rule tossed to the wind. It comforted her that Sam seemed out of sorts also. It would've bothered her had he been too calm, too ready to slide in there and play a role he wasn't sure he had yet.

Nothing about Sam said he was a player or out to scam Hahna, but she'd let Kimberly and Twila get in her head about him. She'd let them make her think she was moving too quickly (she was moving quickly, but it was the *too* that was in question). But Sam was there with her anyway, smiling, staying low-key as he sipped his mimosa on the Brextons' massive lawn at their enormous estate.

If they hadn't been on the island, it would've been too warm for an outside brunch, but the ocean breeze saved them from the worst of the heat. There were chairs and tables, but this was mix and mingle time—two things Hahna really didn't feel like doing on two hours of sleep. She plastered on a smile and powered through. This contract was worth it. She'd be able to subcontract three of her smaller accounts if she landed this one.

"If it isn't the data whisperer," Dr. Hale Brexton said as he

strode toward Sam and Hahna, his decades-younger wife, Jelena, in tow.

"Game on," Hahna whispered. Sam grinned. She hoped that
meant he was ready.

"Dr. Brexton. Thank you so much for this invitation," Hahna
said as she embraced Dr. Brexton and Jelena. "I can't say we
were expecting it."

"You keep calling me 'Dr. Brexton' like we're not on 'Hale'
and 'Hahna' terms. You make me feel like an old man."

"You are far from old, Hale. You're stubborn, not old."

Hahna's rapport with Hale Brexton had taken years to build,
and he trusted her. He'd sent many clients her way, but only
reached out for her services when his top analyst, Shane
Brown, had gone to prison for assaulting his girlfriend.

"I wouldn't dream of having you find a decent brunch when
we have one every other Sunday," Jelena said. "I'm happy we
thought about it in time."

"Hale, Jelena, this is my beau, Sam."

Beau? She'd said "beau." Not "boyfriend," because that was
too much, even though the words were damn near synonymous.
Not "friend," because that wasn't quite enough to describe Sam.
They had bonded even before they'd shared their bodies.

Sam shook Hale's hand, and accepted Jelena's hug. "Pleased
to meet both of you."

"I'm glad Hahna brought a friend," Jelena said. "It's Miami.
Might as well make a getaway of it if you have to be here."

"Speaking of that," Hahna said, "I'm sure we could've ham-
mered this out via conference call, Hale. Why did I have to
come all the way here to seal this deal? What's holding you
back?"

"Get right to it, why don't you?" Hale said with a laugh. "How
do you know I didn't just want to see your pretty face?"

"I'd believe that, except your wife is prettier," Hahna said
with a wink at Jelena. "So, what is it?"

"I'm tightening my circle. Not doing business over the phone.

This thing with Shane put a lot of my trade secrets at risk. The police raided his home and invaded my privacy. Then I found out he'd been invading mine."

Hahna made a mental note to have Corden include in their presentation the off-site, secure data storage solution. It sounded like this was about more than trust. Hale sounded like he had something to hide.

"I hope our proposal meets your needs, Hale. I hate that any of this is happening to you."

"I have a new security guy that I want to have work with you if we get this deal done. His name is Josiah Walton."

"How new? How did you vet him?" Hahna asked.

"He's family. The only reason I trust him. My sister's boy. A cybersecurity genius. He just left the federal government to come and work for me."

"Okay. Just making sure."

"I like the way you think, though, Hahna. Shane destroyed it for any outsiders. That's the reason you're here. I feel like you're family too."

"I appreciate that sentiment."

Hale groaned. "Let's not talk about this anymore today. My doctor has said my life expectancy is decreasing. Too many angry days in a week."

"Sunday shouldn't be an angry day," Hahna said as she nodded in agreement.

"I don't want him angry at all," Jelena said. "His heart can't take it. Let's talk about something else. Sam, I know all about Hahna. Tell me about yourself. What's your passion?"

Sam gave Jelena one of the smiles that had crumbled Hahna's resolve.

"I'm a writer. Coincidentally, it is my passion too."

"Listen. It's either your passion or your poison," Jelena said. "Your work can feed you or kill you. What do you write?"

"Mostly quirky romances and women's fiction," Sam said.

"Fascinating. I used to read more. I was in a book club a few years back," Jelena said. "Then, for some reason, it fell apart. I think it had to do with the wine at the meetings. We had more of it than sandwiches, and some of us just came for the drink."

"I thought that was what a book club was all about," Hale said. "Wine and more wine. Sometimes you all get around to discussing the books."

"Ignore him," Jelena said. "I hope you've managed to find your audience, Sam. The book market is terrible right now. Publishers are dropping like flies."

"I can't argue or disagree with that one," Sam said. "I'm independently published, though. I do well for myself."

"Save your money, and lock Hahna in. Don't let her and her millions get away."

"I don't need Hahna's millions," Sam said.

Jelena cackled. "Who doesn't need millions? Everyone needs millions."

Except that Sam didn't know anything about her having millions. To be fair, neither did Jelena. It was a correct assumption, but still only an assumption.

Jelena looked as if she wanted to query more, but Hale had already given her a look. Now Hale wrapped his arm around Jelena's waist.

"The food should be ready now," Hale said. "Let's stop yapping and start eating."

"You're right, honey," Jelena said. "I mean, seriously, the mimosas are everything, and the shrimp and grits are life-giving. Let's eat."

Hahna slid her arm through Sam's and drew close to him as they followed Hale and Jelena. He felt stiff, and his lips were drawn into a grim-looking thin line. Was he embarrassed that Jelena had assumed anything about his finances and hers? Was his pride wounded?

She would deal with Sam later, after she sealed the deal with Hale. If his feelings were hurt, Hahna wasn't going to let it impact her business. If he was wounded, he was going to have to learn to deal with the fact that she had money.

Hahna was so glad they hadn't declined the invitation. She'd thought that they were being invited to an event with Dr. Brexton's friends and wouldn't be missed. But this brunch had been prepared specifically for them. Not showing up would've probably cost them the deal. She had Corden to thank for the wake-up knock and the win.

Hahna made another mental note to give him a raise.

Chapter 19

The scent of fried chicken and thick, sweet syrup filled the air of the tiny breakfast diner. It had been their favorite in college. Every other Sunday, Big Ron had brought Kimberly and Hahna to this restaurant, and they'd pooled their money to buy chicken and waffles, scrambled eggs, and biscuits.

Kimberly always wanted Ron to ask her just once to come to brunch alone. But he never had.

"You remember our brunch Sundays?" Ron whispered in her ear as they waited for the hostess to show them to their seats.

The whisper made her shiver. She swallowed hard and closed her eyes, trying to extend every one of these precious moments with Ron. In case he disappeared again.

"How could I ever forget? I looked forward to those Sundays."

"I did too. I was broke as hell, though. I would scrape up money from my boys until I had at least fifteen dollars. That was enough for me to pay if y'all didn't have any money."

"It wasn't enough to eat and leave a tip, though."

"Shole wasn't. I bet those waitresses hated to see us coming."

The waitress showed them to their table, guiding them through the tight spaces between the assortment of booths and chairs. The restaurant didn't have a certain type of décor. There were tables, chairs, booths, and menus. And the best breakfast in Atlanta.

Ron gazed across the table at Kimberly, his eyes saying more than he ever said with his lips.

"I just can't believe how beautiful you are."

"Ron. You always said that to me."

"And I meant that shit."

Ron made curse words sound sexy. He used them to punctuate his sentences.

"Then, why didn't you ever make your move back in the day?"

The corners of Ron's mouth twitched in the expression he always made that was between a smile and a grimace. Kimberly didn't know if she wanted to go back to the past already. Maybe it was too soon. They were only an hour into their first real date. But it was tugging at her, the idea that Ron hadn't wanted her in school when everyone had known about her more-than-crush. Her sorority sisters, his fraternity brothers. Everyone. Ron had always acted like he was sweet on her but had never once made a move.

"You were too good, Kim. You were going to be a lawyer and take over the world. You and all of your girls—shit, y'all was the overachiever crew."

"So. That means I didn't want a boyfriend?"

Ron chuckled. "That means you didn't want a boyfriend with a kid back at the house. Did you?"

"I don't know. You didn't give me the chance to find out."

But he was right. She did know. And back then she wasn't trying to be anybody's mama. Much less to a child who wasn't even her own.

"I wish you'd come to the reunions," Kimberly said. "Homecoming or something. I'm there every year."

"Every time I think about going, this or that comes up. I don't do the social media thing, so I guess I just don't keep up with everybody."

"Oh."

"Are you done interrogating me now?"

Kimberly laughed as she swiped her curls out of her face.

Her bangs were covering her eyes, and she wanted a perfect view of Ron. This felt like a dream. Accepting a date with his son and then finding him again. When did things like that happen except in dreams?

"I have missed you, Big Ron, and I've thought of you often. I wish I'd known how to get in touch with you after graduation."

"I married Shawn's mother after graduation."

Kimberly leaned back in her seat and let those words sink in. "Wow."

"Yeah, you know, I felt like I owed it to her. I got to leave and go to college. She got stuck at home, going to Sunday school and church picnics. We had a kid together, but she had all the consequences."

"You loved her, then."

"I wouldn't say I loved her. I felt guilty. She didn't have anybody but Shawn. Everybody was proud of me, and they gave her grief for being a teenage mom. I just . . . wanted to help her, I guess."

"Where is she now?"

This time only one side of his mouth twitched. He narrowed his eyes and sighed.

"I don't know. She'd started using drugs when I was away at school. No one knew. I think she tried to stop once we got married. Maybe she did."

"But she found them again."

"Yeah. Eventually."

"Then you raised Shawn alone?"

"No. I was never alone after we divorced. I had grandmothers, church mothers, church aunties. Everybody raised Shawn."

"Y'all did a good job."

"Thank you."

Kimberly didn't want to keep talking about Shawn, because talking about Shawn made her feel like there was a desperation lurking beneath the surface. More than what Twila had suggested when they'd made their pact. She didn't want Ron to judge her for it, although she wondered if he thought less of her.

"I guess I'm just glad you didn't end up with a white woman."

Ron burst into laughter, and Kimberly did too. They had gotten too serious and needed to get back to safer, more jovial conversation.

"How do you know I didn't?"

"I damn sure wouldn't be surprised."

"I could see Twila being pissed at me about that, but not you, Kimmie Kim. You don't care about interracial relationships."

"I care about my single sisters. I care about single me."

Suddenly, Kimberly felt awash with emotion. She felt the tears well up in her eyes, but quickly blinked them away. There *was* desperation there. She was desperate for Big Ron to change her status from single to wanted.

Ron waited quietly while she dabbed her eyes with the napkin and regained her composure.

"Sorry, I don't know what's wrong with me today," Kimberly said.

"Nothing's wrong with you today."

Ron signaled to the waitress that he was ready to order. Kimberly let him order the same foods they'd enjoyed when they were in college, although she sure didn't need to be eating chicken and waffles.

"You know, Kimberly, I made a mistake not snatching you up back in the day."

"Sounds like you had good reason."

"I thought I did. But I didn't. Making a baby doesn't mean you need to make a home."

Kimberly nodded, although she didn't know about making a baby or a home. She just believed him if he said it was true.

"I'm not gonna give you my sob stories today, but I've been through some pretty rough shit relationship-wise," Ron continued. "Maybe it's because I met my soul mate on the yard and let her get away."

Kimberly's bottom lip quivered, but she was determined not to cry.

"Maybe I did too," Kimberly said, those four words the only ones she was able to muster.

"Since we've found each other again, I think we should give

it a shot. I live in North Carolina, but I'm always here. Every other weekend."

Kimberly was almost too shocked to answer. It couldn't just be this easy. It was never this easy. Not for plus-sized black girls who'd reached middle age.

She thrust her arm across the table. Ron laughed.

"What?"

"Pinch me. For real. 'Cause if this is a dream, I need to wake the hell up."

Instead of a pinch, Ron took her hand and kissed it.

"I'm real. This is real. Let's just see what happens. If it doesn't work, at least we gave it a grown-ass try."

Well, how in the world could she say no to that? She couldn't.

So, she didn't.

"Okay, Big Ron."

Chapter 20

After the brunch, Hahna and Sam had once again separated from Corden and Symone to walk down South Beach and take in the sights. Their hands touched as they moved through the perfectly sculpted bodies. Hahna noticed every one of the bikini-clad goddesses, but Sam didn't seem to be paying any attention to them.

Sam was quiet, but Hahna didn't know him well enough to figure out if his silence was uncharacteristic or if this was normal for him. He *was* a writer. Was he one of the brooding types?

"What are you thinking about?" Hahna asked.

This was a safe enough question. She didn't want to assume that something was wrong or was bothering him, nor did she want him to think she was projecting anything from her own psyche onto him. Maybe she was overthinking all of it. Perhaps she didn't need to be safe at all.

"I was just thinking about how I'm typically not into this type of thing."

"What type of thing?"

"Brunch on Fisher Island with millionaires. Five-star hotels on South Beach. It's just typically not my lane."

"You're not having a good time?"

"I am. But I think it's only because I'm here with you that I'm having a good time. I wouldn't enjoy this if I was alone or with someone else."

"So, I'm taking you out of your comfort zone?"

"It's more that I enjoy being with you so much that it isn't bothering me."

Now Hahna was silent and brooding. This was her life, and she enjoyed it. He made it sound pretentious and shallow, but she had no problem enjoying the fruits of her labor.

"I work hard, Sam. I like nice things."

"I get it. Typically, I steer clear of women like you."

Hahna stopped walking and Sam went a few steps before turning around with an apologetic smile on his face.

"That didn't come out right," he said.

"It sure the hell didn't."

Sam took a few steps backward and slid her fingers through his. He squeezed her hand, and then raised it to his lips and kissed it.

"Women who enjoy the finer things are not usually satisfied with what I'm bringing to the table."

"We've only been dating a few days. I don't know what you're bringing to the table."

"You saw how I live. It isn't lavish. I don't care about it ever being lavish."

"That doesn't bother me. My needs and wants are met."

Sam gently pulled her hand and started walking again.

"I was a marketing director at Raythor Beverages, before I started writing," Sam said. "I hated it. Everything was fake. It was always about convincing people that our unhealthy-ass soda was something they could drink every day."

"So, you quit," Hahna said.

"Not right away. I worked my ass off. Got bonuses every year, because my campaigns were the bomb. I had a condo in Buckhead. Right around the corner from the bookstore where we met."

Hahna didn't respond, because she didn't see anything wrong with what he had done at Raythor. True enough, those sodas were full of sugar, but people knew that when they bought it. There was a nutrition label. People chose the foods they wanted to eat—Sam wasn't tricking anyone.

"Then, I finished a short story that I'd been working on for years. I shared it online and people loved it."

"What was it about?"

"A young man who had pondered suicide but had a kind mentor who had intervened. It was somewhat autobiographical. I wasn't the happiest kid when my mom took us from our family here."

"That sounds deep."

"When I started getting emails from readers that they could relate, or that they let their son or nephew read my work . . . it was everything. I wanted to feel that every day. I wanted that to be my work."

"Then you quit?"

Sam chuckled. "I waited a little longer. I planned. I didn't want to leave my job in debt, and I know, like Jelena so bluntly told us earlier, that there's not a whole lot of money in publishing."

"Why are you telling me all of this?"

"'Cause I want you to know that I'm not rich, but I'm not broke. I had a nest egg. I have investments. I own a four-suite apartment building in Decatur. I don't *need* anything from you."

"I was hoping you'd need *something.*"

"You know what I mean. I'm not after you for your money. I have all I need. It's enough, even for two, as long as that doesn't include five-thousand-dollar trips to Miami."

"Business expense."

He laughed. "I know. I'm just saying."

"Since you're just saying, I never said I had the expectation of you flying me out anywhere."

"That's the thing now, though, right? Women trying to get flown out to some exotic location all on the dime of some rich dude?"

"It is a thing, but not *my* thing. I fly myself out. I'll fly my man out too, honestly. Jelena bluntly talked about my financial status. She's right. I am a millionaire."

"But you have a hard time finding millionaire brothers to mate with?"

She snatched her hand away and frowned. "What makes you think I have a hard time finding a man?"

"It's atypical for a woman of your status to be interested in a brother who is only concerned with necessities. I figured you just decided to lower your standards."

"I didn't lower anything. I just met a guy in a bookstore and had a good time. Why are you trying to make this a plot device in your next women's fiction novel?"

He took both her hands this time. The intensity on his face was real and more visceral than any reaction Hahna had ever seen in a man.

"Because I have never felt about anyone the way I'm feeling you, Hahna. I don't want to be an experiment. If we're going to do this, you have to know that I don't take relationships lightly. I'm monogamous. When I'm with a woman, I'm only with her. I give my all. And I don't want to worry that you're gonna bail when some rich guy rolls up with wads of cash and a private jet."

"I won't, Sam. I've had those guys. And they're not monogamous, and they don't give their all. Most of them are assholes."

Sam bent down and pulled Hahna's face to his, kissing her deeply and weakening every muscle in her body.

Hahna thought about making Sam give her some promises too. To not feel threatened by her propensity to make money or by her power moves. And to not get weird when she wanted to spend money on herself, on him, or just for the hell of it. She didn't want to be his experiment, either.

But that would have to come later. Because now, Sam was running down the beach path to the ocean, and she was following him. And all that mattered was the moment, and the fact that this man wanted her more than he'd ever wanted anyone else. That counted for something. No. It counted for everything.

Chapter 21

Hahna stepped into the Mexican cantina that Kimberly had selected for their girlfriends' celebration of the launch of her Curlpop hair products. Plus, from their text conversations, it sounded like they all had man stories to share.

Kimberly was already in the waiting area. She ran up to Hahna and gave her a hug.

"Where's Twila?" Kimberly asked.

"You already know."

Kimberly shook her head. "I told her to be here a whole half hour earlier."

Twila walked up behind them and poked Kimberly in the back. When they turned around, her lips were twisted.

"Y'all think I'm not hip to y'all's little tell-Twila-a-whole-half-hour-earlier bullshit? I am hip to it, heffas."

Kimberly hugged Twila. "Thank you for showing up almost on time."

"Hush. Hahna just got here. I need a margarita, y'all. Can we sit down?"

Twila gave the hostess a glance, and she pulled together three menus. Hahna grinned. Twila was well known all over the city, because she had so many celebrities as clients. She'd been invited to be on several reality shows too, but hadn't accepted.

So, when she walked into a restaurant, people moved. Hahna loved it. It made her feel A-list.

The three of them crowded into their booth, and before they could even get comfortable, Twila flagged down a waitress.

"We need three mango margaritas on the rocks," Twila said. "Double the tequila in mine. These two are lightweights."

"Yes, we are," Kimberly said. "Thank you."

The waitress smiled, nodded, and walked off to put in their drink order. In high dramatic fashion, Twila closed her eyes, shook her head, and slammed both palms down on the table.

"Girrrrrrl."

Hahna and Kimberly cracked up. That word always signaled the start of a classic Twila story. And it usually was about a man.

"So, what had happened was . . . I saw this dude on Instagram."

"Girl, you told us that part," Hahna said.

"You slid into someone's DMs?" Kimberly asked. "And you invited him over. You told us that part too."

"That's not how it happened. Let me tell my story."

"You better hurry up and tell it, then," Hahna said. "'Cause now I'm worried."

"Oh no, you're not! Not when you met a man at a bookstore and then flew his ass to Miami. You ain't worried about me."

"Touché."

"Anyway," Twila continued, "I saw him on Instagram. He had a video where he's making an eggplant frittata."

"Eggplant?" Kimberly asked. "Oh."

"Yes, exactly. Click bait, but I was aware of that. He was fine, though, a butterscotch complexion, gray eyes, and muscles for days."

"That's just your type too," Hahna said. "You love those light-skinned brothas with light eyes."

"When she knows they went out of style in 1997," Kimberly said.

"Will both you heffas shut up! This story is juicy. Y'all taking all of the fun out of it. Yes, I like light-skinned men, and yes, I am aware they aren't particularly in vogue right now. More for me."

"You can have them. I like my men to be Wakandan plus Zamundan," Kimberly said.

"We know. Like Big Ron's ol' chocolate-dipped ass," Twila said. "We gonna get to that in a second. First, let me tell you about Marcus."

"That's a stripper name," Hahna said.

"He could be one. He has all the equipment."

Kimberly sucked her teeth. "You ho. You done already screwed him? Damn!"

"For your information, I have not, although if I had, it would've been my business. He sent me an image of his equipment to my mobile device."

"He sent you a dick pic?" Kimberly asked.

"That was crude. But yes, I believe that is the colloquial expression for said image."

Hahna cackled with laughter. "Let us see."

Without a second thought, Twila whipped her phone out of her purse and scrolled through her photos. When she found the photo she wanted, she smiled and handed her phone to Hahna.

"Oh, wow."

Kimberly snatched the phone from Hahna. "What in the horse-hung fraggle nackle is this?"

"Right," Twila said as she promptly reached for her phone when Kimberly started swiping left.

"Looks like you sent him a little something back, sis," Kimberly said.

"You are nosy, but yes, I sent him a little treat. My face isn't showing in the pictures, so I'm good."

Tears poured from Hahna's eyes from laughing so hard. The waitress returned right on time with the margaritas, because their fun was just getting started.

Twila held her drink in the air. "Let's toast, heffas. To fine men and sexual healing."

Hahna clinked her glass so hard against Twila's that a little margarita sloshed out on the table. She chuckled as she took a sip. She was excited about that toast. Shoot.

"Did y'all go out on a date yet, or y'all just sexting?" Kimberly asked, going right back to her interrogation.

"Yeah, how did you even meet him?" Hahna asked.

"We've been on a few dates actually, and he came into my office with one of my clients. He was thinking about getting some cosmetic dental work himself."

"Oh, is he an actor?" Kimberly asked. "That explains why he's on Instagram frying up eggplant."

"He's a singer, and he has an incredible voice."

"Really?" Hahna asked. "Is he performing anywhere? We can all go see him."

Twila shook her head. "Not yet, but soon. He's putting some things in place now and recording some original music."

Kimberly glanced at Hahna, and Hahna lowered her eyes. Hahna knew they were both thinking the same thing. This guy sounded like all the women on Instagram. The ones who wore lingerie and said they were aspiring singers. Marcus was the male version of that.

"He's fine, okay," Twila said. "I didn't say anything about falling in love or marrying him. He's fine, and he's fun. Two *f*s down and one to go. If he can land that last one, y'all can kick rocks."

"I know that's right," Hahna said as she high-fived Twila across the table.

"Hahna! You saying that like *you* done freshly experienced that last *f*," Kimberly said.

"I mean . . ."

Twila smiled and sipped her margarita. Hahna sipped hers to keep from responding further.

"You gave that man some booty already?" Kimberly asked.

"I shole did," Hahna said, without one ounce of shame. "And it was good too."

Kimberly frowned for a fraction of a second, but then it melted into a smile. She high-fived Hahna.

"All right then, girl. It's been a while."

"Yeah. Since Torian."

"He's dust," Twila said. "Don't even mention his name. Ashes to ashes."

Hahna did feel strange being the first out of the three to consummate her new sugar mama romance. But it wasn't too fast. Not with Sam. They had a connection that she wasn't even going to try to explain. Plus, she was grown. She didn't have to explain anything, nor were her girls asking her to.

"Well, Big Ron is still as sweet as ever. He went back home to North Carolina after his graduation to marry his baby's mama. They're divorced now, though."

"Shawn was cool, though?" Twila asked. "Poor baby thought he was 'bout to have him a thick cougar."

"I don't know whether he was cool or not," Kimberly said. "I was over him after he took me on that roller coaster. He was *too* young."

"Yeah, but if you hadn't said yes to him, you wouldn't have run back into Big Ron after all these years. Kismet," Hahna said.

"Kismet? That's kinda my line," Kimberly said. "You've never cared about destiny before. What's this about?"

"I don't know. Maybe meeting Sam, and just *knowing* with him makes me feel different on that topic. It's crazy, y'all. It feels like I've known him my entire life."

"Like your souls were connected in the cosmos before you were manifest in the flesh?" Twila asked.

"I mean, yeah . . . I guess?"

Twila burst into laughter. "I just made that shit up. I'm glad you're really feeling this dude, but don't fly away. Keep your feet on the ground. I need to meet him, so I can feel okay about him."

"What about your Instathot?" Hahna said, taking offense. "We need to meet him so we can feel okay."

"I trust both of y'all," Kimberly said. "Y'all grown. I don't need to meet either of them."

"Oh, I know," Hahna said. "Sam is doing a book signing at

this event at the Ritz-Carlton next week called 'It's Raining Men.' We should make it a triple date."

"Bet. I can check out Soul Mate Sam in his natural habitat. You shouldn't even tell him we're coming, so I can see if he tries to holla at me."

Hahna thought about this. Sam would probably be offended if she didn't tell him. He'd think she wanted her friends to spy on him.

"I'm not worried about him trying to holla at you or anybody else. Just bring Marcus, and Kim, bring Big Ron. I'll text y'all the link to buy tickets."

"Okay," Twila said. "Kim, did you think we forgot about Curl-pop?"

Kimberly laughed. "Yes. Y'all started talking about these men and forgot all about my little company, which is the reason why we're here tonight."

"We need another round of drinks so we can toast again."

The waitress must've heard Twila's loud declaration because she came over quickly. "Another round of margaritas, ladies?"

"Yes, I'll take another double, but this time I think we all need a double."

"Well, if we're doing that, can we order some food?" Hahna asked. "We'll take some chips, guacamole, and queso. Gotta soak up some of this tequila."

"Absolutely."

"You're gonna be in stores everywhere?" Hahna asked. "This is so exciting."

"I know!" Kimberly said. "We have to have a launch party."

"We should do it at my office," Hahna said. "I can deck out the whole mansion."

"And Katie can cater," Twila said. "I'll pick up the tab for it."

"Is Katie good? Maybe we should try to find a black caterer," Kimberly said.

Twila frowned, and Hahna sighed. This was a recurring argument that these two always had. And it always ended the same way. Stalemate.

"Katie can cook her ass off," Twila said. "That's not fair that you're judging her cooking just because she's white."

"I'm not judging her, really. It's just that I'm a small business owner selling products made by black women, for black women. Why can't we circulate our money through our community?"

"I have clients of every race and persuasion because my work is the best," Twila said. "As a matter of fact, I have more white, Asian, and Latin patients than I do black ones."

"That's just 'cause black people don't always trust black doctors and dentists," Kimberly countered. "That doesn't have anything to do with this conversation."

"Yes, it does. But look, you can have whatever caterer you want for your party. I was just offering mine, who is one of the best in Atlanta."

Hahna knew it was time for her to play the referee.

"Twila, I'll get her number from you. Maybe we can have more than one. A caterer for each level of the house, and a bartender too. People can go from one floor to the next and get different kinds of food."

Kimberly shook her head. "You're never going to take a stand on this, are you?"

"No, I'm not. Not with you two," Hahna said.

"You're smart not to," Twila said. "There are no winners in this argument."

"Maybe no winners, but our ancestors are crying right now," Kimberly said.

"You got some white ancestors too, with your caramel self," Twila said.

Now, this made Hahna laugh. There was never a boring time with her best friends. She couldn't wait for Sam to meet them, and for them to meet Sam. They were going to love him, just like she did. And then, maybe, they'd stop worrying about her.

Chapter 22

Kimberly had dreaded this moment. In fact, she had avoided her regular Starbucks for days in an effort to not run into Shawn. But she was in a rush to a meeting with a legal client and didn't have time to go out of the way. Not stopping was not an option. This client was an aspiring franchise owner who knew nothing about purchasing a franchise. The questions were going to be exasperating. She couldn't do this without caffeine.

Kimberly stood in the line, trying not to make eye contact, but she could feel Shawn's eyes blazing into the back of her head. She'd thought he wasn't angry when his dad had swooped in and stolen his date, but if his behavior now was any indication, he was big mad.

When she got up to the register to place her order, Shawn pressed his lips into a straight line, deepening his dimples. Now that she was really looking at him, how could she not have known he belonged to Big Ron? The resemblance to his father was unmistakable.

"What would you like, Ms. Kimberly?"

"My usual."

"I'm not sure I know what that is. Sometimes you think you know a thing and then you don't."

Kimberly rolled her eyes. "Okay, then. I'll have a venti blonde roast. Leave room for cream."

Shawn pressed the buttons on the register so hard that Kimberly thought he was going to break the thing. She held up her phone for him to scan it for mobile pay.

"Shawn, can we talk for a couple minutes outside?"

"Let me grab your coffee first," Shawn said. "Tracie, could you cover this register for me for five minutes?"

Shawn set the coffee on the counter instead of handing it to Kimberly, as if he didn't want to take the chance of making contact with her. That stung a little. He didn't have to be like this. It had only been a first date, and not even a good one.

After she got her cream and sugar, Kimberly stepped outside the restaurant where Shawn was waiting.

"Why are you angry?" she asked.

"Because it took me months to work up the nerve to talk to you. Everyone at work was rooting for me. Like, every day they would try to give me tips on how to get your attention."

"Oh . . ."

"And then, when you said yes, they recommended all this stuff I couldn't afford, even though I said something to you about making a reservation. I knew you wouldn't want to go out on a date with someone who can't afford to take you anywhere but the Busy Bee Café."

"I like Busy Bee. Best peach cobbler in Atlanta."

"I'm just saying, I took you where I could afford, and I could tell you weren't feeling it."

Kimberly sighed. "I wasn't, but that wasn't your fault. I didn't give you any information to go on. You didn't know what I would like and what I wouldn't like."

"But my dad, yo . . . That shit is embarrassing."

Kimberly shook her head. "Don't be embarrassed. Just don't tell your coworkers what happened. It isn't any of their business, but you can tell them I was a bitch. I don't care."

Shawn's eyes lit up. "Maybe I will tell them that."

Kimberly laughed. "I didn't mean for it to happen that way, Shawn, seeing your daddy again. But I'm so glad that it did."

"He says y'all were really feeling each other in school."

"Yeah, we were, but he never tried to holla at me. I had no idea he had a little boy back home. He didn't tell any of us. There was a whole crew of us that used to run together."

"That's crazy. I guess I'm braver than he was."

Kimberly nodded, smiled, and took a sip of coffee. "You are braver than he was."

"Maybe I get that part from my mom."

Kimberly didn't comment. She had no idea what Shawn knew or didn't know about his mother, and Kimberly damn sure wasn't going to be the one to fill the knowledge gaps.

"So, you and my dad gonna go out on some more dates?" Shawn asked. The question was innocent enough, but Kimberly knew enough to understand that his pride was still wounded.

"We'll see. He'll have to work for it a little bit. Show me why I should let him holla."

Shawn seemed pleased with this response. "That's right. Make him work for that shit."

"I will . . . and, Shawn . . . this is gonna seem a little bit petty for all the other women my age that you might decide to go out with . . . but find a young lady your own age."

"Naw, Ms. Kimberly. I like what I like. These young girls out here aren't talking about anything. I want to talk about marriage and family. They asking me if I have any pills they can pop."

"Really?"

"You don't understand. Most of these young people in Atlanta go around in a constant state of being high. I'm not with that."

She shook her head. "I can see why you wouldn't be."

"Exactly. So, do you have any friends?"

Kimberly threw her head back, opened her mouth wide, and cackled. Even if she did have any other friends who might be interested in this young of a guy, she wouldn't tell them about Shawn. It was different when she didn't know who he was. He was somebody's son then, but it was a nameless, faceless somebody. He wasn't *Big Ron's* son then. He was going to have to do his cougar fishing elsewhere.

"Should I take that as a no?" Shawn asked.

"You should take it as a hard no."

"You ain't right, Ms. Kimberly."

"And you ain't ready. You're still riding roller coasters and eating food that could pass for a biohazard. Grow up a little bit first."

"If you hadn't chosen my daddy over me, you'd know how grown I really am."

"You're just mannish. Go on back into that job, now, boy!"

It was amazing to Kimberly how quickly she snapped into auntie mode with Shawn. It was usually her demeanor with young men his age. It was safe for them and for her. Only this dare with her girls had her trying something different.

"Good luck with my father. Maybe you'll be the right one for him."

"What does that mean?"

"Nothing. It just means good luck. I wish y'all the best."

That was either shade toward his father because he was angry still, or it was real intel that she needed to pay close attention to. She couldn't tell which, because Shawn was walking back into the Starbucks with a lighter gait to his step. Maybe he was happy because she'd given him a way to save face with his coworkers, or perhaps he got off on being petty.

She sure hoped it was the former, because she wasn't here for any games with Big Ron. If she found out he was a player, Kimberly would reclaim her time quicker than his head could spin.

Chapter 23

Hahna was back in the office wishing she was still on the beach in Miami watching the sunrise with Sam. But she knew better than anyone that all play and no work meant no clients for The Data Whisperers. Besides, she had lots of work to do today to prepare for the arrival of Brexton's data security expert. Josiah Walton was on a flight to Atlanta and would start work as soon as he touched down.

"I knew you and Corden would land Brexton Inc.," Sylvia said as she dropped a stack of folders on Hahna's desk. "Shame you had to go all the way to Miami to do it. He could've just trusted you over the phone all the years you've known him."

Hahna looked up from her laptop screen. "I know. But Hale is old-school."

"He's just old."

"That too," Hahna said with a laugh. "You sound like you're still annoyed that you and Brexton didn't hit it off."

"I didn't want him," Sylvia said. "He's into younger women."

Hahna remembered the last time Hale was in Atlanta before he'd met Jelena. Sylvia was absolutely interested, and Hahna was almost a hundred percent sure Sylvia had broken Hale off a little something at his hotel. But that had happened years

ago, when they were barely a company. When Hahna was working out of a rented little office and could only afford Sylvia
part-time.

"Don't act like you didn't like him," Hahna said.

"I like that he helped you launch this company, even if he entrusted his own data analysis to that crook."

"Hale is loyal. Shane Brown had been with him for years already. Before I started my business."

"Yeah, but he gave you your first corporate job."

"He did. And he's given me many leads and sent me clients
over the years. I don't hold it against him that he had Shane
doing his data analysis. I'm just glad he thought of me when it
came time to clean up the mess."

"Mmm-hmm," Sylvia said.

"Is there an office space ready for Josiah when he shows up?
He won't want to share with anyone."

"Yes. I've already put office supplies, a wireless mouse and
keyboard, and a Keurig in the office in back."

Hahna grinned. "You think of everything."

"I sure do. Now, give me a raise."

"Didn't I just give you a raise?"

"Yes. But there's no limit on that type of thing. I don't think
anyone would be mad if you gave me another one."

Hahna winked at Sylvia. "Another raise comes with more du-
ties. You ready to supervise a new administrative assistant?"

"You're hiring someone?"

"I may need to. Landing Brexton Inc. is going to put us on a
lot of people's radars."

"God is good."

"All the time."

"Speaking of God being good," Sylvia said. "Are you going to
church with me this Sunday to repent of all of your fornica-
tion?"

"Corden has a big mouth."

"Ha! I knew it. Corden only said you brought a man with
you. He didn't confirm any shenanigans went down."

"What else did Corden say?"

Sylvia looked away, letting Hahna know that whatever Corden said was shady.

"Sylvia," Hahna said, "what else did he say?"

"Just that he thought you were paying for everything and he didn't like it. Don't tell him I told you this."

Hahna shook her head. Sylvia should've been more concerned about gossiping about her boss than Corden's little crusty-tail feelings. Corden had no idea what she had paid for and where Sam had paid.

"I don't have to explain anything," Hahna said. "But Corden was wrong. Sam did what Sam needed to do. Corden should stop being so nosy."

"His name is Sam? Why am I just hearing about this Sam? I know you and your girls were having a single friends revolution vacation just a few weeks ago."

"Yes. I met him after. That night I went to the book signing."

Sylvia scrunched her nose. "Hahna, that wasn't even two weeks ago."

"I know."

Hahna waited for the judgment packaged in words of wisdom. Sylvia couldn't help but give unsolicited advice. She thought she was everyone's mother figure, and although she wasn't Hahna's, Sylvia tried to share her mother-wit when appropriate—and when inappropriate.

"I see. Well, I guess you must be all the way grown now."

"*Now* I'm grown?"

"Mmm-hmmm. You 'round here smelling yourself."

"Sylvia."

"Listen, chil'. When folks deciding to be grown, ain't nothing you can do about that."

Now Hahna felt bad. Had she offended Sylvia by not being open to her mothering? Hahna didn't want to hurt her feelings. Plus, Sylvia's advice was usually pretty spot-on.

"I'm sorry, Ms. Sylvia. I didn't mean to be short with you."

"It's fine. I do have one question, though."

"What's that?"

"Did he hurt ya real good?" Sylvia asked. "If it ain't good, it ain't worth sinning over."

"Ms. Sylvia."

"Okay, okay. Minding my own business now."

"Thank you."

Sylvia turned and left Hahna's office. As soon as she closed the door, Hahna laughed. She'd been tempted to answer her question. Yes, Sam had hurt her real good. Over and over again. If Hahna could've swung it without losing a client, she would've stayed home from work, just so he could hurt her some more.

Chapter 24

Twila felt nineteen again as she sat on the hard, wooden stool in the smoky recording studio. Apparently, some things hadn't changed in twenty years. The weed smoke was still mandatory to make a hit record.

Marcus ran scales in the recording booth, warming up his voice, which was smooth and versatile. He had range like Eric Benét and Brian McKnight, and he hit the notes effortlessly. Someone should've already put him on. All these producers in Atlanta, and no one had heard him?

The world just needed to hear about him. As soon as they heard the voice she was hearing, he'd be selling out shows and opening for A-listers. He was going to be an A-lister too, and she wasn't just going to be his manager, she'd be on his arm. Visions of red carpets and celebrity parties danced through Twila's head. She loved being a dentist, but it was hard work. Being a celebrity wife would be easier. Maybe then she'd take the networks up on their reality show offers. No one cared about cosmetic dentistry, but everyone wanted to know how a Grammy winner's wife spent her time.

Twila rewound the tape in her head. First, he needed to record this song, no matter how many takes it took, so that he could record the video. Then the video was going to go viral on YouTube.

"Okay, Marcus, you're warm. Hit me with the hook quick. The bgvs are already laid," said Luke, the recording engineer.

"What's a bgv?" Twila asked.

Luke swiveled around in his seat and gave Twila an annoyed expression. She folded her arms across her chest and cocked her head to one side. She was paying for this, so he'd answer every question she had.

"It stands for background vocals. I had some vocalists come in and do them for me earlier today."

"Did Marcus approve them? Did he even listen to them first?"

Luke scrunched his nose into a frown. "You think this dude Bruno Mars or somebody?"

"Better."

"He's a new artist, who barely has enough studio time booked to record this song."

"How much more does he need?"

"What, you buying or something?" Luke asked.

"How much *more* does he need?"

"Maybe another two for recording and an hour to mix it down."

"Let's do it then."

"Studio time is one hundred dollars an hour."

Twila closed her eyes trying not to present as irritated when she was. She reached into her purse, pulled out her wallet, and produced three one-hundred-dollar bills. She placed the money on the engineering board.

"Let's. Do. It. Then."

Luke spun around in his chair and hit the speaker that let his voice into the recording booth. "Your girl just added three hours to your session. You ready to get this done tonight?"

"Thank you, Twila, but you didn't have to do that. I pay for my own studio time."

Twila rose from her seat and leaned into Luke's microphone.

"It's an investment," she said. "I expect a return."

Marcus grabbed the microphone and ran up and down a scale again. He was ready for this. He only needed a little push.

Three hours later, Marcus's first song, "No Warning," was recorded, and mixed down. It sounded incredible. An up-tempo love song about a woman who'd stolen his heart unexpectedly. He'd written it before meeting Twila, but it still felt like a serenade.

"It's a great song, Marcus. Are you ready to be famous?" Twila asked.

He laughed. "You sound like a judge from one of those singing reality shows."

"You could win every one of those shows."

"Thank you, beautiful."

Twila felt her skin flush at his term of endearment. The studio waiting room was small, and it felt like their attraction and pheromones were taking up the entire space. Twila was seated across from Marcus, each of them in a leather armchair, but the way his scent wafted up toward her nose, Twila might as well have been sitting in his lap.

Luke finally walked out of the studio tech room holding a flash drive in his hand.

"Here you go, completely mixed down," Luke said. "I will master it in a couple days, so just fall back through."

"Is this good enough quality to play at a club?" Twila asked.

Luke nodded. "Yeah, if they have a good sound system. But good luck with that. Nobody knows him yet, so I doubt that would happen."

Twila stood to her feet, took the flash drive from Luke's hand, and tucked it away in her purse.

"Thank you," Twila said, then turned to Marcus. "You ready to go celebrate?"

He nodded. "How're we celebrating?"

"We're going to the club."

Luke laughed as Twila headed for the exit and Marcus followed.

"Damn, you got a boss lady for real," Luke said to Marcus.

"Yeah, I do."

"You got any friends, boss lady?"

Twila looked him up and down. Even though Luke was a little on the chunky side, he was handsome and well-groomed. Plus, he had his own business. Twila was starting to believe her successful circle was sleeping on all kinds of potential. She was starting to like this sugar mama business.

"Maybe I do. I just might send somebody your way."

"As long as she looks like you and is bossing like you, I'm here for it."

Twila winked at Luke and let Marcus open the door for her. Marcus knew she was a dentist, and that was impressive to him just on its own. But she was about to show him her other side—the side that cosmetic dentistry and access to Atlanta's elite had built.

Twila was about to show him how an Atlanta boss lady really moved.

Chapter 25

"What is this place?" Marcus asked as Twila stopped her car in what appeared to be a clearing in a wooded area north of Atlanta.

"Hold on a sec."

Twila took out her phone and sent a text, then put it back in her purse.

"If I didn't trust you, I'd be worried," Marcus said. "This is like the beginning of a horror movie or something."

She chuckled. "This place is called Phenom. It's a secret club. Very few people have access. You'll have it tonight, as my guest."

"Oh, so like a celebrity hot spot?"

She shook her head. "More than that. There are going to be celebrities here, though, so please don't embarrass me by acting like a fan. Act like you're supposed to be here."

"What does that mean?"

"It means, don't ask for an autograph, don't try to network, don't do anything but chill and vibe with me. That's what we're here for."

"You don't think I need to build a network?"

"You do. But not tonight. Celebrities and real billionaires come here to party, not talk shop or make deals. No one will

ask you what you do, because since you're here they will assume
you're supposed to be here."

"And I'm not?"

"Not on your own merit, no. I wouldn't usually either, but
the owner is one of my sorority sisters. I have made many friends
here, though."

As they waited for a response to her text, Twila wondered if
she should've brought Marcus to Phenom. She'd never brought
anyone. Hahna and Kimberly knew about it, but refused to
party there. They didn't have the same level of tolerance for debauchery that she had, and there was more than the usual
amount of debauchery happening inside of Phenom.

"What are we waiting for?" Marcus asked.

"This."

She pointed over to the trees and two headlights shone from
the shadows. A dark van with tinted windows pulled up along-
side Twila's car. A large man got out of the passenger side of
the van and walked toward them.

"What the hell?" Marcus asked.

"Shhhh," Twila scolded. "Trust me."

The big man opened Twila's driver's side door and handed
her a white ticket. She thanked him, put the ticket in her purse,
and gave him a fifty-dollar bill.

"He's the valet," she said to Marcus. "Come on. We have to
ride in the van to get onto the property."

Marcus seemed to relax a little. "Oh, I get it."

Twila climbed into the van first, and Marcus followed her.
She could hear his sharp intake of breath when he saw that the
inside of the van was tricked out like a limousine.

"Hey, Ms. Twila," the driver said. "Where you been?"

"Working. Then I was out of the country for a little bit. I'm
home now, though."

The driver glanced at Marcus in the rearview mirror. "I see
you brought a friend. He's pretty."

"Yes, I brought a friend, and I'm not sharing."

The driver shook his head. "It's a pity. I'd make sure you enjoyed it too."

Marcus frowned and opened up his mouth to respond, and Twila jabbed him in the ribs with her elbow.

"I know you would, hun. What you got chilling over here? Cîroc?"

"There's some chilled and not chilled. Help yourself."

Twila poured double shots for herself and Marcus. She handed him his glass and smiled.

"Let's do a toast," she said.

"Okay, what are we toasting to?"

"To us. We're toasting to us. For a lovely and exciting tonight, and maybe tomorrow."

Marcus leaned over and kissed Twila's neck, sending a chill through her body.

"Maybe tomorrow?" he whispered.

"It all depends on what you do tonight."

Marcus held up his glass. "To us, then."

"To us."

They clicked glasses and downed their shots. Twila closed her eyes as the alcohol burned her throat going down. The driver was right, she hadn't been to Phenom in a while. It had gotten to be too much to come alone. Too overbearing. She came to rub elbows with rich people, but the decadent nature of some parts of the club were not her speed.

After driving for about five miles, the wooded area opened up to a second clearing. It was well lit and easy to see the mansion situated next to a lake. Twila watched Marcus's eyes widen, but he said nothing. She smiled. He wasn't going to embarrass her. Good.

When they pulled into the circular drive, the van started to vibrate from the sound of the bass in the music coming from the mansion.

The driver stepped out of the van and unlocked their doors. Marcus jumped. He probably hadn't realized they were locked in. Abena, the owner of Phenom, took her privacy and secrecy seriously.

The driver opened the door, and Twila climbed out first,

then Marcus. Again, Twila gave a large tip. She also hugged the driver good-bye before he got back into the van.

"Are we underdressed?" Marcus asked as the driver pulled off.

She was wearing a camouflage romper and earth-tone leather sandals, while he wore jeans, a fitted t-shirt, and high-top Jordans.

"No. This isn't that kind of club, Marcus. You don't have to dress to impress. Everyone here is already impressive."

"This next-level shit," he said.

"It is. I want you to remember that all evening, and we're going to have fun."

He nodded and held his arm out for Twila to take it. She smiled, and they ascended the stairs to the front entrance. Twila pressed five numbers into the keypad on the door's handle and it unlocked. Marcus pushed it open.

The entryway was a dramatic two-story foyer with a double winding staircase. The only light came from the chandelier in the ceiling, so there was a hazy glow over the entire area. Marcus probably couldn't tell because it was dark, but Twila knew that there were marble floors under their feet.

There was loud music, but the area was empty No one at all was in the foyer, or on the stairs.

"Where is everybody?"

"Follow me."

The parties—and there were always several different kinds of parties happening at once at Phenom—were behind reinforced metal locked doors. Nothing ever happened in the unsecured areas, in case, for any reason, uninvited guests (like local law enforcement) made their way inside. There was a complex series of alarms and cameras throughout the house that kept Phenom's attendees safe from any prying eyes.

The party Twila wanted was behind the blue door with glitter. On the lower level was the red door. They wouldn't venture there. She knew what was on the other side of that door—a huge, everything-goes sex party. She wasn't interested in sleeping with strangers. She didn't knock the others who attended; it just wasn't her lane.

Again, Twila punched a code into the lock on the room with the blue door. It opened to a two-leveled dance club with a fully stocked bar on the lower level. It was reggae/soul night, Twila's favorite. The dance floor was packed, and the music was bumping hard.

"You want another drink?" Twila asked.

Marcus shook his head and pulled her out to the dance floor. Twila rolled her hips in time to the music, giving him every bit of her Mother Africa blessings.

Twila backed up into Marcus, who was grinding her behind into his pelvis area. She felt his python spring to life and imagined them doing the horizontal tango instead of vertical club twerking. Marcus wrapped both arms around her body and pulled her in closer, leaving no space between their bodies as they rocked to the music.

Marcus's heart raced, probably from both the dancing and the heat. His warm breath on Twila's neck was sweet, so she closed her eyes and savored every moment.

The hard bass beat slowed, and the tempo went from dance hall to slow jams. Marcus turned Twila in his arms and pulled her close again. He gazed into her eyes, and she gazed into his. The moment was intense—their faces close enough to touch. He pulled her even closer, and she tilted her head upward so that her lips brushed his.

Marcus accepted the invitation and kissed Twila deeply. There was no starting off soft and unsure. This kiss sent a message to Twila's lady parts. A surge of heat and moisture told her that they had responded.

They tasted each other as their tongues danced. Marcus let out a low growl when Twila ground her pelvis against his. They separated, and Marcus's eyes opened only partially. He was as intoxicated as she was, and not from the liquor.

"We came all the way here for nothing," Marcus whispered in Twila's ear. "'Cause I'm ready to go."

She giggled and bit his bottom lip playfully. "Not yet. Wait for me at the bar, I'll be right back."

Twila made her way up to the DJ booth, grateful for a moment of reprieve, because she was ready to give it up to Marcus right there on the dance floor. Or maybe even in the room behind the red door. No one would care about them getting it on there. They'd probably even have an audience. But Twila was no exhibitionist.

Inside the booth, the DJ turned around as the set played. His face lit up. He was her sorority sister's husband, Kyle, and they'd all been friends since high school.

"Bena know you're here?" Kyle asked.

"Not yet. I haven't gotten a chance to speak yet."

"Oh, okay. You here by yourself?"

Twila shook her head. "No. Brought a date this time."

"Okay, I see you. You got a special request?"

Twila reached into her bag and pulled out the flash drive. Kyle chuckled.

"You an artist now, T?"

"No, my date is, though. He just did this cut at the studio tonight. Do you mind playing it for me?"

Kyle shrugged. "Lemme listen to it."

He put the flash drive into his laptop and put on his headphones. Twila felt tense as he listened. She thought it was good, but maybe she was blinded by the eggplant frittata.

But when Kyle's head started to bob and his shoulders went up and down to the beat, she knew he liked it. He pressed STOP on his music player.

"Yeah, this is fire. I'll play it. Is this song about you?"

She shook her head and laughed. "No, he wrote it before he met me."

"Maybe it was prophetic, then."

"Maybe."

Twila liked the idea of Marcus writing a song that prophesied her arrival into his life. That was beyond kismet.

"Let me copy it onto my hard drive," Kyle said.

Kyle clicked a few keys on the computer, and in a few seconds, he was popping the flash drive back out of his computer.

"Thank you, Kyle."

"You're welcome, sis. You should've brought your man up here so I could get a look at him."

"I didn't want to bring him in case you said no. Plus, I told his ass not to come up in here networking and shit. Not the time nor the place."

Kyle gave Twila a fist bump. "Good looking out, sis. That's why you have full access here. We're family."

"All day."

Twila slid out of the DJ booth and back to the bar. Marcus was engaged in conversation with another brother—one she knew well. Duran Stevens. He'd tried many times to get with her, but she wasn't with it. He spent too much time in the room behind the red door. He didn't have a monogamous bone in his body.

"Twila," Duran said as he walked up. "I was just congratulating your date. I told him you never bring anyone here, so he must be special."

"He is special." Twila kissed Marcus on the lips to punctuate her sentence.

Duran pressed his lips into a line and nodded. "Maybe I'll see y'all downstairs."

"No. You won't."

Twila turned her back to Duran and flagged down the bartender. She didn't expect Marcus to be able to afford the drinks here, but she was thirsty. Duran scuttled away before the bartender showed up, thankfully. He didn't need to know that she was a sugar mama. It wasn't any of his business.

"You drink D'ussé?" Twila asked.

Marcus nodded.

"Two double shots of D'ussé, neat," Twila said to the bartender.

"Who was that guy? Y'all used to date?" Marcus asked.

"No. He's a cybersecurity expert, someone I've known for years. He's a jerk mostly, though."

"Cybersecurity?"

"Yeah, he investigates when these high-profile corporations get hacked."

"Like WikiLeaks?"

Twila nodded. "Yeah. Like that. I hear he's good at what he does. He's gotten pretty wealthy rich from his work."

Marcus shook his head, as the bartender handed him his drink.

"What's wrong?" Twila asked.

"I mean, that's the kind of guy you could be dating, and you brought my ass here. I feel like this is some sort of elaborate prank."

Twila took a long swallow of her cognac and let it slowly warm her chest. She loved a good cognac.

"Who said that's the kind of guy I want?"

"He's probably a millionaire."

"Billionaire, I think. But I've got my own money. I don't want his."

"So, you don't care that I'm broke?"

Twila lifted an eyebrow. "How broke are you?"

"Broke enough to be renting a town house with two other guys. Broke enough that my car has about two hundred thousand miles on it, and has me scared to drive from point A to point B."

Damn. He was broker than she thought he was.

"But you've got enough to invest in your music."

"That's all I do. I take the money I make waiting tables and spend it all at the studio."

"I like that in you, Marcus. I do."

Marcus took another sip of cognac but set his glass down on the bar when he heard the intro to his song come on. He looked at Twila, and she just smiled.

"You want to dance?" he asked.

"No. I want you to enjoy the crowd's reaction to your music."

Marcus's eyes lit up as the entire club proceeded to get pumped to his song. The bass line was infectious, and his voice weaved in and out of the chords effortlessly. The song sounded even better in the club than it did in the studio.

"Get used to this," Twila said. "Imagine yourself performing it live, and the crowd giving you this much love. Imagine selling out venues."

"Yessss. . . ."

"Visualize it. Put yourself in the picture. Look at this club. These people are going off on this song. Women are twerking and backing it up, men's hands are in the air, they're all whooping and hollering."

The smile on Marcus's face couldn't get any wider. She could tell his imagination was running wild. He could see himself as the artist she knew he could be.

"You know, I've hoped that I could have this career," Marcus said. "But I don't know if I ever really believed it could happen. Not until now."

"It's real. We're going to make it happen."

"No one has ever been in my corner like this before. It feels like a dream."

"Well, wake up. I want your eyes wide open for this journey. It's gonna be fun."

Marcus lifted Twila off her feet and wrapped her legs around his midsection. He kissed her again—this time more passionately than before. His face felt wet, and she thought it was from sweat, but when he put her on the ground again, she saw that the wetness was from tears.

She'd brought a man to his knees before, but never to tears. Twila had never felt this powerful before in a relationship.

She liked it. A lot.

Chapter 26

Whoever had planned the "It's Raining Men" event had done their best to make it feel like an elite, VIP experience for the authors and the readers. They had hotel suites for each of the five authors, a runner to make sure they each had everything they needed, and a red carpet for their arrival.

"Are you gonna walk the red carpet with me?" Sam asked as he held out his wrists for Hahna to put on his cuff links.

Hahna took each of the small, obviously fake rhinestones and clasped Sam's shirtsleeves closed. She'd have to get him some nicer ones if she was going to be accompanying him to events.

"Why would I walk the red carpet? Those women aren't here to see me. They're here for you."

"Are there only women here?"

"That's all I've seen so far."

And there were a few hundred of them, book club members wearing matching shirts and sorority sisters with bags of books. They were in the hotel lobby when Hahna had gone down for coffee. They were dressed to impress, with their sequined tank tops and sparkly miniskirts.

"Are they starting to arrive? The promoters told me they sold out."

"Mmm-hmmm. They're dressed so nice. The older ladies have on their Sunday two-piece suits, and the younger ones are wearing their after-five apparel. It made me so happy to see all those book lovers waiting for the event to start. I love us, man."

Sam sat on the hotel room's sofa. He took in a deep breath and let it out.

"You okay, babe?" she asked.

"I am. It's just . . . these events really take a lot out of me. I'm never sure if my jokes are gonna stick. What if it's a tough room?"

"It won't be. Those ladies are ready to show nothing but love. This is gonna be an easy crowd, I bet."

"At least there aren't any superstar authors out there. We're all at pretty much the same place in our careers. Struggling on the come up."

Hahna sat next to Sam and rubbed his thigh. "You're not struggling. You cater to a niche market that has some of the most loyal fans you'll ever meet."

"How do you know?" Sam asked.

"Because I've read your work, babe. It's incredible."

"I appreciate you. If I didn't sell another book, I'd write them just for you."

"You're gonna sell millions, and you'll write them for me and your hordes of fans."

"Hordes?"

"That's what I said."

Sam kissed her lips softly, lingering to taste her for a moment. She wondered if he was trying to start something, because she was here for it. The hordes of fans could wait.

"Let me stop before I change my mind about attending this event," Sam said. "If you won't walk the red carpet with me, will you at least walk me downstairs?"

"I sure will. You'll get a chance to meet Twila and Kimberly before we go in."

"They're here already?"

"Yes. Kimberly texted me about fifteen minutes ago."

"Why didn't you say something? We could've gone down then."

"I didn't want to interrupt your getting-ready process. My friends are fine anyway. They brought dates."

"Oh, well, that's good. Let's go, though. I can't wait to meet your friends."

"And they can't wait to meet you."

"Really? What have you told them?"

"Only good things. All the wonderful things. That you're fine, brilliant, creative—and fine."

Sam laughed as he stood to his feet. "You said fine twice."

"I know."

"You are damn sure good for my ego."

Hahna stood on her tiptoes to kiss him. He was good for her ego too.

They held hands as they walked down the hotel hallway to the elevator. Sam's palms were moist. He truly was nervous about this event. Hahna gave him a reassuring hand squeeze, because he needn't be nervous.

They stepped inside the elevator, and there was a group of apparent book lovers, all holding their bags of books. Sam turned on the charm and smiled.

"Y'all here for 'It's Raining Men'?" Sam asked.

"Yes, we are, Sam Valcourt," one of the ladies replied. She gave Hahna a mild stink eye, which tickled Hahna. "You brought your girlfriend?"

Sam laughed and kissed Hahna's throat.

"I sure did."

"Well, I'ma still buy your new book. I have to know what happened to Tristan and Diane."

"Thank you so much for supporting me. Even though I brought my girlfriend."

"You know I met him at a book signing," Hahna said, trying to win some points with the ladies.

"You did?"

"Yes, she was there for Eric Jerome Dickey, but I'm the one who got her number," Sam said.

This was met with loud, black-girl-joy laughter. The kind that made other women turn their heads and wonder what was so damn hilarious.

Once they were in the lobby, Hahna immediately saw Twila and Kimberly, but it was because of the crowd that was in their area. Were women taking selfies with Twila's boyfriend? Hahna narrowed her eyes. That was her Instagram boo.

"There are my friends, and that's Twila's date—the one with the crowd," Hahna said.

"Oh, I've seen that guy before. He's popular on book covers."

"He is?" Hahna asked. "Is that like a celebrity thing too? Book cover models?"

Sam shrugged. "I didn't think so, but obviously the ladies want pictures with him, so maybe I'm wrong."

"Well, these are readers. They're here for you, not hot guys. They're probably just taking those photos because they haven't opened the doors yet."

"I thought I was a hot guy."

"You know what I mean," Hahna said as she smacked Sam on the arm playfully.

Hahna and Sam crossed the room, then Kimberly turned to greet them. Hahna's jaw fell—not because of anything Kimberly was doing—but because Big Ron was with her, looking just as fine as he had in college, only a little older. He'd always had the prettiest eyes and eyelashes, and those dimples were just as deep and just as sexy.

Hahna hugged Big Ron. "My goodness. What a blast from the past. You are looking good, Big Ron."

"Hahna, I think they kept you in a time capsule after you graduated, because you look the same as the first time I saw you on the yard," Big Ron said.

"Kimberly and Big Ron, this is my boyfriend, Sam. He's one of the featured authors here tonight."

Ron gave Sam a firm handshake, and Kimberly gave him a friendly hug. She winked at Hahna while she hugged him to let Hahna know she approved.

"It's good to meet y'all. Kimberly, she talks about you all the time, so I felt like I had already met you."

"Awww, she does?" Kimberly asked. "Well, you're *all* she's been talking about to us, so it's good to finally meet you in person."

"What's up with Twila?" Hahna asked.

"All those women wanted photos with her date, so she organized them and made sure that they could take one photo at a time and upload them to Instagram with a tag to his page."

"She organized them?" Hahna asked. "What is she, his manager?"

"Yes," Kimberly said.

Hahna closed her eyes and groaned. This Instagram guy was supposed to be a fun fling. Maybe even a boyfriend. But if Twila was managing him and caring about his career and social media followers, then she was all-in. And all-in Twila was frightening.

"Mmm-hmmm," Kimberly said in response to Hahna's groan. "All-in."

Ron and Sam exchanged a confused glance. Of course, neither of them knew what was wrong. They were witnessing black girlfriends in their natural habitat. They had their own language that was a mix of verbal and nonverbal. They could say entire paragraphs with one look. Their expressions now were speaking volumes.

"Well, I'm going to go inside now. I think we're supposed to be setting up," Sam said.

"Okay, babe. You need any help?"

"No, stay out here with your friends. I'll get to meet Twila later, I guess."

Sam kissed Hahna on the forehead before he headed toward the ballroom. It was the most tender and natural thing. Nothing he did felt forced or for show. Sam was a hundred percent real. He was the tangible and whole thing that Hahna hadn't known she needed. He was only a few footsteps away, and she already missed his presence.

"He seems nice," Ron said. "You never seemed like the type to want a writer, though."

"What does that mean?" Hahna asked.

She was unoffended, but curious about the perspective of another man who'd known her in the past.

"This guy seems mellow, but when we were in college, all your boyfriends were the top dogs at something. Couldn't just be in the Student Government Association, had to be the president. Couldn't just be an Alpha man, had to be the head of the chapter. You've always gone after the overachievers."

"And those guys were jerks," Kimberly said. "It's about time she switched up."

Hahna quietly accepted this observation, but she didn't think she agreed with it. The part about her being attracted to overachievers was true. She just wasn't sure Sam wasn't one. He was just less noisy and braggadocious about it.

One of the event promoters appeared to tell the attendees to line up for their entrance into the event. Finally, the crowd around Marcus dissipated, and both Twila and Marcus walked over to where they were standing.

Marcus extended his hand to Hahna, and she shook it. "You must be Hahna. I love your name."

Hahna smiled. "Thank you."

"Girl, you already know this is Marcus. Did you see me having to pull him away from his adoring fans?" Twila asked. "I should've charged them per picture."

"Do people even pay for that kind of thing?" Kimberly asked.

"Yes, for real celebrities," Marcus said. "Not for a stock art image on the cover of their favorite book. Tyler Kincaid, one of the authors here tonight, has me on the covers of one of his book series."

Twila shook her head. "You are a real celebrity. Remember I said you have to speak these things into existence?"

Hahna looked at Kimberly again, and Kim was shaking her head. This was what all-in meant. She was going to push this man in whatever direction she thought he should be going. Hahna hoped he was ready.

"I do remember, and you're right," Marcus said, and he kissed Twila on the cheek.

"Let's go inside too," Hahna said. "I don't want to miss any of it."

"Can y'all grab us a seat?" Kimberly said. "I need to talk to Ron for a minute."

Hahna lifted her eyebrow at Kimberly, silently asking if everything was okay. Kimberly gave a slight head nod back. So, she was good; she just didn't want to have a conversation in front of the group.

"We'll see y'all in a few minutes," Kimberly said.

And if they didn't, Hahna and Twila would be right out of their seats to see what was wrong. So, Ron had better behave himself. Morehouse brother and all, they would bring him the heat if necessary.

Chapter 27

Kimberly waited until Hahna, Twila, and her boy toy were behind the closed ballroom door, before she spun on one heel and glared at Big Ron.

"What? What did I do?"

"Why'd you say that to Hahna about how she picks men?"

Ron grimaced. "Yikes. I'm sorry. Was that bad?"

Kimberly exhaled and shook her head. "I know you didn't mean anything by it, but we've been through a lot of shit when it comes to men."

"It wasn't a judgment, Kim. It was just an observation. And was I wrong?"

"You didn't tell a lie."

"So, what's the big deal? I mean, if she felt offended by it, I will apologize. I didn't mean to hurt her feelings."

"No, I don't want you to apologize. I just want you to be mindful. She really likes this guy. I can tell. I see it all over her. She's glowing."

"She is glowing. I was serious when I said she looks the same as when were in college."

Kimberly wanted romance for Hahna more than she wanted it for herself or for Twila. Hahna had been hurt so many times in the past, and she was so sweet.

"The single life is hard for us, that's all I'm saying," Kimberly said.

"You act like it's easy for us guys."

Kimberly scoffed. "Man, get the hell out of here, Ron! Most women wouldn't kick you out of bed."

"Men want more than sex too. I know I can get a woman in bed, but can I get in her head? Her heart? Y'all be having more issues than a few, and that shit is hard too."

Kimberly cocked her head to one side. "Issues?"

"You know what I mean, Kim. We go back too far for me to sugarcoat things. I love my sisters, but damn, it's hard as hell to get close to some of y'all."

"Oh, you mean the issues we have when we can't find a man who's educated, because they graduated and found white women? Or maybe the baggage we have because every A-list brotha has a non-black woman on his arm?"

"Not true."

"Or perhaps you're talking about the struggles with coming to terms with the fact that we may never get married. Why? Because all the marrying brothers are marrying white women?"

Ron wrung his hands and stared at Kimberly. She was near hyperventilating as her chest heaved up and down. She couldn't stand when brothas tried to act like the issues black women had were insurmountable. Especially when they had been a party to most of those issues, from not liking the hair that grew out of black women's scalps to buying in to every negative narrative about black women on social media.

Ron took Kimberly's hand and led her to a sofa in the lobby. She sat, and he got her a cup of water that was flavored with oranges and limes. She didn't want to admit that she needed the water, but she did, so she took the cup from his hand.

"Kimberly. You know I love black women, right?"

Kim nodded. She remembered how he'd always cheered for them on the yard when they stepped and tutored every damn body so they could graduate. Big Ron was an ally. A brother. But his words had triggered her.

"I'm about to tell you something, but only because I think

I'd like to pursue something real with you, and if it comes up later, I don't think it'll be good."

Kimberly inhaled, then held her breath. Her heart was still pounding from her rant. She didn't know if she could take any more stimulation.

"My ex-wife is white."

Kimberly was confused. "Shawn's mama is white?"

"No, not Shawn's mother. My second wife."

"Damn. Why, Ron?"

"Because I fell in love with her. It wasn't because she's white. She was just cool, and we vibed."

"Why'd you divorce her?"

"She divorced me. Wanted to get back with her ex-husband and try again. He was her high school sweetheart."

"White guy?"

"Yes. It really got to me, though. The second divorce. I didn't ever think I'd fall in love again."

"What changed your mind?" Kimberly asked.

"Seeing you again. Remembering how good our young and innocent love felt. Me wanting to consummate the feelings that we had in college but never acted on."

Kimberly didn't know how she could feel angry, betrayed, wounded, and hopeful all at the same time. She breathed in and out, trying to calm herself.

"Kimmie Kim? You gonna say anything? Does this make you see me any differently?"

"No. You're still Big Ron to me. Same as always."

"Good. Then I'm glad I told you. I've wanted to get that off my chest since our first conversation, but I didn't know how to say it. You wanna go inside now, and hear Hahna's boyfriend speak?"

Kimberly nodded. She was afraid to open her mouth, because then the words "*I lied*" might fall out. The fact that Big Ron had been married to a white woman did make her see him differently. She didn't know if she could unsee this.

Chapter 28

Hahna could tell that something was wrong as soon as Kimberly and Big Ron sat down at the table. But he put his arm around her, and she leaned in to him like everything was okay. Hahna would remind herself to interrogate Kim later.

Now, though, she was going to focus on her man as he read from his novel. He was the second to go, and the first author had killed it. It was the Tyler guy who had Marcus on all his book covers.

Sam stood, and cracked his knuckles as he made his way to the podium. Hahna wished she could catch his eye and tell him to smile. He looked too serious up there, almost mean. He was focused, though, and wanted to do a good job.

Hahna clapped for him as he went forward, and many of the other women started to clap too. This cracked his façade a bit, and a slight smile teased his lips. Now he still seemed focused, but less angry.

"Um, good evening, everyone. I'm Sam Valcourt, and I'm happy to be here tonight. I want to thank the promoters for inviting me, and my girl for being here to support me."

Sam looked in her direction, and Hahna blew him a kiss. The oohs and ahhs from the crowd were cute, but Hahna wanted them to turn back around and look at Sam, not her.

"Many of you are familiar with my Lovers' Quarrels series with Tristan and Diane. I am working on the fourth book in that series. They are my absolute favorite couple that I've ever written about. In between books, however, I sometimes write things other than relationship fiction. That's what I call them, the stories about the ups and downs of coupledom."

"We want Tristan and Diane!" a lady yelled from the crowd.

Hahna's nostrils flared. It was that lady from the elevator. She wasn't above dragging a chick up and outta here. Even if the chick looked like a Sunday school teacher in her ankle-length skirt.

"Simmer down there, big fella," Twila whispered across the table. "I don't want to have to bail you out tonight."

"She betta shut up, then," Hahna whispered back.

Sam took it in stride, though. He chuckled. "Tristan and Diane haven't gone anywhere. They're still right up here."

He tapped the side of his head and smiled at his crazed fan. Hahna guessed she wouldn't drag the out woman tonight.

"I want to share something else with y'all, if you don't mind. It's a stand-alone novel called *Repetition for Emphasis*. While there are relationships in it, it's not relationship fiction. It's about a man who rethinks all his life choices and wonders what he might do if he had a do-over. If you don't mind, I'd love to read you some of it. And . . . um . . . I hope you like it."

Sam cleared his throat and opened his book. He smiled at the ladies once more before he began.

These gatherings are the worst. None of us are friends, really. We are a collection of married couples who were all raised together like family. Our marriages are damn near incestuous, since we are first play cousins once and twice removed.

I listen to Janaiah tell the story of how I pursued her when we were teenagers. She tells this story at least once a year, and each time she embellishes a new detail. It never occurs to me to correct her, or even interrupt her once she gets going. Janaiah is entertaining as she holds court. Even my wife is among her admirers.

It's not that Janaiah lies. She doesn't. She minimizes or com-

*pletely forgets the things that make her seem flighty and indecisive
(she was) and amplifies the events that make me look heartless
and cruel (I was not).*

*The only one who seems perturbed by Janaiah's retelling is her
husband, Esteban, but after three vodka cranberries he cannot
control what she says. No one can, though. Janaiah says what she
wants and holds people captive with her shine. We all love her,
and we all secretly hate her, all except Esteban, who seems to love
her more than he loves his own manhood.*

*"And then he had his cousin call me on three-way, but he
stayed silent. Who does that? These kids now just text and screenshot
and Snapchat away, but back then, the shadiest thing we had was
that silent three-way, know what I'm saying?"*

She never waits for anyone to answer these questions.

*Janaiah's hair is cut into a style that bounces on her shoulders
when she talks, adding the punctuation that her run-on sentences
lack. Her heavily lashed eyelids blink rapidly when she seeks a reaction from her audience. She bites her glossed bottom lip when she's
finished, letting us all know that it is someone else's turn to speak.*

*I could give these details about Janaiah's face even if I wasn't
staring in her direction. I have memorized every part of her. She is
the first woman I fell in love with, but not the last. I can't fix my
mouth to say that she got away. I never had her.*

*Lucy, Esteban's younger sister and Janaiah's best friend, pours
everyone a fresh drink. None of us needs another drop, but our
gatherings last long into the night, and no one has to go home or
get the hell out of here. When Lucy and her husband, Steve, host,
it feels like a weekend getaway. Their four-thousand-square-foot
home has bedrooms for all, and they cook as if our party of six was
a party of fifty.*

*No one feels as welcome at my house. My wife, Chelle, doesn't
cook. I do, though—or I used to. Cooking was one of the things I
used to pull the ladies.*

*Then Will asked me what I thought of BJ, and I was caught
off-guard. Sure wasn't expecting that. "To tell the truth, I was
hoping Will was going to finally ask me out, finally," Janaiah
continues after guzzling down her cocktail.*

"She said I was shallow," I told the group.

Janaiah looks over at me, standing in a corner, holding up a wall. She squints with what I believe is amusement on her face, but I could be wrong. She could just want me to shut up so she can tell the story the way she always does.

"She said I was shallow," I repeat, *"and she meant that shit."*

"Byron. Language."

I ignore my wife's admonishment. I don't have to watch my language here. This is a circle of trust.

"How could I have meant it?" Janaiah says. "You always say that, but I didn't know you at all. I didn't know if you were shallow or deep. I just thought Will was cute with his little round-headed self. What's going on with him, anyway? Anyone heard from him?"

"I heard he married a girl from Yugoslavia. Czechoslovakia. One of those," Lucy says. "BJ, do you know? He's your cousin."

"I do know, but I'm not sharing." Will hates everything about this life. The gatherings, the conventions, the weddings by the time a young person hits the age of twenty-one (unless they're damaged). He would hate being a topic of conversation here, especially since Janaiah had been the one to bring up his name. Those two share no fond memories.

"Haven't heard from him in a while."

Janaiah reaches for another drink from Lucy's tray. She doesn't seem annoyed that I stopped her stride. She scoots to the edge of a recliner to continue her tale.

"And he wanted revenge on me that whole time. 'Cause I called him shallow. Who does that? Chelle, I am fervently praying for you. Heaven forbid you spill bleach on his favorite shirt. Or give him three lumps of sugar instead of two in his coffee."

"I don't take sugar in my coffee."

Again, I interrupt her tirade, but it's what she wants. I can tell by the smirk on her lips and the lift of her eyebrow.

"I'm the only sweet he needs," Chelle says.

This is tolerated from my wife. Everyone in the room knows the deal with me and Janaiah. My wife came after all that went wrong between us.

Revenge is too strong a word for what I wanted all those years ago when Janaiah insulted me by telling my shallow-ass cousin that I was shallow. My cousin, who was dating three girls and sexing them all. My cousin, who thought nothing of pawning a girl off to his nerdy, virginal cousin. But I was the one who lacked depth. Whatever.

How could I be shallow, as ugly as I was? I wasn't a pretty boy like Rome and Tony, the twin brothers who grew up with us too. They were tall with silky waves for hair, courtesy of their Latin father. One was dark; the other pale with gray eyes. They didn't have to worry about having intelligent conversation or coming across creepy for carrying around a notebook full of poetry.

That was me. Big nose, courtesy of my African American father. Nappy hair that needed to be cut low, so low that it didn't hide my lumpy head. Later, Janaiah told me I had nice eyes and a perfect jawline. That was much later, though.

I was deep because I didn't have anything to offer in the looks department.

No, revenge was never my intention. All I wanted was for Janaiah to know she was wrong. I wanted her to know me, fall for me, and then . . . then I wanted to walk away.

But walking away wasn't an option once we got together. My mother told me light-skinned girls were my kryptonite. Maybe she was right. Janaiah made me weak. She's probably the reason why I chose a darker berry to spend my life with. Chelle allowed me to be the man I didn't know I was.

The man in me is a great husband. The geeky teenager—the one who still lives at the depths of my psyche—his heart aches every day for a love that never matured past awkward sex and amusement park dates.

Drinks were being poured again. I took another. Needed to numb the neurons and nerve endings that fired off in Janaiah's presence.

I forced myself not to compare my wife to my former flame. Janaiah was more than a candle's flicker; she was a forest fire, sucking all the oxygen and life from this confined space. She needed the great outdoors.

Our church also stifled Janaiah. Stunted her growth. It was why she left after me. After she broke me. No. After we broke each other, she left.

Her leaving loosened my shackles enough to choose a wife. But they didn't fall free. The bonds stayed to burden my heart. I've grown accustomed to them now—hence my attendance at these gatherings. Being in her presence isn't enough, but it's all I have.

It was hard for Chelle when we first started dating. It would've been difficult for anyone who'd come after Janaiah. My obsession with her had been legendary, and Janaiah's circle of friends wouldn't let it die. They breathed life into that dysfunction every time they whispered another tale to my wife.

"She was his first, you know.

He's got a thing for redbones.

If I was you, I wouldn't be the rebound girl."

Chelle touches my arm. Communicating without speaking. Healing wounds she didn't know were there.

I hope that Chelle isn't stupid for loving me. I hope because I'm not sure I wouldn't run into Janaiah's outstretched arms if she beckoned me.

Her running away left us unfinished. The only thing keeping us apart when she returned was my wife and the daughter I'd adopted and called my own.

That's what I tell myself anyway. That deep down she still loves me (did she ever?) and that this torture thing she does at our gatherings is out of jealousy.

It could be that she despises me and watching me squirm gives her pleasure.

Pleasing her gives me pleasure—even if it's at my expense.

Sam closed his book and looked up at the room. Hahna wanted to cry, the reading was so beautiful, and from the looks in the room, it seemed like most of the other ladies agreed with her.

"Well, that's an excerpt from *Repetition for Emphasis.* I have copies of it with me tonight," Sam said. "Who has the first question?"

The questions came fast, but Sam was ready with responses.

It seemed the reading had loosened him up, because he was animated and full of fire.

When the book signing began, Sam had the longest line. Hahna wondered if he had enough books for the demand, as she immediately slid behind his table to help.

"What can I do, babe?"

"Can you run the credit card machine while I sign?"

She nodded. "Sure can."

The next few customers had cash, causing Sam's stack of singles and five-dollar bills to dwindle.

"You want me to go and get change from the lobby?"

"Do you mind?"

"I don't mind. No problem."

Hahna slid the tablet for credit card payments back to Sam, so he could take over again. She headed out of the ballroom feeling excited for her man's success. With a writing gift like the one he had, he would soon be a bestselling author.

If Hahna had known what was waiting for her out in the hotel lobby, she would've sent someone else. She would've stayed inside the ballroom with her new love celebrating his success, and not revisiting ghosts of her past life.

Chapter 29

Hahna rushed into the hotel lobby, clutching Sam's fifty-dollar bill in her hand, excited that he had run out of cash because of all of his sales, and pleased that she could be a supportive girlfriend. This felt good, but what felt even better was Kimberly and Twila's acceptance of Sam. Hahna tried to pretend that she didn't care what they thought, but she did, because they knew her better than anyone.

There was a crowd in the lobby. Some elegant affair was taking place in another ballroom of the hotel, because these were real designer gowns and shoes on the attendees, and Hahna spotted a few of Atlanta's longtime black rich. Not the new reality show stars, but the doctors and lawyers who'd migrated north, and then back again. They had generational wealth and weren't the newly minted "I'm a rich bitch" millionaires. It probably wasn't an event she would've been invited to even if she didn't have Sam's book signing happening in the other room.

Two men dressed in tuxedos appeared to direct the guests to the ballroom they were using, freeing up space at the lobby front desk, where Hahna needed to go for change.

She rushed over, trying not to make eye contact with any of

the elite partygoers. Just in case this was an event she should've been invited to, she didn't want to run into anyone and have to make small talk.

As she approached the lobby desk, the sound of his voice stopped her in his tracks. Not Sam's voice. The ghost's voice. Ghost Torian.

She felt frozen as she watched him, looking dapper in his tuxedo, standing at the desk asking a question. There was a woman with him—one he held tightly, his free arm wrapped around her body. On her left ring finger was a monster-sized diamond. It was in the wrong place for costume jewelry. It was an engagement ring.

So Torian had figured out how not to disappear. Or maybe this girl was the reason why he'd ghosted Hahna. Either way, Hahna felt her heart break all over again, when she was supposed to be over Torian.

She *was* over Torian. She'd moved on to Sam, was dreaming of a future with Sam. He was the one she wanted.

But she also wanted the life that Torian was offering this random woman with pale skin and strawberry blonde hair. This was a black girl who stayed out of the sun in the summertime and bleached her hair more frequently than a Hollywood starlet.

She wanted parties like this. Shit. She wanted a ring like that. Sam wasn't buying a ring like this on his budget—even if marriage was on the menu.

Then, Torian looked over at Hahna and smiled. And then he walked toward her, guiding his trophy girlfriend, fiancée, or whatever over in her direction. Why was he coming her way? What could he possibly have to say to her that wouldn't break her further?

"Hahna."

He said her name like it was an entire thought. Like there was a situation attached to her name. There was something attached. The curious upending of their relationship was still unaccounted for, and still unrequited. But Hahna didn't want closure from Torian—not this kind. She'd wanted to hear that he'd fallen upon calamity, that God had done His work and visited Torian with karma.

She didn't want to see him with an upgraded model of herself. A thinner, younger, prettier model who was clearly ready for prenups and baby making. She wanted to see him weeping, gnashing, moaning, and groaning. Maybe even penniless. Yes, especially poor. Poor would break Torian if nothing else would.

Hahna wanted to scream and maybe claw his eyes out, but instead, she returned his smile.

"Torian."

"It's been too long. Have you ever met my cousin Constance? I don't think you did."

His cousin? His cousin. Hahna hadn't met anyone in Torian's family. That was supposed to be coming in the future, but then he'd ghosted.

"I lost one of my contacts, so I can barely see you," Constance said, "but I'm pleased to meet you. I've got Torian leading me around like a seeing-eye dog."

Don't insult the dogs, please. Hahna's thoughts toward Torian were of the unkind variety.

"Well, Constance, she's pretty amazing. Curly hair that loves to escape the topknot she has it in now, gym rat physique although she doesn't work out all that much, and an award-winning smile."

What the entire hell? Compliments? He was going to stand there looking fine as ever and smelling like her favorite cologne. The one that was so costly that he only needed to use a drop and his scent filled the atmosphere.

Hahna didn't know how to respond, although she could tell he was expecting a response. Why was he trying to make her forget that she hated him? Because her memory was getting shaky as she stood here in his presence.

Constance grinned. "You've got good taste then, cousin.

Hahna, I look forward to meeting you when I can actually lay eyes on you."

"Can you wait here for a second, while I take Constance to her seat? I'd love to catch up for a second or two," Torian said.

"Um, okay."

Hahna watched him walk away, then remembered that Sam, her man, was waiting inside. She stepped up to the lobby counter.

"May I have six five-dollar bills and twenty one-dollar bills?" Hahna repeated the request that Sam had made just a few minutes earlier, even though it seemed like hours had passed.

The front desk agent seemed annoyed by Hahna's request. She looked in her drawer and counted out some, but not all the currency needed.

"Hold on a second. I'll be right back," she said, leaving Hahna waiting.

Hahna felt nervous that this was taking too long. She needed to get back inside with Sam so she could feel grounded again. The memories of Torian were coming at her too fast. The plans they'd made together, how they'd been on one accord about everything. How he'd wanted to still try for babies, and how her frozen eggs were at the ready for fertilization.

Finally, the front desk agent returned and handed Hahna the change. She almost snatched the money out of her hand, trying to move swiftly enough to avoid the conversation with Torian. She almost made it back into the ballroom.

"Hahna, hold on a sec!"

She pulled in a deep breath and exhaled. If she was supposed to get away from this conversation, then she would've escaped. Since she hadn't—maybe she was supposed to talk to him. Maybe this chat would help with purging him completely from her heart, because it obviously hadn't happened yet.

"Hahna, are you at an event? A sorority thing? No, 'cause you're not wearing your colors."

"I'm actually at a book signing."

He nodded. "You always were an avid reader."

Why hadn't she mentioned that she was at her boyfriend's book signing? Why hadn't she mentioned anything that would put Torian off the scent?

"I am an avid reader. What is it that you want, anyway? You disappeared one day, and I haven't heard from you since. Why do you want to talk to me now?"

There. She was remembering the anger, hurt, and shame. She remembered how desperate she felt most days before she met Sam, and how he'd solved all that for her. In a few weeks' time he'd made her feel more loved than she'd ever felt before.

"I only wanted to apologize, Hahna. I know it was wrong for me to dip out on you like that."

"But why did you?"

He sighed and bit his bottom lip. "I got a stage-four cancer diagnosis. Aggressive tumor in my gallbladder that had spread to my liver and kidneys."

"What? Why didn't you tell me? I would've been there for you."

"I know. That's why I didn't tell you. The prognosis wasn't good at the time. I guess I preferred you hating me than grieving over me."

With this new knowledge, the anger, rage, and memories dissipated. Hahna went into full caregiver mode. This was someone she'd loved, and he'd been gravely ill.

"You look healthy now."

"I'm in remission. Short one gallbladder, one kidney, and a piece of my liver. I was lucky that I was in such good shape otherwise. The doctors said that helped."

Hahna couldn't stop herself from hugging him. He'd beat cancer's ass. That deserved a hug, even if it brought her face close to the hollow of his throat where he dabbed that one drop of her favorite cologne.

"I wish you'd have let me go with you on that journey," Hahna whispered while still in the embrace.

"You know, I'm saying it was to spare your feelings, and that's mostly what it was . . ."

"But?"

"But I was afraid too. What if you'd left me? I don't know if I would've had the strength to heal if you'd left my side."

Hahna released him. This was not how she wanted to remember Torian. She'd rather remember him as the loser who abandoned her, because outside of his disappearance he was perfection.

"I'm sorry for dropping all this on you," Torian said. "I just saw you and now that I'm well, I just couldn't let you think the worst of me."

"Thank you for telling me."

"I-I'll let you get back to your book signing now."

"Oh, yes, right."

Hahna reached out for the handle on the ballroom door, and Torian covered her hand with his.

"This might be too much to ask, but are you seeing anybody? Can I call you?"

Hahna paused. The pause was too long, but she couldn't force the *yes I have a man* out quickly enough. Sam's glow had faded a bit. Because she'd loved Torian hard too.

"I am seeing someone, actually. He's a writer. This is *his* book signing."

"Oh, wow. A writer? Wow. Well, I am glad I got to see you, and tell you what was going on with me."

"You could've seen me any time, Torian. My number is the same. I still live in the same place."

He nodded slowly. "You're right. I guess I was afraid of *this*. Of you having moved on. It feels how I thought it would feel."

"I imagine it feels as terrible as I felt when you disappeared."

Hahna pulled her hand away from Torian's. "Take care, Torian."

"You too, Hahna."

Hahna pushed open the ballroom door and escaped inside. Still clutching the money in her hand, Hahna rushed across the ballroom to where Sam and his line of fans were waiting.

Some of them were using credit cards, but the ones waiting for change were patient and smiling. He was so good with his readers. He made each of them feel special.

Just like he made her feel special.

And she was just in the hallway considering all the love she'd had for Torian, like it meant anything now. It only meant something in memories and the could-have-beens. Hahna pushed the image of Torian out of her head.

"Here, babe," she said as she handed Sam the change he'd been waiting for.

"Thank you. That was quick," he said.

"Really? It feels like it took forever."

And it did feel like a forever had passed in the time she'd left the ballroom, laid eyes on the past, and then returned. She wondered if Torian was still lurking outside, waiting for another chance to throw her off-kilter with more revelations.

"How did you do it?" one of the book club ladies asked Hahna.

Shocked to hear a question directed at her, Hahna jumped. "Oh, I just went out to the front lobby desk. They'll give you change if you need it."

The woman laughed. "Not how did you get the change. How did you get *him?*"

"Oh, Sam?" Hahna responded with a question and a slow smile. "He was easy. I met him at a book signing and hit him with my serious mack game."

"She is a mack," Sam chirped. "She's been wining and dining me since we met."

On the surface, this tickled Hahna, so she giggled along with the book club lady. But underneath that first layer of psyche, something tugged at Hahna. She didn't mind wining and dining, so it wasn't that. There was something else, though.

A feeling that she was supposed to be the one swept off her feet. A rule that her grandparents had instilled in her about what a man should and shouldn't do. But she had waited for those men to appear and they hadn't. In fact, they'd disappeared even when Hahna had done all the right things. Even when she'd been the supportive, submissive, and sweet girlfriend, Torian had disappeared.

But Sam hadn't disappeared. He wasn't a ghost. He was a real-live man. Maybe the sweeping part was for fairy tales. And *this* . . . finding someone who felt like a soul mate and brought her peace. Maybe that's what she'd been missing. Maybe Sam was *the one* she'd been missing.

Chapter 30

Twila stood in the doorway of her bedroom, a mug of hot coffee in her hands, wearing a small tank top, thong panties, and nothing else. She gazed at Marcus, sprawled across her bed. The muscles in his back flexed even while he slept. She wanted to move closer and inhale his scent.

They'd been in and out of bed for three days—Friday, Saturday, and Sunday. He hadn't gone home. She hadn't asked him to. His overnight had turned into overnights, and now Twila wondered if she wanted him to leave, or if she now had a roommate.

For three days and two nights, Marcus had fed every one of Twila's hungers. In the kitchen he'd whipped up the healthy and the decadent. In the bedroom he'd served the sinful. And she felt well attended to. Wasn't that how a sugar mama should feel?

And she could have that every day if she wanted. Marcus would be a fool not to ditch that roommate situation he was in to move into Twila's Buckhead mansion. And she knew if he moved in, she'd never be hungry. He'd always have—and be— a snack.

But how crazy would she be to move this man into her place after only a couple of months? They'd gotten closer after she'd taken him to Sam's book signing. It was like seeing those women clamor to take a photograph with him had made her see him in a different, more appealing light.

Twila was becoming Marcus's biggest fan.

She needed to wake him, because his video was being recorded today. The video that Twila had paid for to launch his career. The whole budget was out of her pocket—another investment that Twila fully expected to recoup, and she wasn't taking payment in eggplant.

This video, once posted to all social media platforms, was going to spur downloads of Marcus's song. And then, she'd take her cut off the top. She'd probably reinvest it into his career, but he didn't need to know that. Right now, he thought she'd be the first in line with her hand out for her money.

Marcus stirred. It was probably the weight of Twila's stares that woke him. She sipped her coffee slowly and waited for him to rise.

"The video shoot's today?" he said through a yawn.

Twila nodded. "It is today, so don't you think you should get out of bed?"

"I probably should. Is there more coffee?"

"In the kitchen."

"Are you going to get some for me?" Marcus asked.

Her response was a giggle. No one waited on the boy toy hand and foot. The boy toy waited on the powerful woman.

"I guess I'll have to get it myself," Marcus said.

Twila didn't have to wonder what Kimberly and Hahna would think about her having Marcus in her home for days on end. They had already told her several times. But why did they think they were the only ones who got to have hot and steamy love affairs? They should be happy for her, the same way she was happy for them. They had finally let go of everything holding them back, and they were all reaping the benefits.

"I made you breakfast, babe," Twila said. "Or, I should say, my caterer made us breakfast. I just heated it up."

Marcus grinned. "You know you've made it when you have a personal chef."

"Is that when you know? I thought I knew it before that."

Marcus jumped out of the bed and pulled Twila close, nuzzling her neck. Luckily, she had a lid on her coffee mug or it would've been sloshing all over the place because of the commotion.

"That's what I love about you. You're such a damn boss."

Twila kissed his nose. "Well, love it with some mouthwash and toothpaste. I'll see you in the kitchen."

Marcus stumbled backward clutching his midsection as if she'd thrown daggers or shanked him.

"You slay me, lady."

"Stop leaving yourself open, then."

Twila turned and walked back downstairs and into the kitchen, feeling open her damn self. She fixed two plates of her favorite quiche and fruit. It was a light breakfast, and that was all Marcus needed. That and warm tea with honey and lemon. She had that ready too.

Marcus emerged from upstairs, freshly showered. He still glistened from the shea body butter and smelled like sunshine and promises. But he didn't wear his usual smile. His face held a tight frown, and his eyebrows were furrowed—with what? Worry?

"What's wrong?"

Marcus shook his head slightly. "Nothing. Just trying to remember all the choreography for those dance routines."

"Oh. Well, if you mess up you can just do another take."

"I don't want this to go over budget, though. I'll do it right the first time."

"Okay, well, I don't want you stressing me out."

Marcus set his phone on the counter—a habit Twila hated—and plopped on a bar stool. She pushed his plate and mug of tea in front of him.

"Thanks, babe."

Marcus's phone buzzed. He ignored it. That was curious.

"So, we're going to do a marketing campaign for your video and single. I've had my marketing experts research your demographic. Social media is best, but we need you to go viral."

"Well, duh."

Twila cut her eyes at him. "Let me finish. We've got a whole lineup of Atlanta celebrities who are going to share your video on the same day. Mostly reality stars, and other artists."

"Why just Atlanta? I don't want to be a local artist."

"It's called soaking your city, remember? You find your fan base at home, solidify it, and then expand."

Marcus's phone buzzed again. He ignored it. Again.

"Who is blowing you up this morning?"

Marcus closed his eyes and sighed. "Nobody."

"Well, it's somebody, and they have your number on lock. Sounds like you need to get your birds in order."

Marcus looked up at Twila and chuckled. "You actually think I'd let my phone sit here on the counter blowing up if it was a chick?"

"You might, with your arrogant ass."

"I may be arrogant, but I'm not stupid. I know you've got guns, Twila. You always talk about shooting someone."

"Don't worry about my arsenal. Worry about your phone."

It buzzed again.

"If it's not a chick, unlock it. Lemme see."

Marcus licked his lips nervously, but he did as she asked. He unlocked the phone and handed it to her.

Like a digital forensics expert at the scene of a crime, Twila expertly swiped and tapped until she had Marcus's text messages up on the screen.

She scrolled as she read and shook her head. Now she knew why he was worried.

"The sheriff is at your apartment now? Throwing all y'all stuff out?" she asked.

He nodded. "I knew it was going to happen. Khalil didn't have his part of the rent for three months in a row, and we couldn't cover his arrears. The landlord asked us to move. We just didn't have anywhere to go."

"They don't, but you do."

"Twila, I couldn't ask that."

"Then don't ask. I'm offering. You can stay here until you

start making enough money for your own spot. I don't think that's going to take too long."

"Why are you so good to me?" Marcus asked.

"Because you are *so* good to me."

"If I'm being honest, I don't trust it," Marcus said. "Nothing this good has ever happened to me. My life is a Dickens novel, babe. It was the worst of times, and the worst of times."

"Not anymore. It doesn't have to be like that anymore."

He took a bite of his quiche. He moaned with pleasure.

"I need to get your caterer's recipe. I can make this for you. You don't have to pay for someone to prepare your meals while I'm here."

"She won't share her recipes, but I'd love to try yours."

"I will cook every day for you."

"Thank you."

Marcus took a long drag on his tea. "I'm not perfect."

"I know. Your wallet is kinda light."

"Well, that too, but that isn't what I was talking about."

Twila lifted an eyebrow. "What's wrong? I already checked and you have both testicles."

"You are hilarious," Marcus said. "But I'm being serious. I'm jealous. I'm a little insecure. I don't like dogs."

"I don't have one."

"I don't like animals, period."

"What? Why don't you like animals?"

"I mean, as long as they stay in their own habitat I don't have any beef with them, but if they roll up in my space it's a problem."

Twila cleared her throat. "You're living at or below the poverty level. You're jealous. You're insecure. You don't donate to PETA. What else?"

"Isn't that enough?"

"All things considered, it's not that bad."

Marcus laughed out loud. "What all are you considering then? It sounds bad to me."

Twila took another sip of her coffee and sighed. He had no idea what she'd had in her life before. The men who'd hurt her. The men who'd ignored her calls and made her feel thirsty and desperate. The men who were for her and everybody else.

These were the things she considered. These were the men who hadn't considered her.

"Trust me, Marcus. You're all right with me."

"Will you let me know when it's not all right?"

This was something he needn't worry about it. If it became not all right with Marcus, she'd leave him right where she found him. In a bad situation with a bleak outlook. A sugar mama wasn't a real mama. There were limits and bounds to this arrangement.

"Let's go get your stuff before someone steals it," Twila said, not feeling the need to warn Marcus about his less-than-solid foundation. "We've got to hurry so we can still get to the video shoot."

"You're going with me to pick up my things from the street corner? Now, that's some ride-or-die shit right there."

"You're the best thing that's happened to me in a long time."

Twila refused to consider anything otherwise.

Chapter 31

After Big Ron's revelation, Kimberly thought about not asking him to accompany her to her coworker's wedding. It wasn't that she couldn't forgive him for loving a white woman . . . no . . . that's exactly what it was. She couldn't forgive him for loving a white woman. At least not right away.

But she had asked him anyway, feeling that even having that traitor on her arm was better than nothing.

Ron was aware of the impact of what he'd shared. Kimberly had cooled toward him some, and when they'd been hurtling in the direction of stoking the unrequited flames, his previous marital ties had doused it like ice water on a campfire. And so, he was trying hard.

Ron arrived on time to pick up Kimberly for the wedding. His navy suit and bow tie were perfect for his slim frame. He smelled so good that she wanted to undress him and put her face to his chest.

"Hey, Ron. Come on in. Excuse the small mess in here. We're getting ready for my product launch, and there are boxes everywhere. I'm almost ready."

"I don't mind, Kimmie Kim."

He stepped over the threshold and into her foyer. Kim loved the way he took his time looking at her, not feeling shy about lingering on her breasts, which her body shaper had thrust up and out for all to admire.

Did his white woman have all of this?

Kim closed her eyes and shook her head. She had to try to get over Ron's past. This was a good man right here. A good, fine, chocolate man. He had his own money and was responsible. And he was obviously attracted to all her curves.

"I don't get a hug or anything?"

His extended arms were too good an invitation to ignore. Kimberly tried not to move too fast or seem too anxious to feel his arms around her, but when she fell into his embrace and he squeezed her tightly, it had a calming effect.

"You get all the hugs," Kim whispered, "because you give the best hugs."

Like she had a movie reel playing in her mind, she imagined that she'd been married to Big Ron the past two decades, and that they'd raised their own children—a boy and a girl. Why had they taken so long to find one another again? And why hadn't she found him before that white woman?

The thought of *her,* whoever she was, spoiled the moment and the embrace. She tried to squirm away, but not before Ron kissed her deeply and passionately. Now, that was almost enough to erase the memory of his ex-wife.

"I knew I'd have to tell you about her eventually," Ron said, "but dammit, if I'd known you'd react this way, I would've kept my previous marriage a secret until the grave."

"I don't know what's wrong with me. I think it's just because I've been alone too long. And you were always one of the good ones. Maybe, if not for her, you would've come looking for me sooner. I'd be the mother of Shawn's baby brother."

Ron kissed her again, this time snaking his hand through her curls and pulling her in as close as he could. She was breathless when he released her.

"You want a baby, Kimmie Kim? It's not too late."

"Yes, it is. It's too late for me. I'm in my forties. I missed my baby window."

Ron put tiny kisses all over her neck and lips. "We don't have to make a baby, but I want you."

Kimberly knew that Ron wanted her. She didn't have a doubt about that. But was she enough to compete with the memory of all his former loves combined? Could she erase them from his mind? Would he always be with her, while thinking of someone else? Someone thin with straight hair probably. Someone who was the antithesis of Kimberly.

"I want you too," Kimberly whispered, giving words to her truth, even though she still had fears about his loyalty.

Ron slid Kimberly's knit dress off her shoulder and left a kiss there. She shuddered.

"Who's getting married today?" Ron asked. "Can you just send a gift with regrets?"

Ron kissed the small of Kimberly's neck. She shuddered again and moaned.

"What is it that I'm regretting?" Kimberly asked.

"Not this."

Ron slid Kimberly's dress all the way down her body, leaving her standing there in her girdle and bra. She felt herself become self-conscious. This was just another thing thin women didn't have to worry about. Being disrobed and having your armor exposed.

"What's wrong?" Ron asked. He must've felt her body tense up when he kissed her again.

"Nothing. I just feel a bit exposed."

"Well, that's on purpose. I want to see all of you."

"That's the thing. There's a lot to see."

"Kim. You know I don't care about that. I love all this. I should've made love to you twenty-two years ago when we were in school."

Kim felt her wall crumble brick by brick. Ron knew what to say to make her feel at ease while standing in her living room in a girdle.

She tried not to giggle as he struggled to pull the girdle down. This armor was strong and unrelenting. It was why she loved it.

It made her want to cry that Ron didn't make an issue of it at all. He didn't joke or ask how to disrobe her. He didn't make her feel badly for needing what she needed to look her best in a dress. Ron just acted like a man who wanted a woman. *He* was strong and unrelenting. The girdle was no match for his desire.

When he'd gotten the girdle around her ankles, Kim daintily stepped out of each leg. Ron moved slowly up her legs, kissing her calves and then her thighs. Her legs felt like gelatin, so she backed up against the living room wall to keep from melting. That one step created the space that Ron needed to get to the jewel he sought. He pushed her thong panties to one side to taste that throbbing bit of flesh and set her on fire.

"R-Ron," Kim said, her voice quivering, barely able to form words.

Ron looked up from his snack. "Yes, baby."

"I w-want to feel you inside me."

Ron let out a low, hungry groan and stood. Then he squatted and used his powerful legs to lift her into his arms. She hadn't thought that he was strong enough to lift her, but he didn't struggle or strain. She pointed to the bedroom, and he followed her lead.

Kim tried not to cry but felt tears spring to her eyes. She never thought she'd have this fantasy. Never thought a man as fine as Ron would come into her life, and literally sweep her into his arms. She should have known that she was worth all of this, but she hadn't. She thought those were fantasies for women who didn't have extra rolls and stretch marks. She loved every bit of herself, but never thought a man would. Not like this.

When Ron laid her on the bed and made every nerve ending in her body sing, Kimberly knew that she'd been wrong. He could have a hundred white women in his past—she wasn't letting this go.

She'd been waiting her whole life for this feeling. There was nothing that would make her give it away.

Chapter 32

Twila walked into her home at eleven o'clock at night, knowing that she hadn't answered any of Marcus's text messages asking about her whereabouts, and not caring. She had an emergency patient. An A-list model had chipped her front tooth at the gym, was flying out to Milan in the morning, and she had a job as soon as she landed.

Twila didn't even think twice about seeing her. That was how she had grown her celebrity clientele list to its current level, and that had gotten her bank account to its current level.

"What took you so long to get home?" Marcus asked.

Twila looked around the living room. She lifted a couch pillow and peeked underneath the coffee table. Then she picked up a vase and peered inside.

"What are you looking for?" Marcus asked.

"Not what, but who," Twila said. "I'm trying to find who the hell you think you're talking to. I don't answer to you, so don't start interrogating me."

"You were at Phenom, weren't you? Probably in the sex room with that cybersecurity billionaire."

Twila rolled her eyes. This was the reason why she never took men there. Once they knew of the open exhibitionist space, none of them ever believed that she had no desire to participate.

"That was childish," Twila said. "First of all, if I had gone to Phenom, I wouldn't have had to clear it with you. Second, if I had hooked up with the cybersecurity billionaire at Phenom, you would never know. Nothing leaves those walls."

"So, you're saying I'm just never going to know."

"No, I'm saying you sound ridiculous and that you should probably leave the subject alone. I'm not in the mood."

"Twila, I told you I was jealous."

She shrugged. "Sounds like you have a problem—not me."

"I'm not gonna share you with anyone. If you're with me, you're with me," Marcus said.

"That sounds too possessive. I mean, you can ask me not to be with anyone except you. Why don't you start there? Let's see how that works."

Marcus shifted his weight to the other side of the armchair. Twila sensed annoyance. Good. She hoped that he could sense hers too. He was confused if he thought she would be controlled by him, just because he happened to have male body parts.

"Twila, while I'm living here, while we're doing *this*—whatever it is that we're doing—will you agree to be exclusive and not see other men?"

"Whatever it is that we're doing?" Twila asked.

"I hesitate to define it, because you just told me you don't answer to me. The definition I have in my mind is that at this point we both answer to one another. Perhaps my definition is premature."

"Perhaps?"

"Are you going to continue seeing other men, Twila? I mean, that's the whole point of this conversation."

"I'm not seeing other men. That was an assumption you made."

"Okay, you're not seeing other men now. But are you still open to other men? Do you still consider yourself single?"

Twila paused before responding. She knew the pause would be a problem, but still she couldn't give him a quick answer. This thing with Marcus was fun. She enjoyed helping him with his career, and he'd brought the spice back to her bedroom, but . . . she didn't know if he felt like her forever. She didn't want to promise forever if she didn't feel it.

Admitting that she wasn't sure about a future with Marcus was part of breaking her own dating rules. Twila had always let men make her feel obligated just because they were hitting it right. She'd act like a wife even if she couldn't see herself married to the man.

"Why is it taking you so long to reply?" Marcus asked.

Twila could hear the panic rise in Marcus's voice and didn't care for how it sounded. There was desperation there. Desperation wasn't attractive at all.

"Marcus. I don't feel like I'm single. We are together for now."

That was as honest as she could be. As close to the truth as she could come without completely breaking him.

"For now. For now? How do I know when my time is up?"

"You're making it seem like I'm just going to throw you away or something. The time may never be up. I'm just not sure yet."

"But what is it contingent upon? What do I need to do to seal the deal?"

He had gotten up from the armchair and was closing in on her personal space. Twila didn't feel threatened, but as the intensity escalated, she strategized on which weapon she would pull from the underside of the couch or from beneath the lamp if she needed. She wondered how many of the weapons Marcus had found. She didn't hide them, because they weren't for him. The weapons were for intruders.

"I need you to calm down, Marcus. Nothing is changing. I worked late. Had an emergency veneer to do for a model who is on her way overseas."

Marcus visibly calmed, but Twila didn't like this.

"That's all you had to say in the beginning, Twila. Why did you let it go here?"

"Because you need to understand you don't have the right to question me. I'm a grown woman, and you aren't my father."

"What rights do I have as your man? Do I have the right to expect you to be exclusively sleeping with me?"

"You can ask that, and I can decide whether or not I want to comply. I'm not going to lie to you, though."

Marcus sat again. "So, can I ask that you be exclusive?"

"Yes. I already am. If I decide that I no longer want to be, I will tell you."

Marcus wiped his face with his hand and sighed. "Twila, I told you I was jealous when I moved in here. And you said you were okay with it. I've been one hundred percent honest with you, and you've not done the same with me."

"I haven't lied to you. You moved into my home with one perception, and I don't share that perception. Why do you think you have your own bedroom?"

"I thought you were just giving me my creative space."

"You should've asked why before you assumed. I let you move here because you were in a tough situation. Not because we had reached a certain place in our relationship. We're still brand new, and I'm enjoying it so far. When it's not enjoyable, I may decide to do something different."

Twila stood her ground. She was not going to be pushed into anything deeper than what they had now because of his need to feel ownership of her.

"I can't deal with this amount of uncertainty, Twila."

"Okay."

"What does that mean?"

"It means I'm not trying to force you to deal with anything. If you don't like my honesty, then you can choose something different for yourself."

"You sound like one of my homeboys. They never make any promises, but when they break the girl's heart they say, 'I was honest. She heard what she wanted to hear.' You sound just like that."

Well, maybe Marcus was acting like a woman who read between the lines when there was no hidden meaning. Shit, Twila had been that woman. But that was the past. Her new self was honest and expected honesty in return.

"I'm not like your homeboys. I'm not a cheater. I said we're exclusive, and I mean it. I just don't know about forever."

"No one ever knows about forever," Marcus said. "Forever is a long damn time."

"That's my point. I just want you to enjoy what we have right now, in this moment."

Marcus nodded and seemed to be content with this response. For now. And Twila was satisfied for now.

But something tickled at Twila's spirit. What was going to happen when she woke up and wanted forever?

Chapter 33

Hahna was nervous about inviting Sam to her home, even though she'd been to his apartment, and they'd been on a trip together. If she didn't invite him, would he think she was hiding something? Well, she was hiding something.

She was hiding the fact that her house was huge and that it had cost her half a million dollars. Sam said that he wasn't bothered by her taste for finer things, but she felt like he was secretly judging her for it.

Hahna peeked out the window when her doorbell rang. Sam stood smiling and holding a gift in his hand. Hahna exhaled. Maybe he didn't mind her living in luxury as much as she thought he did.

Hahna threw the door open and hugged him. "I missed you," she whispered in his ear.

"It's only been two days since we last saw each other."

"That was two too many days. Come inside. I made you dinner."

The entire lower level smelled like garlic and oregano—the main spices in Hahna's lasagna. It was her best dish, though she rarely made time to prepare it. Her work took away from her domesticity.

"It smells good in here. My stomach just growled," Sam said.

"Good! I hope you're hungry, because my lasagna is a man's meal, babe. You almost need two stomachs to enjoy it properly."

"Oh, well, I packed my extra stomach. It's in the trunk of my car in case I need it."

"Let me give you a quick tour of the house while it finishes cooling, and then we can eat."

Sam smiled. "A quick tour? This place is huge."

"It's not that big. Come on."

Hahna led Sam upstairs and showed him the master bedroom with her closet that was almost the size of a small bedroom. Then she showed him the two guest bedrooms and her shoe closet, which was really another bedroom transformed into a home for her hundreds of pairs of shoes.

"That's a lot of shoes," Sam said as he looked from the floor to the ceiling. "Damn."

"I know," Hahna explained. "It's just that I'll sometimes see a pair that I don't even have an outfit for, but I can't leave them in the store."

"Have you worn all of them?"

"About seventy percent of them have been worn at least a few times. Some I haven't gotten to use yet."

"Oh."

Then Hahna took Sam through all the rooms downstairs; her living room, sunroom, library, foyer, and dining room that was set for dinner. He had no comments on these rooms. He merely smiled. The smile seemed stuck on his face, actually, like he had to try hard to maintain it.

"One more level," Hahna said. "The basement."

Sam glanced out the kitchen window. "You have a pool?"

"I do. I wish I had time to use it more. I love that it's back there, though."

Sam nodded and smiled again as he followed Hahna into the basement. She showed him the gym area, and the entertainment room. The bar was her favorite part. It was stocked better than any bar in town. When she had parties, sometimes she'd hire a professional bartender.

"Well, that's it. That's the tour. You ready to eat now?"

A nod and a smile. Again.

Hahna ignored her impulse to comment on Sam's stoic facial expression. Mostly because if he felt a certain way about her home, it was ridiculous. Thanks to Hale and Jelena, he knew she had millions in the bank. He had to expect that her home would reflect that.

Sam went to the bathroom to wash his hands, and Hahna finished bringing the food out. She looked into the small bag that Sam had brought. Inside it was a candle that smelled amazing. She took it into the living room and lit it before coming back into the dining room.

They sat at her dining room table, which could normally seat twelve, but she had placed the settings side by side so that they didn't have to yell at each other across the table. Hahna hoped they were going to have a conversation, since Sam had been silent since the tour of her home was complete.

Sam took her hand and blessed the food. Only then did his stoic smile crack.

After he was done, Hahna scooped lasagna onto Sam's plate. She'd prefilled the salad and bread plates.

"Your home is beautiful, Hahna."

Finally, Hahna relaxed. "Thank you. It took me a while to get it to where I wanted it to be, but I think I'm done now."

"Why did it take a while?"

"Well, I got the house at a discount. It had gone into foreclosure. So, when I bought it, there was some remodeling that I had to do."

Now Sam gave her a genuine smile. "Ah, I see. Well, that makes sense. I'm glad you were able to save some money when you purchased it. It's enough house for a few families to live in all at once."

"I didn't buy it because it was at a discount, though."

"Oh?"

"I bought it because I loved the house. It was just a coincidence that it was in foreclosure. I would've bought it outright."

Sam took a bite of his lasagna and chewed for a long time. "This is good, babe. You're a great cook."

Hahna stared at Sam, blinking several times. Of course, he'd changed the topic. He had a problem with her house. Just because he was okay living in a tiny home didn't mean she had to, though.

"See, that's why I didn't want to invite you over here."

"Wait, what?"

"Sam, you don't have to say anything. Your face is transparent. You don't like my house."

"I do! It looks like something out of a magazine. It's incredible."

"But?"

"But nothing. You have a beautiful home."

Hahna cleared her throat. "If we got married, would you want to live here?"

The fake smile was back on Sam's face. Plastered on his lips, which should've been saying words of reassurance instead.

"I'll take that as a no."

"I'd want to live wherever you were."

"But it wouldn't be your preference."

Sam closed his eyes. "You see how I live. You know I'd never buy anything like this for myself. But when you're in a relationship, it's not just about you."

"That's true. So, you'd live here for me."

He nodded. "Yep. But would you live in my home?"

He'd caught Hahna off-guard with that question, and she burst into laughter. Sam shook his head.

"I mean, why would we have to live there? It's too small for two people."

Sam nodded. "Mmm-hmm."

"What does that mean?"

"People who love stuff never understand people who don't love stuff. I don't care about any of this, but I can tell that you do."

And there it was. The judgment.

"And what does that tell you about me? What conclusion have you drawn because I need more than seven hundred square feet?"

"No conclusions drawn. I just worry that you wouldn't be happy without the stuff. And you know, sometimes the stuff disappears. Then, all you have is each other."

"You've got me wrong, Sam. This is merely the fruit of my labor. I grew up without extra. Shit, I grew up without the things that I needed. I know how to live without. I just don't want to. You don't have to worry about me."

"Okay, then. Let's enjoy this lasagna, though, because I don't want this part to disappear. The making-me-dinner part. I love that."

Sam leaned across the table and kissed Hahna. She kissed him back, but it didn't taste as sweet as before. Maybe because his words had bite to them. They were a little tart. They tasted like the bitter truth.

Chapter 34

K imberly fluffed her couch pillows, then brought out the good wineglasses—and the good wine. Hahna and Twila were coming over to help her plan the launch party for Curlpop, and she hadn't seen or talked to them since she and Ron had been intimate. She wasn't a virgin, but it almost felt like she'd never been touched by a man. It damn near broke her heart when he had to get on the road to go back to North Carolina. She never wanted him to leave.

But he was wonderful, perfect even. He called every day, several times a day. He wanted to use FaceTime so he could see her face before he went to bed. He was everything.

Kimberly felt like a bad friend, though, because she hadn't talked to her girls much and they all had new things going on. Was this how they were going to be once they were all married? Was their friendship going to fizzle and die? Kimberly wasn't going to let that happen.

Hahna got to her house first, because of course she did. Twila was always the last to arrive everywhere.

Kimberly hugged Hahna, but the hug back was weak. "What's wrong, girl?"

Hahna let out a long sigh and plopped down on the living

room sofa. "I'll wait for Twila to get here so I only have to tell it once."

"Don't tell me you and the author are done?" Kimberly said as she sat next to Hahna.

"No, we're not done."

"Well, as long as it's not that. I like him. What, then? You pregnant?"

Hahna laughed. "Girl, no. I will tell you when Twila gets here."

"Okay, then we can talk about my launch party. We're still doing it at your office, right?"

"Yes, unless you want to do it at my house."

"I really liked the idea you had about having a different caterer on every floor. That would be fun. Maybe different flavors of the African diaspora."

"Ooh, that's good! We could have West African, Caribbean, West Indian, and Southern African American foods. That would be awesome."

The doorbell rang, signaling Twila's arrival. Kimberly jumped to her feet to answer, because she was ready to hear what was going on with Hahna.

Twila came through the door like a hurricane.

"Kim, I hope you got some wine, 'cause this fool got me all the way twisted," Twila said as she kicked off her flip-flops, threw her purse on the coffee table, and fell onto the couch next to Hahna.

"Yes, I have wine. What fool?"

"Tequila. Maybe tequila is better," Twila said. "And I mean Marcus."

"The Instathot," Hahna said.

"Yes, that's him," Twila said.

Kimberly set an open bottle of chardonnay in front of Twila. "I don't have tequila, so you better get into this wine."

Twila poured herself a large glass, then took several gulps. "Oh, that's good. So, Marcus is tripping, but that's what I get for letting his ass move into my house."

Kimberly and Hahna's eyes both widened.

"You moved him into your house?" Hahna asked. "And you were talking about me moving fast?"

"I am not you. I can efficiently kill a man at least a dozen ways. Plus, he had gotten evicted and all his stuff was thrown out."

Kimberly slapped her palm over her face. This was worse than she thought it might be. Twila's man was a bum.

"You're a sugar mama for real," Kimberly said. "Weren't you helping him with his singing career?"

"I have been. Got his music played at a club I go to sometimes. Everybody loved it."

"What club?" Hahna asked.

"You don't know it. You've never been. Anyway, he's got a video done, and as soon as it's edited, it'll be on YouTube. It'll really put him out there."

"Well, then, what's the problem?" Kimberly asked.

"Oh, he thinks I have to tell him where I'm going and who I'm seeing. He's trying to act like my husband."

"You're sleeping with him, right?" Kimberly asked. "That isn't such a bad thing. Maybe he doesn't want to share you with anybody else."

"He ain't my daddy. He ain't paying my bills, and he ain't my husband. If you aren't doing any of those things, I ain't gotta tell you where I'm going when I leave *my* house."

"But why wouldn't you tell him?" Hahna asked. "I know you. You aren't sleeping with anybody but him."

"Because he ain't my daddy, he ain't paying my bills, and he ain't my husband. Talking 'bout he's jealous."

"As long as you're honest with him, I guess he's just going to have to understand that," Kimberly said.

"Exactly. And he's staying in the guest room. I only let him visit my room periodically."

"What does 'periodically' mean?" Hahna said.

"Just about every night, but I kick him out when we're done."

"There is something wrong with you," Hahna said.

"Oh, shut up. What's going on with you and Shakespeare?"

"He writes novels, not plays, but we're good . . . I think," Hahna said.

"What does *that* mean?" Kimberly asked.

"I mean, I almost feel ridiculous saying this after what Twila just said. She's got bigger problems than I do."

Twila pointed her wineglass in Hahna's direction, sloshing the liquid over the top. "Spill it, heffa."

"Okay. Sam is kind of judgy."

"He's judgy?" Twila asked. "That's not even a real thing, and it's not a real word."

"It is a real thing," Hahna said. "He's got this whole haughty higher-plane-of-thinking thing. I invited him over for dinner and he asked me if I could live without all my stuff. My house and my expensive furniture."

"I don't find that to be a judgy question," Kimberly said. "I think it's valid, for him, since he doesn't seem to care about that kind of thing."

"I can live without my stuff. I just don't want to," Hahna said. "And I think he's considering and reconsidering if I'm the one for him every time we have these kinds of conversations. And I need him to stop reconsidering, because I'm falling in love with him."

Kimberly glanced at Twila, but she was no help. She was holding up one finger and chugging the rest of her wine.

"You're falling in love with him?" Kimberly asked. "It's too soon for that."

"Not too soon. Enough time to know."

"You sure you're not just dickmatized?" Twila asked.

"I'm not. I mean . . . I love the sex, but our connection is unreal. We're damn near soul mates, except for the fact that I like fancy things and he doesn't."

"I have bigger problems than both of y'all," Kimberly said.

Twila scoffed. "With Big Ron? He's perfect. What problems do you have out of him? He's too sweet, too kind? Too handsome?"

"He used to be married to a white woman."

"Girl. 'Bye." Twila said.

"That isn't a problem," Hahna said.

"Are you two kidding me? Do you know anybody more pro-black than me? More pro-black family?"

"No," Twila said. "But I think Ron is pro-black too."

"Can you be pro-black and married to a white woman?" Kimberly asked. "How is that even possible?"

"He *used* to be married to a white woman," Hahna said. "And although there's nothing wrong with that, what could you possibly be worried about? He's with you now."

"I thought that would be enough, especially after we made love."

Hahna's eyes became saucers, and Twila jumped up and high-fived Kimberly spilling a little more wine. Kimberly was going to send her the cleaning bill.

"She done finally got a piece of Big Ron," Twila said. "Go 'head, girl."

"Was it wonderful?" Hahna asked. "This is so sweet. You've been in love with him for more than two decades, and God brought him back to you."

"It was better than anything I've ever felt. I don't know if I've ever been with a man who loves me. The difference was unbelievable."

"This should be enough," Hahna said. "You love him. He loves you. Stop caring about who he used to be married to. She's a non-factor."

"Right, and you need to stop anyway," Twila said. "You're racist."

"How am I racist? A black person can't be racist. I don't have privilege and the entire justice system at my disposal to systemically oppress white people. There's no racism here."

Hahna rolled her eyes. "Okay, maybe you're not technically racist, but you are hateful toward a lot of white people."

"Not hateful. I just don't let them get away with shit. But even y'all hate the white women who *only* date black men. Come on. How many times have we gagged over the Kardashians?"

"White women gag over the Kardashians too. They might be universally hated by anyone over thirty," Twila said. "We're talking about you, though. Just like how you won't rock with my caterer. She got a whole white husband and white babies at home."

"I'm just rooting for everybody black. Period," Kimberly said. "I can't even believe I'm having this conversation with y'all."

"Well, you need to, because you're about to let your feelings about white women mess up the first real love you ever had," Twila said. "I swear, if you stop dealing with Big Ron because of his ex-wife, you are straight-up tripping."

"I didn't say I was going to. I'm just trying to deal with what his choice might mean. We may have fundamentally different views about politics and uplifting the black race."

"You just need to worry about Ron uplifting your black ass," Twila said as she poured herself another glass of wine.

"Ugh," Kimberly said. "Hahna, can you at least hear where I'm coming from?"

Hahna nodded. "I know what you mean, but I think it's stupid."

"So, I can't get any support from either of y'all? Really?"

"I support you and Big Ron together, because he's great," Hahna said. "That's all."

Neither Hahna nor Twila truly understood Kimberly's stance, and it seemed that nothing she said could convince them. But they hadn't walked her walk. They'd spent a few years being single, but they hadn't always been single. They hadn't had every man pass them up for someone else—someone thin, someone younger, someone lighter, someone whiter. They'd had loves, and they'd lost loves.

Kimberly had only ever loved Big Ron. She'd loved him from that first tutoring session, and he'd never left her heart. But it hadn't been the same for him. He'd moved around and had fallen in and out of love more than once. It wasn't just with a white woman—but she was the biggest insult. Kimberly had been sleeping alone, when Ron had cuddled with a woman who probably had all the choices in the world.

Her choices had always been few, and she was tired of sharing. Who gave a damn if they didn't understand? Kimberly knew that her feelings were valid. She just had to decide if she was going to allow those valid feelings to keep her from what could be her one shot at love.

Chapter 35

Twila walked back into her home after her girls' night with Kimberly and Hahna. She wanted nothing but to crash in her bed and wrap herself in a thick comforter. She was tired— partially from arguing with Kim's stubborn self, but mostly from the wine.

Marcus stepped out of the guest bedroom, and Twila forced herself not to roll her eyes. She was surprised by her feelings toward Marcus, but maybe she shouldn't have been. Even though he was shirtless, and his muscles shone with oil, his jealousy had made him less attractive in her eyes. In her mind, jealousy was a sign of weakness. An alpha male never had to be jealous, because his woman had no reason to seek out another.

"Hey, beautiful. Did you enjoy your girls' night?"

Twila nodded. "I did. I needed it."

"You were stressed?"

"No, not really. I just hadn't seen them in a while. Needed to catch up."

"Are you mad at me? You're being really short."

"Not mad at all. Just tired. Kimberly always has the best wine."

Marcus grinned. "All liquored up, huh? Well, I can come read you a bedtime story."

Normally, this would've been exciting, and Twila would've gotten aroused just at the thought of Marcus by her bedside.

"Not tonight," Twila said. "I just want to sleep."

"Wow. Okay."

"Don't do this, Marcus. Don't turn into this whiny thing. You've already put me off with your jealous tirade."

"I apologized for that."

"I'm still processing that apology, because what brought you there in the first place is my issue."

Marcus shook his head. "What am I supposed to think when the girl I'm falling for is a member of an exclusive Atlanta sex club?"

"It's not like that, and I'm not a member. My sorority sister owns it. I only took you there because her husband is the DJ and I knew he would play your music."

"You're not a member, but the driver and the doorman knew you by name."

"So, in your mind, every time I'm not in your presence, I'm at the club sexing in front of an audience?"

"I'm a man. Can't help that's what I'm imagining."

"You can help it. You can decide you sound ridiculous, because you do, and maybe you'll turn me on again."

"Oh, damn. I'm turning you off?"

"I'm off. Sorry."

"You want to do something else then, like watch a movie?"

"I just want to sleep. I have work in the morning. Early appointment."

"Okay."

"Good night, Marcus."

Twila started toward her bedroom, but then Marcus closed the space between them and stood in her path. Twila looked up at him with fire in her eyes—but it damn sure wasn't the fire of passion.

"Remember when I said I was grown enough to date you?" Marcus asked.

"I do remember. Not sure if you were telling the truth, though. I think you're not quite old enough to ride this ride."

"I'm old enough and mature enough to admit I made a mistake in questioning a grown woman's whereabouts."

"Mmm-hmmm . . ."

"And I'd like to give you a real apology."

Twila's lip twitched. This could get interesting. She didn't stop Marcus from advancing until the tip of his nose touched hers.

"I don't want this thing we have to be just about sex," Marcus said. "I'd like for us to be much more than that. I envision us as a power couple."

Twila could barely decipher his words. She was envisioning him naked.

"I appreciate everything you've helped me with so far. When this music takes off, I can't wait to take you on vacation."

"Mmmm . . . really? Where we going?" Twila asked, her voice a husky and throaty whisper.

"The Amalfi Coast. The island of Capri. We can jump off the side of a yacht and drink thousand-dollar wine."

Funny, Twila didn't care about any of that. Maybe because she'd already been to the Amalfi Coast. She'd already swum in the Mediterranean Sea next to a yacht. Marcus didn't even know how to upgrade her. He was thinking too small.

"Why don't you just take me to bed. Plan our vacation tomorrow."

"You want that bedtime story now, huh?"

"Nah. Bedtime stories are for little girls."

For the moment, Twila let Marcus make her forget that she couldn't see a forever with him. For now, it was good enough that he touched her the way she needed to be touched. She tried not to think about the future, and about being alone again.

Chapter 36

Hahna pressed and massaged her temples, trying to keep a massive headache at bay. It was Thursday, but it felt like the fourth Monday in a row. Nothing was going right. They'd lost a client today. Not a big one, but one who'd been with them since the beginning. A small Atlanta bakery that was on the verge of starting a franchising operation. The owner, a sista, had told Hahna that she and her business weren't going to be a little fish in a big pond.

This had pained Hahna because she prided herself on customer service, and the ability to make every one of her clients feel important. This Brexton account, though, had taken up so much of her company's available bandwidth that the other clients were suffering. Hiring staff was a must, but it was very difficult finding someone who could come into the Data Whisperers and hit the ground running. Almost everyone they'd recruited had the soft skills and could maybe be a great employee in six months to a year. They needed someone yesterday.

Even looking out her office window wasn't helping Hahna feel at peace. Even though Hale had paid them a quarter million dollars for the first phase of their data transformation,

Hahna was having serious doubts about taking him on as a client. She couldn't lose the rest of her clients dealing with his issues.

The office intercom lit up, and Hahna pressed the button. "Yes, Sylvia."

"You have a visitor."

Hahna quickly ran through her mental calendar, but couldn't think of anyone she'd scheduled to see today.

"It's Sam. I'll send him back," Sylvia said, before Hahna could respond.

Hahna's mood changed. The stress of the workday melted away at the anticipation of seeing Sam, even though she'd just seen him the night before. Whenever he was in her space, Hahna felt better than all right.

"It's lunchtime," Sam said as he walked in, "and I cooked. You liked my uncle's stewed chicken so much that I thought I'd make you some."

"Babe, you are so thoughtful. You're a godsend today."

Sam spread the food out on the conference table. "Come and eat, then. Food will make you feel better."

Hahna got up from her desk and joined Sam at the table. He lifted her up in one arm and kissed her throat before gently setting her back down.

"You always taste so sweet," Sam said. "Here. Sit."

Hahna followed instructions and waited to be served. Sam was perfect at it. He quickly placed a bowl in front of her, and then added rice with little bits of parsley. Then, the stewed chicken went on top. It smelled amazing.

He fixed himself a portion and then took her hand to bless the food. He always did that, every time they ate. He didn't go to church, or at least they hadn't gone to church together, but thanking the Creator for sustenance was important to Sam.

"I didn't just come here to bring you a delicious lunch," Sam said after they'd dug into the delicious food.

"Really?"

"I also have good news."

Hahna's eyes lit up. "Do tell. I need some good news today."

"Remember that editor who came to my table to get her book signed?" Sam asked.

"The one who gave you her card? The one with the tight black dress, schoolteacher glasses, and fat booty."

Sam burst into laughter. "Yes, that's the one. I didn't see or care about all that, though, because you were there."

"Mmm-hmm," Hahna said. "But you knew exactly who I was describing. It's okay, babe. You'd be blind not to notice all of that."

"Anyway, my news has nothing to do with her looks. She's a senior editor at Walcot and Edwards Books. She offered me a two-book deal."

Hahna dropped her fork and jumped up from her seat. She had to hug Sam. This wasn't good news. It was life-changing news.

"Babe, that's incredible," Hahna said between hugs and the barrage of kisses she rained on Sam.

"I turned it down."

Hahna stopped kissing and hugging. "I thought that's what you wanted."

"I want more people to read my books, but I don't know if I want to go the publishing company route. It's good news, because that means my writing is getting noticed."

"I'm confused. I thought the whole point of doing that event with other seasoned, published writers was to get a book deal, so that you can make money off your books. What am I missing?"

"What you're missing is that I don't have any desire to be held to a deadline or have stipulations over how often I can publish or have to get events approved. I like the idea of independent publishing. I just need to do more research."

"You turned down the deal?"

"Yes, but I did leave an open door with the editor."

Hahna got very quiet and focused on her meal. The food was

so good, because Sam was a wonderful cook. She'd never have to worry about eating well while they were together—as long as she bought the groceries.

"What's wrong?" Sam asked.

"You told me this was good news. I don't see any good news. I see you turning down an opportunity."

Sam nodded slowly. "I see. You think I'm leaving money on the table."

"Aren't you?"

"The offer of a book deal, I think, validates me in a way I didn't think I needed," Sam explained. "It's not the money that comes with it, because honestly they didn't offer much, but the fact that an established publisher thinks I'm good enough."

"Your readers tell you you're good enough."

"But there is something more when a professional says it."

That something more was a check. And Sam seemed determined to run the opposite direction of the flow of cash.

Sam wiped his mouth with the napkin on his lap, then folded it and placed it on the table. All of this was done slowly and methodically as if he was pondering the entire time.

"Have I asked you to purchase anything for me? Pay a bill?" he finally said.

"No, you haven't."

"Do I seem broke to you?"

"No."

"Then please tell me why you are so concerned about me making money?"

Hahna considered whether or not she should share what was truly in her heart. If she did and it drove him away, she would forever regret saying the words. But if she didn't tell him, Hahna knew that she was going to have to stop making an issue of his income or lack of income.

"I always thought that the man I fell in love with would be my partner."

"Partnership isn't just about money."

"No, not *just* about money, but that is a part of it."

Sam stood and started packing up the leavings from the lunch he'd brought. Now she'd upset him when he'd come to cheer her up with good news.

"Are you unable to be with me?" Sam asked.

"No. I want to be with you, more than anything. I'm trying really hard, Sam."

Sam closed the space between them. He brushed her curls from her face and kissed her head.

"I don't have to try," Sam said. "I wasn't lying when I said that being with you feels like home. I believe you are the one for me, even though we have our differences. I think you have to decide what's really important to you, babe. I can't decide for you."

"Don't leave."

Hahna's voice sounded distressed. She didn't want Sam to disappear like the others. Not over this. Not for money. Not when she could stop working that day and still have all the money she'd ever need.

Sam kissed her again and sat.

"I'm not leaving, Hahna, but I'm not changing either. I'm never going to decide things based on how much money I can make doing it. I have enough."

"I know."

"And you have more than enough."

"I do."

"I am falling in love with you too, Hahna. Fallen, I should say."

Hahna trembled. His words had power. She felt the vibrations of them. They shook the room.

"What's next?"

"I don't mind you generating wealth, Hahna. Most would say that's very wise. I just want you to love me more than the stuff. Love me even if someday it's gone."

"I do. I will."

"Okay. I believe you will keep trying to do that. I hope that one day you'll feel so safe with me that the material things don't matter. Until then, I'll wait for you."

Hahna breathed in. Exhaled. Shook off the fear of losing him. She loved him more for being patient and kind with her. Sam displayed the definition of love. He was perfect.

So, why was she making him wait for her love in return?

Chapter 37

Kimberly opened one eye when her doorbell rang. At first, she thought it was in her dream. It was too early for company. It was Saturday, and she was getting that good sleep. The kind of sleep you get when you missed a few hours every night the entire week, and your body finally rebels and takes what it needs.

But when the doorbell continued after both her eyes were wide open, Kimberly climbed out from under the comforter and put her slippers on. She peeked out the window in her bedroom to see what car the person had pulled up in.

It was Ron's truck.

Kimberly racked her brain for a moment trying to remember if she'd forgotten some plans. Ron hated being stood up, and she didn't intend on doing that.

Kimberly rushed down the stairs without visiting the bathroom for even mouthwash. He wanted to wake her up at the crack of dawn, then this was what he was getting. Unwashed body and unbrushed teeth.

She swung the front door open and grinned like Ron was Publishers Clearing House telling her she'd won five thousand dollars a week for life. Ron threw his head back and burst into laughter.

"Baby, I don't think I've ever seen you with your hair standing up on your head like that," Ron said.

"This what happens when you roll up on me at the ass crack of dawn," Kimberly said as she fluffed her pouf for emphasis. "Come on in."

Ron came in and made himself at home. He *was* home as far as Kimberly was concerned. He never had to leave again if he didn't want to.

"I know I should've called," Ron said as he went to put on a pot of coffee. "But I wanted to surprise you. Don't you wanna go on a road trip with me?"

"A road trip where?"

She hoped they were going somewhere fun like Savannah, or maybe even Myrtle Beach. Anywhere she could smell the ocean was a place she'd love to be.

"I've got some business in North Carolina, but I couldn't go all weekend without seeing you."

"Of course, I want to go. Just give me a little time to get dressed."

"While you're getting dressed, I'll make you breakfast. Sound good?"

"It sounds perfect, baby. I'll be ready in less than an hour."

Kimberly bounced back up her stairs, excited to be going anywhere with this perfect man. She felt like all the women at church who testified about finally finding the man God had for them. Ron was for her. There was no uncertainty in her mind about that. He loved every inch of her—even the extra ones. He made love to every nook and cranny (although she probably wouldn't testify about that part), and he was hers.

When she was done showering and dressing, Kimberly came back downstairs to the scent of bacon, coffee, and something sweet.

"It smells good down here, baby," Kimberly said. "What did you make?"

"French toast and bacon. Working on this omelet. Your coffee is in your mug."

Kimberly slid in at the bar stool. "I love it when you take care of me."

Ron looked back and smiled. His deep dimples and salt-and-pepper goatee made her heart rate elevate.

"I love that I have the opportunity. This time has been really special for me too."

Ron reached into his pocket and slid a small box across the countertop. Kimberly stared at the box like it was contaminated with radioactive goo.

"Open it, Kimmie Kim. It's not an engagement ring."

Kim chuckled, but exhaled, even though she didn't mean to show him her relief. "What makes you think I wouldn't want a ring?"

"I know you, girl. It's too soon for that."

Marriage was on Kimberly's vision board and she could see it happening with Ron—just not yet. Maybe being over forty made her hesitant, or maybe it was making her own millions. She wasn't yet ready to change her last name.

She opened the box and squealed with delight. It was a charm bracelet, full of charms. There was one with a peach for Georgia, and there was a charm for her sorority. There was a charm with her birthstone and a little comb and brush.

"Ron, I *love* it."

"It took me a minute to figure out what all I wanted to put on it."

"How many charms are there?"

"Twenty. One for every year that I should've been with you but I wasn't."

"Baby . . ."

Ron took the omelet off the heat and slid it onto a plate. He kissed Kimberly softly on the lips, and she moaned from the promise of that sweet touch.

"I know we can't make up for the lost years, but we can start now."

Ron clipped the bracelet on Kimberly's wrist and kissed her hand before releasing her.

"Come on. Eat up," Ron said. "We've got to get on the road."

* * *

Five hours of driving brought them to North Carolina, but not to anywhere she'd ever heard of. It was a little town she'd never heard of called Shady Falls.

"Where are we?" Kimberly asked as they pulled up into the driveway of a cute two-story home. "Is this your mother's house? You're introducing me to your mother?"

Ron smiled, and his dimples deepened. "This is not my mother's house, although we can go over there too. I'm sure she'd love to meet you, and you would love her."

"So, if this isn't your mama's house . . ."

Kimberly didn't even get to finish her sentence before two little girls came running out of the house. They had on cute clothes, but their hair was standing straight up in the air in bushes of curls and tangles. They looked like twins.

"Daddy, Daddy, Daddy!"

Ron opened his car door and jumped out. The girls immediately attacked him with hugs as they climbed up into his open arms.

These girls clearly had their father's dimples, but they didn't have his dark, ebony skin. These babies were the color of fresh hay and cinnamon butter. Biracial babies.

He'd procreated with his ex-wife.

He hadn't just taken a white woman to the chapel and married her. He hadn't just lain down with her. He'd made beautiful babies.

"Carly! Kayla! I said don't run outside. I haven't even combed your hair yet."

And there she was. The ex-wife. In living non-color.

At least Big Ron had picked a beautiful one. She had long, wavy black hair that cascaded down her back in huge ripples. She was very fit and athletic. The knit sundress she wore clung to every curve and her tight abdominal region. Kim sucked her belly in out of habit and self-consciousness. How could the same man be attracted to both of them? A big, beautiful, black woman, and a tiny soccer mom.

"I'm sorry, Ronald, I tried to get them ready. It takes forever on hair-washing day."

Ronald. *Ronald?*

His name was Ron.

Then finally, the soccer mom noticed that Ronald wasn't alone. She tilted her head to one side and gave Kimberly a once-over. Kimberly once-overed her right back.

"You brought a friend with you?"

"Yes, Sabrina, I brought my girlfriend."

Her eyebrows lifted at the word "girlfriend." Did she still want Ron? She was wearing a huge wedding ring on her finger. Was that the one she'd gotten from Ron, or was it from a new husband?

"It's not a problem. We just . . . didn't discuss it."

"No discussion needed. I've known Kimberly since college. Kim this is Sabrina, Sabrina meet Kim."

"Since college? So, you know all about him stomping and clapping all over the place?" Sabrina laughed like this was funny. Kimberly and Ron did not.

"Yes. He's in our brother fraternity. I guess I did quite a bit of stomping and clapping too. But we called it stepping."

"Yes, that's right. Stepping. Well, I'm pleased to meet you, Kim."

"Likewise."

It was a hot and muggy summer day, but Kimberly's words were as frosty as Times Square on New Year's Eve, and nowhere near as festive.

"How long will it take you to get them ready? I want to get on the road."

"Where are you taking them?"

"To Atlanta. To see their brother and visit with Kim."

Sabrina looked nervously from her children to Ron to Kimberly. This transaction was taking too long. Not that Kimberly wanted to leave with these writhing, wiggling, and giggling brats, but she desperately wanted to get away from their mother.

"Ron, can I talk to you alone for a second?"

Ron shook his head. "No, Sabrina. I tolerated it when you brought the man you cheated on me with to live under the same roof as my children. There is nothing to talk about today. How long will it take to get them ready?"

"About an hour. I have to comb their hair. Would you like to come inside? My husband isn't home."

Ron looked at Kimberly, and she rolled her eyes so hard she thought she strained them. No way she wanted to stay at this heffa's house while she combed these kids' hair. They both looked like they'd been electrocuted, so it was going to be a huge job.

"Uh . . ." Ron said.

"It's fine, Ron. I don't mind," Kimberly said.

"We'll be back in an hour, Sabrina. Please have them ready."

As soon as they were back in Ron's car, he started talking.

"That didn't happen how I planned it."

"Damn, Ron. You could've given me a heads-up that I was going to meet your ex-wife today."

"Who cares about her?" Ron said. "I brought you here to meet the twins."

"Yeah."

"Are you okay? This wasn't such a good idea, huh?"

Kimberly chuckled. "This was a horrible idea. I see where your son gets it. Y'all plan the worst dates."

"We're pretty pitiful."

"Are all the girls twins?"

"The second and third best things that have ever happened to me. The first was Shawn."

"Do you get along with Sabrina?"

Ron let out a long sigh. "I wish we got along better. It's hard, though. She's got her new husband in there with my daughters.

"I hate it," Ron continued. "I used to worry that he wanted to be with her because of the girls. You know, single mothers get stalked by predators."

"Does he give you that vibe? Because I can help you get custody."

"He doesn't give me that vibe. The girls love him and he's a nice guy."

"Oh, okay."

"You'd be okay with me having custody of them?"

"I guess. I don't know if I'm good with little girls, to be honest. My brother has boys. I just buy them trucks and blocks. They're easy."

"I think you'd be great with them. You want coffee? Tea?"

"Coffee is good."

"We probably could get a three-course meal. It's going to take her all day to comb their hair."

"She needs some Curlpop."

"We'll ship her a whole case of it. She'll be your best customer."

"Maybe she'll tell the rest of her black men–loving friends so they can buy it for their daughters."

Ron's smile faded and was replaced with a frown.

"What's wrong?" Kimberly asked.

"I hope you can try to get over this thing you have about white women."

"My knee-jerk reaction is to cuss you out."

"You are a great woman, Kimberly. You're smart, you're beautiful, and you're about to be rich."

"I am."

"But this is an ugly side of you. Every white woman isn't the same, and every interracial relationship isn't a fetish. There was a time when I loved Sabrina, and she's not a bad person. She's the mother of my children."

Kimberly took a deep breath. She hated when black men tried to lecture black women on how to deal with the pain of being abandoned by their asses. Seeing *her* with Ron's children was a reality slap in the face. Especially when Kimberly was probably too old to push out her own set of twins.

She looked down at the bracelet on her wrist. Twenty years Ron had missed. Twenty years he could've shared with her. He'd had two wives, and two divorces. Now two baby mothers.

And he had the nerve to lecture Kimberly about her baggage?

"Listen, Ron. There's a whole lot to unpack if you want to really understand how I feel about this. To tell you the truth, my problem isn't really with white women, it's with black men who hold them up on a pedestal. But since I can't help but still love y'all, I take it out on them."

"You shouldn't be mad at black men, either. People can't help who they're attracted to."

"And that's where we will have to disagree. Attraction might be primal, but love and marriage are choices. You chose her, just like you could've chosen any other black woman. You could've chosen me."

"I choose you."

Ron had cut Kimberly off midrant. She was about to go into act two of her tirade where she talked about the economic crippling of the black community when black men refused to marry black women but chose women of some other background. And how when they left those non-black women as widows (because they almost always died first), whatever wealth they had accumulated flowed away from the black community even if they had children.

But she couldn't continue. Ron had chosen her on this day. He hadn't thrown her a bone or a consolation prize. He'd chosen her.

"And to be honest, if I'd come back to Atlanta, I would've chosen you sooner. I guess . . . I thought someone else had found you, and I'd lost my chance after I graduated."

"I'm glad you found your way home."

Ron smiled. "Back home to the sistas?"

"No. Back home to me."

Even as Kimberly said the words, she couldn't be sure. Two biracial children and their mother seemed a bridge too far. But she loved Ron as much as she'd loved him in college, and she would give anything to have his love for the rest of her life.

Chapter 38

Hahna was anxious for Kimberly to arrive for happy hour. She was supposed to be picking up the final run of show for her Curlpop launch party, but Hahna just wanted to talk to her girlfriend. She needed a sanity check, or an insanity check—either one could be accurate, depending on how one looked at the situation.

Hahna was on her second drink when Kimberly finally arrived. She looked just as stressed as Hahna felt.

"Girl, I'm so sorry I'm late," Kimberly said as she slid into the booth. "I got home from the office and tried to take a damn power nap. Woke up four hours later."

Kimberly looked like she'd jumped straight up from a nap. Her curls were all over her head, but still were somehow defined and flawless. Her hair products were the bomb.

"Were you at the Curlpop office or the law office?" Hahna asked.

"You know I'm still closing out some cases."

Hahna lifted her eyebrow. "You sure you're not opening new cases? You can let go, you know. Curlpop is really taking off."

"I know, I know, but it's just that . . . so many years I needed to rely on my steady check while I was mixing up potions in the garage and whatnot. It's just hard to cut that umbilical cord."

"But you can't give them both one hundred percent. Give it to Curlpop."

"You're right."

"You *know* I'm right. I went through the same thing when I left corporate. You just have to let go."

"Let me see this run of show for the launch party. Maybe it'll feel real once we do this."

Hahna pushed the clipboard across the table. "It will feel real, but even more so when you see it on the shelves of the stores. That is going to be what does it."

"And then all the negative reviews flow in, and the homegirls and sorors who I thought had my back start hating on me because of my success. And all the men who want me for my money."

"Girl, what? You cannot be worried about all that, and you got a man anyway. Big Ron doesn't want you for your money."

Kimberly rolled her eyes. "Girl."

"Oh no. What? I was about to tell you about Sam, and you talking 'bout *girl.*"

Kimberly shook her head and chuckled. "You go first."

"I think I'm breaking up with Sam."

"You just said he was your soul mate."

"And that is why this is tragic, because I truly believe he is."

"Then why are you breaking up with him, Hahna? That doesn't make sense. It ain't like soul mates are just running around at the ready."

Kimberly waved down the waitress. She walked straight over with a huge smile on her face. She was overly friendly, but Hahna forgave her for it. She needed to see a smiling face tonight.

"I need something with caffeine in it," Kimberly said. "Let me try a double shot of Tito's with Red Bull."

Hahna made a disgusted face. "I'll have another old-fashioned," she said.

"Don't turn your nose up at my drink," Kimberly said, "while you're over there drinking old man bourbon."

"Bourbon is sophisticated."

"Mmm-hmm. You're a liquor snob."

Hahna's eyes dropped to the table. "Sam thinks I'm an everything snob."

"But does he? Or does he just refuse to do the same things you do?"

"What, like earn a paycheck?"

"I thought he was a writer?" Kimberly said. "I assume there is a check associated with that."

"Not when you turn down book deals."

"What?"

"Yes, girl. This is why I'm breaking up with him. I'm okay with a modest income, but this fool doesn't want to have an income at all."

"Damn."

"Right? I can't deal with it. I didn't mind him making less than me."

"But he has savings, right?"

"He says he does, but he doesn't care about wealth. I do."

"It could be worse," Kimberly said.

"What's worse than a man who doesn't care about being broke?"

Kimberly pressed her lips together as her nostrils flared. "A man who has twins with a white baby mama."

Hahna was confused for a second, and then she groaned. "Damn, damn, damn, Ron!"

"Girl, right. He's got twin girls with that heffa he married. What the hell am I supposed to do with that?"

"I know what I would do, but what are *you* gonna do?"

"I have no idea. I was thinking about forever with him, but that means raising those two girls. Being their stepmother. Co-parenting with Becky."

"Is that her name?"

"Naw. It's Sabrina, but you know what I mean."

Hahna inhaled deeply and exhaled. "So, what are we gonna do?"

"Hell if I know. Where's Twila, anyway? She's the one who got us into this mess with her challenge."

"She's been below the radar. I haven't heard anything about the Instagram model since the last time we all talked," Hahna said.

"This isn't good. I don't like it when she goes dark."

"Right."

Twila had gone silent on them before. After she'd met a man who'd stalked her and assaulted her. He was the reason she had weapons hidden all over her home, and the reason she knew hand-to-hand combat and a dozen ways to kill a man.

"She's over all that, though. That was years ago," Kimberly said, reading Hahna's thoughts.

"I know she is, but whenever I don't hear from her, I think about it."

"Yeah, me too."

Hahna whipped her cell phone out of her purse. "I'm calling her ass."

"FaceTime her. Put her on speaker."

Twila picked up on the first ring. She was in full makeup, and her hair looked freshly styled.

"Heffa," Hahna said. "Where you been?"

"Yeah, heffa!" Kimberly echoed. "Why ain't nobody heard from your ass?"

Twila laughed. "Why y'all going in on me like this? I been working a lot."

"You don't look like you're about to go to work now," Hahna said. "You and Marcus going out?"

The right side of Twila's mouth twitched. "Nah. I'm solo tonight."

Hahna glanced up at Kimberly. "You want some company?" she asked.

"Nah. Y'all wouldn't like this club. Too many young people there."

Hahna and Kimberly locked eyes again. This wasn't good.

"Okay," Hahna said. "You and Marcus good?"

Her mouth twitched again. "Yeah, we good. For now. He's not my Prince Charming, though."

"Who cares about a fairy tale anyway?" Kimberly asked.

"I thought we were looking for happily ever after," Twila said. "I don't think I've found it yet."

"What if it isn't out there?" Hahna asked. "What if everyone we think is in a happy relationship is really feeling just like we are?"

"Wait, ya'll bugging out too?" Twila asked. "Never mind. Don't tell me right now. You gonna ruin my high."

Kimberly shook her head. "I thought I told you to say no to drugs."

"It's not drugs. Just weed," Twila said. "It's all good. I'm gonna call y'all tomorrow, okay?"

Hahna nodded. "Okay. Love you, girl."

Twila winked. "I know."

"Bye, heffa," Kimberly said, and she pressed the END button on Hahna's phone.

"She back going up to that spot," Hahna said. "I know she is."

"We don't know."

"Yes, we do."

Kimberly sighed. "I'm not going there until we know for sure. Plus, Abena and Kyle will watch out for her."

"They didn't watch out for her the last time. We had to go and pull her out of that dark, nasty room."

"I don't want to remember that," Kimberly said.

"Me either, but we have to, because we can't let her go back there."

"She promised never to go back to that part of their club again. I trust that she'll keep her promise."

"And if she doesn't?"

Kimberly sat back and folded her arms across her chest. "Then we'll go and get her again. Pull her out of a dark and nasty room. Again. 'Cause she's our sister."

"Word."

With Twila tumbling down a slippery slope from her past, Hahna's issues with Sam were secondary for the moment. She wondered if Kimberly felt the same way.

"The party plans look good," Kimberly said. "I'm looking forward to it. It's gonna be hot."

"Yes, it is."

"I'm blessed to have you two in my life," Kimberly said.

"Same."

Hahna felt uneasiness in her spirit, and she wasn't one who usually trusted harbingers of doom. But Twila's weirdness and all their relationship woes happening at the same time was a sign of something. She just didn't know what.

Chapter 39

Hahna looked at Sam's cell phone number as it flashed across her caller ID screen. She considered not answering. She was still in a funk about what might be happening with Twila, and she was still on the verge of breaking up with Sam. Conversation wasn't really on her mind.

But she answered anyway.

"Hi, Sam."

"Hey, babe. Are you home?" he asked.

She paused. Didn't know if she wanted to share her whereabouts. Was still musing about her friend and wondering if she'd made it home all right.

"Yes, I'm home," she finally said. "What are you doing?"

"Sitting outside in your driveway. Needing to see you."

She breathed in and out. Wondered if she'd be breaking up with him tonight or the next night.

"Come on. I'll open the door."

As soon as she laid eyes on him, Hahna realized she'd missed him even though it had only been a few days since their last conversation.

"Why is it still hot out there?" Hahna asked as a warm breeze washed across her face.

Sam squeezed her in a hug and kissed her neck. "Atlanta in June. You know."

"Yeah, I do."

"I brought food," Sam said. "Pho."

"I've been having a taste for this. Where'd you get it?" Hahna asked.

"My kitchen. I made it."

"Of course you did."

"Nothing against the restaurants, but I prefer to let my broth simmer all day long, to let the flavors emerge and blend."

Hahna laughed. "Why do I even do this with you and food?"

"I don't know why. You know I'm a chef. I was raised by a chef."

"You are. You should have your own cooking show and call it *The Chocolate Chef*. It'd be a hit."

It was a joke, but Sam closed his mouth slowly. It wasn't like she meant to steer the conversation to ways he could make money. It was just the way she was wired.

"Babe, I wanna share something with you," Sam said. "Come sit down with me."

Hahna followed him, wondering if he was going to be the one to break things off. Hahna wouldn't be surprised. Sam was intuitive. He had to know she was feeling some kinda way.

She sat down next to Sam on the couch, and he rubbed her thigh. She looked at him and smiled. No matter what, he was delicious.

"I took the book deal, babe," Sam said. "They only offered me six thousand per book on a two-book deal."

"That's not too bad."

"If I made six thousand dollars in a year on any other job, would it be enough?" Sam asked.

Five hundred dollars a month wasn't enough for anything. Not even groceries. Sam knew this and what her answer would be.

"No."

"Are you glad I took the deal?"

She was, but not as happy as she thought she'd be.

"Are you happy you took it? I think that's the most important part."

"I am. You're right. Not about everything, but you are about this."

"How so?" Hahna asked.

"This is what I've wanted with my books. Maybe I'm scared I won't be successful, or that I'll be too successful and that I'll change."

"You won't."

"Money changes people."

Hahna scoffed. "So does *not* having money. It makes people hard and anxious and prisoners. Poverty is a prison."

Sam nodded. "I signed it, and I'm glad I did."

"I'm happy for you, babe. I can't wait to help you promote your books."

"You're not breaking up with me now?" Sam asked.

"Who said I ever was?"

"I felt that you were on the verge of it. You'd gotten a little distant."

"I was just . . . evaluating things."

Sam grinned. "I know you were. I could tell."

"Did you take the book deal because of what I thought? Because I was evaluating?"

Sam shook his head. "I would never do that. I'd never make a decision for me based on anything you or anyone else thought. I took it because you were right."

Sam smelled so good to Hahna. His scent did something to her. She knew it was their chemistry—it was perfect.

"You wanna celebrate?"

Maybe Sam could tell by the way her voice lowered a half an octave, or by how she'd started licking her lips. Maybe it was in the way Hahna was absentmindedly stroking Sam's middle back.

"How you wanna celebrate?"

Sam tilted her chin upward and covered her lips with his. His breath was sweet, and his lips tasted of mint. His kiss had dizzying effects.

"I love you, babe," Sam said as he kissed the small of her throat. "You gonna let me make love to you?"

Hahna answered him with a kiss.

Chapter 40

Kimberly narrowed her eyes at the image on her phone. She was scrolling through Instagram while she stretched across her king-sized bed, wishing Big Ron was in town. She stopped when she saw a photo of Marcus. At first, she thought it wasn't him, but when she looked closer she saw that it was him without his low haircut. In this picture, Marcus's hair was curly and fluffed around her head. She couldn't decipher what the caption meant, so she called her internet language expert.

"Hey, Kim."

"Hi, Hahna. I need to ask you a question really quick."

"What's up?"

"What does MCM mean?"

"Depends on the context. Is it fashion?"

"No. It's an Instagram post."

"Oh, that means Man Crush Monday."

"I see."

So, a young lady named Cherry4d on Instagram thought Marcus was her Man Crush Monday. The rest of the post was just hearts and eggplants and peaches. Kimberly didn't need Hahna to tell her what those meant. They had sexual meanings.

"Why? What are you looking at?" Hahna asked with her nosy self.

"Just a post that I see as I scroll. I was just curious."

"Who is the man crush? Is it a celebrity or someone I know?"

"Damn, you're nosy."

"Well it must be halfway important because you called to ask me instead of Googling it. You could've very easily Googled MCM and gotten the correct meaning of the acronym."

"Another question. Do I see people's posts who aren't my friends?"

"Are you on your timeline or the explore page?"

"I think my timeline."

"Well, you have to had followed the person at some point. That's the only way they would come up in your timeline. Click the girl's profile page."

"What makes you think it's a girl?"

"Cause you said you're looking at a man crush post."

"It could be a man having a crush."

"True. So, look at the person's profile page. Do you know him or *her*?"

"You put the emphasis on her," Kimberly said.

"I know. What's her name? Is it some white woman crushing on Big Ron?"

If only it was Ron, this would be easier. Seeing a photo of her own man on someone else's timeline was a pretty clear course of action. It meant phone calls and maybe even drive-bys to see if Ron was doing what he'd said he'd been doing.

Someone else's man posed questions. Should she say anything? Maybe Twila already knew, and the question would come across as irritating and petty. Maybe she didn't want to know. That was always a strange situation, but Kimberly knew there were times when people didn't want to know.

"It's not Ron," Kimberly said, deciding to share if for no other reason than having another person burdened with the information. "It's Marcus. He's on some other woman's wall as her man crush."

"Well, let's not be hasty. You know Marcus has an internet following. Maybe she's just a fan."

Kimberly hadn't gotten the impression that Marcus had a big following, but Hahna was right; maybe it was just one of his fans.

"Scroll through her pictures. Are there any more of Marcus?"

Kimberly started scrolling. Every five or six photos, there was a picture of Marcus. The girl looked familiar in the shots where she posed with Marcus, but she couldn't quite place her.

"There are a bunch of him. And I think I know the girl, but I don't know where I know her from."

"What is the screen name?"

Kimberly spelled it for Hahna.

"Hold on while I look up her profile."

There was no going back now. Hahna was on the case. Kimberly almost regretted telling her, because there was no choosing inaction now. She was going to force a revelation.

"I know where you know her from," Hahna said. "She's in that undergraduate chapter of Gamma Phi Gamma that we mentored over at Clark Atlanta."

"She's a college student?"

"Yep. So, Marcus has a college girlfriend."

"Are you going to tell Twila?" Kimberly asked.

"Um, no! This was your discovery, Kim. I don't have anything to do with this."

"Do you think she'll be mad? She doesn't seem to be all that into this guy."

Hahna clicked her tongue against her teeth. "Girl. This is I-know-a-dozen-ways-to-kill-a-man Twila. This is I-got-guns-and-I-know-how-to-use-them Twila. You already know."

"You're right. She's gonna be mad. That guy is living in her home, though."

"In the guest room," Hahna said.

"But making conjugal visits to her bedroom."

"As long as Marcus doesn't put his hands on Twila, he should be safe," Hahna said. "Or better, Twila will be safe from a felony. I don't care about him."

Kimberly shook her head and looked at the other pictures on Cherry4d's profile. Then, she noticed a detail that she hadn't seen before.

"Oh, shit," Kimberly said.

"Yeah, I know," Hahna said.

"No! Look at that first couple shot. Look at the girl's ankle."

"Her ankle? Let me try to blow it up."

In the photo Cherry4d was wearing Twila's Gamma Phi Gamma ankle bracelet. Kimberly knew that it was Twila's, because when they crossed as a tribute to their sisterhood, Kimberly, Twila, and Hahna had gotten matching ankle bracelets. The GPG was diamond encrusted and surrounded by pink and blue stones—their sorority colors. The bracelets were custom-made—and they'd spent a grip on them.

"Oh no, he didn't," Hahna said.

"He did. Instathot gave his girlfriend Twila's ankle bracelet."

Hahna groaned. "This is not good. I say we go to Twila's when she's at work, get him to pack his stuff and get out."

"Well, we have to get Twila's bracelet back too! That ho has no right to be rocking that," Kimberly said. "We can't do that if we just put Marcus out."

"Do we need to confront the girl too?" Hahna asked. "This is going to get messy."

"Girl, I don't have time for this. I have a product launch. Plus, what if homeboy starts tripping on us?"

"You're right. We need to bring Big Ron with us. Is he in town?"

"He will be tomorrow."

"Well, we go tomorrow, then."

Kimberly's upper lip trembled with irritation. They weren't in college anymore. Nowhere near college-aged, but they were about to be up to college shenanigans.

"You sure it wouldn't just be easier to tell her?" Kimberly asked.

."We have to have each other's backs," Hahna said. "We can't let her catch a case behind this dude."

Kimberly hated when Hahna was right, but there were no lies in what she'd said. They wouldn't—couldn't—allow their sister to be negatively impacted by this mess. If they intervened now, they'd be able to stop Twila from doing something she'd regret.

And if Big Ron had gotten into town that day instead of the next, their plan would've worked.

Chapter 41

Twila stared at her gynecologist, Dr. Sydney Baker, in disbelief. But really, she'd known from the first time her urine burned on the way out. Marcus had given her something—even though he claimed he had a clean bill of health.

"Sydney, just tell me what it is," Twila insisted.

Sydney touched Twila's arm and gave it a gentle squeeze. "Relax. It's just chlamydia."

"*Just* chlamydia?"

"I mean, as far as sexually transmitted infections go, this isn't all that serious. You take some antibiotics and you're good."

Sydney was Twila's friend in addition to being her doctor, but that didn't stop Twila from being embarrassed.

"I can't believe I got burned like I'm in high school."

"Girl," Sydney said, "please know that you are not the only woman in her forties to come into my office with an infection."

"Well, I can't speak for them, but I will say I'm too old for this shit."

"Aren't you glad you got tested?" Sydney asked.

"Yeah, I am, but my life just became way more complicated than it needed to be."

"Are you still with the guy? If so, you'll both need to take antibiotics."

"I don't care whether he takes them or not, because I'm not sleeping with him again."

"Maybe he didn't know he had it," Sydney said. "Men don't always have symptoms."

"He's got me out here looking like I'm an afterschool special."

"Girl, you are hilarious. He doesn't have you looking any kind of way."

Twila hadn't told Sydney or either of her best friends that she'd been terrified when she walked into the doctor's office with a hot crotch. What if Marcus had given her something worse?

"Whether he knew or not, I'm done with this. I mean, it's bad enough he's broke."

"He's broke?"

"Yeah. An aspiring singing artist."

"Is he any good?" Sydney asked. "You know, my brother-in-law is Rod Knight."

"That's right. He *is* good, but I'm not recommending him or cashing in any of my connections to hook him up."

"Okay, well, if you change your mind, I will send any demos to Rod."

"I appreciate you."

"Now, let's get you this prescription, so you can feel better."

"Thank you."

Twila got her prescription, paid her copays, and said good-bye to her friend, but in the back of her mind she was strategizing on how she was going to remove Marcus from her house. Because he *had* to go.

Twila couldn't believe this was happening to her—a grown woman. When Marcus had said he was disease free, she'd believed him. She'd also required that he wore condoms. So, had he taken one off? Had a condom broken?

"You did a pregnancy test too, right?"

"Yes, you're good. Not pregnant."

Sydney knew Twila well. For some "not pregnant" resulted in immediate anxiety. The opposite was true for Twila. And she especially didn't want to be pregnant by a man who would give her an infection.

Twila sighed. "I'll tell his ass when I get home from work. Right before I make him pack his shit."

"You're going to work? You should cancel your appointments for today and go get some rest. This is a lot for you."

"This is a lot," Twila agreed. "It's too much. This is first-year-at-college stuff."

"Wait until you get to the nursing home. One of the highest rates of sexually transmitted infections is in our senior population."

"Chil', Grandma and Grandpa over there getting fire crotch?"

Sydney shook her head. "Yes, girl. They are getting it in. And they're usually not even upset when I tell them."

"They're all like you only live once, huh?"

"Yep. I'm gonna leave you alone so you can get dressed. I'll leave your prescriptions at the desk up front."

"Thanks, Syd."

"Of course. Don't feel bad, Twila. It happens to the best of us."

Twila nodded and her shoulders slumped. "Especially when we're dealing with the worst of them."

Sydney left the examining room, and Twila got dressed. It irritated her when she felt the tears on her face. She snatched a tissue from the counter and dabbed her eyes dry. Why the hell was she crying?

This whole sugar mama thing had been her idea, and she'd allowed herself to break the rules. All of them. Marcus was too young, too broke, too clingy, too bossy, and too needy. You can't add anything to that and still be good. Now he was too diseased on top of it all. Shit, the only thing Marcus had going for him was his looks. His singing wasn't even an asset, because he wasn't making any money from it.

There was another rule Twila hadn't broken yet, though. It was one that was so deeply ingrained in her psyche that she called it a tragic flaw. She had a problem letting go when she'd started fixing a man. Even when she was ready to throw the entire relationship away, she always found something to make her stay a little longer. This time it was sex, but she couldn't imagine Marcus touching her again. The thought of him coming near her made her woman parts chafe like they were lined with sandpaper.

Even though she'd invested her time, Marcus had to go.

Twila just hoped that he'd go easy. She wasn't in the mood to shoot anybody.

Chapter 42

Kimberly was anxious as Ron drove her and Hahna over to Twila's condo. He'd gotten in town a day later than expected. That was a whole other day for Twila to find out about Marcus before they had a chance to convince him to leave and save his life.

"I can't believe y'all got me doing this, like we are still in college," Big Ron fussed. "Why can't we just call the police?"

Kimberly looked in the back seat at Hahna, who just shrugged. This got on Kimberly's nerves. Why couldn't she come up with something? It was half her idea anyway.

"If we call the police, he's not going to want to leave willingly," Kimberly said. "We're trying to make this a peaceful exit."

"So, bringing me as the muscle is going to work?" Ron asked.

Hahna laughed. "You're kinda thin, Ron. We just didn't want to go without a man."

"Doesn't matter if I'm thin. I'm scrappy."

"I hope no scrapping occurs, though," Kimberly said. "When we present our evidence, he'll go peacefully."

"What's this evidence, again? Instagram photos? How do you know this girl wasn't around before Twila?" Ron asked.

"You sound like you're on his side," Hahna said.

"I'm not. I just want to know. If I'm going over there putting a man out of where he lives, it better be for a damn good reason."

"The girl could've been before Twila, but she's happening during his thing with Twila too, because he gave her Twila's Gamma Phi Gamma ankle bracelet."

"She's a soror?" Ron asked.

"Yeah, but I doubt she knows what's going on," Kimberly said. "She has no idea she's the side chick. She's posting about her man online like everything's fine and dandy."

"What if she isn't?" Hahna asked.

"What if she isn't what?"

"The side chick," Hahna said. "Maybe that's Twila's spot."

Kimberly closed her eyes and frowned. If this was true—if Marcus was cheating on his girlfriend with Twila—this would make things worse.

"Let's just hurry and get there," Kimberly said. "We've got to have Marcus packed and gone by the time Twila gets home from the office."

"What time does she get off today?" Ron asked. "In case this takes longer than we want."

"It depends," Hahna said. "She said her last appointment is at four. She's a dentist, though. She could be doing a procedure that takes fifteen minutes or one that takes two hours."

"Let's hope for two hours. We need all the time we can get," Kimberly said.

"Is he home? Does he have a car so we'll know he's home when we get there?"

Kimberly shook her head. "No car. No job. Where the hell is he at if not here?"

"At his side chick's house," Ron said. "What are y'all gonna do if he isn't home? Seems like this whole plan hinges on that."

"It does, and if he's not home, then we'll just make up another plan, Ron," Kimberly said. "Don't be a hater."

"I'm not a hater. I just came to Atlanta to spend time with my woman, and y'all got me evicting Twila's boy toy."

Kimberly couldn't help but smile at the words "my woman." No one had ever referred to her this way before. She considered herself a feminist, but the thought of being cherished by a man made her tummy flutter.

"And Twila has appointments this morning, right?" Kimberly asked. "You confirmed that, Hahna?"

"Yep. I invited her for a morning coffee to talk about your Curlpop launch party. She said she had appointments all morning."

Kimberly gave a satisfied head nod. "See. I told you this was perfect. Marcus will be gone before she gets home."

"If he leaves," Ron said.

"He'll leave. Once he knows that we're on to him, he'll know that Twila will be putting him out soon, anyway."

"Didn't you tell me he doesn't have a place to live?" Ron asked. "Y'all are underestimating how desperate a man can be when he doesn't have a place to lay his head."

"We have evidence, though," Hahna said. "He can't possibly think he can stay with Twila after what we show him."

Ron chuckled and shook his head. "You all are also underestimating the stupidity of a man. I promise he's more stupid than you think."

Both Hahna and Kimberly's phones chirped at the same time. It was a text from Twila.

This motherfucker gave me chlamydia. I'm about to go and put him the fuck outta my house.

Kimberly gasped, and Hahna groaned. This would not be pretty or end well.

"Ron," Kimberly said.

"Yes?"

"I need you to hurry."

Chapter 43

They were too late.

Hahna jumped out of Ron's car first when she saw Twila's car in the driveway of her town house. Twila had left the car door open when she'd exited, and that scared the hell out of Hahna. No way she'd leave the door open if she wasn't on the edge of violence.

Hahna didn't wait for Kimberly or Ron, although later she thought that maybe she should have. She could only think of saving Twila from herself, and from catching a felony case. She gave no cares about what happened to that cheating Marcus.

Hahna pushed open the unlocked door. Another horrible sign. Twila didn't leave doors open or unlocked. She was hyperaware when it came to security after her home had been burglarized. Her hyperawareness was the same reason that she had weapons all over the house.

Hahna shuddered. *She had weapons all over the house.*

Twila's voice was the first thing Hahna heard.

"You must think I'm stupid as hell out here," Twila said.

Her voice was too calm to be confronting a man who'd given her a disease.

Hahna rushed toward the sound of the voices. It wasn't coming from Twila's master bedroom. That's right. Twila made her boy toy sleep in her guest bedroom. This was something else Hahna would think about later. If your man is sleeping in the guest bedroom, is he really your man, or just a dildo with a heartbeat?

The door to the bedroom was open, and Twila stood in the doorway. Twila's body trembled, but it wasn't out of fear. It was rage.

"Twila honey," Hahna said.

Twila spun around. "Hahna? You're here?"

"Of course. Kimberly and Big Ron are here too. It's going to be okay."

"No. No, it isn't. He's brought the diseased coochie up in my house."

Hahna's jaw dropped as Twila pointed into the bedroom. The girl from Instagram—Cherry4D—scrambled from the bed naked. She tried to gather her clothes quickly, but they were spread across the room.

Marcus was brave. He stepped out of the bed and pulled on his underwear (*was that a python, baby arm, shit*), never breaking eye contact with Twila.

"Twila, don't flip out," he said. "You know we're not together like that."

Twila rocked back and forth, shifting her weight from one leg to the other. Her eyes darted to several locations in the room. Hahna thought that might be where she'd hidden a gun or a knife.

Still not breaking eye contact, Marcus kept talking. "We're both doing our own thing, right? You go to that club Phenom and I do my thing."

"You still go there?" Hahna asked. "I thought you said you'd never go back there after what happened."

Twila didn't reply to either of them. She kept her glare trained on Marcus, and she stayed blocking the doorway. The only way out was past Twila or out the second-story window.

Then, Twila tilted her head to one side and stared at
Cherry4D.

"Are you wearing my ankle bracelet?" Twila asked. Then to
Marcus, "You let this ho wear my jewelry?"

Marcus looked genuinely confused. Maybe he hadn't given it
to her; maybe Cherry4D had stolen it.

Cherry4D put both hands up. "Whoa. I didn't know who
Marcus was cheating on me with. If I had known it was you,
soror, I would've never touched it."

Twila had closed her eyes when Cherry4D said *soror*, and she
hadn't reopened them.

Ron and Kimberly's slow behinds finally made it inside and
upstairs to the second floor of Twila's town house. Hahna
grabbed Ron's arm and pulled him to the room, and she gently
pushed Twila out of the doorway.

"Let Ron deal with him honey," Hahna said. "It's going to be
okay."

"It's not going to be okay. We said we would break the rules.
We said we would give the next guy a chance. I gave *this* motherfucker a chance, and he gave me chlamydia."

Cherry4D glared over at Marcus. "You have chlamydia?"

"And apparently so do you, ho," Twila said. "You need to
take my motherfucking bracelet off before I beat the brakes
off you."

"Yes, soror, I'm sorry."

"You are not my soror. You are a ho who sleeps with other
people's men, in other people's houses, and steals other people's jewelry. You're nothing to me."

Cherry4D set the bracelet down on the nightstand.

"Come on, playa," Ron said. "Get your clothes and the rest of
your stuff . . ."

"He ain't got no other stuff," Twila said.

"Well, get your clothes, and go," Ron said. "Don't make me
have to remove you. That won't go well."

Marcus sneered at Ron. "No disrespect, man, but this ain't
got shit to do with you. This is between me and Twila."

"And the ho," Twila said. "Don't forget the ho. We share everything, shit. Bacteria, pathogens, all that."

"This has everything to do with me," Ron said. "Twila is my sister. I'm not going to let you stay here."

Hahna glanced back at Kimberly and shook her head. Kim beamed with pride at her man, who hadn't actually done anything yet except sell wolf tickets. From the way Marcus was sizing Ron up, Hahna hoped Ron had a little action to back up his words.

"Bruh," Ron continued, "I'm going to give you just this one chance to get your things and go. Take your girl with you, and nobody has to get hurt."

"You threatening me, old man?"

Ron closed his eyes. A vein throbbed near his temple. Hahna remembered seeing him fight before. On campus, his senior year. A bunch of guys who didn't even attend Morehouse had jumped one of his fraternity brothers, and Ron had been the first to jump into the melee. He was young back then, though. Probably wasn't thinking about felonies or the ability to get gainful employment.

"He's not worth it, Ron," Kimberly said.

Ron moved so quickly that it seemed like someone had fast-forwarded time while Hahna blinked. One moment, Ron was standing next to Kimberly breathing deeply with the vein throbbing. In the next moment, he was on Marcus with one arm around Marcus's neck squeezing. Ron's other arm was looped under Marcus's arm making that arm go up vertically into the air.

Hahna gasped when she realized that Ron was choking Marcus.

"Ron, don't kill him!" Hahna screamed.

Ron gave a tight head shake, and Kimberly elbowed Hahna in the ribs. Marcus struggled and struggled but couldn't get free. In less than a minute, his unconscious body hung limp against Ron. Cherry4D sobbed with the sheet from Twila's guest room bed wrapped around her body. At least Marcus had enough sense not to take her in Twila's bedroom.

"Where you want this trash?" Ron asked.

"Outside. And take his ho with you," Twila said.

Ron dragged Marcus, and Cherry4D scooted over to the door, still wrapped in the sheet.

"Bitch, if you don't put my thousand-thread-count sheet down, and get out, I'll strangle you myself," Twila said. "Get your clothes on. Ron is gone. We got the same thing you got, ho."

Hahna was still concerned. The fact that Cherry4D wasn't already gone made her still a problem. Cherry4D was taking her time getting dressed, but Twila didn't have the same restraint as Ron did. This still had the potential to go left.

"Girl, hurry up before you get hurt," Hahna said. "You're putting your clothes on like you have time. You don't."

Cherry4D took Hahna's advice and just grabbed her shoes without trying to put them on correctly. She ran from Twila's condo barefoot and looking crazy. Only then did Twila's shoulders slump.

"You okay?" Kimberly asked.

"Hell naw," Twila said. "I have chlamydia and my boyfriend is a cheater. Looks like some of the dating rules needed to stay in place."

Hahna and Kimberly both went to Twila and encircled her with hugs and sister love. Hahna felt badly that she and Kimberly had found good things while Twila languished with more heartbreak.

"I should've known, right?" Twila asked. "He was an Instagram model, for crying out loud. How could I not know?"

"Sometimes our brain knows things, but our heart does something different," Hahna said. "It's okay that you trusted your heart. You'll be smarter next time."

"My *heart* is not what led me to Marcus," Twila said. She laughed, and Hahna felt herself relax. Twila was mad as hell, but she wasn't broken.

"Oh, it was that treacherous little Ms. Kitty, huh?" Kimberly said. "Well, now her ass is on antibiotics."

"Right," Twila said. "Next time, I'm gonna rein her ass in."

"Okay! Ms. Kitty isn't smart," Kimberly said. "And sometimes she a ho."

Ron came back inside. He was drenched in sweat, huffing and puffing.

"One of y'all could've helped me," Ron said. "That dude is solid muscle. I think I pulled something dragging him out."

Kimberly left Twila and went to Ron. She hugged him and kissed his neck. Seeing them together made Hahna's heart feel glad. Everyone had known when they were in college that they belonged together. No one could understand why they weren't.

"I'm too old for this shit," Ron said.

"You're not, though," Kimberly said. "You handled Marcus."

"He didn't know what hit him. You went old-school wrestling on him," Hahna said.

Twila stared at her tainted sheet lying on the floor. Hahna went and scooped it up and ripped the other from the bed.

"Don't worry. I got this," Hahna said.

Twila smiled. "I don't deserve y'all."

"You don't," Kimberly said, "but you're stuck with us anyway."

Twila scrunched her nose into a frown. "Wait a minute. You three were on your way here already. Did you *know* about Marcus?"

Hahna exchanged a glance with Kimberly. Kimberly had procured the intel, so Hahna was willing her to speak up about it.

"All I saw was a Man Crush Monday post on the girl's page. We were coming to interrogate Marcus and possibly put him out," Kimberly explained.

"It's Wednesday, though. Did you see the post on Monday?" Twila asked. "Two whole days ago?"

Kimberly shared another glance with Hahna. It was a *help me* glance, but Hahna couldn't think of anything to offer in the way of help.

"We did see the post on Monday," Hahna said. "But we had to wait for Ron to be in town before we could execute."

"If we had known he was a disease carrier, we would've been over here," Kimberly added. "With his trifling ass."

"I need to sit," Twila said. "Everything in this room is tainted."

Twila pushed past Hahna, who was still holding the nasty sheets, and walked down the hallway and into her bedroom. When the door slammed, Hahna knew she was done talking to them.

"Should y'all go after her?" Ron said. "Is she okay?"

"She will be. She's just mad mostly," Kimberly said. "She's probably in her room telling herself all the reasons she didn't kill Marcus."

"You think we should stay over?" Hahna asked. "Marcus didn't look like he wanted to leave."

"He didn't," Ron said.

"Well, what if he comes back then?" Hahna asked.

"Guess you're on guard duty," Ron said. "Kimberly and I have a date."

"That's how it is, Kim? You just ditch me and your troubled friend to go out on a date?"

"Pretty much. Y'all done already wore my man out before I had the chance to," Kimberly said.

"Ewww . . . y'all nasty," Hahna said. "Just go. Don't get knocked up."

Kimberly, who had already been pulling Ron toward the door, stopped and looked back at Hahna. The look on her face made Hahna want to gobble back her words. Ron had three children with other women. Hahna wondered if he wanted to have one with Kimberly, or if she'd given up on her desire to become a mother.

Hahna wanted to apologize for her joke. Neither she nor Kimberly were laughing anymore.

"We're good," Kimberly said. "Worry about yourself."

As Kimberly and Ron left the bedroom, Hahna was worried. But not just about herself. She was worried about her sisters too. She couldn't help it.

Kimberly seemed okay with his situation now. She had Ron on her arm, and that's all that seemed to matter. Hahna felt the same way when she was with Sam.

But Twila's drama had broken the spell. Had throwing the rules away provided liberation, or had they shifted their own destinies? Hahna prayed that Twila would be all right and find the love she needed.

Chapter 44

Hahna was back in the office, although she hadn't wanted to leave Twila. She'd gone home in the middle of the night and cuddled with Sam. She'd needed to feel his body next to her for reassurance.

As she sat at her desk, preparing for the day, Hahna smiled as she read a note she'd just found from Sam, tucked away in her lunch bag with the leftovers he'd packed for her.

If you're reading this, then I'm probably—no, definitely—already missing you.

In a little over two months, their bond had deepened quicker than any bond she'd had with any other man. Torian and his cancer alibi were a distant memory. Before she'd met Sam, the thought of Torian was enough to bring her to tears.

Hahna was still smiling when Corden knocked on her office door for their two o'clock status meeting. She wasn't necessarily in the mood to think about work. She'd rather let her thoughts linger with Sam, and what she wanted to do with him when she saw him later. She wished she could will time to speed forward until the moment that she was in his arms again.

But the money wouldn't make itself.

"Come in, Corden."

The grim expression on Corden's face irritated Hahna, only

because she knew Corden was bringing her bad news. She didn't want anything to disturb her afternoon fantasies.

Corden sat and placed his notepad on Hahna's desk. His lips were pressed into a tight line, and his forehead creased in concentration.

"What is it?" Hahna asked. She didn't feel like dragging the story out of him. "Is it Aliyah? What did she do?"

"No. Not Aliyah. It's Brexton's data."

Hahna gave a slow blink. This wasn't Corden's weekly "fire Aliyah" rant. This was something else.

"What's wrong with Brexton's data?"

"There are big chunks of time where the financial reporting is missing or incomplete. Also, some of it is just plain inaccurate."

"You're trying to build out a dashboard?"

"Yeah. A financial dashboard."

"Are you sure it's the data? Did we corrupt something when we imported it?"

Corden shook his head. "I thought that too at first, because I let Aliyah do the import. But that wasn't it at all. The import was fine. I went back to the raw data to verify."

"Did you talk to Josiah about it? Maybe he has some intel."

"I wanted to talk to you first. I've never seen a company as big as Brexton's have this sort of data integrity issue."

"Does everything else look okay?"

"Yes, we were able to import all the data from their customer relationship management system. There's a lot of data there that should be more secure, so we're fixing that as we build out the dashboards."

"What kind of data needs securing?"

"Some personally identifiable information like names attached to certain prescriptions."

"Really? I can't believe they've been this sloppy. That's very elementary to lock something like that down."

"Bingo," Corden said. "Which is why the messed-up financials are even more suspicious."

"You're right. I want you to get with Josiah and comb through the data for any more abnormalities. I'm going to call Hale. He should know that Shane might have done more damage than he knows about."

"Right. He might have even been laundering money. He had full access to everything."

Hahna sighed. "That's why Hale sent Josiah here to work with us on site. His trust is completely broken."

"Yep. But I'm ready for Josiah to get the hell out of our office space."

"What? Why?"

"He and Aliyah are hooking up—I know it."

Hahna eyes widened. "Here? In the office?"

"I think so, but I haven't caught them. They both just seem to disappear at the same time and reappear later."

Hahna chuckled. "Well, everyone is grown, and Aliyah is beautiful. I can see a single man wanting to get to know her better."

"Yeah, well, I'm not feeling it. She barely pays attention as it is. I don't need her getting some during the workday. That's not what we're paying her for."

"You're right."

"So, can you do something about her?"

"I'll take it under advisement."

Aliyah was a soror, a lovely Gamma lady, so Hahna wouldn't fire her unless she had no other choice. She would talk to her, though. Just to keep Corden's head from exploding.

"I'm going to call Hale now. Let me know how it goes with Josiah."

"I'm serious about Aliyah, Hahna. She's not a good look for us."

"And I was serious when I said I'd consider taking action. I'm listening, Corden. I just want to ponder a bit on how to handle it."

"Okay."

Corden stood to leave, although he didn't seem convinced that Hahna was going to do something about Aliyah.

As soon as the office door clicked shut, Hahna called Hale on her office speakerphone.

"It's Hahna, the data whisperer," Hale said. His voice echoed off the walls and high ceilings in Hahna's office.

"It is I. How are you, Hale?"

"I'm well. Finally starting to feel like this whole thing with Shane is going to blow over."

Hahna was glad that Hale wasn't on a video chat to see her *oh shit* face. Because she was about to burst his bubble.

"There may be a little bit more to clean up from Shane."

Hale groaned. "Oh, good lord. What now?"

"Corden found missing and incorrect financial data."

"What do we do about it?"

"We're still investigating, but we may need access to bank statements and other paper documents that can help us fill in the blanks."

"Oh, well, Josiah should be able to help you with that."

"Corden is working with him as we speak. I just wanted to fill you in."

Hale sighed. "Thank you, Hahna. I knew I was right to trust you. How are things going with that new boyfriend?"

Hahna laughed. "How did you know he was new?"

"He still had the new man smell to him. Wasn't completely awkward but didn't anticipate your movements like a seasoned boyfriend would've."

"I'm surprised you noticed that."

"I am very observant. I love to people-watch."

"Well, the new boyfriend is still here. The new boyfriend smell is wearing off a bit, I think. He's settling right on in there."

Hale gave a hearty laugh that filled her office space with his mirth.

"That's good. I hate to see a successful woman without a good man at her side. Too many men don't see the value in a gem like you."

"You're making me blush, Hale."

"Listen, if you hadn't brought him to Miami with you, I would've introduced you to some eligible bachelors here. If things don't work out, let me know. That option is still on the table."

"I appreciate you."

And she did, although she didn't think she'd need his match-making service. Sam was going to be there for the long haul. She could feel it.

"Well, I know you'll keep me posted on what Corden and Josiah find out. Jelena is standing here giving me the evil eye, because we have lunch plans with her friends."

"Okay, go take care of her, and send her my regards."

"Will do. Talk to you soon."

"Okay. 'Bye, now."

Hahna disconnected the call and bit her lower lip. She hoped that Corden didn't uncover something too devastating, because whatever was in disarray had happened right under Hale's nose. Something bothered Hahna about this. How had Hale noticed those very small details about Sam—that she hadn't even noticed—and missed an entire catastrophe happening in his own company?

Chapter 45

Twila had rescheduled her appointments for the entire week. Time enough for the antibiotics to run their course, and time enough to breathe. Because she needed cleansing oxygen. And sage.

She knew what the women at Kimberly and Hahna's church would think about her ritual cleansing, but it was something she'd learned from her grandmother. Bad spirits didn't like the aroma of burning sage. She didn't know if it worked on the bad spirits or not. Twila just knew it was good for *her* spirit.

She opened every window and cleaned every space. Normally, she hired a cleaning service for these types of things, but today she needed the physical labor. It had a calming effect. It occupied her hands to keep her thoughts from roaming back to dark places.

When the scents of bleach, lavender, and sage filled the condo, Twila turned on her ceiling fans to circulate the air. She'd removed the mattress from the bed in the guest room. She didn't want anything with Marcus's diseased sexual juices on it in her environment.

She'd packed the rest of his tired possessions and put them in a plastic tub on the front walkway. He hadn't called or texted, but a few days after Ron had put him out of her home, the plastic tub was gone. Either he'd picked it up, or someone else had gone shopping. Either way they weren't getting much.

Twila didn't know what was happening with him. She'd blocked him on social media and blocked his number on her phone.

There was no need to entertain any impassioned speeches about how much he really cared about her, and about how the other girl didn't mean anything. She'd acted stupidly with Marcus, but she wasn't stupid. His time was up.

Twila didn't feel bad about helping Marcus with his career. She didn't need to fall for a man or bring him to her bedroom to help with a business venture. Twila wasn't, however, going to allow him to continue making money with things her finances had provided. That upgraded income-generating video subscription? Cancelled. Gym membership to keep Marcus's abs together for his photo shoots? Cancelled.

He was cancelled. Period. Twila's excommunication game was strong.

She appreciated Hahna and Kimberly, who were tiptoeing around what they probably thought was the real issue—her return to Phenom, after all that had gone down there. She went there for the dancing, the liquor, and the anonymity.

The stalking had happened with a man she met behind the *other* door, and she wouldn't ever go back there. That part of her story was true, although she wasn't sure that Hahna and Kimberly believed it. They'd had to come and get her once. She'd been drunk and high and assaulted.

She'd burned sage for days after that one. And then she'd pumped peppermint and eucalyptus essential oils through her oil diffuser to disinfect the air.

And she'd healed.

She'd heal again from Marcus. He hadn't broken her. She hadn't plunged a knife into his thigh and watched him bleed out. She hadn't choked him out and watched him turn blue. She'd wanted to, but she hadn't.

She'd let Ron take out the trash, and Marcus was gone.

Twila took her ankle bracelet out of her bottom drawer. She blew the sage smoke over the jewelry, hoping to chase away any bad vibes still associated with the piece that was worn by the side piece.

Or had *Twila* been the side? She hadn't tried to check the timeline to see if the girl had come first and she'd come second.

Twila twirled the ankle bracelet on her hand. The jewelry wasn't just a symbol of her sorority. It was symbolic of the unbreakable bond that she had with Hahna and Kimberly. She had decided against going to the Curlpop launch party at first, but she changed her mind. Even though she wasn't in a celebratory mood, her girl deserved to be celebrated.

Her girls deserved everything. Especially the loves they'd found, even though hers had fallen flat. She should've known she wasn't ready. Phenom wasn't yet out of her system, and she wasn't over what had happened to her there.

One day she'd have a good man. One who wouldn't make her ponder all the methods of ending a man's life.

Until then, she would celebrate with her girls, and she would go to Phenom when she felt like it, until that was burned out of her system too.

Twila took a deep breath and exhaled one word that her grandmother always said when the sage burning was finished, and when her spirit was calmed.

"Amen."

Chapter 46

It was the day of Kimberly's Curlpop launch party, and the decorators were at the mansion decorating for the event. It didn't mean Hahna and her team stopped working, though. It just meant that they had a lot of unwelcome people underfoot.

The scents of the catered foods seemed to waft even through the closed door of Hahna's office, although she was trying to keep them out. The dress she'd chosen for the launch party didn't leave any room for a snack attack pouch. She'd eat when the whole thing was over, so she could look svelte in the pictures, because social media was forever. These pictures would be forever too.

The knock on her door made her look at the clock. Was it already ten and time for Aliyah's conference meeting? The day was going by too quickly. The decorators needed to pick up their pace if they wanted to be ready by the time of the party. She was going to start on time.

"Come in, Aliyah," Hahna called.

Aliyah didn't walk into Hahna's office. She trudged like she was on the hot seat for something, but as far as Hahna knew Aliyah had been doing good work. The only thing was her trysts with Josiah, which Hahna had decided not to address.

"What's bothering you?" Hahna asked as Aliyah sat.

"I'm trying to figure out how to tell you something."

Hahna felt herself get a little tickled. Was Aliyah going to ask her for man advice about Josiah? Maybe this was the opening for her to mentor her, so they could buff the rough off her diamond talent.

"I . . . um . . . got another opportunity, and I'm resigning."

Now, this was a shock. She hadn't even known that Aliyah was looking elsewhere for jobs.

"I don't know what to say."

"This has been a great learning ground for me, but I just think Corden will never forgive me for that one mistake I made."

Hahna narrowed her eyes a bit but tried not to glare. "Why didn't you come to me if there were more issues with Corden?"

"Come on, Hahna. You know there were issues with him. He hates my guts."

"He doesn't hate your guts."

"He does. I asked him if he was gay one day, and he's been pissy with me ever since."

Hahna shook her head, not knowing where she'd find someone to replace her skill set.

"When is your resignation effective? Will you have time to train a replacement?"

"Oh, I start my new gig on Monday."

Hahna closed her eyes and sighed. Now, Aliyah knew better than to quit without giving notice. This was something different.

"Aliyah. Is there anything else you need to tell me? This doesn't make sense for you to do this."

Aliyah paused for a long moment. She looked ready to say something. She even opened her mouth and then closed it again.

"Hahna, because we're sorors I will say this. Be careful of what you disclose around Corden. He's not what you think."

What kind of cryptic message was that supposed to be? Plus, she was tripping. Corden had been with her since day one. She trusted him with everything.

"I trust Corden. He is my right hand."

"Would a good right hand be telling your subordinates that your man is broke, and that you can do better?"

Hahna gasped. "He *said* that?"

"His exact words were, 'Hahna done scraped the bottom of the barrel with this one. I guess she out here sponsoring dudes now.' "

"Really? *Really?*"

She nodded. "Ask Josiah if you don't believe me."

"Did Sylvia hear him?" Hahna asked, needing an unbiased party.

"No. Sylvia wasn't there. It was only me and Josiah."

"I'm sorry, Aliyah. I just can't believe he said that."

She nodded and smirked. "I knew you wouldn't. That's why I never told you. But riddle me this, soror. How did I know your boyfriend's financial status?"

"You don't. My man owns property and is a published author. He is far from broke. Wherever you got your facts—they're wrong."

Aliyah shrugged. "I gave Sylvia my laptop and office cell phone on the way in here."

Hahna pressed her office intercom. "Sylvia, did Aliyah turn in all her equipment?"

"She did. I suspended all of her account access as well."

"Have Corden change every system password also."

"Already told him," Sylvia said. "He's working on it now."

Hahna stopped pressing the button. "I guess we're done here."

"I just wanted to say I really appreciate you hiring me right out of college and giving me my first real job."

She sure the hell had a funny way of showing it.

"Listen, Aliyah," Hahna said, "don't belabor the point. I wish you the best in your future endeavors."

Without another word, Aliyah stood, turned on one heel, and marched out of the office. This time she wasn't trudging. The load was off her chest, so why should she? She'd transferred it for Hahna to bear.

Hahna pressed the intercom button again. "Send Corden in here, please."

In less than two minutes Corden pushed the office door open.

"What the hell?" he asked.

"Aliyah resigned."

"I'm aware, and I'm damn sure not surprised."

Hahna cocked her head to one side and grimaced. "You're not?"

"No. Not at all," Corden said. "There's been a data breach."

Hahna stood up from her desk and strode across the room, leaving Corden seated. She went right on out the door too. She was done for the day. Damn the party and everything else. She had to get the hell out.

Chapter 47

Hahna didn't make it past the main party coordinator on her quest to escape the office. The woman whose wig danced back and forth on her head as she talked was yelling at Hahna. Maybe the yelling wasn't on purpose. Maybe this woman just had a voice like Samuel L. Jackson. But Hahna was using every ounce of restraint to keep from yelling back in the woman's face.

"We don't have enough outlets for all of these electric food warmers. What is the problem with using the burners that everyone else uses?"

"Your people were supposed to run power strips and tape them down on the floor under the tables," Hahna said. "It's in the setup information."

The woman used her tongue to make a loud and irritated sucking noise. Then she shook her head.

"This is why I don't do African American events."

Hahna felt the heat climb up her neck and face until it had to go out her body by way of the curls on her head, which were probably electrified to the touch from the heat. She felt like her hair might just reach out and sting this woman like the snakes on Medusa's head. She stood, clenching and unclenching her fists, trying to calm herself, but only feeling more furious.

Corden finally came to her rescue.

"Ms. Deluca, you can go. Your services are no longer needed here."

She looked Corden up and down. "You can't fire me. You didn't hire me. You're the help."

"Yes, I help my boss get rid of her problems," Corden said. "Today, that means you."

"I still require the remaining balance on my payment for services."

"Were services rendered?" Corden asked Hahna.

"Not adequately, no," Hahna responded.

"Well, you can see us in small claims court, Ms. Deluca. You and your nasty attitude can take it up with our lawyers."

Ms. Deluca's bottom jaw dropped in surprise. She wasn't ready for Corden, but Corden never had to get ready. He was *always* prepared with a quip, a comeback, and a get-the-hell-outta-Dodge spirit. And this was why he was her right hand.

"Hahna, please come back in your office and let me finish debriefing you on that other issue. Sylvia can handle the event planning stuff."

"But I want this to be nice for Kimberly," Hahna said as she looked at the complete disarray that the room was in. They didn't look close to being ready for a party that was going to take place in less than seven hours.

"They will be ready, if I have to come out here myself and decorate. Come on, because you need to hear this."

Hahna grudgingly followed Corden back into her own office. She sat down at her desk, because she was the boss. She *had* to sit and listen. She had to deal with consequences, whether she wanted to or not.

"Go ahead and tell me, Corden." Hahna said, but from Corden's demeanor she feared the worst.

"Thousands of lines of Brexton Inc.'s customer information,

including medical histories, medications taken, and insurance coverages, are on the dark web. Probably at this point in the hands of Chinese or Russian hackers and being sold to data traffickers."

There was no punchline. No softening of the blow. Corden was giving Hahna her worst nightmare.

"How in the hell did this happen?"

"A system vulnerability to which we had applied a security patch somehow became unpatched."

"How does a system vulnerability become unpatched?"

Corden inhaled deeply and sighed. "Someone had to do it deliberately. That's what our digital forensics specialist is saying."

"Who would want to do this to us? Does Brexton know yet? Do we have time to do any damage control?"

"That's the worst part. Brexton called Josiah going off. Apparently, one of his close associates had been hiding an HIV-positive status—from his wife. His information showed up with a bunch of other positive folks on a website exposing cheaters. This close associate was getting his HIV medication directly from Brexton Inc. on mail order."

"Shit. Shit. Shit. Brexton knows. What do we do, Corden? How do we fix this?"

Corden sat in the chair in front of Hahna's desk. "I don't know what to do. For the first time, I don't have any ideas on how to fix this."

"Have we, at least, isolated the breached server from the network?" Hahna asked.

"Yes, and the security patch has been reapplied, so at least the hacker can't do any more damage."

"Make sure to change all of the administrator passwords in case Aliyah had something to do with this."

"In case she had something to do with it?" Corden asked. "Come on, Hahna."

"Until we have proof, I'm not going to say that she did it. I just can't."

Corden shook his head. "Why? Because she's your sorority sister? I will have proof soon. When the digital forensics specialist looks at the system logs, we'll know who rolled back that patch."

"Okay, well until then, stop saying it was Aliyah."

Corden rolled his eyes, his disdain for Aliyah evident. But Hahna just couldn't believe that someone she'd helped and mentored would do something to deliberately hurt her like this.

There was a knock on Hahna's office door. She didn't even want to answer it. There could be nothing but worse news on the other side.

"It's me, Josiah. May I come in? This is an emergency."

Hahna closed her eyes and nodded at Corden to open the door. Josiah wrung his hands nervously as he walked across the room. He didn't sit at the empty seat in front of Hahna's desk. He stood.

"My uncle Hale would like to start the notification procedure to customers who might have been impacted by the breach. After what happened with Shane, he doesn't want to wait to notify his customers."

"How bad is it, Josiah?"

"This will probably finish Brexton Inc. This is too soon after the last breach. His stock prices will never be able to recover, and his customers may never return."

"Go ahead and start whatever processes you need to start."

"Well, Uncle Hale wants to know if you are going to contact your other clients. He doesn't want to start contacting people before you've had the opportunity to start that messaging."

Hahna looked at Corden. "Wait. This is impacting all of our clients?"

"Not all to the degree of Brexton. We had critical data for about half our clients on the server that was breached."

"Do we know the hacker only got information on that server?"

"We're pretty sure it was isolated. Our digital forensics specialist is confirming."

This was worse than Hahna thought. This was worst-case scenario. This was break glass in case of emergency and the failsafe inside had already been used. If all her clients' data was out on the dark web—the Data Whisperers would never recover.

Chapter 48

Kimberly glanced out the window of the limo that Hahna had sent to transport her and Ron to the Curlpop launch party. The entire front lawn of Hahna's mansion was decorated with lights, and there were beautiful men and women with all types of curls holding baskets of sample product gift bags to distribute as the guests arrived.

Her heart swelled with joy at the thought of this dream coming to pass. She remembered mixing products in her kitchen, just for her own wild mane of hair. Of using too-mushy avocados to condition her hair and shea butter to make everything soft and manageable. She had gone natural before it was the in thing to do—before there were hair care products on the market. Kimberly had made her own glycerin and aloe gels and knew just how much oil could be added to the mixture before the components started to break down. She'd been a kitchen chemist, like so many black women who'd come before her, and the Lord was blessing the work of her hands.

"This is awesome, right?" Ron said. "Haven't even been inside yet, and I can tell Hahna knows how to throw a party."

"She does. I wouldn't trust anyone except her to execute something on this scale."

"Is Twila coming? Have you heard from her?"

Kimberly nodded, although she hadn't heard from Twila. "She'll be here. She wouldn't miss this."

"I know you mentioned she wasn't doing too much communicating. That's why I asked."

Kimberly was silent on the topic of Twila, because this was Twila's cycle. Sometimes Kimberly thought there was an undiagnosed mental health issue there like bipolar disorder, but she wasn't sure. Twila would be all the way up—going on vacations, meeting people, clubbing, and being the life of the party. But when she was down, she disappeared. Even in her down times, though, she never disappointed Kimberly or Hahna. Not on the important things.

Ron and Kimberly exited the limo at the walkway's entrance. She clutched his arm for dear life as they walked along the sparkling gold carpet that led up to the door. People applauded, and cameras flashed. *This* was it. She was having the best life ever.

When she walked through the door, Hahna's dramatic cathedral ceilings in the foyer gave an even classier feel to the night. There were displays of her most in-demand products in every corner and a huge centerpiece surrounded by more beautiful and glistening black people of every shade. Hahna had turned jars of gel and hair butter into art.

The aroma of food made Kimberly's mouth water. She noticed a station with fried catfish skewers and another with fried green tomatoes on little plates. There was Jamaican food, African food, Puerto Rican food. Every group from the African diaspora was represented here—either through a model or through food.

Kimberly was overwhelmed.

"Baby, is there a cocktail in sight anywhere?" Kimberly whispered to Ron. "I need a glass of wine or something to calm me down. I feel like I'm on level ten."

"You should be, though. This is all about you."

Kimberly closed her eyes and opened them again. She wasn't much for the spotlight, but she knew that it came with success.

"Wine, please . . ."

Ron smiled and kissed her cheek. "Of course. I'll be right back. Just take deep breaths to slow your heart rate down."

How had he known her heart was beating out of her chest? Could he see it through the thin, gauzy fabric of her gown? She'd asked the designer to make her look like a caramel angel, and that's what she'd done. Kimberly's gown was white with sparkly shimmers. It hugged the curves where they should be hugged and flowed where things should be covered.

Kimberly scanned the room for Hahna. She wanted to thank her for bringing her overachiever A game to this party. She hadn't even been through the entire house yet, and she knew that this was one for the record books.

When she couldn't locate Hahna, she looked for Twila. She didn't see her either. Before she could ponder what might be wrong, a young woman walked up to Kimberly. She had a microphone and a cameraman with her.

"Do you mind if I ask you a few questions? I'm Quana, the Black Entertainment Television correspondent here tonight."

BET? Well, of course, she could ask a few questions. Shit. She could ask a lot of questions if she wanted. She could ask all the questions.

"Why did you start the Curlpop line?"

"I remember when I first went natural, and the products I found were either too greasy or didn't provide enough slip and protection for my hair type. I started mixing potions, and then I shared those with my friends. I'm now ready to share my secrets with my sisters all over the world."

"That is awesome! Speaking of sisterhood. I read in your bio that you are a member of the Gamma Phi Gamma sorority. What does sisterhood mean to you?"

"Sisterhood is everything. It's sharing our joys, fears, and heartbreaks. It's praying for one another and pulling a sister's collar when she's out of line. It's about having a sister's back at all times."

"That is a wonderful philosophy. Does that play into what you've done with this product line? Is sisterhood your brand?"

This question, although innocent enough, irritated Kimberly. She smiled to hide her annoyance.

"No, it's not my brand. It's just who I am. Who I've been taught to be by the women who came before me. I hope I make my ancestors proud."

Quana smiled. "Thank you."

Ron walked right up with the wine as soon as Quana and her cameraman walked away. Kimberly took the glass and guzzled.

"I don't know if I can make it through the evening," Kimberly said. "This is a lot."

"You got it, baby. And I've got you," Ron said.

Finally, Kimberly saw Twila, and waved her over. Twila was a stunner in a royal blue form-fitting dress. Her weave was new— bone-straight with golden highlights on the tips.

Kimberly embraced Twila. "It's so good to see you, honey," she said.

"You knew I wouldn't miss this," Twila said.

"But I didn't know for sure if you were coming because I haven't talked to you. What is going on?"

Kimberly did not care that she was at a party launching her hair-care line. She needed to know what was up with her girl.

"You know me. I needed space for a while. I had to get away from all the noise for a bit."

"Well, come back."

"I have. I am."

Ron also pulled Twila into an embrace. "I thought I was gonna have to come evict someone else out of your house."

Twila chuckled. "No. That will *never* happen again. No man is moving into my sacred space."

"What if you meet the right one?" Kimberly asked.

"Then he'll move me to a new home. He won't be living in mine."

Kimberly nodded. Twila was back to her rules on what the perfect man should be. She'd broken her rules and had tragic consequences, but Kimberly and Hahna had broken theirs and found love.

Kimberly knew enough not to try to convince Twila now.

Shit, all their rules were created in response to heartbreak and male shenanigans. She'd just been burned. Throwing up walls and rules was the expected response.

"Where is Hahna?" Twila asked.

Kimberly looked around the area again. More people poured into the front door, grabbing free stuff and putting it into their bags. It was funny that most of the partygoers didn't even realize that Kimberly was the creative genius behind the products.

She needed to put her face on the jars. Next batch.

Corden, Hahna's employee, rushed across the room to greet them. He hugged Kimberly first, then Twila. Lastly, he shook Ron's hand.

"Twila, can you come to Hahna's office with me? She's having a little . . . wardrobe malfunction and she asked for your help."

Kimberly scoffed. "She asked for Twila's help and not mine? Boy, take me to her."

Corden shook his head firmly. "She explicitly said Twila only. She wants you to mingle with your guests, Kimberly. She'll be out soon."

Kimberly watched as Corden took Twila's arm and rushed her along just like he'd rushed when he'd come up to meet them.

"Something's wrong," Kimberly said to Ron. "But they don't want me to know during the party."

"How do you know?" Ron asked.

How did she know? Kimberly knew because she knew her sisters. There was something going down, and it was major.

"Ron, Corden isn't the best messenger, and if there wasn't something terribly wrong, Hahna would've already been out here, at my side. Because she knows crowds are not my thing."

"I think you're overreacting. He said it was a wardrobe malfunction."

"That's what I'm saying. Hahna doesn't have wardrobe malfunctions. She tries on her clothes a hundred times before buying. She has a contingency plan for her contingency plans. She carries safety pins, buttons, and a travel-size needle and thread.

Hahna doesn't have wardrobe malfunctions because she's always prepared. Whatever's wrong tonight—it was something she wasn't prepared for."

"Women know each other so well."

"I don't know if that's true for all women, but it is most certainly true for us."

Kimberly walked toward the stairs, pulling up the bottom of her dress so that it didn't drag on the floor.

"Where are you going?" Ron asked.

"I'm going to see what's wrong with Hahna. You coming?"

Ron shook his head. "I don't see how I have a choice."

Kimberly was glad he realized that, because he didn't have a choice when it came to supporting her best friends. He'd already proved himself worthy when he'd helped them evict Marcus from Twila's home. Kimberly hoped that wasn't a one-off, because if he planned to be with her, he had to accept Twila and Hahna as sisters-in-law.

"I can't wait to bring you back out here to your guests when you find out there's absolutely nothing wrong with Hahna," Ron said as he followed.

Kimberly smiled. She would come back out to her guests, and she'd let Ron lead the way. But only after she knew that her sister was all right.

Chapter 49

Hahna felt paralyzed. She wanted to get up and walk across the room, through the door, and out to Kimberly's party. She wanted to celebrate her friend's success. She wanted everyone to see her pretty gown. But she couldn't move.

The Brexton data breach had hit the news cycle before she and Corden had had a chance to do anything. No client phone calls, emails, or communications had gone out. It was a total blindside. Josiah had disappeared soon after their initial conversation about the breach and wasn't returning calls. His office was empty. No computer, no cell phone, no personal effects. Hahna assumed that was his resignation.

He and Aliyah gone on the same day.

The Google alert that was set up on her phone for the Data Whisperers chimed incessantly. Every news article about the breach had mentioned her company and her name. She was going to lose every one of her clients.

The door to her office opened, and Corden had Twila with him. She appreciated his effort, but Twila couldn't help.

Twila rushed over to the sofa where Hahna reclined. Hahna's floor-length gown draped on the floor, but she'd taken off her shoes.

"Wardrobe malfunction, my ass. Honey, what's wrong? Is it Sam? What did he do? I will beat his ass."

Hahna shook her head. "No, it's not Sam."

"So, where is he?" Twila asked. "You laying up here like this? Lover boy needs to bring his ass."

Hahna picked up her phone to check for messages from Sam.

"He texted he's on his way. He's stuck in traffic."

"Well, he better get unstuck or teleport his ass over here," Twila said.

"Calm down," Hahna said. "He's coming. It's not like I'm dying."

"Have you seen yourself?" Twila asked.

Judging by Twila's grimace, Hahna didn't think she wanted to.

Twila turned to Sylvia. "Get someone in here to fix her makeup. At some point she's going to have to leave this room and she can't look like this."

Sylvia paused for an instant and looked at Hahna, perhaps wondering if she should do what Twila said. Twila lifted her eyebrows and Sylvia rushed out of the room. This almost made Hahna smile. She supposed it was a good sign that she could still find humor when her life was over.

"Don't threaten my staff, girl," Hahna said.

"You better tell them who I am, then."

"They know who you are, but I am the one who signs their checks."

Maybe that should've been in the past tense. Signed their checks. She had no idea how many more checks she'd be signing once all her clients walked away.

"If it's not Sam, then tell me what's wrong. Corden wouldn't say."

Hahna closed her eyes and opened them again. She didn't want to say the story out loud again. And then another time when Sam finally showed up.

Kimberly burst into Hahna's office, and Hahna groaned. She hadn't wanted Kimberly to know about this. Not tonight. This was her night to tell the world about Curlpop, not to worry about her.

Sam stepped in behind Kimberly and closed the door. He gently pushed Kimberly to the side as he made his way over to her on the couch. He kneeled on the floor next to her.

"What's wrong, babe? Tell me," Sam said.

It was as if there'd been a dam holding back her tears and Sam's words had been the dynamite to blow it to smithereens.

"D-data b-b-breach, and . . ."

Hahna sobbed. Corden sighed and scratched his head as everyone looked at him for answers.

"There's been a data breach. We lost a great deal of our clients' private customer data. It is now available on the dark web, and there is evidence that it has been shared or sold."

"That's not the end of the world, right? People get hacked all the time," Sam said.

Hahna couldn't even respond, except by shaking her head. He didn't understand her business or her livelihood, and tonight wasn't the night to explain it all.

"When your business is data," Corden explained, "this is the worst thing that could happen. People trust us with one of their company's biggest assets, and they expect us to turn it into information. What they don't expect is that it will end up on the dark web for hackers to exploit."

"I just love how calm you sound," Twila said, the sarcasm dripping from her words. "Why the hell didn't you keep the data safe? Isn't that what she hired you for?"

"We took every precaution. We had every tool the industry recommends for data security. We even have an IT security company that comes in and does penetration testing, where they try to hack into your servers and they tell you where you're vulnerable."

"Well, why didn't it work?" Sam asked. "Stop giving us the cover-your-ass speech and say what really went down."

Corden shook his head. "I can tell y'all want someone to blame, but it's definitely not me. I think it was an inside job, though. The girl I've been trying to get Hahna to fire for the past few months quit right before we found out about the data breach."

Hahna sighed. "He did try to get me to fire her. She's a soror, though. I wanted to give her a chance to turn her performance around."

"Y'all take that sorority shit too seriously," Corden said.

"Thanks, Corden. That's enough," Hahna said, her tears drying. "You're probably still mad she thought you were gay."

"You're not gay?" Twila asked.

Corden shook his head and frowned. "What difference does it make? I'm about to be unemployed if we can't figure out how to spin this. Look at CNN."

Hahna couldn't bear to bring the website up on her phone, so she handed it to Sam. He tapped the screen until he was on the news site.

"Oh, wow," Sam said. "Hale Brexton is right here on the home page."

"Click the article link," Twila said. "Let me see."

The link took them to a video. Twila pressed PLAY and Brexton was onscreen. Weeping.

"I have failed," Brexton said, "everyone who trusted me to keep their information safe from prying eyes. Everyone who entrusted their secrets to our company to get the medicines they needed."

"What do you want to say to everyone who's listening?" the reporter asked.

"That I'm sorry. I'm sorry I trusted the Data Whisperers to perform my data analytics."

"Did the company come highly recommended?" the reporter asked.

"They did. The owner, Hahna Osborne, is someone I've known for years. I'm sure she is just as broken up about this as I am. No one wants this kind of blemish on the good name of their company."

"Turn it off. Turn it OFF!" Hahna screamed.

"I bet he's doing an I'm sorry tour and talking to whatever media outlet will listen," Corden said.

"How long have y'all known about the breach?" Twila asked.

"We just found out this afternoon," Hahna said.

"And this bastard is already on the news circuit?" Twila asked. "He has something to do with it."

Hahna was starting to feel the same way, even without proof. But with the disappearance of Josiah and Aliyah, how could she think anything else?

"I'm with Twila," Sam said. "His tears didn't even seem authentic."

"But why?" Hahna asked. "Why in the hell would he destroy both our companies? That doesn't make any sense."

"That's the part I can't figure out," Corden said. "Maybe the digital forensics specialist will shed some light on it."

Kimberly had been quiet the entire time.

"Kimberly, what are you thinking?" Twila asked.

"I think this is some bullshit," Kimberly said.

And it was. But Hahna hoped that she and Corden could get to the bottom of it, before all was lost.

Chapter 50

Sam had taken Hahna to his apartment after the party and hadn't left her side since. For an entire day and a half, she'd sat on his sofa, crying and eating, and crying some more.

"Sam, I really don't think I can survive this," Hahna said between sobs. "This is too much."

"You mean your company can't survive this."

"Sam, I said what I mean."

Sam pulled Hahna into his embrace and leaned back on the sofa. The walls in his apartment were so close they felt like weighted blankets wrapping another layer of comfort around Hahna. But still, she sobbed.

The story had made national news. Little old Hahna from Spelman had made CNN, MSNBC, and all the networks. Hale's crying face had been plastered all over every channel. Hale Brexton had dominated the news cycle for an entire day and a half. Had it not been for a summer tornado in Oklahoma, it would've been a day and a half more.

Hahna's work cell phone kept ringing. She knew who was calling. Her clients. They were leaving one by one. Even the ones who knew her personally. Even the ones who didn't have data that anyone wanted. No one wanted to feel violated the way Hale said he was violated. No one wanted to break down like he was breaking down.

And it was all Hahna's fault.

She hadn't broken anything. She hadn't given anyone's information away, but her business, which operated from a "trust us" model, had broken every trust.

"Your phone is ringing," Sam said.

"I don't want to talk to anyone. They will call Corden. He will handle them."

And Corden would. Even in his subordinate role, he was taking the brunt of the fallout, because his boss had fallen apart and couldn't handle it. News outlets had reached out to Hahna to get her side of things. But what side? What could she say that would make any of this better? They had interviewed a man, disguised his identity, and shared his story about how this data breach had cost him his marriage and his career. Not the fact that he was hiding an HIV diagnosis from his wife. No, not the fact that he was having unprotected sex all over Atlanta. That hadn't destroyed anything. It was the data breach.

The secret telling.

Everyone had secrets that they thought would never be told.

"You can survive this, babe. Even though it's your company, it's still only a job. It isn't who you are. It isn't love. It isn't peace. It isn't joy."

Hahna groaned. This was spoken by a man who didn't own a life-changing company. The Data Whisperers had changed Hahna's life. It had taken her from struggling to being able to enjoy paid utility bills and food in the refrigerator. Sam thought it was all about luxuries, but it was about never worrying for the necessities. This, to Hahna, was love, joy, and peace all wrapped into one.

"Sam, you're not helping. Just hold me. That's what I need right now. I can't see past the next hour."

"I can still see forever. I see us walking on the beach hand in hand. I see us chilling in my uncle's restaurant eating stewed chicken. Can't you see me in your future?"

Hahna wasn't ready to envision life without her company. What was she going to do now? Go work at a call center? It wasn't like she was going to walk into any corporation and say, *Hey. I'm great at data analytics. You should hire me.* Her résumé would go right in the trash, along with the ability to pay her mortgage.

"This doesn't have anything to do with us, babe."

"It does. My love is supposed to help you get up and fight."

"Fight?"

"If your company is so important to you, shouldn't you at least try to save it?"

"You just said the Data Whisperers couldn't survive this."

Sam shook his head. "No, I was only repeating what you were thinking. I don't think you should give up yet."

"We didn't get out ahead of it. It hit the news before we even knew what was happening. We didn't have time to investigate or spin. All we had time to do was retreat."

"So, stop retreating. Figure out what went wrong and fix it. Then apologize to the loyal clients you have left. Then start over."

"I just keep thinking about Hale."

Sam scoffed. "I don't like him. Something doesn't seem authentic about him."

"Are you kidding me? The man sobbed on national television."

"I don't know. Sometimes things are just *off*."

"What do you mean?"

"It's hard to explain. Like, remember that black teenage boy who was protesting in Ferguson with his mother? The one who was crying and holding a sign that said Free Hugs?"

"Oh, yeah. He hugged a police officer and that became the photo every media outlet used to give us hope for reconciliation."

"Yeah, well, that boy's mother drove him and the rest of his foster siblings off a cliff. Killed them all. How do we know he wasn't pleading for help?"

"Shit. That's dark."

"I know. I said it to say, something hit me wrong about that boy. I don't know what it was. At the time, I was thinking his family were media whores or something, and that they were trying to go viral on social media."

"You hate social media."

"I don't. I hate what people use it for. I hate that every fake and phony person is given a platform and the means to have a voice. Some people should just be quiet."

Hahna chuckled. He was definitely helping to keep her mind off things.

"But back then, when I saw that boy, I knew something wasn't right. I think he was trying to tell us something, and we all missed it."

"What are we missing with Brexton?"

"His wife, Jelena, was there with him on the news. Stood next to him and didn't shed one tear. What black woman you know can have dry eyes when her husband is sobbing like a baby on television?"

"One that doesn't give a damn about him?"

"Or one who isn't worried at all."

"You're right. If all his money was about to be gone, that trophy bride would be devastated."

Sam's jaw tightened, but he didn't say anything. If Hahna had to guess his thoughts, she probably could.

"Like I'm devastated, huh?" Hahna asked.

"I don't understand why, though. First, your damn money ain't even gone yet. You have millions in the bank, and you're over here catatonic about the potential of losing it all."

"It's easy not to care about losing it all if you ain't got shit."

Hahna hadn't meant to snap back so hard at Sam. He chuckled like it hadn't bothered him, but she knew it had.

"It's too bad you don't see the things you have that are more important than money."

"Shit, Sam. You act like I don't know. My health, my friends, my family . . . my man. I know what's important. Stop trying to school me all the damn time. I get to be upset about my company being destroyed. *This* is an appropriate reaction."

"No, an appropriate reaction is doing your research and

launching your own media campaign, just like Brexton did. But since I ain't got shit, I guess I wouldn't know what the hell I'm talking about."

It was too late to apologize for her words, and even if she did, Hahna knew the apology would be an empty one. She'd meant every word. He didn't know how this felt. He didn't know where she came from, and to where she was never going back.

"You're right about the research and the campaign, babe," Hahna said. "Tomorrow I'm going into my office. While I still own it."

"Mmm-hmm."

Tomorrow, Hahna would get up from her bed of sorrow and carry herself to the front line to fight for her business, her good name, and her cash flow. And after she'd won—because she was going to win—she wondered if she'd have to fight for her relationship with Sam. Or what was left of it.

Chapter 51

Twila had asked Kimberly to meet her for lunch, but only because she needed food to soak up the cocktails she was about to drown herself in. Marcus's betrayal had left a huge, gaping wound. He'd reminded her of things she'd thought she'd left in her past. Hahna was usually her go-to friend for these types of pity parties, but it had been a week since her company's scandal hit the news circuit, and no one had heard from her. She wasn't responding to calls or texts. She'd sent them one message that she was working and that she'd reach out when she was ready to come up for air.

So, she'd have to settle for Kimberly.

Kimberly showed up finally, with her usually perfect curls drawn up into a bun atop her head. There were dark circles under her puffy eyes, and she hadn't bothered to apply makeup to cover them. She looked like she hadn't had any sleep in days, and Twila was sure she'd lost some weight.

Kimberly hugged Twila before sitting. "Girl, what's going on?" she asked.

"What's going on with you? You looked whipped," Twila responded.

"Thank you very much for telling me I look like shit."

"You do."

"Every night is a late night. I haven't gotten more than three hours of sleep at a time in a week, trying to get these orders ready for the distributor. The manufacturer keeps calling me asking if they can swap out ingredients, talking about the price point will go up."

"Oh no. You can't change the formula. Your main customers will know."

"Yes, girl. I know. If that curl doesn't pop like it should, they won't be buying my product again. Folks will think I sold out to get this distribution deal."

"And you know we are some unforgiving asses when it comes to each other."

"Right, but we will have a prayer service for a white man who shot up the damn church."

Twila shook her head. "You are talking right, girl. That's how we do."

"I need a drink."

"I'll second that."

Kimberly chuckled. "You look like you already done had a few."

"Have. And will have a few more. And I shan't be judged by you."

Twila watched the way Kimberly's face lit up when she laughed. That's the way she looked whenever Ron was around. It was the way you were supposed to look when you had a good man, and Ron was the gold standard.

"Where has my brother been?"

"Who? Big Ron? He had some business back home in North Carolina, but he'll be back tomorrow. He's bringing his twin daughters with him."

Twila grimaced. "You gonna be all right, or do you need reinforcements? I can go pick up my niece and we can have a playdate."

"I think I'll be good. He wants us to bond."

"Can you bond with that white woman's kids?" Twila asked. She laughed as she said it, but the question wasn't a joke.

"Honestly . . . I don't know. They're beautiful babies. They look just like Ron. Just caramel-colored instead of dark ebony like him."

"They got his dimples?" Twila asked.

"They both do."

"I can't wait to meet them. Kimberly's gonna be a step-mother."

"Yeah."

"Yeah," Twila echoed. She felt the moment of joy dissipate as her melancholy settled right back in.

"So, what's going on?" Kimberly asked as she called the waitress over to take their drink orders.

"Nothing, and everything."

"Oh lord."

The waitress came to the table and Kimberly snapped the menu shut. "We'll both have pinot grigio. As a matter of fact, just bring the bottle."

"How do you know I want wine, heffa?" Twila asked. "Maybe I'm in a tequila mood."

"Unh-uh. No tequila until I find out what's bothering you. I need you coherent."

"I knew I shoulda called Hahna. You rationing a sista's liquor."

Kimberly nodded. "Yep, I am. Until you tell me why you've been back to Phenom."

One thing about Kimberly that was different from Hahna, Kimberly played no games when it came to getting information. There was no back and forth, no twenty questions. Just open your damn mouth and spill it. That's how Kimberly rolled.

"I just go to dance now. I haven't been back in the other part of the club."

"You can dance anywhere. Why would you go back to the scene of where that man hurt you?"

"Because it's owned by my soror, the music is nice, and the liquor isn't watered down. Shit."

"Those are the only reasons? Do you hope to see him there again?"

Twila scoffed. "He wouldn't dream about coming back in there. He would lose his life."

"Your mind doesn't replay the assault over and over when you go there?"

It did. It was like a movie playing in her mind a million times over. But the movie version of herself kicked her attacker's ass again and again. In some versions she shot him with a concealed gun. In other versions she sliced him until he bled out. And in other versions she engaged in hand-to-hand combat until he was bruised and bloodied. In every version of her dream, she won. The shit felt empowering. It was addictive.

"I think it's part of my healing process. That's what my therapist says."

"So, what's wrong, then? You called me here for a reason."

Twila sighed. "I'm gonna sound like a straight-up hater, but this is me being honest."

"Go ahead."

"I'm tired of being by my damn self. I'm watching you and Ron and Hahna and Sam. The way Sam just pulled up and gathered all Hahna's tears. That shit was awesome. I want that too."

"It's coming, honey. Sometimes we aren't quite ready for what we need. That's why we settle for what we want."

"That's a damn lie. I'm ready. I'm more than ready."

The waitress brought back the wine, and Twila took hers off the serving tray without even giving her a chance to set it down. She guzzled half the glass and knew this bottle was going to be gone in short order.

Kimberly sipped instead. "I'm not sure if you're ready to trust a man. You've still got weapons all over your house."

"I've been assaulted. I have to feel safe."

"I'm not against that. You know I have a gun in my bedside table."

"Well, then, don't come for me over that. I need to feel safe in my own home."

Kimberly sipped again. Her eye contact was unsettling to Twila. It felt like her friend was trying to hypnotize her or something.

"You've gone beyond safe. You've got knives under the lamp-shade and under every couch cushion. Razor blades under your pillows, and under the sofa. A gun taped under the dining room table and in the master bathroom toilet bowl. Like, where did you even get the idea to do that? The toilet?"

"It was a movie. *Godfather* or something. I don't know. I saw it and I liked it."

"I think you'll be ready for a man, when you're ready to let go of some of that stuff."

"I don't need a man to protect me, though. I protect me. So, me having a man shouldn't have anything to do with my wea-ponry."

"Yes, but you live in fear. I don't think love can exist in that same space. Because love requires you to come out of battle mode."

"Who are you supposed to be? Iyanla or somebody?"

"Beloved. You need to listen more and talk less."

This made Twila holler and Kimberly too. They always went to their Iyanla voices when they wanted to break some of the heaviness. And this conversation weighed ten thousand tons.

"I'll be okay, eventually," Twila said. "I'm working through it. But I sure would like some sexual healing too."

"I hear you."

"What do you think is gonna happen with Hahna?" Twila asked, wanting to shift the focus from her dysfunction to some-one else's.

Kimberly sucked in a sharp breath. "I mean, she's going to be okay. Last time I checked her investment portfolio with her accountant, she was at about four million. About a third of it is liquid."

"Well, I know financially she'll be okay, but what about her business?"

"Girl, what about her spirit? Four million dollars is not enough to make Hahna feel secure. You know where she came from. The idea that she won't keep making money to replenish what she uses is going to drive her mad."

"She might push Sam away, because he won't get it," Twila

said. "He's a damn tree hugger. He'd rather be one with nature."

"I didn't know he was all that. I just thought he was a starving artist."

"Hahna said he ain't starving, just damn near."

Twila and Kimberly laughed, but it wasn't at Sam. Twila thought Sam was the best thing that'd ever happened to Hahna, especially after that whack-ass Torian broke her heart. She just didn't know if Hahna knew that.

"She'll be okay. She has us."

"And who needs anything else besides our illustrious selves?"

Kimberly poked her lips out. "Nobody. And if they think they do, they don't know any better."

"I'm lying. I need a glistened-up six-pack with a side of anaconda. I need that today."

Kimberly burst into laughter. "You don't need it, but it's okay to want it."

Twila shook her head and laughed. Her wants and needs were wrapped into one. But Kimberly was right. She wasn't ready, and there probably wasn't a man alive who was ready for her in her current form.

"Will you help me, Kim? I want to get rid of my weapons. I want to do the work that'll help me get there."

"I will help you, sister. I think the first thing you should do is never return to Phenom. That place holds nothing but ghosts and shadows."

Twila nodded to feign agreement when she didn't agree at all. There were no ghosts and shadows at Phenom. There was only the power she felt with victory.

She would stop going when the enemy was completely defeated.

Chapter 52

Hahna and Corden sat in her office, poring over the digital forensic specialist's report. They were looking for anything that would prove their innocence, or at least something they could point to as a cause, to make their clients feel secure.

"How many have gone, Corden? Or should I be asking who do we have left?"

Corden sighed. That sigh told Hahna this was news she didn't want to hear but needed to know.

"All of our major clients are gone. Shale Accounting's chief information officer did an interview about Aliyah's mistake from a few months ago. She said she should've known then that their data wasn't secure."

"Shit," Hahna said. "That was completely unrelated."

"Not to the public. To the public, we're just sloppy with data security."

"The majors are gone, okay. What about my churches?"

"They are the bright spot," Corden said. "They've stood firmly with you, some Atlanta pastors even making statements on your behalf. They're saying that you've done so much good for the community that they back you up on this."

"That's all right. At least we have their support."

Corden shook his head. "It's not enough, though. All twenty-seven of the churches that we service only make up a quarter of our business. We can't keep our doors open with just them."

"I know. I know."

Sylvia's voice came through the intercom. "Hahna, there's someone here to see you. He says he has information that can save your business."

Hahna locked eyes with Corden, and he shrugged. Hahna was curious about who would be bold enough to say they could save her company during this crisis.

"Send him in."

Sylvia opened her office door and let the visitor inside. He walked across the room like a man of purpose, or one who had information.

"You don't know me, but I'm Shane Brown."

Corden looked up and narrowed his eyes. "The Shane Brown that used to work for Brexton?"

It seemed that Brexton only surrounded himself with beautiful people. Shane Brown was tall and dark, with silky curls that made him look Latin. His full lips were sensual, and his eyes were dreamy and expressive.

But Hahna ignored all of this. Shane was an enemy in enemy territory. What could he want that would help her situation?

Shane nodded. "I did work for him, and I can tell by both your expressions that he spread lies on me to you like he did the rest of the financial community. He has ruined me."

Hahna was almost content to let Corden facilitate the conversation, because she wasn't in the mood for talking. She had to figure out how to stop hemorrhaging clients her damn self or she'd lose everything she'd worked for. But she had to ask a question for herself.

"Why are you here? You have to know we're the last people who're interested in talking to you," Hahna said.

Shane sat in the chair in front of Hahna's desk. Both she and Corden gave him the stink eye. They hadn't invited him to sit.

"I came here to warn you, and maybe give you a way out of this."

"Why do you want to help us?" Corden asked. "What's in it for you?"

"If you can prove what I know to be true, then it would clear my name as well," Shane said. "I'm not going to bullshit you. I know we're not friends. But we've got a common enemy—Hale Brexton."

Now Hahna was intrigued. The slobbering, crying Hale Brexton was the enemy? Aliyah had done this—had uninstalled the patch that had allowed the system to be attacked. It was what the system records had shown. She was going to be punished and hopefully would do time in jail.

What did this have to do with Brexton?

"Hale might be your enemy," Hahna says. "But I have to take responsibility for what my team did. We let Brexton Inc. down."

"Stop. Don't say another word accepting guilt."

"Tell us what you're talking about, then," Corden said.

"When Hale hired you, did he tell you he was on the verge of bankruptcy?" Shane asked.

Hahna shook her head. "No, although we did identify abnormalities in some of his financial reporting. The check cleared, so . . ."

"Brexton is broke. I don't know where he got the money to pay you. Probably scammed someone, but his company has been underwater for the past two years."

"What does being broke have to do with a data breach?" Corden asked.

"Don't you have a staffer who's being blamed for this?" Shane asked. "He probably paid her to do it."

"He sent his own person to work with us," Hahna said.

"Let me guess—Josiah Winters?"

"Yes, his nephew," Hahna said.

"He tells everyone that Josiah is his nephew. He's not. Josiah is a computer hacker who was on Hale's payroll long before his personal texts and social media inbox messages were leaked to the press."

"And you did that?" Corden asked. "Why should we trust you?"

"I revealed those screenshots after Hale tried to destroy me. I wanted to go to the board members and investors to tell them that Hale had been reporting inaccurate numbers for years. Of course, he didn't want that."

"Connect these dots for us," Corden said. "Because it just sounds like you and Hale have a beef."

"We do, but that's not the point here. The point is, Hale was in a desperate situation. Desperate enough to sell his own company's data to the highest bidder."

"Do you have proof of this?" Hahna asked.

"No. I'm just giving you a tip, so you know where to look. It might be a way to save your company," Shane said.

"And you?" Corden asked.

"I hope that after you prove Hale's lies and shenanigans, you can tell everyone how I came to you with the tip that changed the course of your investigation. I'm not perfect, but I'm not what Hale says. He's the criminal."

"If this information saves my company, I'll give you a job," Hahna said.

Corden cut his eyes at her. Maybe hiring a potential slime-bucket was a bridge too far for Corden, but she was desperate for anything that would put the Data Whisperers in the clear.

Chapter 53

K imberly's doorbell rang as soon as her blueberry breakfast muffins were ready to come out the oven. She hurried to remove them before she answered the door. The yummy treats had her whole downstairs smelling like a small-town bakery, even though the muffins were from a box.

When Kimberly opened the door, she gasped. Big Ron stood there with his two little girls, Carly and Kayla. Both their heads looked like birds' nests. Ron's sheepish expression was more apology than explanation.

"Hi, Carly and Kayla," Kimberly said. "Who's hungry for blueberry muffins?"

Both girls' eyes lit up, and they squealed. "We are! We are!"

"Come on in and you can help me put butter on them."

Ron smiled. "May I have muffins too, my love?"

Kimberly gave Ron a side-eye. "Girls, you can sit at that round table."

"May we have milk with our muffins?" Carly asked.

"Sure. I have milk."

Kayla shook her head. "I'd like tea instead. Can we have a muffin and tea party?"

Kimberly laughed. "We can have both."

The girls ran to the table, and Kimberly turned to Ron. "Why isn't their hair combed? You can't have children out in public looking like that."

"Sabrina didn't have time to comb their hair. She washed it, but said it was all tangled."

"So, they're supposed to look like that all weekend?"

"Sabrina was concerned about that, but I promised her you'd do their hair. Please tell me I wasn't wrong."

Kimberly sighed. She didn't really have time to tackle their hair. She had work to do. Having them over for breakfast was already taking up more time than she had to give.

But then Ron pulled her close and placed soft kisses on her neck. "Please, baby? I don't want them to look crazy when I take them to the park."

"How about this? I can do one and you can do the other," Kimberly said.

"I don't know how to comb their hair."

"I'm going to show you. Plus, you need to know how to do their hair anyway. Just because you're the dad doesn't mean that you don't have to comb hair."

"Ummm, is this optional?" Ron asked.

Kimberly shook her head. "No. It'll be fun. We'll use Curl-pop and have them looking like beautiful princesses in no time."

She turned to the twins. "Okay, girls, let's have our tea and muffins. Then after that, your daddy and I are going to fix your hair and make it very pretty."

Kayla looked at Carly, and both girls burst into tears. Kimberly panicked. She wasn't ready for crying. Why were they crying? What little girl didn't want to look pretty?

As much as she didn't want to feel moved by their tears, Kimberly did. Some of her fondest memories were of her mother and grandmother detangling her hair, greasing her scalp, and braiding her hair into intricate styles. When she got to have wooden beads at the ends of her braids, she spent a whole day swinging those braids, so the beads could click and clack.

"How about if I promise it won't hurt at all?" Kimberly asked.

"It always hurts," Carly shouted. "It hurts bad!"

Kayla just nodded at her sister's words and cried.

"Girls, listen," Kimberly said. "Look at my hair. Isn't it curly like yours?"

Both girls nodded.

"Do you think maybe I know how to comb curly hair since I have it too?"

Carly and Kayla looked at each other, then back at Kimberly. They still had uncertainty in their eyes.

"Once we get your hair done, we can go and get ice cream."

"For breakfast?" Carly asked skeptically.

"Yep, for breakfast."

"Okay," Carly said. "I'll go first. In case it hurts. I think it hurts Kayla more than it hurts me."

"How about if your daddy makes the tea while I do your hair? We still want tea, right?" Kimberly asked. She wanted a shot of vodka in hers. These little girls were a lot to handle.

Kimberly went into her bathroom to get the tools she needed for their hair. First, a spray bottle filled with half warm water, and half of her Curlpop detangler. Next, the Curlpop hair and scalp oil. Then, her signature Curlpop curl definer for their hair type. Lastly some finishing gel, a wide-toothed comb, and a Denman brush.

She was equipped for battle.

Kimberly invited Carly onto a bar stool. "I need you to trust me that it won't hurt, okay? Just relax."

Kimberly gently separated the girl's massive bunch of curls into four big sections. She sprayed the first section with water and detangler, then she started at the ends of the strands until she worked out all the kinks and tangles. Once she was at the root, she brushed all the way through with a bit of oil.

"It doesn't hurt?" Kayla asked her sister.

"Nope," Carly said. "She's good."

"Can you show our mommy how to do this?" Kayla asked. "She hurts us every day."

"Umm . . . maybe . . . I guess so," Kimberly said.

Ron chuckled as Kimberly expertly finished Carly's hair. Kimberly didn't know what was funny. Combing the girls' hair was one thing. Bonding with their mother was an entire other thing. Kimberly had no intention on saying more than three words to Sabrina, much less bonding with her.

"What if I give your mom a gift set with all this stuff and instructions? Then she could do it herself."

"Make a YouTube video, Ms. Kimberly. Then she can watch," Kayla said. "She watches lots of YouTube videos."

Kimberly couldn't believe she was saying yes to this. "Ron, get your phone out. We're gonna make a tutorial for your ex-wife."

As Kimberly did Kayla's hair, she talked through the steps as she went and demonstrated them. In about ten minutes, Kayla's hair was done too. In a sleek bun on top of her head. And there wasn't a screech or jump the entire time.

"You are amazing," Ron said after he stopped the video and set his phone on the counter. "I know Sabrina is going to appreciate this."

Except Kimberly hadn't done this for her, she'd done it for Carly and Kayla—the beautiful babies who would be her step-daughters one day when she married Ron. She didn't care if Sabrina benefited, but Kimberly wasn't ever going out of the way to help any woman who'd stolen her Ron away from her.

Chapter 54

"Twila, where are we going?" Hahna asked.

Twila shook her head. Why didn't her friends ever just trust what she was doing? Both Kimberly and Hahna always had twenty questions when she told them to ride with her. Hadn't either of them ever heard of plausible deniability? They always wanted all the details.

"Why don't you trust me?" Twila asked. "I said this was important for your business, and you don't believe me?"

"It's not that I don't trust you. It's that I don't want to be out and about," Hahna said. "I'm not ready for all of Atlanta to see my face right now."

"Why not? You didn't do anything wrong."

"No, I didn't do anything wrong, but I've failed. Right now, my only clients are churches. And you. That's it. How in the hell am I supposed to eat off that? I love my church clients, but most of them are on my most affordable plan."

"Don't worry. We're not going out and about anywhere. This is a covert mission."

"Covert."

"Yes."

Twila checked the address to make sure it was correct and pulled into the apartment complex's parking lot.

"Where are we?" Hahna asked.

"Girl, be quiet. You'll know in a minute."

"What?"

"Shhhh," Twila hissed. "Wait for it."

They sat in the parking lot for a few minutes. Every time Hahna opened her mouth to speak, Twila shushed her.

"Now. There she is!" Twila said.

Twila jumped out of the car and rushed across the parking lot to cut Aliyah off in her path.

"What are you doing?" Aliyah asked.

Twila got right in Aliyah's face. "I need you to come with me."

"Bitch, I'm not going anywhere with you."

Aliyah stuck out her hand to push Twila, but Twila snatched the girl's arm, swung it behind her back, and pinned it to her body.

"It'll just be a few minutes, soror. I need some answers."

Aliyah struggled in her grasp, but Twila twisted her arm harder.

"I don't want to hurt you, nor do I want to pull a gun on you. That wouldn't be sisterly. Come with me for a few minutes or get hurt."

"I know you," Aliyah spat. "You're Hahna's friend. The dentist. Ain't nobody scared of you."

"You don't have to be scared to get your ass beat. You did some shit to Hahna's business. You're either going to answer these questions or catch these hands. Now, come on."

Twila pushed Aliyah to the car and directed her to get into the back seat. Twila climbed in right beside her, then closed and locked the doors.

"Twila, what are we doing?" Hahna asked.

"Yeah. What are y'all doing?" Aliyah asked. "This is kidnapping."

"Girl, shut up," Twila said. "We aren't leaving this parking lot, as long as you do what you need to do. Hahna, ask her what you need to ask."

"Aliyah, why did you do this? I mentored you. Why would you destroy my business?"

Aliyah shook her head. "It isn't destroyed. You'll bounce back. It'll be fine. Everyone is having data breaches these days."

"But why?"

Twila was so close to Aliyah's face that the girl could probably smell what Twila had for breakfast. But Twila didn't care. She was about to tell Hahna the truth.

"Okay, you know what? I'll tell you. Josiah was blackmailing me."

"Really?" Hahna asked. "We knew you were sleeping with him. We didn't care about that."

Aliyah shook her head. "I wasn't sleeping with him. Who told you that? Corden?"

"Well, he saw you two sneaking around, so I guess he thought you were," Hahna said. "If you weren't sleeping with him, how was he blackmailing you?"

"He had someone do research on me, I guess. I don't know. But he had a video of me from when I was in college."

"What kind of video?" Twila said.

"The kind I didn't want my mother or my current boyfriend to see. And he was threatening to post it on social media."

Twila scoffed. "We all did ho shit in college. Who cares? You ruined my girl's business over that? You should've let him post it. It might've helped your career."

Aliyah shook her head. "Not this. This was . . . I was taking drugs when I did this video."

Twila cocked her head to one side. "What? It couldn't be that bad."

"It's worse than you can imagine, and to be honest, I didn't think Hahna's other clients would be impacted. Josiah said they were only going after Brexton Inc.'s information."

Hahna slumped down in the front seat. "So, it was an inside job. He did this for money. I feel so stupid trusting him."

"He's a rich old man," Aliyah said. "Why wouldn't you trust him?"

"She shouldn't have trusted you," Twila said. "But thank you for giving us a recorded confession."

"That's illegal."

"No," Twila said. "I need the consent of at least one person in the conversation. I have Hahna's consent, so this is legal, sweetie. You can admit what you've done, and no one will have to know about your video, or we can go to the authorities with this recording."

"Now *you're* blackmailing me," Aliyah said.

"No. I'm just asking you to do the right thing for your sorority sister. For the one who gave you a chance to forward your career. For the one who wouldn't fire you when everyone else thought she should."

Aliyah sighed and hung her head. "Who do I need to talk to?"

"We have a digital forensics specialist who's working with the authorities," Hahna said. "Knowing that this was a deliberate act and that we aren't just sloppy with their data might make my clients feel more at ease. Some may even come back."

"I'll do it. Just don't tell anyone about the existence of that video," Aliyah said.

"We won't," Twila said. "Unlike you, we're trustworthy."

"The forensic specialist will be in touch," Hahna said. "You still have the same phone number?"

"Yes, I do. And Hahna, I'm sorry. If it wasn't for them blackmailing me, I would've never done anything to hurt you. I really do appreciate everything you've done."

"I just wish you'd have come to me. What Hale Brexton did to you was illegal, and we can prosecute him. Do you understand they could have gone to prison for releasing that video? If you had come to me, we could've figured it out before it got this bad."

"I guess I just got scared," Aliyah said.

Twila shook her head and unlocked the door. "Just get out," Twila said. "You're not making this any better."

Aliyah got out of the car and took her walk of shame back to wherever she was going to begin with. Twila climbed into the front seat and started the car as Hahna glared at her.

"Really, Twila?"

"Do you want your business back or what?"

"Yes, but this is grimy, underground type stuff. We don't do this."

Twila laughed. "Who don't? Oh, you. Well, I do."

"I can't believe you recorded that girl. And is it still going? Where's the camera?"

"Girl, there ain't no recording. I made that up on the fly," Twila said. "It worked, though, didn't it?"

Hahna laughed. "You are crazy."

"I am. And this is what you call the crazy friend for. Y'all came through for me with Marcus. I owed you one, sissy."

"Never. You never owe me for being your sister."

"I know it. Love you, girl. Let's go get the Data Whisperers back."

Hahna bit her bottom lip and sighed. "I hope it's good enough. I do."

"And if it isn't, so what? You'll do something else. You'll make money some other way. You've got everything else you need, including an awesome man."

"I don't know about that last part," Hahna said.

"Wait, what? Don't tell me Sam has fallen off."

"Sam is perfect. He's just not here for my foolishness."

Twila put the car back into PARK and sat silently for a moment. She didn't know what to say to Hahna to help with her relationship troubles, but she knew that Hahna shouldn't let Sam go.

"I'm not a relationship guru, so I don't know how to tell you to do this, but you need to fix whatever is going on with Sam. He's the best man you've ever been with. Don't let him go."

"I don't want to let him go."

"Then don't. Show him he means more to you than your business and your money."

"I don't know how, but I'll try."

Twila needed her to figure it out. She needed Hahna and Sam to have a happily-ever-after. Because their love had given her hope for her future. And that hope was one of the few threads keeping her tethered to normalcy.

"Don't try. Do it," Twila said.

"Okay. I will."

Chapter 55

Kimberly and Twila passed out glasses of wine and cupcakes to the group of one hundred sorority sisters they'd gathered in the large conference room of Kimberly's law office. Kimberly had invited these women, the most influential of the Atlanta and surrounding area alumni chapters, because their sister was in crisis. Kimberly wasn't going to allow Brexton's bad deeds to destroy what Hahna had worked for her entire life.

The bad news about the data breach had traveled quickly, and all but a few of Hahna's clients had jumped ship. The news about Hale Brexton's hand in the scandal and his selling of company information hadn't made the news at all. *That* part of the story didn't seem as exciting for the cable news networks. They'd been okay with blasting Hahna's company name, and even her photo, all over the airwaves, but they couldn't get a reporter to respond to anything that exonerated her.

Their sister was in trouble, so Kimberly knew Twila would help with her plan to restore Hahna's business and her good name.

After everyone had drunk their share of the expensive red and white wines that Kimberly had bought for the occasion, she stepped to the podium to speak.

"I want to thank all of y'all for coming out tonight. I know it's a Friday, and you probably have something fabulous to get to, but this is sorority business and I knew you'd answer the call."

Grecia Sanchez, one of their most successful sorority sisters since her husband owned a chain of high-end Mexican restaurants in Atlanta, raised her hand to be acknowledged. Kimberly wasn't ready for questions yet, but Grecia was a ringleader, and very influential. Kimberly had to let her get her say.

"Let's cut right to the chase," Grecia said. "We're here about what's happened with Hahna's business, correct? It's not often that we see a lovely Gamma lady on the news for intentional data sabotage. It was intentional, correct?"

"That's what the streets are saying," Holly Bowles, Grecia's sidekick, said.

Kimberly took a deep breath and exhaled. She had to rein these two in before the entire evening was a waste. The other women were already muttering and whispering. There was a small window of opportunity here, and it was closing quickly.

"It *was* intentional, but it was not Hahna who committed any crimes. What the streets don't know . . . yet . . . is that Hale Brexton sold his client's information because he's broke. His company has been underwater for years. The only thing that grieves me is that he was able to blackmail one of our younger sorority sisters who worked for Hahna."

Several of the ladies gasped, but they were all ears. Kimberly had their attention now.

"Hahna did what we all do, reached back to our alma mater and hired one of our sorors, Aliyah Robinson. Brexton was able to find information on the young lady that she didn't want known by her family and her peers. So, she helped him by causing a system vulnerability that they were able to exploit."

"Why haven't we seen *this* on the news?" Grecia said. "It seems like they'd tell the whole story."

"This is why we've invited you here. We need this part of the story—the whole story—to go viral. Soror Samantha Pike, who writes for the *Atlanta Star,* has written a comprehensive story on this data breach and the causes of it. The national news cycle won't pick it up, because it's barely gaining traction in Atlanta.

We need our three hundred thousand sorority sisters to tweet, retweet, post, and repost. We need e-blasts, and we need church blasts. It must be a concerted effort starting on Thursday. For forty-eight hours, we need to get the whole story out there."

"How do we know it's the truth?" Grecia said.

Kimberly seethed, and Twila looked ready to jump across the room and smack Grecia.

"Everyone in this room knows Hahna. You've served with her. You've seen her build this business from nothing. You've seen her give back to the community. She personifies the ideals of Gamma Phi Gamma—integrity, honesty, and grace."

"Well, she's *your* friend. You would say that," Grecia said.

Sharon Adeya, president of the Greater Atlanta Alumni chapter, stood up. Although she was sixty-seven years old, Sharon was the epitome of beauty and black excellence. Everyone always stopped to listen when she spoke.

"Enough, Grecia. You need not always be the devil's advocate," Sharon said. "We will do this campaign for our soror who has been maligned and mistreated. We will pray for our wayward soror who was blackmailed. Now, I need someone to show me how to tweeter. I am not sure how that works."

Kimberly smiled. "Thank you, Sharon. Although that settles it, I have one more thing to add. If I didn't believe in Hahna's innocence, there is no way I would put her in charge of data analytics for my own company, Curlpop. She is great at what she does."

"She's the best at what she does," Twila said.

"And she deserves our support. I will be sending you all the link to the story via email. I would like for you to make an initial post on your social media sites. Don't just share my posts, create your own. For some reason, that's important to the algorithm on how many people see it."

"Guess who taught her that?" Twila said. "Hahna. Y'all need to get with her on how to market your companies and use data analytics. You're leaving money on the table if you don't."

"Why isn't Hahna here to speak for herself?" Holly asked.

"As anyone can reasonably expect, she is in complete breakdown mode. She is resting and trying to wrap her brain around this."

Twila stood and held up Gamma Phi Gamma's hand sign, both thumbs and forefingers folded into a heart.

"She doesn't have to be here," Twila said. "I am my sister. My sister and I are one."

Kimberly repeated the Gamma mantra with Twila. "I am my sister. My sister and I are one."

The rest of their sorority sisters joined in. "I am my sister. My sister and I are one."

The sound of the chant bounced off the walls in the room. Some of the ladies did the Gamma call, five short claps and an "oh" sound. It transported Kimberly back to the yard during junior year of college, back when she, Twila, and Hahna had crossed. She remembered the bond they'd had then. That bond was still solid.

Kimberly wasn't worried now. She knew their sorors would come through. When the world heard the story of what happened with Hale Brexton, Hahna would get her life back.

Chapter 56

When Kimberly received the invitation for coffee from Ron's ex-wife, she'd hesitated to accept. Kimberly didn't want to talk to the woman, although she knew at some point it was inevitable since she was going to be with Ron for the foreseeable future. At least Sabrina had come to Atlanta—Kimberly's turf.

Kimberly showed up late, but not on purpose. There was an accident on I-285 and the traffic was ridiculous. Sabrina was already seated and sipping on something. She looked nervous when Kimberly approached.

"I'm sorry I'm late," Kimberly said as she sat. "Traffic was crazy. This little café is nice. I've never been here before."

"Oh, it's fine," Sabrina said. "The traffic here is insane. I found this place on Yelp. It had great reviews."

"I see. What are you drinking? Is it good?"

"Café au lait. I think it's Jamaican coffee or something. It's very strong. I ordered it black at first but had to add the milk. I don't know if there's such a thing, but it was too black, and very bitter. The milk helped."

Kimberly blinked. Was this girl trolling her? Or was she unaware that every single last thing she'd said since "café au lait" could carry a double meaning?

"I think I'll have tea. Not in the mood for anything black or bitter today," Kimberly said.

Sabrina gasped. "Wait. That's not what I meant at all. I was talking about the coffee, I swear."

"Oh, did I imply you didn't mean the coffee?" Kimberly asked innocently. "I feel confused now."

Sabrina took a deep breath and sipped her coffee again. Kimberly waited in silence while she pulled herself together.

"I know that we may never be friends," Sabrina said, "but I'd like for us to be cordial. The girls raved about you when they came home, and it made me feel so much better."

"How were you feeling before?"

"I hope it's okay for me to be honest," Sabrina said.

"I don't want you to be dishonest. So, absolutely."

"I was concerned," Sabrina said, "that you would be unkind to my daughters."

"Why would I do that? They belong to Ron, and I love him. I would never be unkind to his children."

Sabrina's lip twitched. "But you wouldn't care about being unkind to me or my children? What if Ron wasn't their father, but another black man was? What if you saw me in the grocery store and didn't know me? Would you sneer at me and my children? Because lots of black women do, and so I didn't know how you would be toward Carly and Kayla. Because there is a lot of hate there . . . sometimes . . . with black women. And I . . . well . . . I'm rambling, but I just wanted to say that I'm glad you were kind to my children."

Kimberly got the waitress's attention. She didn't respond to Sabrina's rant. She wanted to give herself a moment to calm her spirit. Ordering the tea would help.

"I'll have oolong," Kimberly said to the waitress, "and a cheese plate. Does that come with croissants?"

"Yes."

"Okay, I'll have that."

"I'll put that right in for you," the waitress said.

Sabrina was still breathing heavily when the waitress walked away.

"I'm not going to speak for every black woman," Kimberly said. "I can't. I can only speak for me. I wouldn't care about you and your biracial children if I saw you in a grocery store."

"I just want you to know that I'm not one of *those* white women. I don't only date black men. I love everyone. Ron is a very good man. We didn't work out, but he is a good man. My current husband is a good man. I don't see color."

Kimberly wasn't going to respond to any of this. She didn't care. Even though Sabrina was crying. Let her café au lait catch her tears, 'cause Kimberly wasn't interested in them at all.

"Thank you for the video," Sabrina said when Kimberly didn't respond. "The girls made me watch it three or four times. They said, 'Watch it again, Mommy.' I had no idea I wasn't doing it right. I always brushed my hair from the root to the tip. One hundred strokes a night on each side. Like Marcia Brady, you know?"

Kimberly cocked her head to one side. She knew Marcia Brady, of course. She'd watched *The Brady Bunch* reruns like every other seventies baby. But she pretended not to get the reference. Because this heffa was stupid, and Kimberly felt like being petty.

"Well, that's wrong for curly hair. You were probably ripping their hair out."

"I think I was. I thought it was just shedding, but when I did it your way there wasn't any hair in the brush."

"Wonderful."

"Listen, like I said, I know we aren't going to be friends, but thank you for your kindness to my babies. It will be good for them to have a black woman as part of their parenting team."

Now, this was a surprise. Kimberly didn't respond, but not out of pettiness. She didn't know what to say to that.

"I can't speak to what their experience will be like as black women," Sabrina said. "And they will grow up to be black women. I want them to know about the . . . stepping . . . and the sororities, and HBCUs and all that."

"You know you can learn yourself and teach your own children," Kimberly said.

"But it won't be authentic. They will need black women mentors, so I'm glad that they have you."

Shoot. Sabrina was saying the right things. Kimberly didn't know if she was being sincere or not, but it sure felt like it.

"I'm glad to have them," Kimberly said, feeling the ice melt a little. "They're beautiful and sweet."

Finally, Sabrina smiled. "I appreciate you."

Kimberly smiled back. And it wasn't a fake or petty smile. It was real. Maybe this would work, and maybe she could be this woman's friend. She was about to coparent with a white woman. Shit. Twila and Hahna were going to crack up at this one.

"Well, I'm not wearing a ring yet," Kimberly said.

"I'm sure it's coming. I've never seen Ron like this," Sabrina said. "He was never like this when we were together. It gives me peace to know we didn't waste years being with the wrong person."

"Appreciate you for getting the hell out of my way."

Sabrina's eyes widened, and her jaw dropped. Then she set down her coffee cup and laughed. It was a loud and hearty laugh. And Kimberly joined her. Their laughter filled the entire café. Kimberly wondered what people thought about this white woman and black woman sitting in the middle of the restaurant hollering.

Who was she kidding? People probably weren't thinking anything except that these were two old friends cutting up.

Maybe one day, that would be true.

Chapter 57

Hahna linked arms with Sam as they walked into the Gamma Phi Gamma quarterly scholarship banquet. She wasn't going to attend, but Kimberly and Twila twisted both arms and legs and every appendage. She wasn't quite ready to be back out on the social scene, but since her sorority sisters were the reason that the Data Whisperers had a fighting chance at recovering, it was only right that she showed her face.

Gamma Phi Gamma's social media campaign was overwhelming. They'd trended on every platform, and the news outlets had finally taken notice and updated their reporting. They didn't want to be on the bad side of Gamma Phi Gamma. Who wanted to be boycotted by the most powerful group of African American women in the country?

But while the truth was out, and Hale Brexton was being investigated for tax fraud, money laundering, inaccurate financial reporting, and a host of other charges, the Data Whisperers clients were slow in returning. Hahna had expected more loyalty than this from some of her long-term customers, but it was going to take time to rebuild.

"Is it okay for me to be here since I'm not a black Greek?" Sam whispered.

"Yes, of course. If it wasn't, I wouldn't bring you, silly."

"Okay. I don't know the secret handshake, though."

Hahna smiled. "I would teach it to you, but then I'd have to kill you."

"I wanna live," Sam said with a laugh. "My girlfriend is fine as hell. I'd like to spend some time with her."

"How about a lot more time? Like all day, every day."

Sam furrowed his brows with confusion and led Hahna away from the door to the venue to the side of the building out of the flow of traffic.

"What do you mean? Are you quitting your job? How can you quit? You're the owner," Sam said.

"I'm not quitting. I'm promoting Corden. I need a few months off, maybe a year. I want to get my head together and rest before I try to rebuild."

"And resting means spending time with me."

"It does," Hahna said. "You bring me peace."

Sam kissed Hahna's lips. It sent shivers through her. Almost made her want to leave the banquet.

"Do you want to stay at my place? You can be completely off the grid."

"For part of the time, yes. I think that would be awesome."

"What about when you're not at my place? Where will you be?"

Hahna shrugged. "That's up to you."

"What do you mean?"

"Well, I figured you've got this book deal, and you're a serious writer. I thought you might want to go on location. I read that Eric Jerome Dickey goes and stays for months on location. That's why his books are so real. Wouldn't you like to do that?"

"The book I'm writing now is set in Ghana."

"Let's go there, then. Let's go to Ghana."

Sam looked shocked. "For how long? When?"

"For however long it takes. I've never been to West Africa. This should be an adventure."

Sam shook his head. "I can't believe you're saying this. You're not on anything, are you?"

"No," Hahna laughed. "This is all . . . I still haven't come to terms with what's happening to me, and my company. But I do know what's important. I know who I love and who loves me. That is what I want to be wrapped in right now. Love."

"We can leave tomorrow, for all I care," Sam said. "This will be life-changing for us."

"I know."

Sam hugged Hahna and picked her right up off the ground in her floor-length gown. She was happy that he was happy, and she couldn't wait to go away with him. He did bring her peace, but she knew that it had to come from inside to stick.

"Come on, let's go inside," Hahna said. "I don't want to miss any of the program, or the drinks. It's an open bar."

Sam laughed and followed Hahna inside. Before sitting at the table with Twila, Kimberly, and Ron, they all exchanged hugs. Hahna waited to see if Twila was okay, being there with them and not having a date. She seemed okay, as if she'd found her own peaceful place.

"What's on the menu?" Twila asked. "I'm hungry. I hope they give us some soul food."

Kimberly shook her head. "Nope. I think I saw something about baked chicken."

"Man," Twila said. "I'm gonna need to join some of these committees."

"You'll have to come to a meeting first," Kimberly said.

"Shut up. At least I pay my dues," Twila said. "I ain't got time for all those meetings."

"I'm bad about the meetings too," Hahna said, "but me and Sam are going to Africa, so y'all are gonna have to figure that out without me."

"Africa?" Kimberly asked. "That's awesome. You can get lots of sun in the motherland. I'm jealous."

"Excuse me," Ron said. "I'll be right back. Some of my frats are here."

Kimberly shook her head. "Don't be long. I think the program is about to start."

"Okay."

When Ron was gone, Twila leaned forward and gave Hahna a hilarious I-got-some-gossip face.

"What, girl?" Hahna asked.

"Did you hear Kimberly had high tea with Ron's ex-wife?" Twila asked.

"She did what?"

Kimberly laughed. "It was not high tea. It was coffee. And she just wanted to tell me she was fine with me being around her daughters."

"You went out with Ron's white ex-wife. In person. Lord, have mercy, Jesus," Hahna said. "I need to repent of all my sins. I swear the rapture is gonna be tomorrow."

"First of all, I hate y'all," Kimberly said. "Second, it was rather nice. She was okay. I can deal with her, I think."

"Hey, are they about to start stepping?" Sam asked as he pointed over in the direction of Ron and his fraternity brothers.

They weren't about to start stepping, they *were* stepping. They transported Hahna back to freshman year to Fridays on the yard. She, Kimberly, and Twila had drooled over the fraternity boys who didn't pay them any mind because they were sweet babies.

Everyone in the room clapped and called, as they snaked their way through the crowd. It was obvious that they were coming to their table, so Twila cut up the most out of everyone.

Ron led the line until he and his brothers had stopped, in formation, right in front of Kimberly. They did a few more moves in unison, until Ron dropped to one knee. Twila hollered, and Kimberly's eyes widened. Hahna just giggled with glee at what was happening. She'd had an idea that Ron was going to propose soon.

"Baby, I remember when I first saw you on the yard," Ron said. "You were thick as what with a smile that stopped my heart. I wasn't man enough to do it then, because I still had lots to learn about life and what matters most. But I'm man enough now, and I need you. In this life and the next."

Kimberly shook as tears rolled down her cheeks. Ron opened a box that held a huge blue sapphire. Ron was so perfect for Kimberly. Only he would know that she'd prefer a sapphire to a diamond.

"I would be honored to have you as my queen. Will you marry me?"

Kimberly didn't speak. She simply nodded and hugged Ron.

"I think that's a yes, y'all," Twila hollered.

The room thundered with applause, hoots, calls, and whistles. Hahna shed tears along with her best friends.

They'd made plans to break rules, date men who made them blush, and maybe find love. But Hahna thought they'd done more than that. They'd cemented their sisterhood bond. It was already strong, but the adversity of the past few months had made it unbreakable.

Out of all the things Hahna knew she needed—love, joy, peace—she should've known that her sisters would be the ones to hold her down. They always were. With or without a man, she had their love and it was pure.

"Y'all gonna be in my wedding?" Kimberly asked when she was finally able to formulate words.

"Of course," Twila said. "And that bachelorette will be *lit*."

Hahna nodded. "Girl, you already know."

Kimberly smiled. She *did* know, like they all did. These were things that didn't have to be said, promised, or vowed. These were sister things. Even without being said, they were understood.

Sam kissed Hahna's neck and squeezed her hand.

"What was that for?" Hahna asked.

"Because I love you. That's all."

Hahna smiled. She squeezed his hand back and returned his kiss. Out of all the things she knew for sure, this one was her favorite. With Sam and her friends, Hahna had all that she needed.

She had love.

She had joy.

Her peace was on the way.

We hope you enjoyed
ALL THE THINGS I SHOULD HAVE KNOWN
by
Tiffany L. Warren.
As a special treat, we've included an excerpt
from her last book
THE OUTSIDE CHILD,
available at your favorite retailers and e-retailers.
Turn the page for a peek at this
remarkable book!

Chapter 1

Two years ago

My nerves are shot.

I should be ecstatic, thrilled, overwhelmed, and every other adjective to describe a makeup artist on their first big celebrity gig. It's in Jamaica, for crying out loud. That alone should make my spirits soar.

But all I can think about is my brand-new ex-boyfriend, Cody. He was supposed to be here with me. We were going to make love in our suite during my downtime. We were going to lie on the beach and plan our future. We were going to have the time of our lives.

But he couldn't keep his penis out of other women's vaginas.

Every time I close my eyes I think of what I found on his phone. I wish I hadn't looked, because everything had changed after that. Two weeks ago, everyone had looked to us as their relationship goal. Now, we are irretrievably broken.

I remember the events of that night. We had gone out to dinner to celebrate his birthday, had great sex, and were resting in his huge bed.

I'd picked up his phone, intending to text myself the cute selfie we'd taken at dinner. His phone had been unlocked, because he always kept it unlocked. We'd trusted each other.

I'd clicked on his photo, and found the selfie, but I mistakenly clicked on the video that was next to the selfie. It played, and my jaw dropped.

It was Cody and some random girl. He was taking her from behind as she cried, "Happy dirty thirty, Daddy."

I hadn't even roused him from his sleep to argue. I'd gotten dressed and snuck out of the bed and his condo. I'd sent him a text later, congratulating him on his birthday conquest. He'd called me insecure and petty.

So instead of holding hands with my man and looking out at the clouds, I'm on this first-class flight with my best friend and assistant, Kara.

"I can't believe we're about to land in Montego Bay," Kara says as she peers out the airplane window.

"I know. I've never been out of the country."

"If I had a boo, it would be perfect. Maybe I'll pull one of these ballers with this thong bikini."

Kara will pull someone this weekend, even if it's a temporary fling. Late last year, she'd hopped another flight to the Dominican Republic and had all the fat sucked out of her size-fourteen stomach and pumped right into her booty. She'd already had big breasts, so now she looked just like the letter S, with a teeny, tiny waist.

The flight attendant announces that we're about to land, so I make sure my seat belt is fastened, my tray table stowed, and my seat is in the upright position. Kara does none of the above.

The landing goes smoothly, and we emerge from the plane into the Montego Bay airport. I have to say, I was expecting more from an international airport. It's small like a regional airport in the States, and it's sweltering hot, like the air conditioning is broken.

Kara fans herself and cusses as we stand in the long line for customs. I can't even get worked up about the wait. I think after crying for two weeks, I've emptied myself of emotions.

We walk toward the hotel shuttle van that has been reserved for the concert attendees. I see people pulling tickets out of their wallets and bags—everyone except me and Kara.

"Were we supposed to have a ticket?" I ask.

Kara made all of the arrangements for this trip, with my credit card, of course. I haven't seen any of the confirmations, because Kara has booked travel for me before.

"I wasn't provided any tickets."

"Oh, okay."

I walk over to the pile of bags next to the shuttle van, to make sure mine and Kara's luggage is there. It is.

"Are we supposed to have tickets for this shuttle?" I ask the bag porter.

"Huh?"

"Tickets. Do we need tickets?"

The porter's eyes widen. "Oh, you think I work here?"

His American accent immediately makes me know that I've made a mistake.

"I'm so sorry. It's just that . . . you have the same kind of outfit as . . ."

Kara walks up with a huge smile on her face. "You're already meeting celebrities, I see, and we haven't even gotten to the resort yet."

My stomach drops with embarrassment. Who in the world is this guy? I feel like an idiot that I don't know and Kara obviously does.

"Brayden Carpenter," the porter lookalike says as he extends his hand to me. I return his firm handshake, but I still have no idea who he is.

"She's not into sports," Kara says. "He plays for the Dallas Knights. NFL. I'm Kara."

"Oh!" I say. "I'm sorry. I didn't mean to mistake you for a bag porter. It's just that I see everyone with a ticket, and . . ."

"She's just nervous," Kara says.

"Not a problem," Brayden says. "Are you guys going to the Tropical Get Down?"

"Yes, of course," Kara says.

"Well, maybe I'll see you there," Brayden replies.

"I'll be working," I say.

Why did I say that? I'm one hundred percent sure he's just

being nice and doesn't care whether he sees us or not, but I had to tell him that I'm working.

He smiles. "Are you an artist? You sing?"

"Oh, no, nothing like that. Chenille Abrams. I am a makeup artist."

"I heard that. Get your money, then."

Brayden gives us a nod and then walks toward the limo bus that's probably taking him to the resort. As soon as he's out of earshot, Kara bursts into laughter.

"Girl, I can't believe you just called one of the hottest players in the NFL a bag porter."

"It's not my fault! He looks Jamaican. He's tall, muscular, and dark. He had on the same outfit."

"Um . . . no, he didn't. His polo was Tom Ford and his shorts were Ralph Lauren."

"Whatever. Did you find out about our tickets?"

"Something went wrong with our shuttle reservation, but they agreed to take us over to the resort anyway."

"How kind of the driver."

"It might've had something to do with the fact that I said I'd go dancing with him before we leave."

I shake my head. "Girl, why did you lie like that?"

"It wasn't a lie. He's hot, and I bet he is packing heat, chile. That's what they say about these Jamaican men."

"What kind of heat? The burning, you-gotta-take-antibiotics kind?"

Kara rolls her eyes and drags me over to the van where the other passengers (who have tickets) are boarding.

"I still can't believe you didn't recognize Brayden Carpenter."

I shrug. "It doesn't matter. You're the one here to meet a baller. I'm here to network for Beat by Chenille."

"Of course you are, but that doesn't mean you can't have some fun, too."

Lord knows I need some fun after what happened with Cody. But the last thing I need is an NFL player. They're even bigger cheaters than the average man. If Cody is videotaping himself with women, who knows what shenanigans a man like Brayden would get into.

No, as fine and as chocolate and as muscular as he is, Brayden Carpenter isn't for me. Maybe Kara and her brand-new, bodacious hips can score him instead.

ALL THE THINGS I SHOULD HAVE KNOWN

ABOUT THIS GUIDE

The suggested questions are included to enhance
your group's reading of Tiffany L. Warren's
All the Things I Should Have Known.

1. At the beginning of the story, Hahna, Kimberly, and Twila make a pact to go out with the next man who asks them on a date, regardless of their previous dating rules. Have you ever thrown away your dating rules? Does breaking the rules equal "settling?"

2. Can a financially successful woman have a solid relationship with a man who makes substantially less money than she does?

3. Kimberly's date with Shawn was a complete nightmare from the start. What is your most hilarious first date story? Did it end in a love affair?

4. When Hahna runs into her ex at her current boyfriend's event, she feels conflicted. Did this bother you? Was Hahna wrong for having these feelings?

5. Twila decides to have a no-strings-attached fling with her Instagram model. Is this even possible? Can two people have amazing sex without catching feelings?

6. Is Hahna materialistic? Does her boyfriend have a point, or should he just get over it and let her enjoy the finer things in life?

7. Is Kimberly racist? Would helping to raise your man's biracial children be a deal breaker? Why or why not?

8. Which character's back story would you like to see explored?

9. What things did you discover as a woman at 25, 30, 35, 40, 50, and beyond that you feel you should've known? What has been your life's biggest a-ha moment?

Connect with Us

Visit us online at
KensingtonBooks.com
to read more from your favorite authors, see books
by series, view reading group guides, and more.

for sneak peeks, chances to win books and prize packs,
and to share your thoughts with other readers.

facebook.com/kensingtonpublishing
twitter.com/kensingtonbooks

Tell us what you think!

To share your thoughts, submit a review,
or sign up for our eNewsletters, please visit:
KensingtonBooks.com/TellUs.